I0645692

Total-E-Bound Publishing books by Patricia Pellicane:

The Cove
The Best Present Ever
Sophie's Pleasure
To Save Emmy
Happy Birthday Baby

TELL ME
YOU LOVE ME

PATRICIA PELLICANE

Tell Me You Love Me
ISBN # 978-0-85715-075-2
©Copyright Patricia Pellicane 2010
Cover Art by Natalie Winters ©Copyright 2010
Interior text design by Claire Siemaszkiewicz
Total-E-Bound Publishing

Published in 2010 by Total-E-Bound Publishing, Think Tank, Ruston Way, Lincoln, LN6 7FL, United Kingdom.

Total-E-Bound Publishing is an imprint of Total-E-Ntwined Limited.

Manufactured in the USA.

TELL ME
YOU LOVE ME

Dedication

To my family for suffering through all my moans and groans, thank you guys, love you.

Chapter One

Thunder crashed overhead. Anything that wasn't tied down swirled wildly around them. A huge branch had already hit her. Matt hurried his pace as he carried an unconscious Kiya inside the small cabin, surprised to find it empty. Apparently, the men who guarded her father's sheep were tending their flock lest the storm frighten the animals into dashing off the nearby cliffs.

A fire burned in the large, black stove, warming the little cabin against outside elements gone suddenly insane. A table, two chairs and a small bed filled the tiny shelter, leaving almost no floor space.

Matt placed her upon the rumpled bed. She was soaking wet, her lips blue. He hadn't a doubt if left as such, despite the warmth of the room, she'd soon take chill. There was nothing to be done for it, and with no further thought on the matter, he set out to quickly dispose of the lady's clothes. It took some effort, but he managed to keep his gaze mostly averted — mostly but not entirely.

His heart pounded, and his hands shook. His lips thinned to a tight grimace resembling pain and a fine sheen of sweat added to his already wet frame as he managed at last to tug a blanket over her, leaving her in her frilly drawers and lacy chemise, both of which were nearly as transparent as gauze when wet.

Granted, he'd known his share of women, but this one confirmed his previous imaginings and then some. She was even lovelier than he had supposed. The top of her head barely reached his shoulder. Her skin glowed with a delicate lustre as if cut from porcelain, while full pink lips almost exactly matched the soft colour of her cheeks.

Her hair when dry was a riot of yellow and silver curls. While riding she had lost most of her pins and curly confection swirled wildly behind her in the wind. Unrestrained, those wild locks reached to her waist.

Matt forced aside his reaction to the sight of her near nakedness. He hadn't meant to look. Indeed, he had not looked as he might have liked.

Thankful for something that took his mind from the woman and her all too vulnerable state, he tore a piece of cotton from her petticoat, pumped water and applied the wet rag to the swelling on her forehead. The flying branch had not broken her skin but had left a small, red mark above a growing knot. She'd suffer some discolouration, perhaps even a black eye, but hopefully nothing more serious than that.

Matt hung her wet clothes over a chair near the stove. As he waited for the lady to awaken, he pumped more water into a kettle and set it upon the stove. Moments later, he washed out the tea pot and cups left on the table. Next he searched for towelling. Finding none, he took a pillow sheet, flipped it inside out and pressed the linen cloth to her wet hair, drying what he could. It was important that she not take a chill. Had he not been so absorbed in her and their earlier conversation, he would have noticed sooner the coming storm. He should have, and because he hadn't, he felt some responsibility for her injury.

After a time, he coaxed, "Kiya, wake up," and then repeated it again in a deep voice that allowed no option.

She moaned softly. "Go away."

He grinned. "You need to wake up."

"No, I don't."

She'd taken a blow to her head. She did need to wake up. "I've tea ready."

For the first time, Kiya realised she was in bed, while talking to a man. She opened her eyes with a frown and was surprised to find herself in a strange cabin. "Where are we? What are we doing here?"

"We were caught in the storm, remember?"

"Oh," she said as the memory came. Her head ached, and she reached a hand to the injury. "I got hit with —"

"A branch, I know. I saw it," he interrupted as he looked at her eyes. "No real damage done, I think. You've a small lump over your eye. Does it hurt much?"

Kiya thought that question particularly ridiculous. She glared her annoyance and returned with, "Only when I breathe."

Matt grinned. She was a sarcastic little brat but the most beautiful he'd ever come across. "Here. Hold this wet cloth to the swelling. I'll get the tea."

A moment later, he stripped off his soaked shirt and hung it near the stove beside clothes that looked just like hers.

Kiya's heart began to beat far harder and faster than it should have, drastically hampering her ability to breathe. He'd taken off his shirt. Just what did he think he was doing?

"Excuse me," she said then asked, "What are you doing?"

He glanced behind him and frowned. Was the blow taken harder than he'd first imagined? "Getting the tea, remember?"

"And you can only do that while half dressed?"

Matt glanced at his bare chest and grinned. "Our clothes are wet."

Kiya stared at him a long moment before she mouthed the word 'our' and then slowly came to a sitting position just as she lowered her gaze to her own chest. Changing positions allowed the blanket to fall to her waist. She gasped at the sight. She might as well have been naked! Good God in heaven! She jerked the blanket tightly to her neck. "Are you insane? What have you done?"

"You couldn't stay in those wet clothes without taking a chill. They had to come off."

"Oh my God," she moaned softly, unable to raise her gaze to his. Kiya had no doubt the man had had himself a good look while going about the business of disrobing her. She couldn't meet his gaze. If the beast dared smile her way, she was apt to kill him on the spot. "And you took them off?" she asked her voice barely above a whisper, clearly aghast at the thought.

He didn't bother to respond. Both of them knew what had happened. No one else was here.

She moaned softly her embarrassment.

"There's no need to distress yourself. I covered you as quickly as I could."

"Indeed?" she snapped and asked in disbelief, "And how quickly was that?"

Matt chuckled softly at her nasty comment, his eyes sparkling dark with something Kiya couldn't name, something mysterious and frightening, something that caused a chill to race up her spine. "Shall I tell you I didn't look?"

Kiya's cheeks burned.

"I promise you I didn't." And the words were almost true. A glance couldn't count as a look, could it?

His statement did little to ease her suffering. That combined with a god-awful headache left her in something less than a good mood. She couldn't remember a time when she'd been half so mortified. Very softly and with hardly a tremor at all, she said, "My father has pistols in his library. When we get back, I'm going to shoot you."

"Are you?" he smiled, knowing a stab of almost overwhelming tenderness at her obvious suffering. "I have pistols as well, you know?"

"I don't care." Her eyes suddenly and unexplainably filled with tears. Her head was killing her, and this beast was making it hurt all the more.

"Don't cry, Kiya." He crouched before her, taking her hand in his. "I didn't mean to upset you. I couldn't leave you wet." His thumb wiped away a lone tear as it travelled down her cheek. "Your lips were blue, your skin as cold as ice. Suppose you took a chill and died? It would have been my fault."

Matt never imagined his actions would have caused this lady such distress. Of course, he hadn't undressed many true ladies, so he couldn't have known how one might react at finding herself, all but for a meagre wisp of lace, naked before a man who was not her husband.

Kiya pulled her knees to her chest and pressed her face against them. She had a raging headache. No doubt that was the main cause of her unusual lack of self-control. No doubt, she was making far too much of this unseemly situation. It was his fault. Even though the man had done what he'd deemed to be right at the time, it was more than his actions. It was the man himself. It was the way he looked at a woman—in this case herself-as if he could see things no one else could, as if he knew her innermost secrets. His gaze most always left her jittery and oddly nervous. She'd never suffered these effects at another's glance. Why so his? Kiya couldn't imagine. She only knew she'd feel ever so much better if he would simply attach himself to another and leave her in peace.

She fought for control and, after a few minutes, raised her face from her knees and looked him in the eye. "First of all, I never cry," she said, belying the tears that were only now drying. "Second, don't call me Kiya. Third, thank you for your help." She choked a bit on that one but managed the words just the same. "And fourth I'd like some tea, if you please."

Matt came to his feet and grinned as he turned away from her to pour the tea. Having had a bit more experience than the young miss in his care, he was fully aware of the sexual tension that had sprung to life from the first moment they'd met. She might not understand her unusual emotions, but he knew the reason behind her soft blushes and inability to look him in the eye. She was afraid. She wasn't sure why, but she most definitely was. Matt hadn't a doubt she felt much the same things as he did, only because those feelings were new, they confused and frightened her.

Kiya glanced in his direction and wondered why she was so conscious of the man. She knew a measure of annoyance and wondered how he managed to upset her. Well, perhaps upset was too strong a word. Still, there was something about this man that left her oddly unsettled. Why? Certainly, he never said or did anything to deserve her wrath. Still, she was convinced he was somehow too forward and in need of a good setting down.

Moments later, they sipped at their cups in companionable silence. He sat at the table; she reclined against the wall, while holding the blanket in place, her headache nearly gone.

"Were you always a guard?" she asked after some uncomfortable silence.

"Pretty much," he returned, offering her nothing more.

"Who have you guarded before?"

"Rich men and their families, mostly in London."

"Any of the Royals?"

"One or two."

She raised one brow and shot him a disparaging look. "My my, a fountain of information, I see. Which one?"

He grinned at her sarcasm. "The King's nephew. There were rumours of a possible kidnapping."

Kiya dismissed the possibility that his smile might have any effect on her. Her stomach had certainly not trembled. She was simply hungry. Still, impressed, she commented, "I read about it in the papers. Are you the one who prevented it?"

Matt nodded, while allowing a slight shrug, "Myself and others."

"It sounds exciting."

"It sounds like it," he agreed.

"Meaning it's not?"

"Meaning, if there is any excitement, it's over in an instant. Quite a bit more time is spent waiting and watching."

"I'd like to do something exciting."

"Would you? What exactly?"

"Among other things, travel I think. I'd like to see for myself the things I've read."

"Travelling is often uncomfortable," he warned. "Beds are usually far from soft and none too clean. Water for bathing is hard to come by. Water for drinking is often bad. Mayhap you've romanticised what you've read."

Kiya dismissed his warning with a laugh. "Perhaps. I'll let you know when I get back."

"When are you going?"

"I have to wait a bit, but I'll be of age soon."

Matt knew without a doubt that she would. "But not alone."

"I'll take a servant with me, I'm sure."

"And you expect a servant will protect you? Have you no prospects?" Having already looked into the matter, he knew she did not. "No future husband who might travel with you?"

"I won't be marrying, so there'll be no husband. Perhaps, I'll hire a guard."

His eyes widened with shock. She wouldn't be marrying? "Why? Why won't you marry? Is something wrong?"

"With me, you mean?" she asked on a laugh. "I'd simply rather not is all."

Matt couldn't fathom her response. "You'd rather not? Don't all young ladies want to marry?"

Kiya shrugged. "All but me, I suppose." And then answered his puzzled frown with, "It's simple. When a lady marries she is no longer herself but merely her husband's property. She owns nothing, becomes nothing, is nothing." And then she added in all sarcasm, "I simply prefer to forgo such an outstanding temptation."

Matt was temporarily at a loss for words. It was a long moment before he went on. "And your father agrees with this decision?"

"He knows my feelings on the matter. Once I'm of age, he'll have no choice."

Matt grinned at last. So her father was not in agreement with his daughter's outrageous notions. He thought that might be the case. "So you'd hire a guard rather than marry? You should know men are not to be trusted."

"Now you sound like my father," she interrupted.

Matt shrugged. "Men know how men think."

"Indeed? Perhaps because men are wicked at heart?"

"Many are."

"You're not. Perhaps, I'll hire you."

Matt thought this woman would surely be alarmed should she know the way of his thoughts, for at this moment, he'd like nothing better than to show her firsthand just how wicked a man could be. Still, lest she bolt from the cabin and into the rain, he remained quiet and offered no comment to her last remark.

"Besides travelling, I should one day like to captain a ship."

"Indeed? Have you experience in sailing?"

Kiya dismissed the experience she *did* have, knowing he spoke of ships, not boats large or small. "No, but I could learn."

And at his look of disbelief, she reminded, lest he believe her ridiculous, "There have been lady pirates. The idea is not impossible."

Matt nodded. "There have and you're right, it's not impossible."

"So it shouldn't come as a shock that a woman might want to travel, to captain her own ship."

"I'm not shocked," Matt returned, and in truth, he almost wasn't. "I have a ship. Perhaps, you'd like to captain her."

Kiya grinned. "Do you? And you guard people in your spare time, for your amusement then?"

"I don't captain it," he said, ignoring her taunt. "I hire people to do that."

"Do you? Is it a pirate's ship?" she asked in clear disbelief.

"It was. My brothers and I captured it and ..."

Kiya laughed delighted in his teasing. "You captured it? From pirates? And now what? You use it to travel?"

"To trade mostly. I haven't travelled too much lately." Aware of her disbelief, he thought it would only increase that scepticism should he tell her more. Wisely, he kept the rest to himself.

"What's her name?"

"The Sea Witch, of course."

"Of course," she laughed softly, delighting in his imagination. Obviously, the man could be amusing when he set his mind to it. "You'll have to show her to me."

"Or what, you'll not believe me?"

"Certainly not. Of course, I believe you," she lied. "I only meant I'd very much like to see her."

"That was very good," he said of her quick recovery. "But it's a sin to lie."

Kiya laughed again, never realising she was growing more comfortable and at ease in his company. "You have a family then?"

Matt nodded. "I have three brothers. I'm the oldest. And then there's my mother, of course."

"Four boys," Kiya mused. "That must have been trying for your mother."

"I've no doubt. We were a rowdy bunch at best."

Kiya smiled and shook her head. "You have that look in your eye. I believe you were a terror." And still might be, she imagined then thought it best to keep that notion to herself.

Matt didn't bother to dissuade her of her thoughts. She was closer to the truth than she knew. "Why have you an exotic name and your sisters not?" he asked, changing the subject.

"Oh, we all have unusual names," she returned. "My mother was an avid student of ancient Egypt. Merry's name is Merytaten—she was a Queen in the Eighteenth Dynasty. Amy's is Amon, god of fertility, I think.

"Our clothes should be dry," Kiya said, nodding towards the hot stove.

"It's still raining. We'll only get wet again unless we wait a bit longer." As if to profess the truth of his words, the wind howled all the harder around the small cabin, rattling its door and shaking its one window, while rain slashed in fury against the tiny shelter.

"Indeed, but in the meantime, I could get dressed."

"If I step outside while you dress, I'll get wet again. Why don't I turn my back or close my eyes?" he offered.

Kiya shot him a no-nonsense look. And without a word spoken, he was apprised of her thoughts on the matter. She wasn't about to get dressed while he stayed in the cabin.

He sighed. "Wonderful," he muttered none too happily. "I'll be right back. You'd best get to it."

"Count slowly to a hundred," she said as he reached the door.

Matt muttered something unintelligible, telling clearly his displeasure. Still, objecting or not to her wants, he did as she asked.

"Count fast to a hundred," he countered. The door slammed behind him.

Kiya moved as quickly as she could. In seconds, she had her clothes in place and was just closing the last buttons of her riding costume when the door crashed open.

"I hope you're happy," he said, drenched again as he staggered, clearly breathless inside. "I'll probably come down with fever and die just because you couldn't wait a bit to get dressed." He gave a violent unexpected shiver and reached for the small linen to rub dry.

Kiya bit her lip. She'd thought at first he was teasing, but his shiver gave her cause to believe he was truly cold. She moved to him, took the linen from his hands and dried his back. He shivered again. Besieged with guilt she said, "Oh Lord, I'm sorry. I didn't think. I should have waited. I never thought you'd get so cold."

He turned to face her as she continued the chore. It never occurred to her that she should not be doing this, touching him. Reaching high she dried his neck, his shoulder and side quickly and without thought. Then his chest... She moved slightly slower then slower still, as if she'd just discovered what her hands were doing, the cloth went to his stomach at a snail's pace. His skin was smooth but for a patch of dark hair centred upon his chest and a thin line of the same that ran over his stomach and disappeared into his trousers. Water dripped on her hands from his hair. She looked up to find him totally still, entranced, his dark eyes watching her without a flicker of their usual humour. Dark, hungry, they seemed to hold her in place, taking her will from her.

She might not have meant to show it, but her admiration was obvious as the cloth again moved slowly over a dry chest and stomach.

She heard his sharp intake of breath as her gaze rose to meet his and felt a shiver of something like excitement race through her body.

Had he said he was cold? God, he was suddenly hotter than he'd ever been in his life. If she continued to touch him, he'd likely burst into flames.

Her hands stopped their movement. The cloth, forgotten, fell away. Her fingers lay motionless against his bare flesh. She never seemed to notice.

I should move, she thought. She was standing too close. He was dry now. So why didn't she? Why didn't her legs obey the dictates of her mind? She felt a wave of dizziness and took a deep steadying breath. She almost moaned aloud as his scent filled her lungs, her mind and her senses, causing the dizziness to grow tenfold. Lord, this man smelled good. She leaned just a bit closer, luxuriating in the delicious scent. In her innocence, she never thought she should not.

A pulse beat in her throat. Her lips parted as she suddenly struggled to breathe. She was lost in the darkness of his gaze, unexpectedly gasping for air as if she'd been running some distance or holding her breath. What was the matter with her? Why was she breathless? Why was her heart suddenly pounding? She couldn't seem to hear anything but the roar of her blood as it rushed through her veins.

His mouth lowered just a bit, his face—his dangerously handsome face—coming closer, his dark eyes blocking out all else but his hunger—a hunger they suddenly both knew. His mouth brushed gently against hers, and all thoughts but one simply vanished. Her younger sister had once remarked that he was lovely to look at. Only Kiya knew he was even lovelier to taste.

Her body tingled from her lips clear to her toes at the simple brush of his mouth on hers. Oh my goodness. She'd never thought a man could smell or taste so good. That probably wasn't a good thing because he looked and smelled better than cherry pie. And nothing was better than cherry pie.

"Pie," she muttered thoughtlessly against his insistent mouth.

He didn't seem to hear her, at least not at first.

"Mmm better," she murmured as he deepened the kiss.

He smiled as his lips parted, and his arm wrapped possessively around her waist, lifting her some while bringing her tightly against him.

"Cherry pie," she said against his delicious mouth.

Kiya knew a touch of amazement. She'd never thought one could talk while being kissed, but she was being kissed and delightfully so. Still, she couldn't seem to resist telling him how much she liked it.

"Are you hungry?" he asked at her mention of food, while never taking his mouth from hers.

"You taste so good," she returned, never noticing her words, never thinking to control or deny the sweetly ingenuous delight that filled her. "Better than cherry pie."

He growled at her luscious response. "Open your mouth for me."

She did as he asked and was shocked to feel his tongue dip gently between her lips. "What are you doing?"

"Kissing you."

She meant to laugh at the nonsensical response, but the soft sound turned oddly into a groan. "That's not a kiss."

"Isn't it? Don't you like it?"

"I think I do," she managed, strangely fascinated by this unusual occurrence. "But do you think you should do that?"

"Oh, I think I should."

"All right then," she agreed. "You're probably right." Anything that felt this good had to be right.

He gave a low deliciously sexy chuckle at her eager acquiescence even as he took her bottom lip and sucked it gently into his mouth. He heard her soft moan of pleasure.

"Mmm, that feels lovely, doesn't it?"

"It does," he agreed

"But I'm almost positive, this isn't kissing." It never occurred to her that she shouldn't be allowing this. Kiya was too taken by the moment, too instantly absorbed into the pleasure that she never thought at all.

His tongue moved over her lip, and the tingling sensations increased.

"You have a beautiful mouth."

"Are you sure you're kissing me?" she asked.

"Absolutely sure," he returned.

"It feels like you're eating me."

"Not yet," he promised. "But I will."

Kiya frowned just a bit at his words. She didn't understand. But most of all, she didn't really care. What he was doing was too lovely to bother thinking on his confusing comment.

"I didn't know a man could taste like you do."

"Oh my God," he moaned. "Do you know what you're doing to me?"

"No. What?"

Matt didn't dare answer the question. To do so would snap her from this delicious moment. Instead, he coaxed her deeper into the magic. "Watch this. Tell me what you think."

His hand came to the back of her head, his fingers threading through her hair as his tongue pushed into her mouth. Breathing her scent, he took her taste as his tongue ran over her smooth teeth, the roof of her mouth then sucked her tongue into his mouth. He allowed no quarter but absorbed all he could of her essence.

She'd been kissed before but never anything like this. It was too much. Her knees buckled as her whole being seemed to flow into liquid heat.

His arm tightened around her as he brought her to the bed.

Kiya neither felt the bed beneath her, nor the buttons of her short jacket and blouse as one by one they came undone. All she knew was this man, his taste, the feel of his mouth on hers, the softness of his lips, the scratching of his beard, the harsh quick sounds of his breathing, sounds that matched her own.

And when his mouth freed hers at last, his face tucked into the sweetness of her neck. She gasped for breath and said weakly and more innocently than she knew, "I think you forgot to kiss me and tried to eat my mouth instead."

He laughed as his lips moved to her shoulder. Amazingly her shoulders were bare and her blouse somehow lay open. She never wondered how that could have happened. All she knew was the lovely sweet thrill of his mouth, his tongue dragging over her skin and the way it caused her toes to curl. "I like that."

"I thought you might. You're going to like this even more," he said as his mouth returned to her neck then lowered to the suddenly exposed flesh of her chest.

A moment later, her chemise was pulled down exposing her breast to his view. In the back of her mind, she knew she should object, only she couldn't seem to find the words to tell him to stop. All she could manage was a weak mechanical, "You shouldn't..." then a deep groan as his mouth, his burning hot mouth, covered the pink tip and sucked it into a pit of fire. The sounds she made were foreign to her ears. It couldn't be her. Someone was in pain, only this was as far from pain as night was from day. She gasped for air as her head fell back, her chest rising, lifting her breast to both their pleasure.

He moaned his appreciation. God, but she was beautiful, no doubt the most beautiful woman he'd ever known. From the first moment, he'd seen her, he'd wanted this, longed for this, ached to know the scent of her, the silkiness of her skin. He'd waited months. Waiting, watching, longing to touch her, to hold her in his arms, to taste her, to breathe her, until he'd thought he'd lose his mind. Now, at last her taste... He forced himself to hold to his control for she was about to drive him over the edge of reason. He had to have more. He had to see more, feel more.

Kiya moaned. There were no words. The wet tip felt suddenly cool as his mouth moved to discover its twin. Nothing had ever felt this good. Nothing ever would. Only she was wrong. His hand moved up her leg, unerringly under her thin, delicate drawers. He rested for a long moment on her thigh. She felt a flicker of surprise. No man had ever touched her there. Matt shouldn't... And then she forgot her thoughts as his mouth returned to hers, dragging her again into the sweet drunken haze of desire and a furnace of blazing, aching heat.

Her hands moved to his neck, pulling him closer, unable to get enough, feel enough or taste enough. Her fingers threaded through clean, dark hair. How had she never imagined a man's hair could feel so soft? Hard man and soft hair. She groaned at the delicious difference.

His hand moved. Higher, higher, it came, closer to the heat of her. His mouth pulled free of hers. His eyes were dark, hungry, watching for her response.

The air was thick. She couldn't breathe. A soft hum filled her ears. What was happening? She felt slightly bewildered unable to understand what had happened or what was about to happen.

He saw her confusion and knew her for the innocent she was. Had she been another, that look alone would have stopped him, but she wasn't another. She was Kiya. No one had ever looked like her or felt like her. No woman had ever come alive as she had in his arms. None had ever, in her innocence, taken his strength and returned it a hundred times over leaving him more a man than he'd ever been before.

His finger slid into the fold of her body, contacting the hot, wet, delicious heat of her, centring on the tiny nub of her building passion.

Her body jerked. Until now, she hadn't known the sensitivity. No one had ever touched her there. A soft gasp came just before her gaze began to clear. "What? What are you doing?"

"Touching you," he said as he smiled at her obvious uncertainty.

She shook her head. "You shouldn't."

"Yes," he countered. "God, yes, I should."

Kiya closed her eyes and sighed as his mouth snatched away the last of her resistance and her last rational thought with it. She was in sudden agreement that he most definitely should.

She moaned softly, her mouth opening greedily beneath his. This time, she sucked his tongue into her heat, and Matt groaned at her eager response and the agonising surge of lust that threatened his sanity. As his tongue filled her mouth, her hips rose against his hand, her legs parting further to the deliciousness of his ever-moving finger.

Kiya's only thought was the pleasure. Like a crazed being, she only wanted more. In truth, she was helpless but to demand more. It only vaguely occurred to her that this shouldn't happen, for the exquisite sensation derived was so overwhelming, so mind shattering, she'd only managed the most meagre resistance.

Her body grew hard, achingly hard, heavy and wet. She tore her mouth from his, her lungs starved for air, and she gasped. A heaviness settled over her stomach. It urged her hips to rise of their own accord, to rise to his wondrous fingers. She whimpered even as her gaze filled with burgeoning fear. She hadn't a notion as to what was happening.

Her body felt weighty, thick, oddly disconnected from her as it throbbed with life, with need and longing, but for what?

"What?" she asked breathlessly, almost desperately. "Please," she urged as her hips moved higher, her need beyond belief. She didn't know what she needed but was frantic for him to bring an end to pleasure that had grown to sudden torment. "Please," she begged again, her head falling back, her throat arching to his mouth, her blue eyes dazed, unseeing and her body stiff as it demanded release.

"Easy, sweetheart, easy. It will come," he breathed against her mouth.

"You have to..." she began then suddenly found it impossible to form words as guttural groans...something...someone...took possession of her body. It was no longer hers, but a wild creature's, straining towards unseen, heretofore unknown pleasure.

She gasped at the pain? Was it pain? She didn't know. She couldn't think. She could only feel as something inside clamped hard over her stomach, pulled tight, tighter, oh God tighter then achingly almost agonizingly tight. At long last, at the very moment she thought she was about to die, something broke and a delirious, cramping wave of ecstasy came then another and another then more, oh God, more in mindless wave after endless wave of debilitating insane pleasure.

She never wanted it to end. She didn't care if she died; she just wanted it to go on forever. She couldn't stop the luscious aftershocks, the throbbing, the aching rolls of enchantment, the sweet release, the sweeter exhaustion. She couldn't remember a time when she'd felt so soft, so weak, so utterly spent or so perfectly replete.

"Did I die?" she moaned, unsure if she had or not.

She heard his low chuckle. "Sweetheart, you don't know how good you are for a man's ego."

Kiya opened one eye a slit, her mouth barely wider. She'd been an innocent. She hadn't known. And because she hadn't, it was something of a struggle to take his obvious good humour in stride. Guilt hadn't set in yet. At the moment, all she felt was outrage that this man should have dared do the things he had done. "And by all means, we want to make sure your ego inflates to its full size."

"Aw, honey," he groaned at her less than sweet tone. "Don't be upset now."

"I wouldn't think of it. Don't call me honey. And get off me."

"It was beautiful. Watching you was the most beautiful thing I've ever seen."

"So happy to oblige. I said, get off me!"

Matt was about to show her the error of her thinking with another delicious assault of her senses when he heard the sound. "Someone's coming. Fix your dress."

Chapter Two

She never saw him move. He was simply, suddenly seated across the room from her, dressed again, the cup of cold tea in one hand, while his free hand lay as if by chance over his gun.

Just as she managed the last of her buttons, the door crashed open, the wind slamming it against the wall behind it. The huge form of Lord Winston staggered into the room, gasping for breath against a wind so fierce it tore even that from a man's body. "Good heavens, what a storm. I don't think I've seen anything this bad in years. Is it a hurricane, do you think?"

And then upon noticing for the first time who already occupied the cabin, his surprise turned into a sly, weasel-like grin, his gaze narrowing, barely concealing his eager lecherous thoughts and the delight that providence had thrown the two of them together for the next few hours.

"Good afternoon, Kiya. Because of the storm, I thought to take a shortcut across your father's property," he explained. "What a delightful surprise to find you here."

Kiya quickly brought her neighbour the linen towelling and smiled. "That's very sweet of you to say, your Lordship. I'll be thanking my father upon my return home. If it weren't for these cabins, I might be out in that squall still." A moment later, she seated herself once again on the corner of the bed.

"But you're not wet."

"Matthews and I made it to the cabin before the worst of the storm came. Our damp clothes soon dried in this warm room." Kiya hadn't known she had it in her. Not only was she spinning the man a yarn, but she was doing it without a tremor in her voice. If she didn't allow her mind to linger, she almost believed the innocence of the afternoon.

"Matthews?" he mumbled in some confusion then turned to his left. For the first time, he seemed to notice Kiya was not alone. To say he was disappointed was to put it mildly. "You mean you've spent the afternoon in here, alone with a man?"

"I hardly had a choice in the matter, did I your Lordship? This is Mr. Matthews, my guard."

"Oh yes, I heard your father had hired on some men."

Matt stood and offered his hand to the obese gentleman. "Matthew Chase at your service, sir."

Kiya nearly moaned aloud. Matthew Chase. She'd been with a man, had allowed him carnal knowledge of her body and hadn't known his name. Good God, could this situation be worse? Could she? Kiya couldn't imagine what had come over her. How had she permitted such an illicit afternoon? She couldn't think of it right now. She couldn't look in his direction. No doubt, she'd never look or talk to him again. Still, it wasn't possible to dwell on those thoughts now. The viscount was saying something, and she hadn't heard a word of it.

"I'm sorry, sir, but I was thinking on an appointment I have this evening, and I didn't hear you."

"I was simply saying it was fortunate I arrived when I did. We wouldn't want rumours to abound that a lady like you was found in an indelicate situation."

Matt grinned at the look of pure rage that flashed in her blue eyes then turned sweetly innocent within seconds.

"A rumour you say? In truth, I can hardly imagine such a happening. Indeed, no one knows I took refuge from the storm in this cabin, but for you, of course. And you are too much of a gentleman to damage an innocent lady's reputation."

"You're right, of course," he blustered hurriedly. "I meant if another had come upon you."

Kiya nodded and smiled sweetly. "Little likelihood of that, I suppose. Few are out in this weather."

"You're father will worry, I think, if you're delayed overlong."

Kiya only responded with a half smile. "I don't think so. He knows I'm perfectly safe with Matt." Now all she had to do was convince herself of the truth of that statement. "Would you care for tea?"

"Now that I'm here, you should send your guard to tell your father that you are safe."

This wasn't the first time this toad had tried to get her alone. No doubt it wouldn't be the last. "Never fear, my father won't worry."

"I'd stay with you while he's gone, of course."

"That is very kind of you sir, but no need, I'm sure," Kiya returned.

"I won't be leaving, sir," Matt interrupted the man and his insistence. "My job is to stay with her at all times. I'd be remiss in my duties if I did anything less."

The viscount made some noises, pretending agreement as he rubbed his face and hair dry. "Um, yes, I'm sure, very good, my boy. I'll have that tea, Kiya, my dear."

The viscount sat at the table opposite Matt as he sipped his hot tea. While drying his hair, he'd forgotten to see to it that it lay flat on his head. The thin wisps that had tried in vein to cover his pink scalp stood up almost straight, leaving him with a look that bespoke a terrifying fright taken. Kiya could barely keep a straight face, especially since the man seemed as always to have one thought in mind.

"Don't you think you could protect her all the better if you stationed yourself outside?"

"No."

Kiya quickly turned her unexpected laugh into a cough then a soft clearing of her throat.

"I hope you're not coming down with something, my dear."

"No. I'm sure I'll be fine, Lord Winston."

But the viscount was intent on one subject and returned to it the moment he was able. "That way you could see if someone approached the cabin from any side."

"There's only one door. To get to her, they'd have to come through it. I could kill at least three before they got me," he said, fingering his gun as well as the long knife that sat sheathed at its side. "I'm sure you could stop a few, Lord Winston."

"Of course, of course," he repeated. Both Matt and Kiya could almost hear the man's mind working on this problem. He was damn near desperate to get Kiya alone.

That was more than obvious, but Matt wasn't about to let that happen. "I think I hear something."

"Don't worry. It's just the wind."

"No, I think it's a rider."

"Perhaps another neighbour needs shelter," Kiya offered, but she hadn't heard anything.

"The storm is close to ending. The wind is lessening." Matt looked directly at Kiya as he finished with, "We'll be leaving soon, I think."

* * * *

She didn't speak to him again that day and thought she probably would not for the rest of her life. In truth, she was aghast. The horror of what she'd done was not to be borne. And there wasn't anyone to blame but herself, unless she shifted the entire culpability to Matt's shoulders where, after some thought, she realised it belonged.

Still shifting the blame to him did little good. Despite the fact that it was all that beast's fault, she couldn't stop berating herself for her part in it—her very *small* part in it. Her face flamed every time she allowed herself to remember. Granted, she hadn't known what he was about. At least not at first. Except, of course, when he'd kissed her. It was then she should have stopped him. Oh Lord, how could she have allowed it? God in heaven, she hadn't even known his true name! There wasn't a doubt in her mind that she'd never know another moment when she'd suffer a greater degree of mortification. What in the world had come over her?

Any number of times, she could have simply told him to stop, and she hadn't a doubt he would have done just that.

But had she? No, she certainly had not. Instead, she had allowed a man, almost a perfect stranger—strike perfect, for he was far from that, but a stranger in any case—the most intimate knowledge of her body. And God help her, she had loved every minute of it. He had done things she had never imagined. How had he learned them? There was only one way, of course. He must have been with dozens of women, perhaps hundreds. She shivered her disgust at the thought of becoming one of the many. Too late to worry on that score, she reasoned, for one of the many was exactly what she had become.

She tried to force aside her intense sense of shame and think more clearly on the subject. Exactly what did it mean? Exactly what was it she'd done? Was she a fallen woman, ruined, no longer a virgin? She thought she was still a virgin, at least in the strictest form of the word. Kya had been born on a working farm. She knew what it took to reproduce, and they hadn't done that. The problem was she didn't know what they'd done. And there wasn't anyone she could ask, except perhaps the villain who had initiated the entire business in the first place. And that wasn't about to happen since she was never going to talk to him again.

* * * *

"I don't care what it takes. I want her brought to me." Jim Willis nodded at Lord Winston. They stood behind the town's tavern in the near dark of evening. "She is not to know the where or the why. Keep her bound and blindfolded at all times."

"Aye, sir," the man said in return as he hefted the two good-sized sacks of coin. Carting off that much money in gold was cumbersome indeed, but a bank draft was out of the question. He was being paid an enormous amount of money. Part of it was to keep his mouth shut. No one could ever know who was behind Kiya Harrison's kidnapping. "I'll take care o' it, sir."

"Do not try to contact me. Just bring her where I told you and leave her there. You have the key. Make sure the door is locked. I'll have my man deliver the final payment. Here, same time, in two days hence." He eyed the man for a long moment before continuing with, "I'm sure I don't have to remind you that she is to be left unmarred, in every way. Should you or one of your thugs dare to touch her in ways I need not mention, not only will the second half of this payment not be forthcoming, but you will, to a man, be hunted down and disposed of. Have I made myself clear?"

"Aye, sir," he said stiffly, hardly put at ease by yet another threat, and threatened he was every time he involved himself with one of the gentry. There had been bodies aplenty spread out and grotesquely positioned over the countryside. He wondered if they were to this bugger's credit. Jim hadn't a doubt that this one of the bleedin' gentry meant what he said. Jesus, but he was tired. Tired of kissin' his bloody arse, tired of his bloody fuckin' highness, lordin' it o'er everyone, thinkin' he was better than any man, when in fact he couldn't get it up unless some poor gel was strung up an bleedin'. Jim thought it was high time the bastard knew what it felt like to find a knife at his throat. After this job, his last, for this bastard, he'd be a rich man. He wouldn't be bowin' to gentry trash again.

* * * *

"We'll be back tomorrow, Father, the day after at the latest," Merry said as she dropped a small bag inside the coach. Amy's bags were tied to the back of the coach. Kiya watched a servant place a huge basket inside which would provide all a picnic lunch midway. It was a lovely day. They were leaving early so that they might arrive at their uncle's by late afternoon. Kiya expected an easy time of it for the roads to their uncle's home were the best in all of England.

"Goodbye, my dears," Mr. Harrison said as he kissed all three of his daughters and helped each into the coach. With the door secured, they adjusted yards of ruffles and lace, while their father went on with, "Have a good trip."

He directed his gaze to the two riders who would watch over them. "See to it that they are kept safe."

"Yes, sir," the two men replied in unison.

Before all three ladies had settled themselves inside, the carriage sprinted forward, leaving the older gentleman in a cloud of dust. The sudden movement jarred the women, sending Kiya, who hadn't as yet gained her seat, to the floor of the coach with a hard bounce to her rear, her feet and stocking-clad legs thrashing wildly, for an instant, above her head, almost lost amid a stiff white petticoat. Merry alone waved her hanky and called out goodbye while Amy nearly dissolved into a fit of giggles at her sister's mishap.

"Mr. George, please," Kiya called out to their driver, while struggling to straighten her hat and secure her seat. "A little less vigour, if you will."

Matt followed to the left of the coach, while Jake Carter, his partner, rode on the right. Matt hadn't missed the sight of a black-clad leg, exposed almost to the knee amid a flash of white ruffles and narrowed his gaze upon the lady attached to that trim appendage. He darted a quick glance to his right and had an odd moment of relief upon realising Carter, positioned as he was, had missed the luscious sight.

He hadn't spoken to her since their afternoon together two days past. She hadn't again taken her horse out riding. No doubt, the lady suffered some sense of embarrassment over the intimacies they'd shared, but Matt wasn't about to allow that to stop them from repeating those luscious delights — delights he'd savoured for the last two nights while sleep eluded him. Hour after hour, he'd lain helpless but to remember the feel of her, the scent of her, the taste of her skin and mouth until he thought he might go mad. With relish, he'd relived those luscious moments as he'd initiated her into the first stages of lovemaking. And when he slept at last, it was she who haunted his dreams, leaving him on the verge of insanity. Indeed, he was eager to see to it that she remembered well what they had done. He hadn't a doubt that they were to do that and more again.

As the vehicle left the long drive and turned onto the country road, Amy was still laughing. "Kiya, it was the look on your face. You were so shocked."

"I'm delighted to have been able to entertain," she remarked sarcastically.

"God, you're so stodgy. You fell. It wasn't a catastrophe. What happened to your sense of humour?"

A good question, Kiya thought. Her sense of humour had disappeared along with her innocence upon entering her father's cabin some two days past. She stole a glance at her tormentor once she'd found her seat, only to realise he'd seen the fall and, no doubt, half her leg to boot. God, what else? He'd already seen just about all there was to see and felt most of the rest. Lately, to her dismay, she'd found it impossible to keep her clothes in place while in the man's company.

She sighed at her thoughts. All right, perhaps that was an exaggeration. She could only blame her extreme distress. After all, what lady wouldn't be upset? Likely, she'd never get over the incredible scene at the cabin. Lord, it was simply too much for any innocent young woman to manage. She sighed softly to herself. There would come a day when she'd think on the matter with some fondness and perhaps a touch of amusement, say when she reached ninety-three or four. Until then, she'd know only torture especially since Matt had, from the first, been assigned as her guard and would no doubt continue as such.

What reason could she give to find another now? There were none. None she could think of at any rate. Lord, what in the world was she going to do? Could she never ride her horse again, walk in her garden or visit a friend? She had made a terrible mistake. One she had no idea how to go about correcting. She wished she could talk to Merry, but Merry would be aghast. Any one of her friends would be equally horrified should they come to know what she'd done.

"You've been quiet these last few days, Kiya. Are you feeling well?" Merry asked.

"Indeed. Very well, thank you," she returned with a soft smile, loath to cause her family worry.

"Is something troubling you then?"

"No. Nothing at all."

"She's in love," Amy said with a wicked snicker.

Merry smiled. "Is she? With whom, I wonder?"

Kiya thought to bring to an instant close any further discussion, lest they come to some erroneous conclusion. "Please, do not discuss me as if I were not present. Amy is mistaken. I most certainly am not in love."

Amy ignored her declaration and continued on in the same vein. "Mmm," she murmured as if in thought then said, "I've got it! It's Matthews."

"You are a wretched, wilful child," Kiya said, her eyes narrowing with annoyance. "I've just told you I'm not in love. Take that silly thought from your mind this minute."

"I'm not a child, and I don't have to listen to you. Besides, you are only four years older than me, so don't act so high and mighty. And your face is red," Amy gloated as if that fact alone proved the truth of her words.

"You'd best listen to me before you run amuck. And why shouldn't I be red? With such a foolish notion, it is a wonder that your face is not red, as well."

Merry smiled as her sisters squabbled. "I'm going to miss this nonsense when I'm gone." Merry was due to marry in three weeks time. All too soon, she'd be the Countess of Binghamshire.

"Indeed, it would be the only thing I wouldn't miss," Kiya returned, careful not to protest too vehemently, lest she give her sisters something to think on in earnest.

"I wish he looked at me the way he looks at you. He looks scrumptious."

Kiya merely sighed and shook her head. One could hardly consider the man scrumptious. Granted, it posed no hardship to look at him, and she imagined her sister correct to a point. He was attractive, but in a hard, rough manner, a bit too dark and too obviously male for her liking. He always needed a shave and looked somewhat disreputable, perhaps even frightening, and certainly not the sort to perk her interest.

From the first, Kiya wasn't overly thrilled to find herself guarded. He was hired by her father, for a murderer roamed the countryside and her father sought to ensure his daughters' safety. Still, the man rarely spoke and mostly left her to her own thoughts while in his company. And yet, there was something about him, something she couldn't understand, something that kept her continuously on guard. She couldn't say what the problem was. All she knew was he made her oddly uncomfortable, while her cheeks often grew warm beneath his dark all-encompassing gaze.

The problem here was that Amy had been in a continuous state of passionate love since the age of twelve. Of course, every month, a new prince charming had caught her eye. So far, thank the Lord, nothing had come of these brief, if all consuming, love affairs, and her sisters were set upon keeping it that way. She was but a girl of ten and five, far too young for such nonsense. Still, she managed some truly outrageous thoughts. *In love indeed!*

"I'm sure he is merely diligent in his work," Merry remarked, trying to ease the tension between the two sisters. "No doubt, he is simply being very careful that no harm should befall her while in his care."

"You turn every word or look into an all-consuming love affair," Kiya said as she watched the scenery pass and purposely ignored the man who rode just behind and to the left of the coach. "I, for one, will be happy when you outgrow such nonsense."

"I shall never outgrow it," Amy declared. "I shall marry a man who loves me to desperation. And we shall live forever consumed by a love that has no equal."

"One can only hope you find him soon," Kiya returned dryly.

* * * *

Some hours later, the coach came to a stop at a small clearing near a shallow bubbling stream. Cook had assembled a lovely luncheon of cold chicken, cheeses and bread, as well as a huge jug of apple cider and some fresh fruit. All partook in the small feast, including their driver and the two bodyguards. Kiya was careful to keep her attention on her food while Matt hardly noticed what he ate since he was so absorbed by the lovely lady sitting across from him.

After lunch, Kiya walked away from the small group. "We have things to discuss, Kiya. Hiding in your house is a cowardly route, wouldn't you say? Besides, no matter how you hide, they're not going to go away."

Kiya looked up to find Matt standing at her side. She hadn't heard his approach and was surprised to find he had followed her to the small stream.

He was dressed in black—his trousers, shirt and coat were always black. He wore a gun, tucked into a holster at his waist, hidden by his coat. The trouble was the gun was the only thing that was hidden. His narrow hips and thick thighs were all too obvious in his tight trousers, while polished boots reached to his knees. He reminded her of pictures she'd seen of pirates, missing only a straggly beard and evil grin. In truth, he looked at least as dangerous.

"I'm not hiding at all," she hotly denied. "Whatever gave you such a notion? And we have nothing to talk about."

"You didn't ride yesterday." He pushed his point. "Why not, unless you're hiding? You ride every day. And we need to talk about what happened at the cabin."

"If it is any of your concern, I was busy preparing for this trip. And nothing happened."

"Nothing happened except you damn near melted in my arms, and if Winston hadn't come upon us, we'd probably still be at it."

She took a quick step away from him as if to deny the truth of his words and returned with a sharp hiss, "Good God, but you are obnoxious."

"We need to talk about it."

She turned her back to him. "It was a moment of insanity. I'd be grateful if you would simply forget it ever happened."

He chuckled softly and moved close to whisper near her ear, "Forget it happened? Forget you turned into a man's dream at my touch? Forget the heat of you? Forget your taste? Not bloody likely."

"You must. Please. You must." She turned to face him again, her blue eyes pleading. "We should never talk about it, never think about and certainly never do it again."

Matt grinned. "You think it is easy? I'll wager you'll never forget it."

She knew the truth of those words. Still she sought to deny them. "I have every intention of forgetting it. As a matter of fact, I already have." She looked him straight in the eye and asked, her tone calmly polite as if discussing the weather, "What was it in particular that we were talking about?"

His unexpected laughter was so genuine, deep and masculine that Kiya found her heart suddenly pounding and her cheeks flushing hotly. She couldn't name the wild explosion of emotion that came upon her. In denial, she silently insisted she felt no emotion. The strange twist in her chest had nothing to do with the fact that this man outshone any other. His looks, of course, were of no consideration. She'd simply eaten too fast. No doubt the apple hadn't been ripe enough.

Kiya staved off the quiver of her own lips. She wouldn't join him in laughter. There was nothing the least bit amusing about this conversation. If anything, it was terribly embarrassing, nothing to laugh at to be sure. She turned away and reached into her pocket for her pipe and tobacco. She wouldn't look at him. The way he threw his head back, the way his teeth flashed white against his tanned skin, had no effect on her, none whatsoever. She wasn't going to eat another apple for some time, she thought as her chest tightened again.

"Do you have any idea how delicious you are? If we were alone I'd kiss you senseless for that."

Kiya pulled herself up to her full five feet two inches and fixed him with her most forbidding glare. "Mr. Chase, I've no doubt I'm already beyond the point of good sense to be listening to this rubbish in the first place, and you will please refrain from mentioning kisses in my presence."

He grinned at her sudden show of arrogance. "There's no point in mentioning them if not in your presence."

She searched her pockets only to realise she had no means to light her pipe. She knocked the tobacco from it and replaced it in her pocket as she remarked coolly, "Then don't mention them at all."

He couldn't control his need to smile. God, she was something. He thought her particularly sassy and adorable while holding a pipe between her small teeth, her blue eyes flashing in fury. "There is something between us. Don't you think we should discover exactly what it is?"

"There is nothing between us," and at his look of doubt, she thoughtlessly added, "except perhaps lust." Her cheeks grew pink with dismay as she realised she'd blurted out so daring a word.

He nodded, his eyes dark with remembered pleasure. "Lust is good."

"It's not good," she countered, her cheeks growing darker still. "It's not good at all."

"It's a start."

"It's the worst of starts."

"Should we start again then? Should I court you?" Matt was shocked as he realised what he'd just said. He hadn't intended to offer for her. He didn't want to marry her. Not any more than she wanted to marry him. Still, he thought perhaps there was a flicker of merit in the notion. Something he needed to think on. After all was said and done, one glaring truth remained, he very simply wasn't about to allow another the pleasure he knew when she was in his arms.

Kiya laughed at the shock in his eyes. Obviously, he hadn't meant to make her an offer. "What?"

"Should I?" he insisted, despite his own surprise and already growing a bit more comfortable with the thought. "Should I speak to your father? Should I make you an offer? Is that what you want?"

"What I want is to end this ridiculous conversation." Then without thought she blurted out, "My sister already thinks—"

"What?" he asked as she came to a sudden stop. "What does she think?"

Kiya shook her head as if to discount the thought. "She's a child. She thinks she's in love. She thinks everyone is in love."

"She thinks *you* are?" His gaze narrowed at her lack of response. "With me?"

"I told you she is a child."

"Are you?"

Kiya laughed at the ridiculous notion, laughed even more that he should even bother to ask. "No. I'm not."

"You're in lust then."

"Oh my God," she groaned and turned beet red before she snapped, "You will abstain from using such language in my presence."

He grinned. It was all right, he supposed that she could use it, but she blushed to the roots of her blonde hair when he did. "Will I? Tell me you wouldn't love it if I kissed you right now. Tell me you'd hate it if I sucked your tongue into my mouth or bit your luscious breasts, ran my tongue over your nipples or slid my fingers between your smooth, hot, wet thighs again."

She spun suddenly away, amazed that she had the strength to move never mind actually walk, for his words caused her knees a weakness she'd never believed possible. She shivered.

"I can see your nipples tightening. You want it all right."

"You are a monster. I'm not listening to this. I'm going back to the coach. It's time we got started again."

"One moment," he said, touching her arm and bringing her to a stop. "Do you want to marry?"

"I most certainly do not."

Matt nodded. "Then you will ride again tomorrow. The moment we get back."

"I will not, and you will kindly —"

"In that case," he interrupted, "I shall be forced to tell your father what we did in the cabin. I'm sure he'll immediately arrange our marr—"

"What?"

"I think you heard me." Matt grinned as he walked with cocky arrogance back to his horse. He had her. There was no way this little spitfire would get away from him. So she didn't want to marry. No problem. Either way, he would bed the little wretch, bed her until he died from the pleasure of it, until they both did.

She was so upset she followed him back to his horse. Never thinking they were being watched, she grabbed his arm and forced him to turn and face her wrath. "And what would that prove? That you are the worst of all beasts?"

"It's very simple. Ride with me, or I tell your father."

"Mr. Chase please, you must know I was an innocent. I never realised what you were about. You cannot force me into accepting you because of one mistake."

If he'd wanted this tasty morsel just a tad less he might have relented at her heartfelt plea. But the truth was, he wanted her more than she could have imagined, and no amount of pleading would serve her well. "Can't I?"

"I'll deny it."

"Will you? Do you know you have a small beauty mark just under your right breast? Do you think your father might wonder how I came to know of it?"

"I don't."

"Look in the mirror."

"Matt," she groaned. She wanted to fling herself at him, to beg for a reprieve. "Why are you doing this?"

Matt gave her a look that told her clearly she knew better than to ask such a question.

"There are other women. Others who wouldn't mind the things you do."

"You didn't mind them either," he returned in all male confidence. "And you won't mind them the next time we do them. Shall I tell your father we plan to marry, then?"

She shook her head. "I need time to think."

"Time to try to get out of it, you mean?" His voice grew suddenly hard. "I'll have your answer the moment you return home." He nodded towards the coach and the young lady standing beside it, her eyes wide as she watched the strange goings on. "You'd best come up with a good story. Your sister hasn't taken her eyes off us."

"Oh my God," Kiya moaned, as she turned and took in Amy's eager expression. Kiya had been so distraught that she'd forgotten all about her sisters. Her lips never moved as she snidely remarked, "No doubt just one more thing for which I should thank you."

Matt gained his saddle then leaned down to whisper in return, "If you are talking about the way I kissed you and touched you, you're very welcome. Indeed it was my pleasure." He laughed as her cheeks grew dark and her blue eyes darker still as they promised untold revenge.

She turned towards the coach, lost in thought. She wouldn't marry him. It was out of the question. She hardly knew the man. How could he possibly believe she'd marry him, and why would he want her to? He didn't. Of course, he didn't. He was simply trying to force her to his will. What would he do, she wondered if she called his bluff? He wouldn't tell her father. She knew he wouldn't. Didn't she?

The remains of their luncheon were soon packed away, and the three ladies were once again inside their coach, more than a bit anxious to see this journey at its end. The coach rocked as it hit one rut and then another preventing its occupants from gaining even a moment's sleep, despite full stomachs and the afternoon's unusual heat.

The fact that Kiya couldn't sleep was just fine with Amy, she was nothing if not full of questions. Kiya needed to think. She didn't want to be bothered answering nonsensical questions right now. Still, she must or else allow the girl to come to her own wayward conclusions.

"We were talking about Jezebel. Matt, I mean, Mr. Chase is entering his horse in a race and thought I might be interested in doing the same."

"All that time?" Amy asked in disbelief. "You were talking about a race all that time?"

Kiya shrugged, trying to act as casual as possible. "We spoke of a possible wager on the outcome. I suppose we spoke of a few other things, as well. Why?"

"You looked furious most of the time. What was he laughing at?"

She shrugged. "I can't remember." Lord, but she was getting good at lying, thanks to a certain abominable man.

"What did he say about you smoking?"

"What did he say?" she asked as if she couldn't fathom such an outrageous question. "What should he say? It's none of his business, is it?"

"Do you mean he likes women who smoke?"

"I mean, my dear sister, I have no knowledge of Mr. Chase's likes or dislikes." That wasn't exactly true of course. She knew some things the man liked well enough, but Kiya wasn't about to correct any inaccuracies in her statement. "Whether he likes women who smoke or not is hardly any of my concern, is it?"

"Do you think I should start?" Amy mused half to herself. "If it means I might attract a man such as him, it's a thought, isn't it?"

"I'm sure you are mistaken about an attraction. And I think you can do whatever you wish once you're of age."

"You're not of age, and you smoke."

"As you continually point out to me, I'm four years older than you." Kiya gave a weary sigh. "Amy, must we go on about such nonsense? Do whatever you will. I've no doubt you'll do it in any case."

"I don't like the taste. It made me terribly ill."

Merry and Kiya smiled. So the little twit tried it already.

"Good," the two older sisters said in unison.

The words were barely uttered when the coach came to a sudden jarring stop. Kiya thought Mr. George might do a better job of starting and stopping this coach. She'd never known him to drive so recklessly. As it turned out, it wasn't Mr. George's fault at all. A fallen tree lay across the road. All three women craned their necks trying to see the problem from the coach windows. Matt and Jake rode towards the tree and dismounted. Seconds later, the tree was easily moved to the side of the road.

They were about to regain their saddles when three masked horsemen suddenly, almost silently, appeared from the thick woods that bordered the road. One of the three pointed a gun in the direction of the two guards, forcing them to throw down their weapons.

"Oh my God," Merry whispered softly. "Highwaymen."

Another of the three quickly took possession of all the horses, including the pair that pulled the coach. Loosely tying all together, he led them away, while the third man opened the door to the coach and peered inside at the three terror-stricken ladies. This wasn't the first time Kiya wished she had a gun. Only this time, if she'd had the weapon, she wouldn't have hesitated to use it.

"Mistress Kiya, please step out," a deep voice ordered, only slightly muffled by the mask pulled over the lower half of a dark face. His eyes were dark, small and mean the brows thick and black. There wasn't a chance the man wouldn't be instantly obeyed, unless the lady in question was frozen in place with terror as now proved to be the case.

Kiya barely heard the command, for at the mention of her name, her mind seemed to shut down.

Merry interrupted, "Please, you've stopped the wrong coach. There is no Mistress Kiya here."

The man chuckled evilly. "Good try, lady. Might you be the lady in question?"

"My good man, I've told you the truth of the matter. You've stopped the wrong coach." Merry pulled the arm locked around her neck away, for Amy in her fear hardly allowed her sister the ability to breathe. The youngest of the sisters couldn't stop her soft sobs as Merry repeated, "We don't know of any Kiya."

He laughed again. "Then I'll have to take you all, won't I?"

His words only caused Amy's sobs to grow stronger and considerably louder.

"No," Kiya managed finding her voice at last. "I'm the one you want."

Merry moaned her disappointment, for she had laboured under the misconception that, if she'd had a few more minutes to convince the man of his error, they might have been left to themselves.

Matt thought his heart would stop as he watched Kiya come alone from the coach. Her face was white. He knew she was terrified. Even from twenty feet away, he could see her tremble yet she put on a brave front, allowing the men to take her without any womanly wiles. No screams, no fainting, no tears, she met her fear straight on, braver than most men he knew.

No, a voice screamed in his head. *No, you won't take her.* And when the man closest to the coach, took her against him, with one hand around her waist, and dared to run his free hand over her breasts, Matt lost all sense of reason. He roared his rage as he charged the man, but was shot down halfway to his target. He lay upon the dirt road, while blood gushed from his head.

The sound of gunfire startled the horses. All four reared to their hind legs, pawing wildly at the empty air before them. The man holding them instantly let go and took cover, nearly trampled as they ran free. The two from the coach charged blindly into the woods, while Jake's and Matt's horses ran down the road some good distance. The horses were allowed to go their way. Pursuing and gathering them again would take time, thereby adding unnecessary danger to the three men and their evil quest.

Kiya never felt the man's touch. She was so frightened his depraved actions never penetrated her senses. But watching Matt fall to the road, seeing the blood gush from his head, she screamed, and with a short quick shot of her elbow to her captor's jaw, she broke free of her kidnapper. Instantly at Matt's side, she held his bloody head in her lap. "Matt," she cried. "Matt, are you all right? Damn you, why did you do that?"

Jake was at her side. She hardly realised that fact since she was so absorbed with the puddle of blood in her lap. She pressed her skirt to his bleeding head hoping to staunch the flow. Unnoticed by Kiya or their attackers, Jake slipped something into her pocket.

"I'll find you," Matt said, shaken but already conscious again. The bullet had only grazed his scalp, leaving a small, bloody, but very shallow mark just over one ear. It was a close call. Had the shooter been a touch better marksman, the bullet would have torn off most of the side of his head. Still, he knew a wave of dizziness and some measurable discomfort. "Don't be afraid."

A moment later, she was yanked away from Matt and carted towards one of the remaining horses. Her hands were bound behind her, a blindfold tied over her eyes. Like a sack of potatoes, she was thrown over the animal's back just before its rider gained the saddle.

Matt was left in the road, Jake kneeling beside him as the three men rode away with Kiya.

Chapter Three

Motionless, all five stayed for endless seconds as if frozen in shock, even the usual soft flutter of fabric remained oddly still on that small lonely patch of country road. The only sound above the territorial squabble between a lone squirrel and a shrieking blue bird was Amy's continuous whimper.

"What are we going to do? We have to find her!" she said softly and seemed to snap the scene alive once more.

Jake gave a sudden shrill whistle. Moments later, his and Matt's horses came trotting back to where the coach stood. "I'm going to bring her back. In the meantime, I want all of you to walk over that hill." He pointed behind them and to their right. "You'll find a small farm. Wait there for me."

He looked at Matt, who now sat in the road, holding his head and moaning softly. The gushing of blood had slowed to a mere dribble. "Are you all right?"

"I'm fine. I'm going with you." Matt looked at least as bad as he felt. One side of his face, neck and a goodly portion of his shirt were completely covered in blood. Mixed with the dirt and gravel of the road it added a layer of mud to his skin, while dust coated his usually meticulous black clothes and shining boots, leaving them a dull brown.

"I can move faster alone."

"I'll keep up," he said, and no one within hearing doubted for a second that he would. He wobbled as he came to his feet but felt better when once again on his horse.

Jake noticed the obvious dizziness and asked, "You sure?"

"I'm sure."

"One more thing," Jake said as he turned from his horse and walked quickly towards the two women. "I should have done this before," he said just before he took a startled Merry in his arms and kissed her full on the mouth, with an appreciating growl telling of his obvious lusty enjoyment.

When he released her, she stumbled slightly striving for a balance that momentarily eluded her. One lone fingertip came to her throbbing lips as if she would hold and savour the pressure of the kiss, the taste of it. Her blue eyes glowed with pleasure, and her heart pounded leaving her a bit breathless. Her cheeks gained colour as she returned without the slightest hesitation, "Yes, you should have."

Jake grinned at her response and was greatly tempted to kiss her again. He promised himself he most certainly would, but that promise would have to wait a bit.

Amy's eyes were wide, her mouth hung open in shock. Jake touched a finger beneath the young girl's chin and, with little pressure, brought her lips together. He smiled as he said, "Take care of your sister."

Merry murmured softly, "Be careful," just before he returned to his horse and sighed with relief as she watched him take a gun from a small saddle bag. A moment later, both men left without another look or word spoken.

Within seconds, the sounds of their horses faded to silence in the thick foliage as they trailed Kiya's kidnappers.

"Thank God, they both have extra weapons," Merry murmured.

Amy's tears suddenly dried as her mind turned to other matters at least as startling to her way of thinking, as the last five minutes had been.

"Oh my God, oh my God," she exclaimed. For the first time, she realised she'd been watching the wrong couple. Vaguely she remembered her always demure sister and Jake speaking after their picnic lunch, their voices low and intimate. Now that she thought on it, their heads had been a bit closer together than might be considered decorous. Still, she had hardly noticed, she was so absorbed in the unusual goings on between Kiya and the dashing Matthews. "And all along I thought it was Kiya and Matthews."

"The man's name is Matthew Chase, Amy, not Matthews. And I do believe you were right on that score. Mr. Chase seems to hold some tenderness for our sister, doesn't he? He very nearly got himself killed on her account."

"I know, I know, but I never thought Jake and you." She came to sudden stop. "Wait a minute. What about the Earl?" She blinked her obvious shock, while trying to wrap her mind around this new and totally outrageous discovery. "Aren't you getting married?"

Merry smiled. "We'll talk about that later. Let's get off the road for now." She took her sister's hand and, with Mr. George trailing behind them, started off through the woods towards the hill and the shelter Jake had directed them to find.

"Suppose they can't find her," Amy muttered worriedly, her tears once again at the ready.

"They'll find her, miss," Mr. George returned. "Have no worry on that score." He knew capable men when he saw them, and those two were as skilled in what they did as any he'd ever seen.

"Do you know he growled when he kissed you? Oh my heart," Amy said, as her hand fluttered in the general direction of the mentioned organ. And then she frowned. "Don't you want to be a countess?"

Merry might have smiled at her sister's dramatics had the immediate situation been less crucial. "Father wants me to be a countess," she returned noncommittally.

"So you're not going to marry the Earl?"

"Let's just see what happens, shall we?"

"Oh my God, I'm so excited. Do you love him?"

"Who?" Merry returned her thoughts on her sister and the terror Kiya must be suffering.

"Merry, will you stop teasing? Do you? Do you love him madly?"

She allowed her sister an affectionate smile. "Let's say I haven't thought through my feelings yet."

"But he kissed you, while we watched, and you let him. Has he done it before?"

"The circumstances were extreme, Amy. Let's just see what comes of it. First, and most importantly, we have to get Kiya back."

Of course, Amy couldn't take that for an answer. Between worried remarks about Kiya, she bombarded Merry with questions for the hour it took to reach the farmhouse. Merry wasn't sorry to be part of this inquisition, for it helped to keep her mind from the paralyzing terror that threatened to assault, terror that could easily drive her to hysterics should she not keep the emotion under the strictest control. She couldn't have been more worried for her sister, even though she knew somehow, someway, Jake and Matt would bring her back. She could only pray they'd find her before it was too late.

* * * *

"I told ya. Didn't I tell ya? He said no 'arm should come to 'er or we're dead men."

"I did 'er no 'arm, mate. A little feel ain't gonna 'urt 'er none."

"Just keep your bloody 'ands off 'er."

Just as he said the last, Kiya screamed as a hand reach under her skirt and travelled the length of her leg. The hand had reached her backside when a shot rang out and the man's hand fell away as his body slid from the horse to the ground, almost taking her with him. Kiya hadn't a doubt she'd suffer some serious injury should she fall on her head from this height. Thank God, the man had fallen back and away from her.

Oddly enough, after the gunshot, someone began to scream. It was a woman to be sure. Vaguely, Kiya wondered who it might be. Had there been another kidnapped? Was she not alone? Someone pulled her roughly from the horse. On her feet, she swayed dizzily while all the while the screaming never stopped. The man shook her violently. Her head snapped back and forth. The screaming stopped, almost as suddenly as it had begun. It was only then that Kiya realised it had been her. Her throat felt scratchy and sore.

"What the bloody 'ell's the matter wit ya? Scream like that again an I'll gag ye."

"Jesus, Jimmy, did you 'ave to kill 'im? He weren't doin' nothin' so bad."

"I told him, damn it! Didn't I tell 'im?"

Until this last half hour of her life, Kiya never knew the true meaning of the word fear. Her stomach and chest ached miserably as each jarring step of the horse had bruised her ribs and threatened to steal her breath. Her hands were tied so tightly behind her they were actually growing cold. Still, she would have taken that discomfort a thousand times over rather than this terror of the unknown.

All she could do plea for her life. "Please, you must listen to me. My father is rich. He'll give you anything you ask. Anything! I swear. How much were you paid? He'll give you more. I promise, much more." Her voice trembled terribly, so badly in fact that she wondered if they could hear or understand her. It clearly told these awful men of her fear. It gave them the power. All of it. She didn't care, for in truth the power already belonged to them. That wasn't important. She had to let them know she could best any offer.

Kiya felt like crying as she was hauled up and flung over the horse again. No one responded to her entreaty. No matter how she implored, no matter the promised reward. No one said another word as she continued to plead for her life, while swearing to these villains untold riches in exchange for her safety.

Some time passed, perhaps twenty minutes, but it could have been anywhere from five to an hour. She'd never realised it before, but while riding in her current position, one completely lost all sense of time.

They stopped at last, and Kiya was pulled off the horse. She stumbled beside her kidnapper as she was lead towards some unseen objective. A door opened on hinges that were in desperate need of oiling. The high-pitched, grinding sound alone sent a shiver down her spine. A moment later, she was thrust inside some sort of damp, dungeon-like room. An unexpected shove sent her sprawling to her knees. An instant later, the door shut, the ominous grating again causing her another shiver. A lock tumbled into place, securing her occupancy for as long as they wished. Or did it?

Kiya was no weak, simpering miss. If an escape was possible, she'd take it. She listened as they moved from the door. She called out for the last time, "Please. Don't do this. I'll make sure you're rewarded. I swear it, *please*," she begged. She might as well not have bothered for nothing but her own panting breath came as a response. The silence was deafening. Never in her life had anything sounded so still or so horribly, thickly dense. She was alone. Of that she had no doubt. The only sound was the pulsing of her blood.

The room smelled of damp earth. She wondered if she weren't underground. Was she perhaps in a mine or a tunnel of some sort?

But there were no tunnels or mines in this part of the country, were there? She stepped on her dress and tore it at the bodice as she struggled to her feet. Slowly, she moved, forcing herself to investigate her surroundings. An earthen wall stood some five feet to her right, another ten feet or so to her left. The back of the room was maybe ten feet from the door. She could discern no windows and no door but the one she had come through. The room held not even a chair. She sat on the dirt floor, her back to the wall and tried to think. The first thing she needed was to get her hands free.

She could find nothing sharp. The ground was soft dirt, the walls a bit firmer but still no rocks or shards of glass made themselves known. There was only one way. She had to bring her hands under her body and wiggle through the small circle that would make. Sweat coated every inch of her by the time she finally managed to bring her hands before her. She trembled with the effort and was, no doubt, covered with dirt. With her teeth, she worked feverishly on the bindings. It took some time, but she finally breathed a sigh of relief as her hands came free.

The instant blast of pain in her hands caused her a deep groan. God, she'd never have imagined the rush of blood would hurt to this extent. She rubbed her hands together. Finally, after some long moments the worst of the discomfort was finally gone.

The blindfold was the next to go, although that seemed to make little difference. Her tiny prison proved just as dark with eyes opened as closed. Almost.

She wasn't mistaken. There was the smallest slit of light. Upon closer inspection, Kiya realised there was a crack in the door, allowing little more than a soft almost negligible glow. She tried to look through it but found it wasn't big enough to detect movement or sound.

She tried the knob. Nothing. The lock held against her struggles.

Kiya paced the small enclosure. She tried to think. There had to be something she could do, something that would get her out of here.

She'd been kidnapped, of course, but why? Who would do this? Who would even think to do something so evil?

At first, she'd thought it was the madman who had killed those girls, but soon she'd discounted the notion. There were three of them. She'd heard them talking. They were working for someone. Could it be they worked for the madman? Had he hired a crew to find him women — Women he could torture and kill for his sick perversions? She thought not. Should the murderer be so foolish as to involve others, he chanced much. It would leave him vulnerable and open to blackmail. No, this wasn't the murderer's doings, at least not this particular crime.

This dastardly deed had been ordered by someone else. Someone at least as sinister, to be sure, but not, she thought, the murderer who currently plagued their countryside. Still, it was someone to be feared. The men who took her were afraid. So afraid, in fact, that they killed one of their own without hesitation, because he dared to disregard an order. She remembered now. Remembered what was said, while she'd hung helplessly over the horse. "He said no harm should come to her. Keep your hands off her." At the time, she'd been almost paralyzed with fear and the words had hardly registered.

She tried to think it through but could make no sense of it. If she'd been kidnapped for the purpose of ransom, why would they worry over her being touched? To be sure, she was thankful to be left reasonably unharmed, but why would that be so important to her kidnapper?

Kiya moaned in frustration. She could find no answer. What she needed was a smoke. A few minutes with her pipe would ease her nerves and allow her to think. She reached for her pipe forgetting she still had no means to light it. Her hands touched something heavy and hard. What in the world?

Kiya frowned as she pulled a gun from her pocket. She wasn't familiar with this type of gun. It was very small. How had it come to be in her pocket? Had Matt put it there while she'd held his head in her lap? Could he have reached her? She shook her head. It mattered not how she'd gotten it. All that mattered was what she did with it.

At first, Kiya thought she might shoot the lock from the door but, moments later, thought better of the notion It was too dark. If she missed, she'd waste a bullet, one she might desperately need later on. In truth, a bullet might not work. She'd wait. Wait until her kidnappers came back. The moment they opened the door, she'd put a bullet in the first one who crossed the threshold. God willing, once out of here, she'd take his horse and soon find help.

Kiya knew she could do it. It might take some cold, deliberate calculating, but if and when her kidnapper came, she had no choice but to put him out of commission for his intent could only be to do her harm. She had no doubt of it.

Time passed slowly as she waited in a small, dark, earthen room. Kiya couldn't be sure, but she thought

Patricia Pellicane

perhaps an hour had gone by before she heard the sound of men's voices. She stiffened with fear and dread. It was one thing to swear she would shoot, but when the time came, she knew it would be harder than she thought to squeeze off the needed shot. Still no matter how hard, she'd do it. Her very life depended on it.

"Kiya, are you in there?"

Kiya's knees almost gave out as she recognised the voice. "I'm here. I'm in here."

"Step away from the door," Jake called. "Did you hear me?"

She heard a mighty kick, another then another. The door trembled but held fast. He used his shoulder next. Again and again and still nothing. "I'm going to shoot the lock. Did you hear me? Step away."

It took five shots before the door finally opened. Jake stood just outside of the room, but Kiya only had eyes for the man at his side. Kiya took in the sight of Matt's injury. Blood had run down his face and coated his clothes. Even now, fresh blood dribbled from his wound. She moved towards him. "You shouldn't have come for me. You've been hurt."

Kiya might have said he shouldn't have come but she was never happier to see him. "How did you find me?"

"They left trail a child could follow," Jake said. "Not to mention a body along the way. Obviously they had no fear of being followed."

"I have to tell you the dead man gave me a start." Matt's gaze, filled with relief, never left her small form. He wanted to crush her against him and kiss her until neither of them could think of breathing again. His voice cracked a bit as he went on. "I thought if they'd kill one of their own, what might they do to you?"

"Are you all right?" she asked him. He looked ready to fall on his face.

"I'm good. Did they hurt you?"

She was covered in dirt. It streaked her face, her neck and hands. It coated her hair and dress and yet in his eyes she'd never looked lovelier than at this moment.

"No," she shook her head. "They just shoved me in there and locked the door. From what they said, I think someone is coming for me."

"Is he now?" Jake's wolfish grin matched the twinkle of burgeoning anticipation in his eyes. He wasn't the sort to forgo certain physical encounters. Indeed, he eagerly looked forward to some. "In that case, why don't I wait a bit?" he remarked perhaps a bit too ingenuously. "You can get her back, can't you, Matt?"

"I can't do much, but I think I can manage that," Matt said as he pulled himself into his saddle, despising the trembling in his arms. He couldn't remember when he'd felt weaker or more disgusted with the fact. A moment later, with Jake's help, Kiya sat in front of him. His arms came around her, silently urging her to lean against him. "All right?" he asked.

Kiya nodded, knowing she'd never feel more all right. Tears sparkled in her eyes as she leaned into his warm embrace. God, he smelled so good and felt so warm. She hadn't realised she was cold. Not until his arms came around her. She shivered.

"Cold?" he asked.

"Not now," she returned and said nothing when his arms pulled her closer still. She hadn't cried, not once during the worst of today's horror. Not once had it even occurred to her yet now her eyes shown brilliant with unshed tears as her rescue proved true. She knew nothing but relief.

"You're not going to cry, are you?"

"I told you once before. I never cry."

"Go to the Miller farm. The others are there waiting for you. They'll give you a wagon to get home."

Matt nodded and turned his horse, leaving Jake to await the arrival of the man responsible for Kiya's kidnapping.

Kiya, sitting sideways, lifted her gaze to Matt, studying the damage done. Her fingers touched his blood soaked hair, just below the slowly oozing wound. "You look awful. Are you sure you're all right?"

"I'll be fine, just a little dizzy."

"You need bandaging. The wound is still bleeding a bit." She shook her head and small teeth worried her bottom lip. "Matt, you shouldn't have come. You should have rested."

Matt groaned as he gave into the need and snuggled the uninjured side of his face against her cheek, her ear, her hair. "God, I almost went mad thinking about what they were doing to you. There was no way I couldn't have come; no way could I have rested."

Something tightened in her chest at the sound of his desperation, and she found herself comforting gently. "They didn't do anything except shove me into that room." Kiya glanced behind her and realised the small hill. Obviously, the room was built into its side. "Why would anyone build a room into a hill?"

"The work of smugglers, likely. Boats have been racing over the damn channel for a hundred years. Depending on the darkness of the night, this area no doubt teems with wagons of contraband. I'd say the room is or was a temporary safe house, a place to drop off and pick up merchandise."

They travelled some half mile in silence before Kiya felt Matt reach for his gun. A moment later, to Kiya's surprise, Lord Winston atop his huge horse suddenly blocked their path.

"What is this? What are you doing?" Lord Winston asked, clearly aghast to find Kiya in her current dishevelled state. "Kiya what happened?"

"She had an accident." Matt said, loath to allow any mention of what had truly transpired, lest this one and no doubt others come to believe the worst. "Her horse threw her."

"Oh my dear, are you all right? Please, we aren't far from my place. I insist you must come and rest. I'll send one of my men to tell your father."

"There's no need. I've already sent one of my men to do just that. Mr. Harrison is awaiting our arrival." And should the man harbour any further thoughts that he might persuade the young woman to accompany him, Matt added, "Just for my own peace of mind, of course, I've sent another for the doctor."

The viscount scowled and shot him a murderous glare, never once asking why Matt was covered in blood if it was Kiya who had taken a fall, or why they were a good two miles or more from the nearest road. "Of course," he returned. "Well then, since you have everything under control, I'll leave our dear Kiya in your capable hands." He nodded and moved off towards the road, while offering nothing in the way of explanation as to why he should be riding through woods that were miles from any road and farther still from his estate.

Barely five minutes after leaving Lord Winston's company, Kiya felt Matt sway drunkenly behind her. A sharp look in his direction convinced her of his suffering. Where his skin was not covered with blood or mud it appeared less tan than ashen grey. "You're not all right, are you?"

"I'm wonderful," he groaned thickly. "Now that I know you're safe, I'm better than wonderful." A moment later, no doubt due to the loss of blood, he slid into dead faint. His weight heavy against her almost knocked her from the horse.

Kiya slid carefully down the side of the animal as Matt slumped forward. His head lay upon the stallion's neck, an arm hung loose on each side. She wasn't strong enough to ease him down. She'd never be able to take his weight without causing him further injury. She couldn't let him fall. No doubt an added blow to his head would bring about some permanent damage. She had no choice but to force him to remain on the horse. Holding to his arm and leg, pulling and pushing against him when necessary, she somehow managed to keep him in the saddle as they moved slowly through the brush.

Branches and thorns seemed to reach out to her tear at her dress and tangle in her hair. There was no path. Through Herculean effort, she somehow forced the animal through the thickest underbrush she'd ever known. So it was with no little degree of relief that she finally mounted the hill behind the Miller farm.

The sun was low on the horizon, and Kiya trembled with exhaustion and breathed a sigh of relief to find her sisters pacing impatiently behind the distant farmhouse. She whispered a prayer of thanks, her legs barely able to support her as Mr. George came running.

* * * *

Kiya sat in her tub until the water grew cold. She had never known this degree of exhaustion, and she wondered if she had the strength to stand. She ached in places that had never ached before, but it was her feet that had suffered the worst abuse. Having no idea they would be needed, she hadn't worn boots. Her soft kid slippers had proved largely useless in the way of protection against jagged rocks, burrs and broken dagger-like sticks that had littered the uneven forest floor. In the end, her feet were scraped, cut and bruised. She thought it would be some time before she'd walk again with any degree of comfort.

She had just come from the tub when a soft knock sounded on her door, and Amy slipped quietly into the room. "How are you feeling?"

"Better now, except for my feet. Would you ask Nora to fetch salves and bandages?"

"Yes, but first there's something I have to tell you."

"What?" Kiya asked when her sister appeared unwilling to go on.

As it turned out, Amy was far from unwilling but had merely waited for a dramatic pause before she began. "Jake kissed Merry. On the mouth. Right in front of us."

Kiya's eyes widened with some surprise. "When?"

"Just before he went after you. Out on the road, with Mr. George and myself watching."

Kiya smiled. "And what did Merry do?"

"Wait. First he said 'I should have done this before', and then he kissed her and then she said, 'Yes you should have'." Amy swung herself in a circle, her ecstatic expression as dreamy as any Kiya had ever seen. "Isn't that the most romantic thing you've ever heard?"

Kiya laughed. "Indeed it is. What did Merry say about it?"

"She said she had to think about it."

"No doubt," Kiya returned.

"Kiya," Amy almost whispered as if she could hardly believe it. "He growled. When he kissed her, I heard him growl."

Kiya laughed. "Did he? He enjoyed it then?"

Her eyes were huge with excitement. "That's what it sounded like."

"And that was it? He just kissed her and said nothing more?"

"He told me to take care of my sister."

Kiya sat on her bed and laughed again. "Did he? But what about the earl?"

"That's what I said. But Merry kept saying, 'we'll see'. Oh my, what a day! We were so worried about you, I could hardly stop crying and then he kissed her. I was so shocked. I didn't know what to think." Amy threw herself on her sister's bed and gave a great sigh. "But the most shocking part was Merry wasn't shocked at all. Do you think he's kissed her before?"

"Did Merry say he had?"

"I asked her that, too. She won't tell me anything."

Kiya laughed at Amy's dramatics.

"I'm going to write in my journal." Amy jumped from the bed. "I don't want to forget anything that happened today."

"Ask Nora to come with the bandages first."

* * * *

Almost an hour later, with a barely noticeable limp, Kiya left her room, dressed in her night dress and robe with soft slippers on her bandaged feet. Her hair was still damp, but with Nora's help, it had been combed into smooth waves down her back.

Matt occupied the room next to her own. According to her father, he deserved nothing less than the best care and accommodations considering the damage suffered while trying to protect his daughter. He had called for the doctor and assigned a nurse from the village to see to his needs.

Kiya knocked and entered the quiet, shadowy room. The nurse, Lena, sat reading in a corner, a candle on the table at her side. Kiya smiled at the woman who often worked in the parish nursery. "If you'd like to get something to eat or drink, I'll sit with him for a spell."

"Oh thank you, miss. I was only now thinking a cup of tea would be just the thing."

Kiya nodded and took the nurse's vacated seat. "Take your time."

"I'll be right back, miss, and thank you."

Kiya nodded, and the nurse left the room.

"Are you thinking to take advantage of me now that I'm too weak to fight you off?"

Something happened inside her as she listened to his teasing words and spied a flash of white teeth from the shadows of his bed, something that caused her chest to squeeze and her heart to flutter. Kiya couldn't imagine what it was. All she was sure of was her relief to find him well enough to talk nonsense. For some reason, it brought her a moment of absurd happiness. Kiya allowed a low chuckle as she came to her feet and approached the bed.

"That would pose a hardship, I've no doubt," she teased in return.

"I'm sure I can endure whatever you want to do to me. Indeed, I'm stronger than I look."

"What you look like is a disreputable pirate. You lack only a ring in your ear." She studied his dark features for a moment before saying, "I think you grow more dangerous looking every day."

He gave a soft laugh. "You think so? And yet, I've not been able to put fear in you."

"Would you rather I was afraid of you?"

He grinned, his teeth a flash of white against the dark shadow of a beard and his eyes shining with wicked humour. "It could only further my cause."

She smiled knowing some surprise. Some hours ago, she was nearly speechless with rage at his daring and now? Now she only knew a sense of ease in his presence, while a smile hovered about her lips. Kiya didn't want to think why that should be. It was enough that it was. "I see you're feeling better."

"Now that you're here," he breathed. "Have you just come from a bath? You smell gorgeous."

"People don't smell gorgeous."

"You do."

Kiya refused to further that topic and asked instead, "Have you a headache?" His head was wrapped in white bandaging, starkly white against dark skin and hair.

"They made me drink this awful stuff."

She grinned. She could almost imagine him as a boy. For just a moment, he sounded like one. "What did the doctor say?"

"That I'm a terrible patient. He hopes I get well soon because he hates tending to my sort. And I should get lots of bed rest."

Kiya sighed and nodded. "You should be your old self soon enough. I wanted to thank you. Had it not been for you and Jake, who knows what might have happened?"

"You need not thank me in words. A kiss should suffice."

She gave a slow shake of her head. "Shame on you."

He grinned. "Jake did most of the work, but I forbid you to kiss him. Come closer. It's dark in here. I can hardly see you so far away."

She moved closer. "You were injured because of me."

He grasped her hand and pulled her until she sat at his side.

She looked at their joined hands and remarked, "I see you've already regained much of your strength."

With her hand in his he asked, "Are you all right? I'm afraid I don't remember much after we left His Lordship."

"You fainted. You'd lost a lot of blood. And yes, I'm fine. Just tired."

"You could crawl in here. There's plenty of room, and I promise you, I wouldn't mind."

Kiya chuckled again, amazed. Earlier, this very same teasing would have left her stiff with rage. Now at his wicked smile, soothing warmth invaded her chest and caused her the slightest inability to breathe. "You wouldn't mind?" she asked as she teased in return. "Are you sure?"

His eyes widened with anticipation. "Are you giving it some consideration?" he asked hopefully. "Open your robe."

"You are very bad. How in the world are you going to get better if you lie here thinking this nonsense?"

"Just for a minute. I promise, I won't even touch you."

Kiya frowned. "Just for a minute what?"

"Open your robe."

She shook her head. "Mr. Chase, you're far too ill to be thinking such foolishness."

He momentarily changed the subject. "Don't you think it most peculiar that Lord Winston should show up where he did, when he did? He was miles from his own land. What business could he possibly have had in those woods?" His eyes warmed as he reached for a lock of long, clean, sweet-smelling hair. "And looking at you could only make me feel better."

Kiya shook away the spell he'd hoped to weave and, responding to the first of his questions, said, "I haven't given it much thought. Why?"

"You said someone was coming. I think his sudden appearance was a bit too much of a coincidence. Don't you think it might have been him?"

"Lord Winston? I doubt it." Kiya felt no tenderness for the man but couldn't imagine him behind such an appalling act.

"Why would you doubt it? Have you noticed the way he looks at you? The man is a weasel."

"I'm sure you're mistaken."

"That the man's a weasel? I don't think so. Suppose I died and never got a chance to see you again. Wouldn't you feel terrible? Open your robe."

"Behave. Lena will be back at any moment."

"I don't want to see Lena. I want to see you."

Kiya couldn't keep her soft laughter at bay and realised their relationship had somehow taken on a completely new perspective. Suddenly, she not only felt as if she'd known him for ages but felt a tenderness she hadn't before realised. Kiya decided not to think too closely on these new feelings but rather to take one day at a time and enjoy his gentle teasing. "Be good."

Matt grinned. "So what do you think?"

"About what?" she asked warily.

"About Lord Winston, of course."

"Oh, of course," Kiya agreed. "I think he'd like nothing better than to get me into a compromising position believing I'd then be forced to marry him. Still, I can't imagine him capable of something so evil. He once offered for me. Did you know that?"

"He's about three times your age," Matt said, clearly shocked, then his mouth hardened. "What I know is I'm going to kill him."

"He's twice my age, and no, you're not."

He watched her for a long moment, a smile tugging at the corners of his mouth. "If I promise not to kill him, will you kiss me?"

"If you promise to go to sleep, I might," she teased.

"I promise," he returned all too quickly.

Kiya smiled and leaned closer. Their lips were a hairsbreadth apart. She waited for him to close his eyes then quickly pressed a kiss to his forehead. She grinned at the promise of retaliation in his eyes just as Lena's voice came from behind her.

"Is everything all right, Miss?"

"Yes, Lena, thank you. I was just checking to make sure Mr. Chase suffered no fever." She gave him a pointed look as she remarked, "He was rambling a bit of nonsense for a time." She shrugged. "A dream no doubt."

Chapter Four

Amy opened the library door and announced. "I just saw them. They were holding hands then they walked around the back of the barn. Do you think he took her there to kiss her again?" She sighed as she flung herself into the chair facing Kiya. "Oh I wish I could have seen that."

Kiya put down her book. "Amy, you're not following them, are you?"

"A little."

"What does 'a little' mean?"

"It means I've been watching to see what will happen next." She sighed with some despair. "I wasn't able to get a word out of her. Do you think she'll marry him? Will he ask father for her hand? Don't you think this is exciting?"

"Amy," Kiya said, her tone showing clearly her disapproval. "Do you think Merry would be happy to find you spying?"

"I can't help it. She won't tell me anything, and I have to know."

"Know what?" her father asked as he entered the room and moved to sit at his desk.

"Know if we're going to the ball next week," Amy returned, not missing a beat nor, to her sister's surprise, showing a shred of conscience at the outright lie.

Her father frowned. "I'm sorry dear, but I've cancelled the ball. Your sister tells me, she won't be marrying the earl, after all."

"She won't?" Amy asked, her eyes growing huge. She looked ready to burst with excitement and the need to know all.

"It seems our Merry has fallen in love with another."

"She has?" Amy had a time of it controlling her need to laugh. "Who?"

"Mr. Jake Carter."

Pretending ignorance, she exclaimed, "Her guard? Is she going to marry him? Has he asked for her hand?"

Mr. Harrison nodded. "Actually he has, this morning."

"And your answer?"

"Do you think I could refuse? It appears the young man is at least as clever as he is brave. His father left him reasonably well off and Jake managed to turn a modest inheritance into a fortune by investing wisely." He smiled at both his daughters. "We can be assured Mr. Jake Carter is not marrying our Merry for her money."

"Why is he working as a guard if he's rich?" Kiya asked.

"He and Mr. Chase are partners in the company. It seems they have their own motives for personally working this particular case. I'm not privy to their reasoning."

"The earl is bound to give you a spot of trouble, I think," Kiya mused. It was common knowledge that the man was hard put to meet his debts. "God's truth, he was counting on Merry's dowry."

"I've no doubt we will work out an amount that will soothe His Lordship's damaged ego and restore his good humour." He nodded as he leaned back in his chair. "In the meantime, I want your promise—*both* of your promises," he amended, "not to leave the house without at least one guard and not to leave this property until further notice."

"Father, you can't mean to keep us in seclusion indefinitely," Kiya asked, her tone incredulous.

"For a time, dear."

"How long of a time?"

"For however long it takes to make sure all of you are safe."

"Father, Matt—I mean, Mr. Chase—mentioned he has men investigating the kidnapping. But suppose nothing comes of it?"

"Let's hope something does."

"Or?"

Mr. Harrison shrugged for an answer.

"It's impossible. I cannot hide for the rest of my life."

"What about the wedding?" Amy ventured. "Surely Merry will want to wear a new gown. That means we have shopping that must be done. We have to go to London."

Mr. Harrison nodded. "We'll work something out, dear."

* * * *

Kiya knocked, and when no sound came from within, she assumed the patient still slept and quietly entered the chamber. The breakfast tray was placed on a table near the foot of the bed. The room was unusually dark, cast in deep shadows as heavy drapes were drawn securely over the double doors. A balcony ran the entire length of the second floor and each bed chamber opened to it. Kiya moved towards the doors and reached for the heavy drapes blocking the sunlight, only to give a short startled shriek as Matt's voice came close to her ear.

"Have you come to pay the debt owed?"

Kiya gasped for breath, her hand over her heart as if to keep it in place as she spun to face a grinning Matt. "I thought you were asleep. Where is Lena?"

"Gone back to the village, I expect. Doctor Bennett pronounced me well enough to leave the bed for a few minutes each day. She was needed elsewhere."

His hair was damp. A towel hung around his neck. He'd shaved. A spot of soap lingered still just under his ear. Obviously, she'd interrupted his morning ablution. He must have been behind the screen when she'd entered the room.

Kiya swallowed even as she wondered with some confusion, how he managed even unwell to look so appealing? His hair was uncombed, and his shirt hung open. His feet were bare. And yet, she thought he'd never looked so tempting. Kiya frowned at the thought. How odd to imagine a man to be tempting? Kiya couldn't imagine how such a thought should come to mind.

Then she realised his scent. He smelled of tooth powder, soap and Matt. Kiya tried not to breathe too deeply — hardly an easy chore since the man seemed disinclined to allow her even the most minimal personal space. Still, she didn't know what she might do if she breathed his scent deeper into her lungs.

Her voice trembled a bit, sounding oddly strained and far huskier than usual when she tried to remark lightly, "I see he took away the bandaging. Good. Sit down. I want to see the wound."

Matt did as she asked.

"Not on the bed. Over here." She pointed to a chair, "It's too dark over there."

"Bring a light. I'm feeling a little dizzy."

She fussed unhappily as she lit two candles and placed them on the bedside table. "How long have you been up? You're still too weak. I don't care what the doctor said. You should have waited another day, perhaps two, before you got up. I want you to eat everything on that tray." She nodded towards the breakfast she'd brought. "You understand?"

"Yes, dear," he said with a grin.

"It's not a laughing matter, Matt. Do you want to get well or not?"

"What I want is to know what you were thinking."

"What?" she asked with a puzzled frown. "When?"

"When you were staring at me a few minutes ago."

"I have no idea, and I certainly was not staring at you."

"But you were. And now your cheeks are red because you're being a bit less than honest."

"You, sir, are no gentleman, or you'd never accuse a lady of lying."

Matt chuckled. "To my mother's everlasting dismay, I've never been mistaken for a gentleman. Are you afraid to tell me?"

She bent at her waist in order to examine the injury. The skin around it looked healthy, with no swelling or redness. She breathed a sigh of relief, knowing he was well on his way to recovery. "There's nothing to tell."

"Kiya," he warned gently, merely shaking his head.

She straightened to stand before him, her hands on her hips. "All right, if you absolutely must know, I was thinking, 'What would a big ugly toad like you—'"

Kiya dissolved into a fit of giggles as he grabbed her waist and flung her on the bed beside him.

"I'd say your strength has returned and then some."

He leaned over her, holding her in place with one hand to her shoulder, while his gaze moved to her laughing eyes. "Tell me."

"Why?"

"Because you made my heart squeeze then turn to thunder with that look. I want to know what it meant."

She tried to make light of it. "It's silly really."

He said nothing but waited for her to go on.

She sighed and grudgingly began, "I see I'll never hear the end of it if I don't tell you. Fine. I thought you looked tempting," she blurted out. "I know it's odd to imagine a man to be tempting, but for some reason, the word came to mind."

Matt closed his eyes and took a deep breath, while offering a silent prayer of thanks. "What else?"

Now that she had begun, the words seemed to come with some ease. "That you smelled good. That you shaved and looked dishevelled and yet I thought you never looked more appealing." As she spoke, her fingers settled his uncombed hair into some semblance of order.

He said nothing. His gaze darkened as it continued to move over her.

"Now I'm embarrassed, and it's your fault."

"Don't be embarrassed. Thoughts like that are natural. Women and men think things like that all the time."

"That's not true. I've never thought them before."

"Good." He lay back and turned towards her, so that they faced each other almost nose to nose. "You know what I think of when I see you?"

She fluttered her lashes with pretended innocence and inquired, "Angels, harps and the pearly gates of heaven?"

He smiled at her teasing. "Close. Angels, at least. I think you're the most beautiful woman I've ever seen. I think God couldn't have created an angel to compare."

Her eyes widened at the compliment then a moment later she shot him a wicked grin. "And then you think I should take my clothes off."

Matt laughed and wondered if another had ever brought such delight. "The thought certainly intrigues, and I, for one, would surely not be averse, but whatever made you think such a thing?"

"I'm not sure. Of course, it couldn't be because I never see you lately that you don't ask me to open my dress."

"Oh yes, you're right, there is that. But I haven't asked you today, yet."

"No, you haven't, but your hand is at my back. Are you opening my dress?"

"Me? I wouldn't think of it."

"No? I'm sure you wouldn't. What would you think of then?"

"What I'm thinking is, while I was very ill, a beautiful young lady promised to kiss me. Now it's been more than two weeks, and although I've seen her nearly every day, she has yet to fulfil that promise."

"If she kissed you now, would that satisfy?"

"Satisfy? Oh, I doubt that. It will be a while yet before I'm satisfied. Still it would go far towards easing my need."

Kiya frowned at his words. "Well, if it's not about to satisfy, why bother?"

"You see, the lady in question is delicious, better than cherry pie, in fact." He smiled, his words reminding her of their first kiss and what she'd unthinkingly said then. Kiya's cheeks, having just returned to their normal hue, coloured again. "And kissing her luscious mouth is just about the best thing a man can dream of doing. God's truth, he can't stop thinking of kissing her again. And should she be generous enough to kiss him, well even the thought of it is almost more than a man could bear."

Her eyes widened with pleasure. "My goodness, I never realised how good you are with words. I thought you to be more the strong silent type."

"Stop stalling." He gave her a warning look that only made her laugh again.

"Do you mean for this beautiful lady to kiss you now?"

"I've waited long enough, wouldn't you say?"

"Perhaps you have. I'd best go get her."

She made to get up then dissolved into a fit of laughter when he grabbed her and began to tickle her mercilessly. "Why you little…"

"Stop!" she said, desperate to escape. She held his hands, with no little strength, as she climbed upon him and sat on his belly. "No tickling," she said with fierce determination, leaving him without a doubt as to her feelings on the matter.

"Get down here."

Never thinking to disobey, and without the slightest hesitation, she slid down until she lay full length upon him, belly to belly, thigh to thigh. He loved it, and she never even thought of her lack of decorum. Her arms crossed his chest supporting her chin. "Here?"

"Closer."

"If I get any closer, I'll be behind you."

"Closer," he continued to insist.

She scooted up a bit, her arms on each side of his head. "How's this?"

"Better."

She nodded her agreement. "Well, now that I find myself this close, our mouths are almost touching, you know?" She said the last in a half whisper as if revealing a great confidence. "I should probably take this opportunity to kiss you."

Matt's eyes glowed with tenderness as he grinned. He wondered if she realised just how at ease and confident she'd lately grown in his company. Relaxed under his gentle teasing, her devilish sense of humour and slightly sexy remarks grew bolder daily. Over the last few weeks, the demure, sweet young lady had grown into a woman whose eyes sparkled, whose laughter echoed throughout the house and whose smile and soft blush was as close as a glance in his direction.

Now that he thought of it, this luscious lady showed all the signs of a woman in love. The more he thought of it, the more sure he became that she was poised on the periphery of that tantalising emotion. And just as sure as he knew his own name, he knew she hadn't a clue.

Idly, he wondered how he might go about pushing her over the edge into the madness that awaited them both.

"Being that you look so appealing today, I think I'll start here," she said as she ran her tongue down his cheek then teased his jaw and chin with her lips, tongue and teeth.

"Lovely," he murmured, his eyes closed, relishing the delectable tasting, "but that's not a kiss."

"Give me a minute. I'm getting there," she murmured as she nuzzled the warm flesh of his throat then moved up to his mouth where at last she sucked his top lip into her mouth. Her tongue ran over it, under it, discovering again his delicious taste and his oh so special texture. And when she released him, she followed his lip with her tongue into his mouth.

He moaned a low sound of pleasure as their tongues played, tastes were rediscovered and textures explored. The kiss went on and on, a dizzying assault on both their senses.

She gasped for air as she suddenly pulled her mouth away. "I don't know what it is, but I get so weak when we kiss. Perhaps, I'm holding my breath too long, or maybe it's simply the kiss itself. It does tend to cause the heart to race, don't you think? Do you suppose it would feel the same if I were kissing another?"

Matt figured he knew what ailed but wasn't about to tell her she wouldn't grow weak while kissing another. She wasn't going to kiss anyone but himself. He said instead, "You're getting better and better. It shatters the mind to think what you might do in say a year or so."

She grunted a sound that might have been a laugh. "The debt is settled. I need no longer hear, 'Kiss me, are you going to kiss me? When are you going to kiss me? Are you here to settle the debt?'"

Matt laughed. "Have I been nagging you?"

"Let's just say, I've been gently reminded at every opportunity."

She lay still upon him, her hand supporting her head, so totally at ease that she never thought to move away as her finger traced an eyebrow then his nose then his lips. Finally she asked, "Do you know that every part of you feels a little different? I never realised a man would feel like that. Actually, I never gave it any thought at all."

"What do you mean?"

"Well, your mouth is soft and deliciously slippery and hot yet somehow firm, while your face is hard, your cheeks and part of your throat is usually scratchy, while your forehead is smooth. Don't you think that's unusual?"

"I'm different, I'll grant, while you are soft and smooth everywhere. What about the rest of me?"

"I haven't discovered the rest of you yet."

"I like that."

"What?"

"That you said 'yet'. So you intend on discovering more, do you? I wonder if I should allow it."

Kiya laughed. "You are such a fraud, Mr. Chase. Allow it, indeed. It's a miracle you still have any clothes on. I have no doubt you'll be nagging me on that score soon enough."

"Nagging you about what?"

Kiya shot him a stern glare, reading correctly the humour in his eyes. "I'm not going to say it, and I'm sorry I brought up the subject."

Matt laughed. "You're no fun at all."

"What? Another lie, Mr. Chase? Keep it up, and you'll need to go to church Sunday."

"I'd go anywhere, as long as I'm with you," he said as he nuzzled his face into her neck.

She tried to move, but his arms were fixed across her back, disallowing any movement on her part. "I need to get up."

"In a minute. I was thinking since you did such a lovely job paying your debt that I might return the favour."

"You'll have to wait until later for that. A friend of mine is coming for a visit."

"When?"

"She'll be here in about an hour, and I have to change now that you've thoroughly wrinkled my dress."

"It will only take a few minutes. I want to show you something," he said as he turned them and leaned over her.

Kiya didn't know how he did it. Yes, she'd felt him fumble a bit at her back, but he'd managed to open every one of her buttons which allowed him to pull both dress and chemise all the way to her waist, exposing her breasts to his view and trapping her arms to her sides.

"How did you—"

His mouth sucked the tip of one breast into a volcano of heat, and she suddenly didn't care how he'd managed it. All she knew was she was terribly glad that he had.

They moaned in unison, each delighting in the feel of his mouth on her. He licked her, he bit her, he sucked her flesh deep into his mouth, marking her in places where no one would see but himself. Kiya thought she might have died and gone to heaven.

His hand slid under her dress, his finger finding the moistness at the juncture of her thighs. He played there a moment, allowing himself the delight of touching her, but refused to give her what her moving hips told him she wanted. Not this time. He'd have her promise to marry him before allowing her a repeat of that particular pleasure.

His hand came away, and he rubbed first his lips then hers and finally coated each luscious nipple with her sweet, moist essence. Seconds later, he licked her lips then sucked her tongue into his mouth again. "You taste so good. God, I can't believe how good."

"My sister said once that you're scrumptious. I'm beginning to think she had a point," Kiya said, careful of his wound she threaded her fingers through his hair when he returned to play with her breasts.

He pulled sharply away, his shock never more obvious as he frowned. "Merry said that?"

"Not that sister."

His mouth returned to nuzzle the sweet, dark tips so lusciously available to him. His hands held her, pressing the soft, firm flesh together so that he could play at his leisure with the beautiful display. He rubbed his face over, around and between them, dragging his mouth back and forth. "Amy should be sent off to school."

Kiya laughed.

"Or married off at the first opportunity. She's bound to give us all a spot of trouble." He continued to nuzzle and playfully extend her nipples with long, lovely pulls of his teeth and lips, covering Kiya in delicious, shivery chills.

She might have once thought it impossible to actually carry on a conversation with a man while he had her nipple in his mouth, but upon further consideration it seemed to be a perfectly lovely way to converse. She was sorry she'd never thought of it before.

Matt licked at a pointy nipple as he continued their discussion. "Talking about marriage, don't you think we should? A few more of these encounters, and we might find ourselves in a bit of trouble."

"What kind of trouble?"

"Kiya, we need to get married."

He knew her thoughts on the matter. She had no intention of marrying him or anyone else for that matter, and she tried to keep their conversation light and teasing. "Why? Are you in a family way?"

"Don't be smart," he said as he gave her butt a playful tap then groaned softly as his hand remained there. It slid under her skirt again for a long delicious investigation. "I'm serious."

"Why? What's wrong with what we're doing?"

"What we're doing is very nice indeed, but I want more. I want to make love to you. I want you naked and able to stay naked for hours, maybe for days at a time. I want to bury my mouth between your legs, to suck in the taste of your sweet pussy and lick you here," he said. His finger playing with her clit told her exactly what he meant.

Kiya groaned at the picture he painted. She hadn't ever imagined a man could suck or lick her there. Suddenly she couldn't wait for him to do just that and her stomach tightened with the need of it.

"And then, once you're all soft and hot and wet for me, once you come like you did at the cabin, like you're going to come now, I want to slide deep inside you. I want to watch you when you come again, when you lose all control, when your muscles tighten around my cock. I want those muscles to suck me deeper into you. And I want to do it forever."

He was driving her mad as he continued to play with her and his soft sultry words created a delicious scenario. "You did it again, you know?" she gasped breathlessly.

"Did I? What was it I did?"

"After the last time, I swore I'd never let you touch me like this again."

"Did you? Who did you swear it to?"

"I swore to myself."

"Next time, you should probably swear it to me."

"You're right, of course. Next time, I shall."

Matt laughed as he pulled her closer. "God, I love the way you feel." He hadn't planned to do this again. He was going to tease her until she begged for his touch, swore she would marry him, but now that he'd started, Matt hadn't the strength to deny her or himself this pleasure. In truth, he hadn't the strength to deny this woman anything she wanted.

"Mmm," she moaned "And I love the way you feel me."

He laughed again, even as something fluttered in his chest at the sound of her sweet purring. She was just the most delicious woman. Gently, he continued her pleasure.

She moaned again as her hips rose from the bed. "Matt, this feels so…"

"I know sweetheart. I know." He licked her nipple, blew on it and bit it gently. "Just let me do this for you."

She couldn't hold back yet another moan as the pressure began to build. Her stomach grew tight, her muscles straining towards the ecstasy she knew to exist. Her hands gripped the bedding as she anxiously strove towards it. "I need…Matt please," she gasped, her breathing desperate irregular pants of yearning. "I need… Oh God. Matt."

"Go with it. Let it come, easy now."

"I can't," she muttered, but his finger continued to move and she knew she could. She knew nothing could stop the delicious torment as her clit grew soft and then hard, harder, longer. "God, this is… I love this…"

Her hips rose higher, higher. She couldn't get enough, he couldn't touch her enough. Her muscles were tighter than anything she'd ever imagined. A band of near pain crushed her stomach as she strove towards pure enchantment. And finally it was there, just beyond her reach. She groaned, waiting, gasping for every breath until finally, finally and it crashed upon her. Without thought, her body jerked forward and jerked again, and once more as his mouth covered hers absorbing her tormented cries of delight.

And Kiya found it impossible to utter an intelligible word for some long minutes to come.

She was in her room changing her clothes before she realise he had never once said he loved her. He wanted to marry her yet had never declared himself. Kiya laughed at the oddity. Still, she didn't care how wonderful he was in bed, how delicious the thrills, how luscious she felt when he touched her or when he bit and sucked at her. He'd have to be madder than the sorriest inmate in Bedlam if he thought she'd ever marry anyone.

* * * *

Charity Wells and Kiya, friends since childhood, sat on the terrace enjoying a cup of morning tea. "You're up early today," Kiya remarked considering the hour of her visit. "I've never known you to rise until well after the noon hour."

"I've yet to go to bed. In truth, I can't remember the last time I've slept more than a few minutes at a time."

Kiya's eyes widened. Her friend was obviously distraught but had managed control of her emotions until this moment. "What's the matter?"

Charity wrung her hands together, her dark eyes telling clearly her ever-increasing panic. She came to her feet and began to pace. "I'm faced with possible catastrophe if I can't find a solution. The French captured Richard."

"Oh my God," Kiya gasped. "How? Why? What about your wedding?"

She shrugged for an answer, telling clearly she didn't know why then went on tell what she did know. "You know Richard is involved with the government. I don't know in what capacity. In any case, the French have him or rather had him." She gave a deep unhappy sigh. "And I'm afraid our wedding will be delayed a bit."

"Lord," Kiya moaned. "What are you going to do? Have you tried to contact the Foreign Office? Father knows somebody who knows the Prime Minister. Maybe…"

Charity shook her head. "They can't help. Our governments have no diplomatic contact. At war again, who hates each other more than the French and English?

"Richard's associates have come to his aid. They hired a group of men, cutthroats, if the truth be told. Still, I imagine they were honourable enough for they carried out the job they were hired to do. It took vast amounts of money for bribes and no little brute strength when bribes wouldn't work, but they managed the impossible. Richard is free and in hiding. Of course, the longer he stays in France the more dangerous it becomes. The hired men have blended back into the populace, but it has become imperative that Richard leave the country at the very first opportunity.

"A group of smugglers was contacted. I don't know how they were found or who hired them. In any case, for a fee they will bring him home. All is set, but for where to dock. It's imperative they find a place nearby. Richard is ill, I think weakened from the time spent in prison, and to tax his strength with excess travel would be to court disaster."

Charity was obviously desperate as she clasped her hands together and leaned towards her friend. "I don't know who else to turn to."

"What do you mean? Do you need us? Shall I contact Charles and Harry and...?"

Five years ago on a dare between Kiya and two of her school chum's brothers—a ridiculous dare only a foolish fifteen year old would consider—audacious excursions had begun. Once a month Charlie, Harry and Kiya plus a few others would meet to cross the Channel, on the darkest of night, in a small boat in order to smuggle contraband from France to the caves beneath her father's home. Of course, Charity being her closest friend was well aware of her escapades. In the beginning, Kiya had thought she might never know a greater sense of excitement or a more excellent rush of fear.

Still after the first excursion, she thought to be done with it, until she realised the money that could be gained by smuggling and all the good that could come from that money. Because of these ill-gotten gains, huge anonymous amounts had been donated to the parish. A new nursery had been added to the parish poor house and schooling made available to a dozen or more orphans.

A few more excursions found her addicted to the excitement, for it proved incomparable. Despite the danger, she was gripped in the throes of a compulsion perhaps for life or until the inevitable day came when she was caught.

"No, as I said, a group has been contacted. Everything is set. What I meant was the caves. I need to use them. And the tunnels that run to my barn, of course. It would take almost no effort to bring Richard through them. In minutes, we could be home."

"If you need to use them, go ahead."

"That's a problem. I don't know the tunnels. Every time, I've gone there, I've gotten lost. In the dark we might roam them for..."

"Don't worry about it. I'll guide you through." Kiya and her sisters had played in the tunnels as youngsters. She knew them as well as she knew her own bed chamber.

"Would you? Oh God, I'd be so grateful. I'll be with you, of course."

Kiya shook her head. "It's no problem. When will they come?"

"I'm not sure. Perhaps early next week. The moon is about to go into quarter, and the nights are growing darker. I'm told they'll move the first night it grows overcast or rains."

"That soon? Are you sure?"

She nodded. "I know this seems sudden to you, but I've been waiting for this for weeks."

"How will I know when to meet you?"

"I'll send my maid with a note. You won't be missed will you?"

Kiya smiled. "They won't even know I'm gone. Instead of a note, just visit and stay the night."

Charity nodded. All was set.

Chapter Five

The Earl of Binghamshire snarled as he entered his coach, leaving behind that sonofabitch Harrison with a brisk, good-day nod. It wouldn't due at all to let the man know of his intense hatred. When the day came for his revenge, blame couldn't be allowed to fall on his shoulders.

He had at first taken the wedding postponement in stride, considering Merry's illness — or supposed illness as it turned out — but to cancel a wedding scheduled only weeks away was more than any man could take. Whether it was meant to or not, it left him a laughingstock.

If Harrison thought he'd stand for it, he was more the fool. He needed the bitch's money, and the pitiful sum he was forced to agree to in order to soothe his hypothetical devastation would barely pay off half of his creditors. How the hell was he to live? It would be months, perhaps years, before he'd find another prospect half as rich or one so fair.

All right, so his tastes usually ran towards women a bit less refined, but he could have managed to bed her easily enough. And truth be told, he'd only need to perform his husbandly duty on occasion. Most of his time could and would be spent as always with those who catered towards what he liked to refer to as his earthy delights. He liked to think of himself as a connoisseur of female flesh. That he kept a near harem of luscious goodies of all shapes and colours was well-known amongst his cronies. He'd been forced of late to begin charging those who frequented his lovelies. Even so, it was getting harder all the time to maintain his particular lifestyle. What kind of a world was it where a man could no longer afford such basic luxuries?

He wasn't about to put up with it. He didn't know how, but he was going to bring the bastard and his bitch of a daughter to their knees. In the meantime, he needed to vent his rage. He called out for his driver to head for London. What he needed was a few days spent with an array of conciliatory lovelies to put him in a better mood.

* * * *

"I want him watched around the clock."

Jake nodded. "Do you think he's likely to exact some sort of revenge? Should I double the guard on Merry?"

Matt shrugged. "Anything is possible. After you marry, you might want to take her away for awhile. After what he did to my sister, I wouldn't put anything past him. He's an earl, and as far as he's concerned, that puts him above the law."

"You don't know for fact that he did it."

"I know he did it. I just can't prove it." Matt drove his fingers through his hair and sighed. "I was just a kid, and I knew. He beat her. I don't know if it was because she was leaving him or he just got off on it, but her back was covered with the marks, old and new. It damn near killed my mother when we found her. Lizzie didn't live long enough to say who did it, but we all knew."

"You've been living with this hatred for years, Matt. It's bound to eat you up inside if you don't get rid of it."

"I'll get rid of it when we get rid of him."

* * * *

"What's the matter? Are you in pain again?"

Matt watched Kiya walk towards him and smiled. "No. I'm fine. Just thinking. Have you come to kiss me again?"

"Lord, but you do keep a thought once you've gained it, don't you? I was going to ask you if you are hungry."

"That depends what are you offering? Open your dress."

"Matt," she snapped not at all happy with his answer.

He laughed and closed the door behind her. Kiya's father had set him up with an office of his own. A desk had been installed in one of the smaller sitting rooms, allowing him a bit of room to carry on his work.

"I was only teasing," he said as he took her in his arms. "You're a bit jumpy today. What's the matter?"

"Nothing. Dinner will be ready soon. Rev Simmons and his family are coming." She breathed a sigh, enjoying the feel of his arms around her. "I was just wondering how much longer do you think you'll be here."

"Why? Do you want me to leave?"

"Actually, no, I want you to stay. I want Merry to stay. I want everything to stay exactly as it is."

"She's only getting married, sweetheart. She won't be going far. And she won't be going anywhere until we find the murderer. Jake has decided, after the wedding, to move in for a spell. We both agree Merry would be safer here."

He pulled back just a bit so he could see her face. "You know things never stay the same, don't you? You know, one day, you'll marry just like your sister. Move away from here. Have your own home and your own children."

She shook her head. "I told you, I'm not getting married. I'll never want to marry. And if someday, by some miracle I should, good God, it would never be to one of the titled. Thank the Lord, Merry had the sense to call off that abominable match."

"Do you believe all the titled are like the Earl?"

"No, although I wouldn't doubt many are. In general, I think them to be a spoiled self-absorbed lot who put themselves above the law. What I do know for certain is that they are arrogant, obnoxious, vicious, back-stabbing, gossipers who think more of their snuff boxes than of their fellow man."

Matt's gaze widened then twinkled with humour. "Kiya, you really should try to be a little less wishy-washy in your opinions."

She laughed. "I'm afraid I have first-hand knowledge of the deplorable characters."

He tipped his head, obviously waiting for her to explain.

"We were invited to court a year before my mother died. I heard their snide remarks about the country bumpkins. I watched how they tore apart every well-meaning gesture, scorned our dresses, mocked us for the most minor mistakes." She shivered at a particular memory then with deadly menace went on. "They weren't worthy to touch the hem of her skirt yet they looked with derision upon my mother.

"She was like Merry, at least as pretty and, if you can believe it, sweeter and even more gentle." Kiya hesitated, swallowed, fought back a sob and almost made it. She cleared her throat and went on, her voice tighter, her eyes dry and filled with hate. "She was ill, but she never told us how seriously at the time. She died never saying one harsh word against them. I wanted to kill them all. I swear I would have if I'd had the means then laughed all the way to the hangman."

"God help us," Matt gasped as he pulled her tighter against him, knowing she meant every word she said. This one was like a tiger protecting her own. He'd never suspected her to be so violent in thought. "Remind me to never make an enemy of you." His hand ran down her back in comforting strokes. "Sweetheart, I promise you all are not so immature and ridiculous."

She shook her head and offered a sad smile. "Sorry, but you won't convince me."

"Ah, Kiya," he began a bit uncomfortably. "We should probably talk."

"About what?"

"Well, the thing is I don't want you to get upset."

"And you're going to say something that might upset me?"

He shook his head. "It shouldn't."

Kiya smiled at his obvious discomfort. "Why don't we try this? You tell me what the problem is and I'll let you know if I'm upset or not."

"It's not a problem really." He bit his lips together and tried for a weak smile. "The thing is…" Matt almost sighed aloud his relief as a knock sounded at the door interrupting his words.

Merry looked in and smiled at the couple still standing in an embrace. "Hurry and dress," she encouraged. "Their carriage is coming up the drive."

Kiya nodded then turned to the man before her, waiting for him to go on.

Matt shook his head. "We'll talk later."

* * * *

The Earl of Binghamshire, lay naked in bed, a young equally naked girl knelt between his legs while two more, one on each side of him provided him with a deliciously erotic massage. The women began to fuss as each looked forward to performing her best, after all it was a known fact that the more eagerness he found in his lady, the more generous he proved to be.

"Don't fuss, ladies. I've enough for all of you. Be patient, and you'll each have a chance at me."

Someone knocked at the door, and Shelby called out for them to enter. Bessy, the woman who ran his establishment said, "Your Lordship, Mr. Connery is waiting to see you."

"Show him in."

A moment later, a tall, thin, darkly tanned man entered the room, his gaze widened with pleasure. "Jesus, Shelby, I never knew you to be so greedy."

The earl grinned. "I see you're back. I'd shake your hand, but as you can see they are a bit busy."

Connery laughed as he watched the man play with both women. His fingers were between their legs, while the third girl held his member in her mouth.

The earl asked, "How long are you staying this time?"

"I've a bit of work to do then I'll be going back."

"I should take you up on your offer to accompany you back to the island."

"You wouldn't be sorry. I can guarantee it. Do you mind if I have a go at one of these beauties?"

"Not at all. Susie, help out my friend, will you?"

Susie looked a bit disappointed. After all, she was in the midst of some pleasure of her own. Still she said not a word as she followed Connery from the bed to the table near the door.

"We've had ourselves a time or two haven't we Susie. You remember what I like?" Connery said.

"Yes sir," Susie replied as she sat on the edge of the table and pulled her legs up high and wide, allowing for a man of most any size to stand between them comfortably. The woman was a study in strength for he could and had kept her thusly posed for an hour or more yet she hadn't once complained.

He smiled at the sight before him, "Lovely," he said and pulled a chair to the table to make himself comfortable. "First, why don't we finish what our lordship started? Would that be all right with you?"

"Oh yes, sir. I'd be grateful. Thank you," she said.

He played a bit with her breasts, studying the size and weight of them as he pinched the nipples to hard nubs. "Still a good handful, aren't you, Susie? I do hate a skinny whore."

He sat then played with her until he heard her breathing grow short and gasping. Whores never faked it with him. He made sure of that. It didn't matter how long it took, there were certain things he took pride in. One of those things was the ability to make any woman climax. But it was more than insisting that a woman achieve climax. Her pleasure only increased his own by ten-fold.

Once he saw her muscles twitch and watched the liquid squeeze from her, he instantly rammed his sex deep inside, all the while keeping his finger rotating on that little nub of pleasure. "I like it when you go tight like that around me."

"Yes, sir," Susie managed weakly. It wasn't often that she actually gained some pleasure in her work, so she was apt to appreciate the effort a man sometimes bothered to take.

It didn't take but a minute of her spasms sucking and pulling at him before he came without the necessity of moving a muscle. "That was very nice, Susie. I see you've still got those lovely strong muscles." He almost laughed aloud at the understatement. She was one of his favourites for he never had to exert an instant of energy yet found pleasure with her time after time.

Susie smiled as he stepped back and sat again. She knew what this man wanted and, without another word spoken, knelt before him and took him into her mouth.

An hour later, both men, decidedly spent, sat in Shelby's small office and sipped at snifters of brandy as they discussed business. "I want her dead. I don't care how you do it, just make sure she suffers. And if you throw in the father as well, I wouldn't object?"

Connery studied the golden liquid swirling in his glass and grinned. "You want him dead or not. What's this 'wouldn't object'?"

He shook his head. "Perhaps not. It should look like a robbery gone bad. If you do the father as well, it might look suspicious."

"And you'll be?"

"Like the last time, out of the country, of course."

"She was a damn fine piece, your wife. I enjoyed her for some time, I must say. I even toyed with the notion of taking her back to the island with me."

"Jesus! And if she'd escaped? It would have meant disaster."

"Which is why I didn't do it." He smiled again. "Can't blame a man for being tempted."

"She wasn't dead when you left her."

"What? She most certainly was."

"She wasn't. Someone found her and brought her to her mother's place. She died there."

"She didn't say who?"

Shelby shook his head. "She didn't live long enough."

"I can't believe it. She lost the baby and was bleeding like a stuck pig."

"Next time, cut the bitch's throat."

Connery nodded, knowing he most certainly would.

* * * *

The manor house buzzed with excitement. Not a speck of dust dared to show itself as the house was cleaned from attic to basement. Rugs were beaten, mattresses aired, drapes taken down and washed, furniture polished to a rich glow. All within began to take on a sheen that proudly spoke of fine china, delicate crystal, elaborate silver and the warm deep lustre of fine wood. Within a week, the baking would begin.

It was decided that the family would travel to London tomorrow. Merry would wear her mother's wedding dress, and they needed expert seamstresses to work it to fit. Once there, they would stay for a day or more in Mr.

Harrison's townhouse. While being fitted during the day, they hoped to take in at least one play before returning home.

In the meantime, Matt had sent for extra men, uncaring that a skeleton crew was left to work his other jobs. He was desperate that no harm should befall any of these women, most especially not his lady. The men arrived daily, and each sister was designated three guards around the clock.

Today, a country fair with perhaps four dozen tents and at least as many tables groaned beneath the weight of everything from quilts, rolls of delicate lace, linen, crystal, baskets of flowers, pies, cakes, candies, fruit and of course copper from the tinkers who were always present at any country gathering.

Spirits ran high as all three ladies were eager to see it all. It had been a year since the last fair, and each was anxious to join in the festivities.

Somewhat less anxious were the men emotionally involved with these women, for they couldn't have cared less about a day's festivities. Rather they found themselves a bit more keenly aware of the dangers that lurked at every turn.

Kiya sat before her mirror playing with an obstinate curl that peeked from beneath her straw bonnet and put the last touches to the bow beneath her chin when in the mirror she spied her bedroom door opening. Matt silently entered then leaned against the door, smiling at her reflection as if he'd just performed some magnificent feat.

"I didn't hear you knock," she said as she came to her feet and moved towards him. "I could have been half dressed."

"You didn't hear me knock because I didn't. Someone might have heard me."

Her eyes widened at the nonsensical statement. "Isn't that the point?"

"Not when a man knocks on a woman's bedroom door. Someone else might have heard, and what excuse could I give to want entrance to this room?"

She grinned as she noticed the lusty expression in his eyes. "You could have said you needed to search it. That perhaps a man entered uninvited, and if he did that, you wanted to make sure he knows how to properly kiss the lady who sleeps here."

"A proper kiss is hardly worth the effort, wouldn't you agree?" He smiled as she moved closer and said without a flicker of conscience at the obvious lie. "And if you were half dressed, I would have closed my eyes."

Kiya laughed in disbelief. "Of course, you would have."

Matt didn't bother to respond, for they both knew he'd lied. He said instead, "Open your dress."

"What again? Was it not you who waylaid me on the way to breakfast asking me that very same question?"

"If I'd laid you on the way to breakfast, you wouldn't be asking if it were me or not."

"Waylaid," she repeated, with a bit of insistence, her cheeks growing pink at this outrageous conversation. "You're getting worse every day."

"And you're getting better."

She shook her head. "I swear I'm not up to this kind of teasing."

"Just looking at you has managed to get something up," he promised, and Kiya didn't dare respond, knowing well enough to what he alluded. "Hurry, open your dress."

She didn't hesitate but to do as he asked, even as she reminded, "They're waiting for me."

"I know, but I need to see you before we go."

"You'll be with me all day. Won't you see me then?"

"I'll be watching for bad guys. I probably won't do more than glance your way once we get there."

Kiya didn't believe a word of it yet did as he asked. She smiled as her bodice parted.

Matt couldn't have been more delighted. Her shyness was long past. She never thought to deny either of them this pleasure, and for that, he could only thank God, knowing he was slowly disposing of all her inhabitations.

"You mustn't wrinkle me, or I'll have to change and that will only bring more questions as to why I was so late."

"Don't worry, I'll help you change."

She grinned at his mesmerised gaze as her fingers hurried with the chore. "Oh yes, and that would only delay us for a day or two."

"God, if I could only tell you what you look like," he managed in a voice tight with longing. She stood before him, the large bow of her bonnet beneath her chin. At once the prim and proper miss and a wild Jezebel, the contrast was enough to drive a man out of his mind and filled him with a shot of wrenching lust so strong he wondered if he'd survive. "If I could paint, I'd paint you just like this."

Kiya smiled then gasped her delight as he reached for her and sucked a pink nipple deep into the flame that was his mouth.

"I wish you could go like this," he groaned, pulling her tightly against him.

Kiya's laugh was low seductive, nearly pushing him over the edge of reason, leaving him dazed but for the need to have more of her. "Would you like that?"

"No, I'd kill anyone who looked at you."

"You're confusing."

"No, I'm not. I'm mad. Before long, I'll be a blithering idiot."

"Poor baby," she soothed, her tone a bit less commiserating than the words implied. Kiya laughed as she met his warning glare and leaning closer, offering her mouth to his. "Kiss me, Matt," she murmured against his mouth.

Helpless but to accede to her will, he sucked her bottom lip into the heat of his mouth. A moment later, dazed from the swirl of hungry lips, ravenously tongues and the tantalising graze of teeth, he gasped, "Oh my God, you're killing me."

"They're calling me," she whispered. "We have to stop."

"I know. Tonight, I'm coming to your bed. I've waited long enough."

She closed her bodice as she glanced up into his dark, hungry eyes, her own filled with questions. "But I thought…"

"I know what you thought. There are other things we can do."

* * * *

At least fifty tables fronted accompanying tents, each table piled high with goods of every type imaginable as they circled a huge meadow just north of the village. Folks from near and far matted the tall grass at the circle's centre where jugglers and acrobats performed for a few coins dropped into a hat.

Kiya smiled at the gypsies gathering around tents and tables that held copper pots, plates, candlesticks and jewellery. A small corral to one side contained the finest horseflesh. They wore startling bright clothing startling, their jewellery dazzling against dark skin and black hair that gleamed in the sunshine.

Kiya couldn't imagine a more beautiful sight. "Aren't they beautiful?"

Matt grinned. "You're asking the wrong man. If your looking for true beauty, all you need is a mirror."

She smiled. "My, we are glib today, Mr. Chase."

"Not glib, honest."

Kiya shot him a warm smile and briefly touched his hand, bestowing a gentle squeeze.

"If I don't get you alone soon, I swear I won't be held accountable for what might happen," he said.

Kiya turned quickly to face him, her expression brooked no nonsense, and as delicious as she had been half naked, Matt wasn't sure if this particular look wasn't at least as luscious. The truth of it was Matt found himself so besotted there was nothing this woman did that did not intrigue. "You'll do absolutely nothing that might embarrass me. Am I right?"

Matt grinned, finding her adorable and didn't hesitate to say as much. "Let's have our fortunes read."

"It's a waste of money."

He shrugged. "It's my money."

She smiled then suddenly noticed her father's tenants Tom and Abigail Brown. "Oh Matt, look at the baby. Isn't she lovely?"

Of course, Kiya was instantly Abigail Brown's most honoured friend the moment the mother heard those words. She smiled at the younger woman. "Would you like to hold her?"

Kiya took the baby into her arms and laughed with delight at the tiny face. "She doesn't look like a baby at all does she? She looks like the tiniest adult I've ever seen. You're so lucky, Abigail."

"I know, miss. God has truly blessed us."

While Kiya and Abigail spoke of babies, Matt and Tom conversed on matters of farming. Matt offered his opinion as to crop prices this coming harvest, while Mr. Brown mentioned he'd managed to secure a prize bull whose service was presently gaining enormous stud fees.

Kiya was surprised for she hadn't imagined Matt knew anything of the day-to-day running of a farm, never mind the possible profit to be made should a farmer harvest a certain crop.

Sarah, the Brown's oldest daughter who looked to be perhaps ten and four, soon took the baby. Kiya and Matt wandered off towards the gypsy tents and waited their turn. Soon enough, they were guided into one particular tent and motioned to sit before a woman who appeared to be at least a hundred.

"How much?" Matt asked.

A price was agreed upon and paid. Moments later, the old lady began to murmur gibberish then clearly said, "You will live a long life and have many children."

Kiya grinned shooting a look in Matt's direction, that spoke, *Oh my how unusual.*

"I see laughter, happiness, a man who loves you. You think you don't want him, but you do."

Kiya frowned. This time the look she sent Matt held a definite glare.

He almost laughed aloud, for her thoughts were easy enough to read. She was wondering how he'd managed to tell this woman what he wanted Kiya to hear. He shcok his head in silent denial and whispered, "I didn't. I promise, I didn't."

The gypsy went on with, "There's a dark man—a tall dark man. Be careful. Be very careful. He means to hurt you."

Kiya stiffened, her eyes wide as she gasped.

Matt came instantly to his feet, his chair falling to the floor behind him. "You're frightening her. What's the matter with you?" He took Kiya against him, his arms almost crushing her to his chest. "Why did you scare her?"

A moment later, he pulled her from the tent, never thinking to take his arms from around her. "Are you all right?"

"I'm fine." Kiya thought it possible that the gypsy had scared Matt more than she had herself. "No, truly, I am. Let me go, Matt."

He pressed her against him, his arm like steel around her, while his hand moved up and down her back.

"Matt, let me go."

He did as he was told with some obvious reluctance. "You're sure?"

She nodded. "Very sure," she said as she smoothed imaginary wrinkles from a perfect skirt.

"Let's go."

Kiya frowned. "Let's go? You just dragged me out of there. Now you want to go back?"

"I meant let's go home."

"I'm not leaving, Matt. I came to enjoy the day, and I expect to do just that."

Kiya had barely finished her sentence when she glanced up to watch a tall man with darkly tanned skin happen to cross her path. No doubt the man would never have been noticed had it not been for the gypsy dire prophecy. He exactly matched the old woman's description. Because he did, Kiya stared when a lady most assuredly would not, and the man returned her look with a smile. The smile itself was quite a bit more licentious than charming. Kiya shivered at what should have been a beautiful smile, for the man was handsome in the extreme yet she somehow knew only fear.

Matt, always conscious of his lady and her immediate surroundings, did not miss the man's daring look nor Kiya's involuntary shudder as she for the first time in her sheltered life looked pure evil in the eye.

Of the three men who continuously shaded her every movement, Matt nodded to Johnston.. Without a word spoken, Johnston, small, wiry, unobtrusive, left the small group to mingle unnoticed into the crowd.

Because of his size and colouring, Johnston proved the perfect agent and often went unnoticed, but in this case, no one realised the acute sense of self-preservation in their adversary.

Connery was not only evil, he was far more clever than most and very much aware that the look bestowed upon a certain lady would not go unnoticed. The game he played only intensified his victory should his adversary prove himself worthy. Where was the fun after all if a woman should be taken with ease? What then was her worth? Not only did she subsequently prove to be less desirable, but the game consequently held little fascination. No, excitement could only be gained by outsmarting the most laudable foe.

Therefore, ever aware of any and all consequences, Johnston and his inconspicuous attempt to mingle into the crowd, did not go beyond Connery's notice.

Patricia Pellicane

* * * *

As the afternoon wore on and evening approached, a
small stage was set up at the centre of the fair. The stage
was surrounded by short poles poked into the ground and
put to flame. The townsfolk made themselves comfortable
on the grass.

Merry sent to their carriage for blankets, lest the
dampness penetrate their clothes, and soon, all sat, eagerly
anticipating an hour's entertainment. The play was most
delightful, the actors easily as good as those in London's
best playhouses and everyone enjoyed their first sample of
The Taming of the Shrew.

After much applause, the final curtain was called, and
the delighted audience came again to their feet, clapping
loudly their appreciation.

The moment it was reasonably quiet again, Amy
announced her intent to become an actress. Kiya groaned
at the very thought, and Matt grinned as she rolled her
eyes towards the heavens as if asking for help.

"A convent...aye, definitely a convent," she muttered.

"Are you Catholic?" he asked.

"We'll convert."

Matt laughed aloud and pulled her to his side with a
quick hard hug, wishing as he did that he could kiss her
senseless. "Someone should talk to her."

Kiya nodded. The idea held some merit except for the
fact that she knew Amy never listened to anyone. Kiya
had no hope her sister would listen in this case. She was
about to say as much when a gun suddenly discharged.
The sound was soon followed by yet another and a young
girl's terrified scream.

Johnston, with a tankard of ale still in hand, lurched quietly, a discreet distance behind the stranger, pretending a degree of inebriation. For most of the afternoon and early evening, he was simply ignored — until Connery decided a particularly pretty young girl would suit his purpose for the night.

Johnston followed with a seemingly aimless stagger, the last of the ale in his tankard sloshing as he stumbled through the fair a number of times, always keeping the dark stranger in sight. Suddenly, the man slipped between two tents.

Behind the tents, it was dark. Barely five feet separated the back of each tent from thick woods. Johnston stepped into almost total blackness. Had he tried he couldn't have seen his hand before his eyes. Therefore, the man who stood to his left blended perfectly into the night and was never noticed.

Connery chuckled as his most recent fan slumped at his feet. Within seconds, the girl he'd kept in sight was in his arms as her young man surrendered to a hard blow taken to his head. With his arm around her, he easily pulled her towards the woods and his waiting horse. He would have made good his escape had the shot he'd fired left Johnston incapacitated. As it was, Johnston recovered just long enough to squeeze off a shot of his own before succumbing to the ever-beckoning darkness. Had he known his shot had hit its mark, he might have gone on to the next life with a bit less of heavy heart.

At the sounds of gunfire, a prearranged plan was put instantly into effect. All who worked in Matt's employ gathered those attending the fair into a large circle at the meadow's centre. Surrounded, they were forced to remain in place, protected by Matt's agents, while Matt, Jake and one of his best men, Pete Landers, raced towards the girl's cries.

Abigail Brown screamed for help. "It's Sarah. He's got my Sarah."

Immediately, Tom Brown broke from the crowd, only to be instantly returned by a burly guard.

"It's my daughter. He's got my Sarah," John argued.

"You won't be rushing off into the woods sir, lest you be mistaken for the villain and laid low. Let those trained for this job take care of it."

Tom moaned as he took his wife into his arms, unable to hold back the horror of what was happening.

Connery cursed as the shocking blow taken to his shoulder left his arm instantly useless. The girl nearly escaped, even as she kept up that god-awful screeching. He tried to muffle the sound against his chest but couldn't manage the chore, not when his arm hung uselessly at his side. She kicked and pummelled him with all her strength in a desperate attempt at escape. Granted, it would have been as nothing to hold her and keep her quiet had both arms been available to him. As it was, Connery found himself struggling to attain his goal.

Nearby, he heard the men trampling through the woods, easily following the girl's piercing cries. A moment later, he dumped her to the ground, believing the effort it took to take her was not worth the prize, especially since he was within yards of being captured.

He left her with a solid kick to her belly, lest the bitch think she'd bested him.

Connery groaned as he sat his horse, forcing aside his weakness as blood dripped down his sleeve, over the horse to the ground. Within minutes, he'd left the fair and its attending multitude some distance behind. His shoulder and arm ached like bloody hell. He thought the bullet taken had gone through the fleshy part just beneath his shoulder, for he felt a warm flow of blood down his back. He sighed at his sudden spurt of bad luck and wondered if the bullet had not left him permanently damaged, for he'd been shot before and the previous injury had not caused his arm to grow totally useless.

He shrugged at the thought. Connery wasn't the sort to bemoan a fact. Certainly it mattered should he be left nearly a cripple, still an arm was only that and he reasoned, if need be, he'd manage well enough with what was left. The only thing that annoyed was his recuperation would take some time. Always a restless sort, he did not look forward to weeks spent idle, hidden away at Shelby's.

* * * *

Matt and Jake brought the party home with no further incident. The family soon retired for the night, for they were to leave first thing in the morning for a shopping trip to London. Before visiting with his lady, Matt made a quick trip to a neighbouring estate. It took a few minutes to bring the man from his bed, but Lord Winston soon entered his library where Matt waited.

Lord Winston was obviously unhappy to find his evening interrupted and said as much while insisting he know why the man had come to his door.

"It's simple, actually. I've come to find out exactly how involved you were in Kiya's kidnapping."

"I had no part in it, I assure you." He shook his head as if the emphasise the truth of his statement. "I was merely on my way to visit a friend when I came upon the two of you."

Matt nodded. "It's as I thought," he said almost to himself. Not a hint of a rumour of Kiya's kidnapping had leaked beyond the circle of her family. Matt smiled. "Now how do you suppose it's possible for a man to know where and when a crime has been committed yet not be part of it?"

"I'm not. I swear, I had no part in it."

"Indeed? Who told you then?"

"I suspect it's common knowledge."

"You might suspect that to be true, except for the fact that it's not common knowledge. No one but the man responsible and those he hired knows of the kidnapping." Matt sat one hip on the edge of the viscount's desk. "Now, the men he hired, I've no doubt, will keep their mouths shut, especially since one of them committed a murder. That leaves the man who initiate the fiasco. Do you think he's apt to brag about the crime?"

The viscount was horrified. Had he just admitted to a crime? Could he be arrested? He shook his head. No, no one would take the word of this ruffian above that of a lord of the realm. Indeed. If anyone was in trouble it was this hooligan. "How dare you come into my home and accuse me —"

Matt leaned forward threateningly, bringing his gun to within inches of the man's chest. "Here's how I dare. You have knowledge of a kidnapping that no one else is aware of. Don't you think that is a bit odd?"

Winston knew he was trapped. He'd tell the truth, lest he lose his life for a lie. Should this bastard tell the law, he'd simply deny it. "I swear to God, I never meant for anyone to get hurt."

Matt nodded. "Why did you do it?"

"I was supposed to find her, quite by accident, of course."

"Of course," Matt repeated. "And thereby become her hero?"

"I want her. I've always wanted her. I thought perhaps this time…"

"You thought she'd agree this time."

"Please," Winston murmured. "I swear I meant no harm."

"No harm?" he asked in obvious disbelief. "Do you realise the fright a young woman would suffer while being taken from the comfort of her sisters, to be treated with no consideration, to witness a murder then be thrown like a worthless sack of potatoes into a dark, earthen room and be held there with no light for untold hours?" His lips tightened with disgust. "Only a woman as strong as Kiya could come from such a horror unscathed."

"I didn't mean her any harm. I swear I didn't," he moaned as he watched Matt cock the gun. "Please don't kill me. Please."

"I should kill you. Were I another, you'd already be dead." With those words, Matt came to his feet and just before he quit the room he hissed, "Know this. Kiya is mine. She's always going to be mine. We will marry soon. Should anything untoward befall her, there's nowhere on earth that you'll be safe."

Chapter Six

Kiya sat before her mirror and slowly pulled a brush through her long hair as she waited and wondered if it wasn't already too late. She'd thought Matt would come to her room, but after they'd arrived at home, he'd disappeared, no doubt looking into the murder of Mr. Johnston.

She shivered at the thought. It was possible she had looked directly into the face of evil today. What else could account for the day's awful happening? She hadn't a doubt the man Johnston had been sent to follow had killed him. Who else? Kiya felt sick at the thought. Poor Mr. Johnston. She'd barely known the man yet he'd given his life to protect her.

Kiya sniffled loudly and blew her nose just as her bedchamber door opened and closed. Instantly alert, Matt came quickly to her side. "What is it? What happened?"

"I feel so bad. I've been thinking about Mr. Johnston. He died because of me.

Have you ever heard anything so awful?"

"Sweetheart," he murmured as he straddled the bench, joining her before her mirror. "Ah, sweetheart," he said again. He turned her so her back lay against his chest. His fingers moved aside her hair as his mouth nuzzled her neck and he breathed her scent deep into his lungs, thanking God as he did that this woman was safe. "Don't think of it like that. Johnston didn't die because of you, my love. He died very simply because a man, a very evil man, killed him. Today, that man took notice of you. Had it been another, another who was unprotected, he would have taken her. If Johnston hadn't followed him, he would have taken Sarah. Believe me, you were not the cause of this. If anything, because he was noticed, Sarah was saved."

It took a few moments, but she soon turned to face him. "I think you're right. Thank you."

Matt took her brush and pulled it through her hair. "You have beautiful hair. Do you do this every night?"

"If I don't it's a rat's nest in the morning."

Matt grinned, unable to believe this woman could be anything but gorgeous, whether upon awakening or any other part of the day. "You're a beautiful woman. I think you know that."

"Thank you." Kiya shrugged as she glanced towards her mirror. "I suppose I'm not apt to give children nightmares."

Matt chuckled. "I agree. Still you are getting a bit long in the tooth."

She shot him a wicked grin and leaned closer so she might peer into her mirror. "Do you think so?" she asked, turning her head this way and that. "I'd say I have a year or so left."

Matt shrugged. "A year or two," he agreed. "Three at the outside."

Kiya giggled and shot him a censorious glare. "You are so mean."

"I didn't say it to be mean," he returned in supposed innocence. "I only mentioned the fact because you might, thinking you have plenty of time, suddenly find yourself beyond the age of marriage."

She blinked in surprise. "Is there such an age? I would have thought people could marry right up to the hour of their death."

"Yes, you're right, of course. One can marry at any age. What I meant was an age when a man might want you for a wife."

"Oh, I see," she returned. "Thank you for worrying on my behalf."

"You're very welcome."

"Are you hinting that we should marry?"

"Now, Kiya, I know how you feel about the holy state. Indeed, I never would have thought to hear you ask me. I profess I'll have to give this some thought."

She frowned, her blue eyes filled with suspicion. "Give what some thought? What do you think I asked you?"

"You just asked me to marry you."

"Did I?" Her eyes widened then she blinked her surprise. "How odd not to remember something so extraordinary. What did I say exactly?"

"I believe your exact words were 'we should marry'."

She shook her head. "You know that's not what I said or what I meant."

As if she hadn't just denied it, he simply nodded. "I should talk to your father about it."

"About what?"

"About your proposal, of course."

"Oh, of course. And what do you think that might accomplish?"

It might accomplish any number of things. The most important would be to push her closer to marrying him. Still, he was wise enough to respond with, "I'm not sure I know what you mean?"

"No doubt," she agreed with no little sarcasm. "You might as well know I won't be bullied into marrying anyone, Matthew."

"Come closer so you can kiss me."

Kiya did little but look in his direction. "Kiss you? I've been thinking about that."

Not a good sign. Thinking was the last thing he wanted her to do. "About what?" he asked then in all confidence remarked, "I'd wager you like kissing well enough."

"There was a time when I was a very moral, shy young lady. I never realised I was at the time. Only now as I look back, I see the change in me." It was easy enough to see she was having some second thoughts and found herself embarrassed and suffering some confusion. "Do you think decent women enjoy kissing quite so much?"

Matt's heart pounded at her unrealised admittance. "Do you think you're no longer a decent young lady because you enjoy kissing?"

"I don't know."

"I do."

She shook her head, still obviously unsure.

He gathered her closer. "Tell me what you're thinking, Kiya. How will I know if you don't tell me?"

"Matthew, a woman..." She shook her head again. "How can I claim to be a lady when I feel these things and do these things? A lady doesn't..."

He frowned. "Who told you that?"

"I don't think anyone ever told me. It's just common knowledge that a lady doesn't enjoy kissing. She allows a man to kiss her for his pleasure."

Matt grinned. "Does she? And she doesn't enjoy kissing at all?"

Kiya shrugged. "Well, I'm sure there are some who enjoy it," she said, knowing she enjoyed this man's kisses, as well as the shocking things he managed to do *while* he was kissing her, quite a bit more than she should. Still her enjoyment didn't make it right. She looked him straight in the eye and said, "I know I've kissed you before, but…"

Matt laughed. "You call that kissing? Do you mean the pithy response given only after I begged you for weeks?"

"You think my kisses are pithy?" she asked, not at all sure she wasn't insulted.

"Well, perhaps not pithy exactly, but definitely stingy and hardly freely given." He pulled her closer still. "We need to get a few things straight. First of all, a man loves it when a woman kisses him. And the more she kisses him, the more he loves it. And she should kiss him whenever she feels the need. He should never have to ask her."

"Any woman?"

"The right woman," he returned. "And a lady most certainly does kiss a man."

"And if she does, he doesn't believe her to be obvious?"

"Sweetheart, you need to understand something about men. We're not all that complicated. The truth is men love the obvious."

"Do you? How do you mean?"

He smiled and gave a slight shrug. "All right, say you were to answer your door at my knock."

"You never knock."

Matt couldn't hold back his grin. "I know, but say that I did. Say when you answered the door that you were...shall we say less than completely clothed."

Kiya's eyes widened with shock. "You don't mean naked surely?"

Damn but she was the most adorable woman. Matt had a time resisting the need to crush her to him. "We're just imagining here, right?"

"Right," she returned dragging out the word, her voice holding more than a little scepticism.

"Well, if such a happening should occur, you'd no doubt believe you were being obvious, am I right?"

"And I wouldn't be?"

"That's just it. You would be, and I'd love every minute of it."

"Oh my," she exclaimed, her fingers at her lips as she studied his smile. "I had no idea a man's mind worked like that." A few minutes of silent concentration went by before she asked, "And after all that, you'd still think I was a lady?"

He laughed as he pulled her tightly against him. "God, but you are the most adorable creature. Do you think I'd want your kisses so desperately if you weren't a lady?"

"Is that true? Do you want them desperately?"

"No doubt I should have kept that bit of information to myself," he said with a low groan. "I think I've only given you a weapon to use against me."

"Are you growing desperate now?"

"Terribly."

"I take it you'd like it if I kiss you."

"All right, here's the next thing."

She laughed. "I thought you said men aren't complicated. How many more things are there?"

He grinned. "I think this is the last one."

She nodded, waiting for him to go on.

"I kissed you this afternoon, am I right?"

She nodded.

"So now it's your turn."

She pulled back a bit and blinked her surprise, surprise clearly mixed with disbelief, her lips curving into a gentle smile. She watched laughter lurk in his dark brown eyes. God, this man was a rogue. "Are we to take turns, then?"

"That's the way it's done," he said in all seriousness as if the matter was indeed true and beyond his control.

"Truly?"

"I'm afraid so."

She laughed softly as she tried to glare into his oh-so-smug expression "I think I've gotten myself into a bit of trouble here."

"I think you're going to love this kind of trouble."

Kiya laughed.

"I'm still waiting."

She laughed again as she snuggled against him, her mouth lifting to his.

"Wait. This isn't any good. I can't reach you like I want to. Here," he said as he turned her to straddle her bench, facing him. Gently he raised her legs to drape over his, pulling her closer than ever. "Isn't this better?" he asked as he slid her white robe from her silky shoulders then pushed the straps of her gown down her arms, baring her to her waist.

"Mmm...ever so much better," she agreed.

"Would you like to take this off?"

"And sit like this naked?" she asked, obviously shocked at the thought.

Matt nodded. "We'll wait until we get to the bed," he said then sighed with relief at her soft murmur of agreement, his heart pounding with happiness for she seemed to think it was all right to be naked as long as one was in bed.

She leaned closer, her hands on his chest, sliding inside his open shirt. Her mouth pressed against the heat of his throat, tasting the salty clean maleness found there then moved higher to his jaw, her teeth and tongue finding his taste irresistible. At long last, her mouth dragged lusciously back and forth against his lips.

He pulled her closer, his eyes closing in delight with the feel of her against his chest. God, he'd never get enough of the feel of this woman. He pulled back just a bit, to allow his hands to come between them. Cupping her breasts, he weighed the soft luscious flesh as his thumbs ran over the tips then he gently twisted the nipples, bringing them to hard aching buds in desperate need of his mouth.

"Would you like to watch this, Kiya? Would you like to watch me touch you?"

"Could I?"

"For a time. Next time, we'll bring a mirror to the bed." He turned her then, pulling the bench out so he sat behind her, while she leaned back against his chest, proudly offering her generous breasts to both their delight.

His hands were on her shoulders, dark skin against ivory white. She thought she'd never seen anything so lovely. His mouth came to the side of her throat as his hands lowered to her softness, to lift pink crested, delicious morsels, teasing the tips with his fingers as she moaned, dazed at the unbearably erotic sight.

"Matt, oh my God, Matt. I can't tell you how good this is."

"Mmm," he murmured his lips against her throat. His lips moved to her ear, tugging at the lobe. He turned her enough so he could reach one breast, and she watched as his dark head lowered, his teeth tugging her softness deep into a luscious pit of fire. "I can't wait any longer. You have to kiss me now"

Kiya turned again to face him. "Yes," she murmured for she wanted nothing more than to kiss this man.

Senses already teased almost beyond bearing, it took no more than the merest touch of her lips on his for his hungry growl then for mouths to open, eager for tongues to search out and luxuriate in tastes and textures and for them to lose all thought but the urgent need for more. The heat of him seemed to sear her soul. She hadn't remembered he tasted this good, felt this good. Every time he kissed her, it was like the first.

Matt was drowning in her taste. He tried to control his emotions and his desperate need for her lest the evening end almost before it began. His hands moved down the length of her, closely followed by his mouth, to nuzzle at her breasts to suck and bite to lick to drink of the flavour of her skin. He smiled at her greedy sound of need as her back arched, silently asking for all he could give as she offered all for both their pleasures.

His hands at her waist, he brought her to her feet. Her gown slid down the length of her, its loss never noticed as he carried her to her bed.

He'd touched her before but had never seen. She was beauty beyond belief. "I can't imagine a sight more lovely," he murmured against her mouth. "Kiya, my God," he moaned against her throat.

A tremendous ache of mindless need overcame Matt, leaving him helpless as a newborn babe as her hands moved over his chest and his stomach, to slide inside his trousers.

He stiffened. "God," he groaned, his heart pounding as if he'd run miles as her uncertain fingers closed around him. "Kiya. Easy, sweetheart," he moaned as she opened the tabs of his pants and lowered the garment to his knees.

Matt knew she'd never seen a naked man and wondered if she'd be afraid. He pulled way the last of his clothes and sighed with relief at her gentle smile.

Raised on a farm, she was well aware that the male form was different from her own. She wasn't afraid and yet some apprehension wasn't far from her thoughts, for she hadn't imagined him to be quite so big.

Her gaze moved from his broad shoulders to his hard chest, following the thin line of dark hair over his flat belly, down thickly muscled thighs and then back to his groin where the dark line fanned out to cupped his maleness.

"You really are beautiful."

Matt grinned. "Am I? Men aren't supposed to be beautiful, you know?"

"I know, but you are."

Matt knelt on the bed, his body easing gently over hers.

His heart thundered at the feel of her. God, she was so luscious, so soft and so warm. He thought he'd never touch her enough. He stretched out over her, sliding against the warmth of her silky, heated skin. His lips brushed gently over hers.

Shivers of delight raced down her spine and curled her toes. Then he sucked her bottom lip into his mouth to run his tongue over it and absorb her soft moan with a hungry growl.

"I love this," she murmured, and an explosion of lust rushed into the pit of Matt's belly. He felt himself grow harder than he could ever remember, and he trembled as he fought to control this aching need. He'd never get enough of this woman, her taste, her scent or her touch.

His mouth, hotter than she'd ever known, ravaged hers until not the smallest part was left untouched. A low buzzing filled her brain as he took, leaving Kiya feeling heavy and weak from the sweet ecstasy. In unison, they moaned their approval as their tongues grew bolder. Their hunger grew out of control until their breathing became short jerking pants of desperate need.

He wanted her more than his own life and knew, after tonight, there was no way he could wait much longer.

For the longest time, his mouth refused to release hers. His tongue imitated the tremendous hunger of his body. She couldn't breathe and didn't care. All she could think was he should never stop. All she wanted was the feel of him, and the taste of his mouth forever. All she could imagine was heaven couldn't hold more delight than this.

Then he was gone, leaving her aching at the loss as he slipped from her mouth to her jaw to her throat. The scratchiness of his cheeks scraped deliciously over her chest. His teeth and lips nibbled at her breasts and filled her belly with a desperate, unbearable need.

And then he left her again to slide over her midriff, to breathe all he could of her luscious woman's scent, to find her soft belly and kiss her there while he nuzzled his face against her warmth.

Kiya hardly realised his daring, delicious touch. When his tongue slid beyond the protective curls covering her pussy, she gasped and fought against the need to cry out.

"Matt," she choked. "What are you...Matt...what?"

She hadn't imagined this. He'd touched her there before, and touching her had brought her the most exquisite pleasure, but this...this was so much more. A bit shocked at first, it took only seconds for her to realised this was the best moment in her life. She wanted it to never end.

"Mmm," she murmured as her hips lifted helplessly towards his pleasure-giving mouth as she felt his tongue slide hot, thick and wet against her. "Oh yes.".

She became a mindless craving creature, knowing but one need, that he should never stop. Her breathing grew choppy as she was drawn under the luscious spell of his ever-moving tongue and searing hot breath.

She felt the heaviness, the tightness slide over her belly, but fought against it. This was too good to give up — to *ever* give up. She knew what awaited her, but she didn't want this to end. Not this soon. Oh please, not now.

She had no real choice. Her muscles stiffened despite her wants. The need took control no matter her yearning. It came faster than any time before. Harder, more desperately fierce. A distant cramp was soon pain then a squeezing tight ache then a clamp of suffocating madness where she lost the last of her control to burst into agonising, white-hot ecstasy.

"What do you think?" he asked as he slid up the length of her.

She mumbled something incoherent.

"How do you feel?" he asked as his hand replaced his mouth allowing him to feel the last of her aftershocks.

"What?" she barely managed as if drugged on the passion.

"How do you feel?" he repeated.

She frowned as his questioning finally pulled her from the sweet lethargy. "With my hands."

He grinned and gave her a tiny shake, obviously needing to hear praises sung. "Kiya," he said in warning.

She laughed. "Like I'm floating. Go away so I can enjoy it."

"If I go, you can't enjoy it. I'm the one who gave it to you."

"All right, stay then. Just don't talk."

Matt laughed as he snuggled her closer, delighting in her scent as he breathed her deep into his lungs and waited for her senses to return.

"How did you like it?"

"If you mean what you just did, I suppose I thought it mildly amusing."

"Did you?" he grinned. "Strange, I didn't hear you laughing."

"That's because I was polite enough to hold in my laughter. I didn't want you to feel self-conscious."

"Thank you for worrying about my feelings. That was very nice of you."

"I'm a very nice lady."

"You're a brat, you mean?"

She pulled her head back and looked up at him. "Oh, are you still here?"

He gave a light tap to her rear and warned, "Behave yourself."

She giggled then came suddenly to her knees and sat back on her feet. For the first time in her life, she was totally comfortable in her nakedness. "I thought it was lovely. I thought it was the most perfect thing that has ever happened to me." She smiled at his cocky grin, figuring just this once she'd let him get away with it. After all, if anyone had the right, he did. "Now, I suppose you'll be looking for something like it in return."

Matt rolled to his back, his hands under his head, his body totally relaxed as he eyed her beautiful, naked form. "I was hoping you'd be supposing that."

"This isn't like kissing, is it? I mean I won't have to wait until next time I see you before I can do it, will I?"

"No, it's not like kissing. You can do whatever you like, anytime you like."

For just a moment, she looked a bit uncertain. "I'm not sure I know..."

"You don't have to be sure, and you don't have to know. Just do what you feel like doing."

Kiya moved to kneel between his legs. "Is it all right if I stay here?"

"It's better than all right."

Kiya grinned at his flagrant display. She couldn't imagine ever being so at ease that she could lay before him, with all her senses about her and her legs apart. "Men don't have problems with modesty, do they?"

"I've never heard of any."

"Mmm, I didn't think so." She watched him as he tried to control his obvious need for her to begin. "I'm not too sure what I should do. Would it be all right if I told you my plan?"

Matt nodded.

"And then you could tell me if there's anything you don't like."

He shook his head, his eagerness not to be denied. "I like everything."

Kiya laughed. "I wonder if you'll always be this agreeable."

He didn't respond. He couldn't.

"All right, let's see if you like this. I was thinking I might start here," she said, leaning forward, placing her finger against his lips. Her swaying breasts brushed against his chest. "Suppose I kiss you the same way you kissed me. Suppose I do it until you're dizzy and weak and helpless beneath me."

He groaned.

"Suppose I lick my way down your body, suppose I bite you just a little on the way then roll my tongue over each bite." Her hand trailed lightly down his body from his lips to his belly.

He gasped, and his body hummed, vibrating with need.

"And then when my mouth is about here," she said, her fingers brushing through the thick hair that cupped his sex, "suppose I kiss this." She suddenly lowered her mouth and ran her tongue up his hard shaft. She and felt his body jerk beneath her touch. "Suppose I lick you here," she said, while her tongue played at the tip. "Suppose I suck you here."

"You're killing me." His voice was gravelly and thick.

"Would that be all right?"

He could hardly breathe. "Why don't you try it and see?"

She smiled and said, "That's a thought. Why don't I?"

She lay full length upon him and grinned into his tight features. "You look to be in some pain."

"I think I can safely testify to that."

"I never felt this kind of power before. I think I like it."

"Don't get carried away with yourself," he said, trying to glare and failing miserably.

Kiya giggled. "Do you know how good you feel? You're so warm and hard. Except for that stick poking my hip, you'd make a perfect bed."

He grinned. "Sleeping is a bit far from my thoughts at the moment."

"And mine," she agreed as she brushed against his mouth in a tantalising tease. Again, again, her lips moved over his.

She was driving him mad.

"Don't touch me, Matt," she warned as his hands came to the back of her head. They fell to his sides when she refused to complete the kiss even as his head rose from the pillow, his mouth trying to capture hers.

"Let me do this. Let me make love to you."

He groaned helpless but to allow her what she wanted.

Her tongue slipped into his mouth, and he sucked hard, trying to absorb all he could of her taste into him. And then she pulled back just enough so her teeth could grab at his lower lip. She sucked that lip played with it, rubbed her tongue over it, inside it. "I love the way you taste. I wish I could always do this, always taste and smell you." She groaned, delighted with her discovery. "I never knew a man could smell or taste like you."

And then her mouth was at his jaw, running along the scratchiness of his cheek and throat. "When did you shave?"

"This morning. I didn't have a chance tonight. Is it too much?"

"No. I like it. It feels wonderful. You feel wonderful."

Matt only managed a low moan in response. He couldn't imagine a woman more captivating than this one. He'd never known another so conscious of his every nuance, so aware of him, so anxious to discover all there was about him and, to his delight, so obviously satisfied with her discoveries. She made him feel more a man, stronger than ever before.

She didn't touch him except with her lips, teeth and tongue and, God help him, the swaying of her breasts as she leaned over him. He trembled as her mouth moved to his chest, lingering in a mind shattering assault on his senses. She sucked at his skin and teased his nipples. His body jerked at almost every touch. She bit him, and he moaned at the gentle pain then moaned again as she rolled her tongue over the tiny injury.

She slid lower. Had he ever known torture such as this? Had he ever felt such desperate need? He gasped for every breath.

And then she nuzzled her face against his groin, sighing her pleasure as she breathed, delighting in the warm musky scent of him. She kissed him, her lips trailing up the length of his cock, her tongue tasting him along the way. She lingered at the tip, absorbing all she could of his flavour and texture.

Matt wondered what he'd ever done that God should allow him this luscious woman. He was dying and wondered if he'd live through this magic. Unable to hold back any longer, he groaned and pulled her up the length of him. His mouth took hers in a kiss that stole the last of her strength. She was his to take and do with as he would. Only he wouldn't. Not yet. In an instant, he pressed her to her back and half upon her moved his hips against her belly, desperate to find his release. His mouth on hers, he moaned as the pleasure came.

"God," he gasped. "Oh my God," he said again then, exhausted, collapsed heavily upon her. "You are the most beautiful, wonderful woman."

They lay quietly together for endless moments before he finally managed to bring his breathing under some control. Suddenly, he jumped from her side and ran for a towel at the dry sink. Within seconds, he had her dry and was drying himself.

"It does make for a bit of a mess, wouldn't you say?"

"For now."

She frowned, trying to understand. "What do you mean 'for now'? Will there come a time when it won't?"

"When we make love, it won't."

"Oh, I see," she said then laughed softly. "Taking for granted we will make love, you mean it won't make a mess on *you*."

Matt laughed and grabbed her in a tight embrace. A huge, satisfied grin teased his mouth as he returned the towel to her body and seemed to take an unusual amount of time rubbing an area which she'd believed already dry.

"If I'm not mistaken, you've cleaned there before."

"I know. I'm just making sure I've got it all."

"You got it all five minutes ago."

Matt grinned. "You don't want me to touch you?" he asked, knowing the opposite to be the truth.

"You're not touching me. The towel is."

Matt laughed and threw the towel on the floor as he pulled her to his side.

As she cuddled against him, she said, "It's best we aren't to marry, Matthew, for we'd never suit."

"Wouldn't we?" he asked, pulling her half over him. "I wonder why?"

She never thought but to speak the truth as far as she knew it. "You're far too big. You could only hurt me."

Matt grinned at the unrealised compliment and hugged her tighter against him. "It's not size that matters, sweetheart. If a man is gentle with his lady, his size is of no consequence."

"Truly?"

"Truly," he returned as he snuggled his face into the warmth of her neck. "I don't want to leave you."

"Then stay," she offered, more than happy to find herself in his arms.

Matt thought that might be one of the better ideas he'd heard in some time. "There's one problem with staying. We might not get too much sleep."

Kiya smiled. "I've always thought sleep was a bit overvalued. Wouldn't you agree?"

Matt grinned. "I have an idea."

"Mmm," she murmured. "I d say you're a man of many ideas."

"What would you say if I started from your toes and worked my way up your body, licking you everywhere?"

"Sounds lovely," she murmured. "But not in church, surely."

"What?" he asked, frowning at her remark, perhaps she was closer to sleep than he'd imagined.

"You said you'd lick me everywhere, and I said, not in chur—" She yelped as he grabbed her and began to tickle her mercilessly. A moment later, she sat upon his chest, proving herself wide awake and of equal, if not superior, strength than her partner, at least for a short, desperate spurt of time. "I told you once before, no tickling."

Matt grinned as he pulled her to lay over the length of him.

"All right," he soothed, while rubbing his hands up and down her back, "since you insist, I won't do it in church. But you should know, now that you've mentioned it, I won't be sitting at your side again without imagining the luscious taste of you."

"Oh Lord, no doubt I'm bound to get some odd looks because now I'll be thinking that you're thinking, and I'll probably burst out laughing, in the middle of a sermon.

How did I ever involved myself with the likes of a man so terribly wicked."

"If I remember correctly, it was raining and you were kind enough to worry about me taking a chill. You tried to dry me off."

"A serious mistake on my part, no doubt."

Matt ignored her teasing remark, knowing it didn't matter how this love affair had begun. She might not have realised it, but it had been destined from the first moment he'd seen her. He brought the subject back to where it had begun. "Where else shouldn't I lick you?" he asked, his mouth already about the chore as he nibbled at her toes.

"The kitchens. There's always someone in the kitchens."

"The kitchens are out. Where else?" he asked as he moved up her leg. He lingered for just a moment then raised her leg and, to her delight, nuzzled behind her knee.

"The dinning room?" she murmured in a voice growing thick, low and choppy with anticipation.

"Mmm," he murmured thinking over her suggestion. "No doubt, that table could be put to its best use."

Kiya hadn't a clue as to what he meant by that and was about to ask him to explain when she lost all train of thought as his mouth approached a particularly sensitive area. "Where else?"

"Mmm?" she breathed as he nuzzled against the sweet moist heat of her pussy at last. "What?" she managed although she couldn't have said how. "Oh, I think you were right from the first when you said 'everywhere'."

Matt chuckled, knowing he'd caused her to lose all sense of reason and thought once again. It was another hour before he left her sleeping and crept silently into his cold bed, vowing it wouldn't be long before he'd have this woman for his own forever.

* * * *

Matt had made an appointment with Mr. Harrison the previous evening. He knocked on the man's office door early the next morning, feeling some nervousness as a voice called out for him to enter.

"I realise I'm a bit early, sir, but I have yet to assign the guards for the trip to London, and I thought I should talk with you first."

Mr. Harrison nodded. There was a moment of silence then he asked, "What was it you wanted to discuss? Have you found the man who killed your agent?"

Matt shook his head. "Not yet, but we will. No, what I wanted to talk to you about is...I find I'm in love with your daughter, sir. I'd like your permission to marry her."

John Harrison knew nothing but confusion. Marry her? Marry his daughter? Didn't Matt know his friend had already asked for her hand? Didn't he know Merry was already engaged? What in the world did he mean by this?

"You're probably surprised, I'm sure."

"You might say that."

"I know she's a bit young, but..."

John frowned. So it wasn't Merry Matt spoke of. Young had to mean Amy. But that couldn't be. Amy was naught but a young girl hardly ready for marriage. What could this man be thinking?

Mr. Harrison shook his head. "I don't think..."

Matt cut him off. "I realise this must come as something of a shock. Indeed, I'm sure the lady is blissfully unaware, as well. Still, I'm sure I can convince her, given a bit of time."

"Might you make yourself a bit more clear, sir? Which of my daughters is it you wish to marry?"

"I want to marry Kiya, of course."

Mr. Harrison almost laughed aloud. Apparently, Matt had no knowledge of Kiya's fervent objection to marriage. After a long pause, he tried to ease the man's rejection. "Indeed, sir, I'm afraid you don't know Kiya. She's professed her reluctance to ever marry on many occasions. I think she won't be changing her mind for some time."

"I think she will."

"Do you? And what, pray tell, allows you to believe she'll change her mind? Has she said as much?"

"No, but I believe she feels something for me. Soon enough, I expect she'll realise that fact."

Mr. Harrison smiled. "You believe, yet she hasn't said as much?"

"She will. I have every confidence she will."

Mr. Harrison nodded, knowing this man was setting himself up for some disappointment. He wasn't the first to proclaim his love for Kiya, and she hadn't yet allowed any would-be suitor to believe she might be interested in the holy state. Mr. Harrison couldn't imagine anything had changed in the last few weeks. "Supposing she does come to feel something for you, sir. Exactly what can you offer her?"

"I'd appreciate your complete confidence in this matter, sir."

"Of course."

"I understand that you are aware of my partnership with Jake in this security firm."

"I am."

"Well, there's a bit more to it than that. I am the Duke of Stratford."

Mr. Harrison's gaze filled with doubt. "The Duke of..." He shook his head. "My good man, I'm afraid—"

"I realise this is a lot to take in, sir. But the truth of the matter is I have a great many interests, and this is but one of them." Matt reached into his pocket, pulled out a billfold and handed Mr. Harrison his card.

"I realize this is a bit of a surprise. You need not take my word for it, sir. You may contact my solicitor at your convenience." Another card was added to the one already in the man's hand.

To say Mr. Harrison knew some surprise at the young man's response was to put it mildly. He felt the need to caution, "My dear sir, you should know of Kiya's aversion towards—"

"I know, sir. Indeed, I do know."

"Then I think the question is, does she know?"

"Not as yet."

Lord, this was bound to be a problem, even should he accept the young man and his excellent offer. Of course, in the end, it was up to his daughter. He couldn't insist. She'd never agree to a marriage should he try to force her. In truth, he didn't doubt she'd run if it came down to that. "I hope you know this won't be easy."

"I'm sure it won't, but I think she's worth any effort."

Mr. Harrison smiled as Matt left his office. To be sure both of these thick-headed young people were in for a time of it.

* * * *

Outside her father's office, Kiya nervously paced the hallway, wondering what on earth Matt was about? What was he doing? Why was there a need to speak with her father?

"What did you want to talk to my father about?" she asked the moment he stepped into the hallway and shut the door behind him.

"Excuse me?"

"What did you—"

"I heard what you said."

"Then answer me," she snapped in a none too gentle tone.

Matt grinned at her bossy attitude, knowing she was unsettled. A moment later, she found herself thrust into a small sitting room across the hall, the door closed firmly behind her, her small form pushed up against it.

"Lower your voice."

"What are you doing?"

"I thought you needed some privacy. We're better off talking in here than in the hall, wouldn't you agree?"

"Why were you talking to my father?"

"Why are you asking?"

"Because I want to know."

"Do you suppose I told him about your proposal?"

"Matthew, you didn't," she gasped. "I didn't."

"If you must know, we spoke of the ride to London," he said, shrugging off the half truth. He *had* mentioned the trip. "Of how many men we'll need and their placement. Shall I tell you the whole of it?"

"No," she returned. "Are you sure?"

He laughed, partly with relief. "I'm sure. Kiss me."

"I kissed you last night."

"That was four hours ago, and I kissed you last. I need more."

Chapter Seven

The three women and their father occupied the coach as it entered the outskirts of the city, surrounded front to back by a near army of men on horseback. Inside, Amy related the rumours currently spreading through their neighbourhood.

"How do you know that?" Kiya asked, clearly shocked. "I promise you, I've never heard any such thing."

"They call it a love child."

Merry moaned.

Kiya gasped that her younger sister should even know of such a thing, never mind mention it. "It's not true, and I think it's awful of you to be party to such rumours."

"How do you know it's not true? Ellie heard it from Mary. Mary heard it from Elizabeth who heard it from Annie's brother. And he heard it—"

"One can hardly imagine any circumstance that might cause a young lady to speak of such things with the brother of her friend. In truth, Mrs. Coventry is too old to be with child."

"She is not," Amy countered. "I've heard tell a woman can have children well into her forties."

Kiya turned her attention to their father and asked, "Father, are you going to do something?"

"What would you have me do, Kiya?"

"The girl needs a firm hand, lest she bring disgrace upon us all."

"Why are you blaming me? I didn't do it," Amy countered. "All I did was hear of it."

"And repeat it." Kiya said. "It's ghastly to think you might so easily contribute to the ruin of a lady's reputation."

"Time will tell if it's rumour or not, I'd wager."

"That's enough, Amy. You're sister is right. There's a lady's reputation at stake here." John Harrison knew the lady in question She was a special friend of his, in fact, and was in the city at the moment. He thought he'd drop by her rooms the moment he'd settled his daughters in his London townhouse. It had been weeks since he'd last spent time in her lovely company.

"The sad truth is a woman alone is often the object of unjust and hurtful rumours. You might remember that, dear," he said, referring to Kiya and her irregular views on marriage. "The time could come when a man at your side might prove advantageous."

Kiya only grunted in response, for she thought many a woman might seek to hold a man to her side but would never know the same in return. Indeed, once his wife, she'd hold less status than any of his children and would be relegated to the same affection as the rest of his possessions, held in awe only as much as his favourite horse.

Granted, many a woman needed the protection of a man. There were many, as well, who did not, yet sought it never the less. Her own sister for one. Kiya couldn't imagine why a woman would willingly give up the rights of any English citizen for the substandard status of 'wife'.

Of course, the time so far spent in Matt's company was more than enjoyable. It was lovely, at times earth-shattering, still no woman with half her wits should trade a few moments of pleasure for a life of second-class existence.

Kiya thought her father's sister, Annabelle, had the right idea. Never beholden to a man, she lived her life as she pleased, and if she pleased to take an occasional lover, it was done in so discreet a fashion there was never a hint of scandal. Kiya thought she rather liked that idea and wondered if, in the years to come, she might not live as her aunt did.

Moments later, the conversation turned to the upcoming nuptials and the thoughts of what the ladies might be wearing.

* * * *

It was late. The three-storied townhouse had long ago grown quiet. Matt, in Kiya's bed, gasped for his every breath, his face against her breast as her hand eased its manipulations of his cock. He put his hand over hers and groaned, "Damn, you almost killed me that time."

Kiya laughed softly. "One can only wonder why a man would choose to put his life at risk for a minute of pleasure at best."

He'd brought linen towelling with him to the bed and rubbed it over her stomach and his, cleaning away the evidence of this last half hour of play. "Because that minute of pleasure *is* the best. In fact, it's closer to a few minutes of heaven." He bit her nipple then sucked it deep into the blazing heat of his mouth. At her soft gasp of pleasure, he said, "Tell me you love me."

She groaned, instantly drawn into delicious pleasure as he licked the stiff, sensitive tip. "Oh God, I love you."

Matt grinned, pulled back and said, "You mean you love *this*. Now tell me the same with a clear mind."

She chuckled softly as she stretched, thrusting her breasts towards his mouth in graceful, purposeful seduction. "Would you have me lie, Matthew?"

He pulled her against him. "You little wretch. Tell me."

"It loses some of its value if you insist."

"If I don't, I'll be ninety before I hear it again."

Kiya giggled and snuggled her face into the warmth of his neck. "I love you."

"And you'll marry me?"

She sighed as she snuggled closer to his side, her head on his arm, her leg thrown familiarly over his. "Matt, you should have seen Merry in her bridal dress. It was our mother's. The seamstress fit it to her perfectly. She is breathtaking."

"I've no doubt. You didn't answer me."

"And Amy... As usual, she wanted a dress that was far too old for her. It was out of the question, of course. By the time we left the shop, she wasn't talking to any of us." She shook her head and sighed. "Lord, I don't know what I'm going to do once Merry leaves for her own home. How will I see to the girl? She fights me at every turn."

"Unlike her sister, of course."

"I presume you're talking about me. I'll have you know I never gave my father a minute's worry."

"Indeed, you've saved them all for me."

Kiya grinned and raised herself to her elbow so she could look down at him, her naked breasts only inches from his mouth. "Have I given you cause to worry, darling?"

Matt's heart nearly melted at the endearment. He couldn't get enough of them. He never would. He pushed her to her back and leaned over her. "Am I truly your darling, Kiya?"

"Of course."

"Then you *will* marry me?"

"Matt, why must you insist?" she asked then whined almost childishly, "You're ruining everything."

"Am I?" he asked, his voice tight with annoyance. "Exactly what is it I'm ruining?"

"Our time together. I don't want these lovely moments to end with an argument."

"But these lovely moments always end, don't you see? And I need more. I need to fuck you. God damn it! I need to fuck you until we both come to know nothing but the pleasure of my cock so deep inside you. I might never take it out again. It's damn near an obsession, almost all I ever think about. Only it will never happen as long as you insist on being a thick-headed little fool."

"How charming of you to let me know I'm held so warmly in your thoughts," she said stiffly. "Thank you very much. Now, if you don't mind, I'd appreciate it if you left. I'm tired." She wiggled from beneath him and, as if he were already gone, dismissed him from her thoughts. She stood at the side of the bed and slid her nightdress over her head.

"And that's it? You tell me to go so, like a trained monkey, I'm to do as you say?"

Kiya said nothing. She got back into bed and turned away from him. She curled into a comfortable position and sighed.

"You're going to sleep?" Matt felt damn close to strangling her as she continued to ignore his presence.

Again no response.

"God damn it, Kiya! What the hell do you want?"

She turned suddenly to face him. "I want nothing but a night's sleep. Please leave."

"I know you love me."

"I don't."

"You do so don't give me any of your bullshit."

"Matt," Kiya gasped. "Is it necessary to use that kind of language?"

"Does it upset your delicate sensibilities, little hypocrite? A gutter word makes you blush but having an affair is well within your comfort zone? And yes, I'm afraid it is necessary as long as I have an obstinate fool for a—"

"My my," she interrupted. "Love words to turn any lady's head, I'm sure."

"I could force you," he gritted between clenched teeth.

Her eyes narrowed into slits of warning as she dared to whisper, "Try it."

And Matt knew she'd make his life a living hell if he did. "All right, so you don't want love and you don't want marriage. Sex is enough for you. Am I correct?"

"You are so ugly."

"Am I? Speaking the truth is ugly?"

"Leave me alone."

"Let's look at this rationally with no emotion involved. Tell me exactly what it is you want?"

"You mean in return for ownership?"

"Is that the problem?" Matt groaned as he rubbed his hand over his face. "Where the hell did you pick up these ideas?" He sighed and then said, "All right, we'll play it your way. In return for owning you, what do you want?"

"Freedom."

"Freedom?" he mused in some confusion, while wondering how either could be free if pledged to the other. He considered the word for a long moment before he thought perhaps he understood her meaning. "Good enough. Let's see what we can do. Suppose I allow you your freedom. What then?"

"What do you mean 'allow me my freedom'?"

"I mean suppose I sign papers agreeing to your every want. Equal in everything. Equal is freedom, is it not? You don't want more than equal, do you?"

"Equal would be fine," she said stiffly.

"Wonderful. So if we're equal in all things, do you suppose it would be expected of you to bring something more to the marriage than a dowry? I mean, if a man has to support you and his children, I can't see how that would make you equal. Do you see what I mean?"

As they sat on the bed with legs crossed, facing one another, Matt wondered if her back could grow any straighter or her anger any stronger before she burst into a furnace of raging flame. Still, she managed to keep her voice moderate, her fury completely under control as she returned in a voice that trembled with raw emotion, "I do, and thank you for making yourself perfectly clear. According to you—and I have every reason to believe most men would agree—I wouldn't be equal to my husband, even though I came to him of my own will, not as a slave but as a free English woman in good standing.

Since I was so foolish as to be born female and of such little value and consequence, I'm to merely bear his children. Not *ours* you understand," she made sure to clarify, "but *his* children. And raise them while he goes about the business of doing whatever it is a husband does. Certainly, I could never be considered his equal, for any could do what a wife does, is that not right?" She didn't wait for an answer. "As a wife, I'd be merely another of my husband's possessions. What I once owned would no longer be mine, from my properties to my hairbrush. What I do, think, feel, believe, desire and dream would be of no real consequence, except perhaps to myself. That, my dear sir, is simply the way of things. I pledge to you even if I come to know the greatest love thus far bestowed upon mankind, it could not persuade me to ever marry."

A long, silent moment passed between them as he seriously considered what he'd believed at first to be ridiculously outrageous opinions. Oddly enough, the more he thought on them the more he realised her views held some merit. Sitting across from her, he silently studied her slight form, her delicate manner, her beautiful face and the steely determination in her blue eyes. He couldn't deny it. Her words made perfect sense. She was right. She was more than right. In her place, he'd be loath to give up his personal freedom in order to marry.

Finally he said, "In truth, Kiya, I think you are above all men, and you do yourself a disservice by wanting to be equal. If you were mine—yes, *mine*," he repeated as her eyes narrowed with warning. "Mine as much and as surely mine as I'd be yours. I'd hold you forever in my heart and deem your wants, desires, dreams and, feelings of the utmost importance. If you want papers signed to that effect, I've no objection."

Kiya looked away. She wanted to believe him. She ached to believe. Could she trust him? "We need time, Matt. We need to come to truly know one another."

He grinned. "Indeed, that's simple enough." His brows rose and fell in wicked amusement. "I know of one particularly delicious way to get to know you."

She laughed. "I think you know me well enough on that score, Mr. Chase."

"Hardly true, Mistress. We've been talking for some few minutes, and I've since come to know a whole new side of you. Opinions, I confess, that are somewhat startling. Opinions I haven't until now given much thought."

"Much thought?" she inquired, looking to make clear his meaning.

"All right," he grinned. "I've never given them any thought."

"But you will now?"

"You might be safe in assuming as much. And while I think on it, and just for my own information, you understand, I'll need to remind myself that it's equal you want to be. I am correct on that score, am I not?"

"You are," she returned, her eyes brilliant with laughter.

He reached for the hem of her gown and began to inch the silky material up her slender form.

"As you can well attest, Mistress, I am sitting here naked, while you are clothed in a night shift. Do you think that makes us equal?"

"What I think, Mr. Chase, is that I'd best be careful of everything I say lest you use my words against me."

"I'd rather use something other than words against you."

She frowned at a loss to understand his meaning.

"Things like my lips, my teeth, my tongue."

"Oh, those things," she said, unable to hold back a soft giggle. She laughed as she shook off her gown and faced him, completely at ease in her nakedness. "Are we equal now?"

Equal? He prayed to God she'd never realise just how superior to him she actually was. "We might have to work on it a bit."

For a brief time, the soft sound of her muffled laughter filled the room.

* * * *

"It's beautiful," Merry said as she raised her hand towards the light shining through the shop's window.

"Do you like it?"

Merry, her gaze brimming with tenderness, raised glowing blue eyes to Jake. "You don't think it's too big, do you?"

"I love you," he said, thinking his soon-to-be wife beyond adorable.

"In that case, I love it, and I'm going to love being your wife."

Matt and Kiya stood nearby as they watched the loving couple pick out their wedding rings. At Merry's comment, Matt quickly pulled his lady outside the shop.

Jake couldn't resist. He gave Merry a quick, hard kiss on the lips.

"Jake," she admonished, knowing the shopkeeper and his wife had not missed the goings on. Merry's cheeks were pink with embarrassment as she pressed her hands to his chest, creating some space between their bodies. "You mustn't."

Jake laughed. "We'll be husband and wife in little more than a week."

Merry shook her head and shot him a warning glance. "Don't do it again."

"Yes, ma'am. I wouldn't think of it," he professed then continued quite a bit more softly for her ears alone, "Until I get you back in my coach."

"You're being very wicked, and you must stop."

"I'd best, sweetheart," he agreed. "Lest your cheeks burst into flame."

* * * *

Outside, Kiya held to Matt's arm as he shot her an astounded look. "Did you hear that? She said she was going to love being his wife. Some women have the most peculiar way of thinking, wouldn't you say?"

Kiya shot him a look that promised untold suffering, which only caused him to laugh aloud. "I think you say entirely too much, Mr. Chase."

"Do you not think it peculiar or, at the very least, a bit strange that two sisters born of the same mother and father and raised together in the same home, with basically the same teachers, schooling and advantages should, upon reaching adulthood, have such startlingly dissimilar ways of thinking?"

Kiya chuckled and shook her head at his supposed confusion.

He nodded over his shoulder towards the shop they had just vacated and the lady still within. "Did you ever wonder what could have happened to the poor girl?"

Kiya laughed. "I believe I've mentioned on more than one occasion that you are a beast."

His chuckle was low and far too dangerously appealing. "Indeed, you have, but what has that to do with this truly odd turn of events?"

She smiled but refused to look in his direction, her gaze instead seemed to suddenly study the startling extremes of London's skyline. "Not merely a beast, Mr. Chase. A wretched beast."

London was enjoying a spell of particularly lovely weather. The nights were chilly the days long and warm beneath a summer sun. Kiya hardly needed her shawl and only wore it because it was easier than carrying the garment.

Matt smiled at his lady and placed her hand upon his sleeve. "Would a lady care to join this wretched beast for a bit of refreshment?" he asked as he nodded towards the inn.

Kiya smiled. "Lord, you must be bored to tears watching three ladies shop."

"I suppose I'll survive, especially if we find a dark corner inside where I can steal a kiss."

She shook her head. "Behave yourself."

And as if she were the one looking for a kiss, he patted the hand on his arm and admonished, "You needn't fret, sweetheart. I know how you yearn. Later will be time enough for kissing."

She was laughing at the wicked light in his eyes and his outrageous disregard of the truth when she stumbled forward just a bit and her shawl was snatched from her shoulders.

A man cursed, and Matt snapped, "Grab her."

Kiya turned to see the problem and watched in amazement as a ragged little girl, who appeared no more than five, was plucked from the sidewalk by the back of her shabby dress and made to hang for a moment with Kiya's shawl clutched in her small grubby fingers. Along with the shawl, Kiya was amazed to find her hanky taken unnoticed from her skirt pocket. She reached for her pocket and found the three coins once within were gone as well. The youngster was immediately brought into the huge arms of one of the guards. Not the least bit afraid, or perhaps more afraid than anyone could have imagined, she bit the man holding her and almost broke free as he cursed again and momentarily loosened his hold.

"Get your goddamn, bloody hands off my sister, you cur," a boy of no more than six fiercely ordered.

A moment later, he was held in place by yet another guard. The remaining four men pulled evil-looking guns from somewhere on their persons, waiting lest this be a ruse to bring harm to the lady currently protected by Matt's arms.

"God help us," Kiya murmured as she took in both brother and sister. They were ragged and filthy, hair uncombed, faces in dire need of washing, clothes in tatters and dirty feet bleeding and unshod. "What in the world?"

Of course, Kiya had seen begging children in the city before, but never had she heard such vile curses directed to their marks as plans were foiled.

"Where do you live?" she asked and received yet another curse for her inquiry.

"Answer the lady," a guard called Thomas warned, and he twisted the boy's arm behind his back. It was easy enough to see, even beneath a coating of dirt that the boy's face turned white.

"No," Kiya murmured as she leaned her back into Matt's strength.

Matt instantly concurred with a quick shake of his head. "Easy on the boy, Thomas. We'll find a constable. No doubt, he'll know where these children belong."

"Please, Miss," the little girl cried, her tears leaving white marks as they streaked her tiny face. "I promise to never do it again. We was 'ungry is all. Please let us go n' I'll never. I promise, please."

"Shut up, Lizzie. They don't care 'bout the likes of us."

"Find out where he lives," Matt ordered the hulking giant as the boy was dragged into the bakery behind them.

Thomas returned a moment later. "Baker says in the alley behind the alehouse."

Three men, the two children, Kiya and Matt all walked to the next alley. In their absence, the remaining three guards moved with a nonchalant air to stand guard outside the jeweller, waiting for Merry and Jake to exit the store.

Kiya and Matt were little more than two feet from the ramshackle hut when a man opened the door and grabbed both children.

"Stealin' again?" he growled. An instant later, the children were pulled inside, and the door was slammed. The adults never said a word but looked at one another then shrugged, realising they had no say in the way the man chose to chastise his children.

"I warned you little sonsabitches."

Kiya stiffened not only at the cursing bestowed upon two young children but at the clear crack of a whip.

"I told you what I'd do if you got caught again. Do you think we'll make it if you find your stupid arses flung into Newgate? Or maybe you'd be lookin' for a stay in the colonies. Is that it? You little bastards lookin' to getaway from your dear old da?" Again the crack of a whip. "How many times have I told you not to get caught? How many times will I have to show you what happens if you do?"

"No, da, please, no!" came a childish cry, and Kiya shuddered at the sound of a whip hitting against tender flesh.

"Stop him," she pleaded. "Oh my God, please stop him."

Matt crashed through the flimsy door, only to find both children stripped from waist to foot, their arms above their heads, leaning against one wall, their scarred buttocks ready for yet another taste of the whip.

Matt slammed a fist into the father's gut, knocking him instantly to the floor. He grabbed the fallen whip. "Suppose I show you what it feels like to be on the receiving end of this?" he asked, while pushing the whip roughly into the man's face.

Kiya touched his arm, bringing instant sanity to the situation. She looked at the two trembling children, and said to the boy, "Pull up your trousers, my good man, and give a hand to your sister, if you will." And then looking behind her she said, "Charles, would you and Thomas please take these two to my father's house? Please ask my maid, Cook and the housekeeper to keep watch over them until I get back. Will you tell them I said these two are to have meat pies, milk and whatever cake Cook has at the moment?" She glanced down at the children's opened-mouth shock and smiled. "Plus any other confection she might have on hand. And if they should want two of everything, that would be just fine."

And then she turned to the man who still lay upon his dirt floor. "Your name, sir?"

"Edwards, Tony Edwards. Would you mind telling me—"

She cut him off. "And the boy's name?" She didn't ask the girl's having already heard her called Lizzie.

"Seth. What do you think you're do—"

"You won't be looking for them, Mr. Edwards. These children no longer belong to you."

"What? You'd leave me without my youngins'?" he whined in a most pitiful tone. "With not a farthing to this poor man as compensation."

"If you are thinking I will pay a penny to a criminal like you, you couldn't be more mistaken."

"Criminal is it?" He came to his feet and glared meanly at the lady before him. His efforts did nothing to cower her as he had expected and did much to annoy the man at her side. All heard Matt's low, menacing growl before Mr. Edwards continued a bit more gently, "Lady, you've got no call to label a god-fearin' man."

"Were I you, Mr. Edwards, I'd fear my God to be sure, for you've much to answer for."

"I'll go to court. You're not allowed to take—"

Again she cut him off. "Do that, and I'll have you taken into custody. Do you think a judge might frown a bit upon a father who forces his children to steal for him?" Her gaze took in the empty bottle of cheap whiskey on the rough-hewn table. "Steal to keep their good old da deep in his cups?"

"Just because you're rich, you think you can do anything you please."

"You're right about that," she sneered and, for the first time in her life, flaunted her wealth into the face of another far less fortunate. "I am rich and I can do anything I please. You might thank me for taking those little children off your hands and thank me further for not pressing the matter of seeing you put where you belong."

Kiya turned on her heel and, without a backward glance, walked out of the shack.

Behind her, he called, "Keep the bloody little bastards. They cost more than they're worth."

Matt leaned over the man, and with his most severe manner and eerily calm tone, he imparted, "Mind me well on this, Mr. Edwards. You will tell no one of this matter. You will never try to contact my lady. Should harm befall her, should she get a damn splinter, I will lay the blame at your feet, and you'll not live to see the next sunrise. You'd best pray hard for her good health and long life, sir. You will never try to contact, what are now and forever will be, her children. Should I hear that you've tried, you will find yourself whisked from England before you've had a chance to even think about begging my forgiveness. You will then be settled in a penal colony, a difficult and demanding environment at best. You will remain there for as long as I live, and I do intend to live a long life, Mr. Edwards. Should you doubt that I speak the truth, I urge you right now to put me to the test." There was a long moment of silence where Edwards, visibly distressed, struggled to keep his suddenly wobbly knees stiff enough so he might remain upright. "Do we understand each other, sir?"

"We do," Edwards managed, shaken to the core of his being, for to look in this man's eyes was to stare death straight in the face. It was beyond his ability to control the trembling in his voice. "I promise you we do."

* * * *

If Kiya thought saving the children from a life of petty crime and the horror of living in squalor beneath the thumb of an abusive drunkard would bring grateful enthusiasm from two latest members of her household, she was soon disappointed. Upon reaching her father's home hours later, she was astounded to find the place in near shambles. Broken glass littered half the rooms downstairs, small tables were overturned, flowers lay trampled, vases broken, while piercing screams, vile curses and running footsteps filled what should have been the quiet tranquillity of the third-floor nursery.

"Oh dear," Kiya murmured as she took in the devastation and the noise that now filled her once-peaceful home. The quiet she had taken for granted might be a dear memory for some time to come.

Matt grinned as a young voice from above screamed, "You're fuckin' killin' me!" amid gurgling and watery choking sounds, along with an adult voice promising someone *would*, within the next few minutes, drown if they weren't instantly docile.

"Do you think your maid is having a problem bathing one of them?"

Kiya smiled as she righted a small table. "It is indeed possible."

"Should we offer our help?"

Kiya smiled and, with only the slightest trepidation, nodded. With a mighty sigh, she said, "Let's see what we can do."

On the third floor, with the exception of a hallway littered with torn clothes, the destruction had been mainly relegated to one of the larger bedchambers. Inside said room, a boy sat in a tub, while two servants stood near the door holding towels and a clean change of clothes. Milly,

Kiya's maid leaned over the boy in a distinctly threatening manner, holding a bar of soap.

"Are you in need of some help, Milly?"

"I could do with a bit, Miss Kiya."

Kiya moved to the tub and looked down at the shivering boy. "What's wrong?"

"I don't want no bath," he said, almost in tears, his hands beneath the water protecting his private area from sight.

Taking into account his crouched position and the way he clutched at his privates, Kiya knew what troubled him. "Do you want the ladies to leave the room, Seth? Is that the problem?"

"I don't take my clothes off in front of no goddamn cow."

Milly's lips tightened at the insult.

Kiya shot Matt a helpless look.

He grinned in return then whispered for her ears alone, "Give him a few years."

She rolled her eyes towards the heavens and shook her head. "He can't bathe alone. Do you think you…"

He nodded.

"Girls, we will leave Seth in Mr. Chase's capable hands," Kiya said. As they left the room, she asked, "Has Lizzie had her bath?"

"She has, Miss. She's having her cakes in the nursery."

"I'm sorry to have put you through that, Milly. I'm sure they gave you a bit of a hard time."

Milly only stood there in silence.

"Tomorrow, I'll contact the agency and immediately begin interviewing for a governess and nurse."

Milly nodded with some relief.

"You can have the rest of the day off."

"But downstairs…"

"I know. I saw it. I'll have the staff take care of it."

Inside the nursery, at a child-sized table, Lizzie sat eating small, sugar-covered cakes. One of the housemaids sat in an arm chair nearby.

As Kiya entered the room, Lizzie dumped the two remaining cakes into her lap, obviously protecting what she thought to be hers alone. It would likely take awhile before either child realised their new circumstances and came to understand most any kind of food was theirs for the asking and the adults in charge wished them no harm. At the moment, they had no reason to trust. Because of the years spent under the worst of circumstances, that particular emotion might be some time in coming.

Kiya's eyes widened at the sight of blonde child. "Is that you, Lizzie?" she teased. "Annie, is this the little girl I found?"

"It is, Miss."

Kiya smiled and came to sit at the child's side. "Aren't you a pretty little girl. Who brushed your hair?"

Her eyes wide, Lizzie looked at the lady she'd first seen on the street She shot the housemaid a quick look, silently telling it was Annie who had taken care of her hair.

"The ribbons are very nice, don't you think?"Kiya asked.

A small hand covered the ribbons, to claim them as she had her cakes.

"The ribbons are yours, Lizzie. There's no need to hold on to them."

Despite the comment, one hand tried to hide the cakes in her lap, while the other continued to hold to the ribbons in her hair. Kiya smiled, wondering which one she'd give up.

"I have something I think you might like." Kiya moved towards the shelves and reach for a box. From the inside, she pulled out a doll, dressed in a sleeping gown and wearing pink ribbons much like the little girl who stared in wide-eyed fascination. "Would you like the doll? It's yours if you want it. Trouble is, you only have two hands. How are you going to hold it?"

Lizzie gave up ownership of both the cakes and her ribbons as her arms reached for the doll and hugged it tightly to her thin little chest.

Kiya put the cakes back on the plate. "Do you like it here, Lizzie?"

The little girl nodded vigorously. "Uh huh."

Kiya smiled. "Have you had your meat pies and milk?"

Lizzie nodded again. She didn't say it, but this was the first time she could ever remember being full.

A moment later Seth came into the room tripping over the hem of a long sleeping gown. Anger flashed in his eyes, and a sneer twisted his small mouth.

"I'm not wearing this," he announced loudly. And with as much derision as he could managed, he said, "Girls wear dresses."

"Most men wear sleeping gowns. Is that not correct, Mr. Chase?"

Matt nodded. "Most."

"Sleeping gowns and caps," she reiterated.

"I want my drawers."

Matt shook his head, his gaze meeting Kiya's over the boy's head. "Rags. Useless."

"Tomorrow, you'll have new clothes. Tonight, you'll wear the gown or go naked."

Lizzie giggled at the thought while Seth's face turned red.

"Have your cakes and milk, Seth," Kiya said and watched as the boy downed half a dozen in near as many seconds. She'd never seen anyone eat so fast.

In the past, only little girls had used this room so the toys here wouldn't be of interest to Seth. Tomorrow, while shopping for their new clothes, Kiya would look for something more appropriate. Perhaps wooden boats, soldiers, farm animals or trains, maybe even a carousel. She wondered if he'd like that.

Kiya pointed to the beds. "You'll sleep here, Seth. Lizzie, you'll sleep here." She watched both climb into their respective beds and wondered if they'd ever had a bed as comfortable, warm or clean. She imagined they'd soon grow used to the luxury, and perhaps, in time, even forget the horrors that they'd already suffered.

She hoped they would.

Once they were settled, Kiya and Matt left the children with Annie. As they moved down the stairs, he said, "It's not going to be easy."

"I know." She sighed, knowing the seriousness of her decision. "I had no choice."

"Would you mind if I told you just how wonderful I think you—"

"Don't, Matt." She shook her head. "I don't take children off the street on a whim or out of the goodness of my heart."

"You don't? You just did. You could have left them or brought them to an orphanage, or—"

"I couldn't. Didn't you see their eyes? Didn't you see the despair? How could I leave them with that monster?"

"What is that to you?"

Kiya stopped and turned towards the man beside her. A frown creased her forehead. She shook her head, knowing he bestowed upon her ideals and qualities she didn't possess. "Matt…"

His heart melted at the sight of her trying to explain away the tenderness that was simply part of her makeup. "Step over here for minute, will you?"

A second later, he opened the door and shoved her into the linen closet. Following her inside, he squashed the both of them against the shelves and slammed the door behind him.

"What are you doing?"

"I thought this was a room."

Kiya laughed. "Why did you push me in here?"

"I want to kiss you."

"Matt, we were talking about—"

"I know, that's why I wanted to kiss you. You're so damn adorable. I don't know another lady in all of England so generous that she would care about or bother with a lost little girl and a wounded young boy. I can't even tell you how many times I've wanted to kiss you and touch you today."

"Did you? One wonders what stopped you."

"Probably the fact that a certain young lady would have killed me if I had." As he spoke he began to open the buttons down her back. "I can barely get you to hold my arm while in public."

Kiya laughed. "And you think this young lady won't kill you now?"

"I think in just a minute or so she'll have other things to think on." His mouth moved over her cheek and jaw as he spoke.

"What kind of things?" she gasped as his lips moved down her throat and over a naked shoulder.

"Just a second. I'll show you."

The bodice of her dress had fallen to her waist, trapping her arms at her sides. Her breasts were cupped in his hands, his mouth fastened to the tip of first one then the other. She moaned, "Oh God, how can this feel so good?"

"I don't know. I'm just happy it does."

Some moments later, he groaned, his forehead against hers after tearing his mouth from a mind-stealing kiss. He shuddered, desperately trying to bring his needs under control. "God, why do I do this to myself?"

Kiya laughed. "And yet, despite the suffering, you seem most anxious to do it."

"We've got to go. It will be time for dinner soon."

Both of them breathed an unhappy sigh.

Moments later, her dress restored to order, she said, "Open the door."

He reached behind him and found only smooth wood where a knob should have been. "Ah Kiya," he began, knowing she wouldn't find this the least bit amusing.

"What are you waiting for? Open it."

"There's no knob on the inside."

"What? Why not?"

"I don't know. Maybe because no one thought it would be needed."

"I hope you don't think this is the least bit amusing."

Matt laughed. "You just said in almost the exact words what I thought you'd say."

"I'm happy to offer amusement," she snapped, dismissing his comment. "Now, stop laughing, and get us out of here. Push against it. We can probably snap it open."

He grunted a number of times as he slammed up against the door. It was solid and held firmly against the force of his shoulder. He couldn't get much momentum within the limited space but tried his best. His best wasn't enough. The door was held in place by solid oak woodwork. It wasn't about to move. He soon gave up. "It's not moving."

"Matt, for God's sake," she almost moaned then snapped, "Get out of my way. I'll do it."

"Do you think you're stronger than me?" he asked in amazement.

"I'm more desperate than you."

"We don't have a choice, Kiya. We'll have to call for help."

"I'm not calling for help."

"Well, I am." He opened his mouth in order to call out, only to find her hand suddenly cutting off his words.

"No, you're not. No one can find us like this."

"Why not?"

"Matt, be serious. If my father heard us—"

Suddenly, as if by magic, the door opened, and Kiya heard her father say, "If your father heard you...what?"

"What?" Kiya gasped then whispered a silent prayer of thanks that he had not opened the door a few minutes earlier. "Oh nothing. We got locked in here by mistake."

"I figured as much. Why?"

"Um..." Kiya did her best to come up with a reasonable explanation as to why two adults would be found locked in a linen closet, an explanation beside the obvious, of course.

Matt enjoyed himself as he watched her bluff her way through the situation.

"Matthew needed fresh towels."

"He needed fresh towels so you both went into the closet and closed the door?"

"The door closed by itself. It's a good thing you heard us. I was getting a little desperate."

"Were you?" he asked, taking in the sight of his daughter's swollen lips and slightly mussed hair. Having bedded a woman or two in his time, he easily recognised the signs of some serious foreplay and wondered when this child of his would use the good sense God gave her and agree to marry Matt. By the looks of her, it couldn't be too soon. "Odd then that you didn't call out."

"We were about to, weren't we, Matt?"

Matt hadn't until this point said anything but wisely agreed. "We were."

Kiya, hardly prone to lying, found herself stumbling over her words and knew her cheeks were red as cherries, even as she wished herself anywhere but here. Nervously, she checked the timepiece pinned to her bodice and announced with no little relief, "It's time to dress for dinner."

As she said it, she turned her back on the men and made quickly for her room, but not quite quickly enough. Because the closet was so dark and the space so confined, it had proven impossible to turn. Buttoning her dress was not done with exact precision.

"How much longer?" Mr. Harrison asked, obviously unhappy with the goings on and hoping they weren't any more serious than what he'd just discovered.

"She's almost ready," Matt returned, praying his words held at least a modicum of truth.

"Are you sure?"

"Positive."

"I have every confidence that the servants are aware of all that goes on in a household. I'll not see a hint of scandal attached to her name."

"Nor I, sir."

"Do get on with it then, man."

* * * *

"Do get on with what? Exactly what has my father given you permission to do?" Kiya had slipped into Matt's room as silently as one of the house cats.

He straightened his cravat before the mirror and patted a lock of hair. His delaying tactics didn't help. He hadn't imagined she'd heard any part of his conversation with her father or he would have had a response ready. Now, he couldn't think of a damn thing. There was nothing for it but to play dumb.

"What do you mean?"

"I heard him say 'get on with it', Matt."

He shrugged. "I don't remember."

"And that's the best you can do? Apparently, you're not as quick as I thought you were."

"What do you mean?" he asked again, knowing exactly what she meant. Not being the sort to lie easily, except perhaps by omission, he couldn't seem to do more at the moment than simply deny.

"It took you a few minutes to think, and that's the best you could do?"

Matt grinned and desperate for any answer. "Your father and I have a wager."

"What kind of wager?"

Matt quickly gave up on that premise, knowing would she press the matter and it would only result in even more lies. "All right, here's the truth. I told your father I want to marry you."

Kiya gasped.

"I also told him you won't have me."

Her eyes widened in shock. He couldn't have. Oh my God, he couldn't have. What was she going to do?

"And the wager?" she asked, desperate for him to tell her he was only teasing.

"There is no wager. I told him I'm wearing you down. He said to get on with it before we create a scandal."

"Wonderful," she moaned, "just wonderful. Why did you do it?"

Matt shrugged. "He knows something is going on between us."

"How could he know?"

Matt figured there was no need to tell her he'd already spoken to her father on the matter. The truth was, if her father had had no previous knowledge of the circumstances between them, finding them in the closet had left him without a doubt. "Because your lips were swollen, your hair a little mused and your dress was buttoned crooked when he opened the closet door."

"Oh my God." She reached behind her, knowing almost immediately he was right about the buttons. She began to pace. "This is exactly what I didn't want to happen."

"There's no need to be upset."

"Isn't there?"

"None at all. He's not angry. He can't force you to marry me, am I right?"

She muttered a sound that might have been agreement, even as she sat in a chair near the door, looking as if ready to make an escape.

"So if he can't force you, what are you moaning about?"

"You don't know my father. If he even suspected us of doing what we've already done, I'd be walking down the aisle tomorrow with a special license or forced into a nunnery."

Matt turned from the mirror. "You just said he can't force you. What do you mean?"

Kiya reasoned there was force and then there was *force*. "When I said he can't force me, I meant, he wouldn't drag me down the aisle by my hair or anything like that. But the thing is it will be two years before I come into my own money."

Matt shrugged. "So? I don't want your money."

"You don't understand. I'm not legally independent. If he insisted, I'd be hard put to refuse, especially if he thought we were doing something," she hesitated, her fingers twisting the material of her skirt, "something we...shouldn't...be...doing."

"But you could still refuse."

She shrugged. "I suppose."

She didn't sound at all positive. Matt couldn't have been more delighted. There wasn't a doubt in his mind, if this lovely lady didn't want to marry him, no amount of pressure could bring about that happening. "I think I have the perfect solution."

She narrowed her gaze wondering if she could trust him and thought she probably couldn't since he was the cause of her problem in the first place. Still, she was desperate enough to ask, "What?"

"We'll tell him we're engaged."

There was a long moment of shocked silence before she breathed, "Amazing." She sighed, her gaze lifting to the ceiling. "For a minute there, I thought you were going to say something preposterous. You came up with that all by yourself, did you?"

Matt laughed. "What I mean is, we'll tell him we're engaged then in a few weeks you can break it off. I'll be gone once we catch the madman in your area then you'll be on your own again. What do you think?"

"I think you are entirely too happy about this whole business."

Matt laughed again, his heart light. If she truly did not want to marry him, a herd of elephants together with the King's own dragoons could not have stopped this little terror from insisting that she wasn't about to marry him or anyone else for that matter. Instead, although obviously a bit upset, she seemed almost agreeable to his ridiculous plan. Matt knew he was making progress and could barely contain the thrill that knowledge brought him. "What do you mean? I'm always happy. I'm a happy fellow."

* * * *

He seemed set on proving the truth of those words the entire evening for he laughed through the whole of it. He laughed when he lost at a game of whist. He laughed when he lost at the word game that followed. And he laughed every time Kiya glanced in his direction.

"I know you said you're a happy fellow, but truthfully you appear close to hysterical."

Matt grinned. "I think we should tell them."

"Tell them what?" Kiya asked, her body suddenly stiff, the terror in her blue eyes telling him she knew exactly what.

He ignored her question. "Do you want me to do it, or will you?"

"It's your idea. You do it."

"Kiya," her father said, from across the room, interrupting their conversation. "I'm told we have guests."

She turned to face him, a small glass of sherry in one hand and moved closer so there was no need to raise her voice. "Not guests father. I've taken in two children, a brother and sister to be exact." She finished her drink. "They were being terribly abused. And they won't be going back."

"So you thought to allow them to abuse my home instead? I understand it was in a sorry state of disrepair shortly before I returned."

"It was, but I think there's little chance that will happen again."

"The boy wasn't at all happy about being bathed by a woman, and he put up a bit of a fuss," Matt offered.

"I see." Mr. Harrison nodded.

"I'll send for one of the grooms the next time," Kiya offered.

"Shall I have Mr. Morgan make up the appropriate papers then?"

Kiya shook her head at the solicitor's involvement. "There's no need. I've already told their father he won't be seeing them again."

"What? They have a father?"

"He calls himself a father, but in truth, he is a man who whips them, who forces them to steal for him, who leaves them constantly without so he might fill his cups. I told him I was taking the children and his only concern was money. He said, 'What!? Without a farthing?' I told him he would not get a penny. They belong to me. I meant it."

"Still, you'll need something a bit more legal, lest the man later insist on his right to them."

Matt had every confidence that the children's father would not, at some later date, further his cause but did not comment on his threats after Kiya had exited the shack.

"I'll talk to Morgan tomorrow. We'll see what we can come up with."

"But Kiya," Amy remarked, "what about when you marry? What will become of them?"

Kiya almost told her sister that she wasn't about to marry, but a glance in Matt's direction, when he cleared his throat, reminded her of their absurd bargain, and she thought better of the notion.

"I promise you it wouldn't matter if she took in ten foundlings." His arm circled her waist and tugged her a bit closer to his side in a far too familiar fashion that left no one ignorant of his intent and her acquiescence. "They'd all be welcome to come live with us," Matt announced. "Isn't that right, sweetheart?"

For some long seconds, nothing moved nor did anyone utter a sound then suddenly, as if everyone understood at once, they all began speaking at the same time, effectively covering Kiya's low groan.

No one questioned why Matt's grin should grow so broad, for all imagined it was less that of a conquering hero, of which Matt felt every inch, but rather a grin any future bridegroom might exhibit.

While Kiya accepted kisses and hugs as well as wishes of happiness from her sisters and future brother-in-law, Mr. Harrison shook Matt's hand. "I'm happy to see she's come to her senses at last." He shot his daughter a quick glance and asked, "Have you told her the whole of it?"

"I thought one shock at a time, sir."

Mr. Harrison laughed, happy he wasn't in this man's place, for he hadn't a doubt things weren't about to run smoothly for these two, thick-headed, young people for some time to come. "Good thinking."

Chapter Eight

Shopping was accomplished, the wedding preparations were almost complete, the coming nuptials were only a week away and the family retired once again to the country estate. The house was in a turmoil. Delivery men were forever at the door. Everything was polished to a high sheen, mirrors, glass and candelabras glittered, the house smelled of lemon oil and clearly boasted of hours spent whipping up deliciously sweet confections.

It was Tuesday, and Kiya spent every Tuesday at the parish nursery caring for the orphaned children housed there. On this summer day, the nursery took full advantage of the warmth. Pots of water stood heating over fires, bedding was changed, soiled laundry was washed, and little children were bathed. There was much to be done before the treats Kiya always brought with her could be enjoyed.

"The children love to see you come, Miss, even if it means they must bathe."

Kiya grinned at the nurse. "Indeed, I understand the suffering involved, poor little mites," she returned with a laugh as yet another voiced his loud objection to water and soap as he was almost flung into a huge tub of sudsy, warm water. Before he had a chance to blink away the water that had splashed his face, soap was rubbed into his hair then rinsed away. While he sputtered his outrage, another worker took him into the folds of clean linen to rub him dry and yet another boy prepared for his turn at this dreadful happening. "I've no doubt they believe us monsters to inflict such punishment."

Later, Kiya was inside the orphanage in one of the boys' bedrooms. In the back of all the rooms, ceiling to floor shelves held sheets, linen for towelling, changes of clothes, nightdresses and row after row of shoes. The rooms were empty during the day, especially on good days where the boys could play outside. Kiya, having just finished changing the last bed, sat upon one bunk while folding clean laundry and spoke with Michael, the handyman who had built these shelves and did all the needed repairs in the small cluster of parish buildings. Kiya had known him most of her life. Michael's father was one of her father's tenants. A few years Kiya's senior, every Tuesday found them together as they discussed the parish buildings and needed repairs.

"I'll be leaving here next month, Kiya."

Kiya nodded as she smoothed a sheet free of wrinkles. "And I for one will be sorry to see you go, but the truth is we all know you've magic in your hands, and you'd be wasting the talent God gave you should you stay."

Judging from the work already accomplished, Kiya knew the man to be but a step away from a master craftsman. With the right teacher, he'd no doubt reach his full potential within a few years. Kiya had seen to it that her father had put in a word to a business acquaintance, and Michael had been offered a coveted position at a small woodworking shop in London.

"I know it's you I have to thank for the opportunity."

Kiya laughed and discounted her efforts with a dismissive wave of her hand. "All I did was offer a suggestion. It will be up to you to make good on it."

"You make it sound as if it were of no consequence."

Kiya smiled. "Perhaps one day you will make me a special piece, and I can boast to all my friends that I know the master who created it. And then I can send them to your shop lest they settle for inferior workmanship."

"Are you ready?" Matt asked as he came to the door. "The children are already enjoying your treats."

Kiya smiled, "I'm nearly finished."

Matt entered the room and the two men shook hands. "I understand you are leaving us for the city. I know Billings. You won't find a man more capable or fair."

"I have your lady to thank for this."

Matt grinned, enjoying the sound of those words 'your lady' and turned to see Kiya's frown. A moment later, Mike left them to be about his work.

"How does he know?" She snapped a piece of towelling in the air then smoothed it into folds with sharp angry movements. "What did you do announce our engagement upon our arrival?"

"Is there a problem? A reason why he shouldn't know?"

Her hands stilled, and she glared at him. "What is that supposed to mean?"

"Have you tender feelings for the man?

She took a deep breath and exhaled loudly before answering, "You're ridiculous."

"Am I? The man is in love with you. Are you telling me you don't return his feelings?"

"What's the matter with you? He's certainly not in love with me. I've known him since we were children."

"Why did it anger you for him to know?"

"It doesn't anger me that he should know."

"Indeed, I can see where I was mistaken. Surely, that was a smile I saw not a frown."

"There's no need to be sarcastic, Matthew," she said, her tone softening appreciably as she came to stand before him and smoothed the collar of his shirt. "Are we not pretending to be engaged? Why then should anyone outside the family know of it?"

"Because your family won't think to keep it a secret. Won't it appear strange that the loving couple said nothing?"

Kiya smiled as she studied his expression, her gaze holding a glimmer of doubt. "Are you sure that we are pretending? I think you're acting like man who is truly engaged."

"Am I? And how would an engaged man act?"

"Possessive." She shrugged. "Jealous."

"How would a man who is in love act?"

Kiya laughed, her eyes widening. "I see what you mean."

"I think the lady could use a taste of it?"

"You mean love? But I'm already..."

Matt grinned as her words came to a sudden stop. "You little wretch. If we're not to marry what difference could it make if you tell me your feelings?"

"I'm already in love," she stated simply.

He nodded. "That's better. But I was thinking of jealous. I think you could use a taste of that particular emotion."

"And now you're going to set out to make me jealous just because I was talking to a friend?" It was her turn to be sarcastic. "Oh yes, how I've longed for a loving relationship. Why I can't count the nights I've lain awake praying for one. Indeed, now that I have it, it's something to —"

He pulled her stiff form against him, cutting off her ranting words as he pressed her face to his chest. "Don't be angry. Indeed, you must believe me to be a brave man. I swear I wouldn't dare."

Kiya laughed as she mumbled into his shirt, "You're squashing my nose."

* * * *

Seth and Lizzie were in awe. Not nearly accustomed to the townhouse, they had been suddenly whisked off to the country estate, a house at least twice the size of the first. Big, brown eyes tried to hide their fear but were unable to disguise their apprehension as they took in everything. They said little and tried to blend into the background lest someone take notice and realise they didn't belong. Obviously, neither child could make sense out of the fact that they no longer lived on the street and dreaded the moment they would be thrust back there. They couldn't understand why the lady had taken them. They didn't trust.

Food was horded, wrapped in towels and hidden under beds for the time when it would no longer be offered. They couldn't believe that time would never come.

"Do you think Da will beat us when we go back," Lizzie asked her brother while she petted her doll, holding it close in a loving embrace. She might be five years old, her brother seven, but underfed and ill-treated, both children looked far younger. Yet both were older than any of their own age.

Seth shot his sister a contemptuous look, telling his beliefs on the subject as he conducted a battle between opposing soldiers while beautifully carved cows and horses grazed along side the skirmish.

"Suppose we don't go back."

"What do you mean?" he asked in some confusion. They both knew they'd go back. Where else could they go?

"I mean after they tell us to leave," she nodded towards the walls around her, implying the collective they, "we could go somewhere else. Yesterday, I went to the village with Kiya, and I saw a girl sweeping in a store. She was only a little bigger than you. Maybe I could do that."

Seth shrugged. There was no way he could know if anyone would take them in and let them work for their keep. Still, he offered, due to his newfound love of horses, "I could work in a barn or stable."

Lizzie smiled. With that settled, she felt just a bit more secure. They had little choice but to wait. When they eventually told her and Seth it was time to go, she'd know only relief that they wouldn't go back. They'd find a village, maybe like the one close to this house. They'd find work there.

Kiya entered the room and sat near the children as they played.

"Guess what we're going to do."

Both children waited in silence, each knowing in their hearts it was already time to go.

When no response came of her question, she asked, "Aren't you going to guess?"

"We have to go back," Lizzie offered sadly.

Kiya's brow creased, obviously puzzled. She hadn't expected anything like that. "What? Go back where? You mean to the streets?"

"Can I take my doll?"

Kiya frowned. "Where?"

Seth threw the wooden soldiers, horses and cows on the floor and sat, his arms folded over his small chest, a hard look in his eyes, his mouth a straight forbidding line as he waited for Kiya to order them to go. And at her look of surprise, he said, "I bloody didn't want them anyway."

By the looks of them, both children believed their surprise was hardly anything to their liking. "All right, wait a minute. Forget about guessing. Just come with me."

Both children looked at their beds, knowing the food hidden under them was lost to them forever. They were leaving, and neither had a chance to grab any of it.

"Lizzie, leave your doll."

Lizzie reluctantly placed the doll in its crib. She wouldn't cry. It was only a doll, after all. And she didn't like it all that much anyway.

A moment later, Kiya had both children by the hand, leading them from the nursery down the stairs. Just beyond the kitchen garden stood a saddled horse. Beside it was a pony hitched to a small buggy.

"What do you think?" she asked, waiting for either child to show a trace of happiness or excitement. She waited in vain, for only silence came as a response. "Do you like them?"

Seth nodded.

Lizzie nodded.

Neither knew what to make of it. What did she want? Why was Kiya showing them a buggy and a horse? Both looked her way with solemn eyes filled with questions. What did she want them to say or do?

"I see I haven't gone about this the right way. Seth, I'm going to teach you to ride a horse. We'll use this one for now. She's old and gentle. Once you know what you're doing, we'll get you something a bit more impressive.

"And Lizzie, this buggy is yours. My sisters and I used it when we were little. With a pony just like this one. I'll teach you to ride, too, but for now, I thought a little girl should know how to use a buggy. What do you think?"

Her eyes huge with wonder, Lizzie almost smiled but was still unsure.

"Do you want to drive it?"

"Can I?"

"Here, let me help you." Kiya lifted the little girl into the buggy and handed her the reins to the pony. She gave her some simple instruction then smiled as Mark, one of the stable boys, walked at her side while the pony and pint-sized buggy pulled away. Lizzie's laughter caused all within hearing to stop whatever they were about and look towards the little girl directing a pony around the small paddock.

Kiya smiled then said to Seth, "All right, now, put your left foot in my hands and reach for the saddle." Kiya bent a bit and cupped her hands, only to find herself moved quickly aside.

"Hold it," Matt said. "I'll do it."

A moment later, Seth sat upon the horse.

Kiya smiled at the boy and swore his eyes couldn't grow larger. Still, not a trace of a smile hovered near his mouth. "What does it feel like up there?"

"High," he returned, his voice breaking a little with fear.

Kiya chuckled. "It always does, especially the first time." She shortened the stirrups to fit the length of his legs as she spoke.

The first time, Seth mentally repeated. Did she mean this was going to happen again?

A moment later, another of the stable boys walked Seth around the corral, while Kiya and Matt looked on.

"Why didn't we take them with us yesterday? They might have enjoyed the children at the orphanage."

Kiya shook her head. "They're very unsure of themselves and of me. I want them to grow secure before I let them see how others live."

"You mean you don't want them to think they'll end up in an orphanage?"

Kiya shrugged as she watched them both. "I think they've suffered enough, don't you? You know what they said when I asked them to guess what we were going to do? They thought I was taking them back."

"It'll take awhile, sweetheart."

"I know. Both of them looked at their beds with some longing as I took them from the room. I think they're hording. "

Matt grinned. "Probably cookies or cakes."

"Do you think they'll ever get used to it? I mean having what they want?"

Matt stood behind her, his arms wrapped casually around her middle as he pulled her to lean against him, his jaw resting on her head. "Eventually. How about we leave them for a bit and go upstairs."

Kiya shook her head and flashed him a dazzling smile. "This always happens when you touch me."

Matt grinned, quick to deny any ulterior motives. "What happens? I was only going to suggest we look under the beds. Could be they have the house silver under there."

Kiya laughed. "Be good."

"Until tonight."

"Oh, I forgot to tell you, my friend Charity is spending the night." Kiya had received a note that morning. She couldn't help her friend if Matt was in her bed.

"What? Spending the night in your bed?"

"I'm afraid so."

"Damn," he muttered then almost whined, "Why?"

Kiya laughed and patted his hand. "That's all right, dear, you can come tomorrow night."

Matt grinned. "And I fully intend to."

Kiya shook her head, laughing at the double entendre. "How long is she staying?"

"Just for tonight. I told her about us."

He stiffened. "What do you mean?"

She shot him a look that clearly told of her confusion. "What do *you* mean?"

"What did you tell her?"

"That we're engaged. What did you think I told her?"

Matt breathed a long sigh that sounded oddly enough like relief. "God only knows. I was afraid to ask."

Kiya laughed and turned in his arms. "Did you think I'd tell her about the things we do?"

"No."

She looked up and smiled as his cheeks coloured. He was actually embarrassed. "I never thought I'd live to see this. You thought I told her *that*. Why? Who have you told?"

"Jesus, no one. I'd never."

"Neither would I."

He smiled. "Good girl, now let's go upstairs."

She grinned. "Charity will be here in a few minutes. She's coming for tea and staying on."

"Great," he murmured mournfully. "Just great."

* * * *

After their first riding experience, Kiya returned the children to the nursery. Upon entering the room, she asked Annie if she could find two boxes. Once they arrived, Kiya asked both of the children to take whatever they had stored under the bed and put it in the boxes. She offered no comment as they took out half-eaten cookies, cakes and meat pies plus stale rolls and a few pieces of liquorice. The meat pies were discarded lest they poison themselves with bad meat. Kiya marked each with a child's name and place them on the shelf beside their respective toys. "If anyone touches your things, you just let me know. Your new governess, Mrs. Stevens, and Nurse Rochester will arrive tomorrow. I'll tell them about your things. They won't be disturbed. Nothing more under your bed. Is that understood?"

Both children nodded, their eyes wide with amazement. They'd thought for sure they were in trouble once she'd asked them to take the things from under the bed. But no. She hadn't beat them. She hadn't called them names or shouted curses. She hadn't even raised her voice. Neither Seth nor Lizzie knew what to make of it

Still, before the night was over, both boxes were again under their beds.

* * * *

Kiya and Charity were in her room, and Kiya's face turned white with anxiety. "Why didn't you tell me sooner? I could have had Charlie and Harry gather the men."

Charity shrugged. "I didn't think. God, Kiya, I'm so desperate."

"Cancel it. We'll go tomorrow night."

Charity shook her head. "It's too late. They'll be waiting for me at eleven. Besides, we can't be sure of the weather tomorrow night, and I can't wait any longer."

"Damn," Kiya muttered. She wasn't at all comfortable with the thought of rowing across the channel with six strange men. She shook her head, and Charity knew she was about to refuse. "Please, Kiya, come with me. Richard is waiting. I can't leave him there. Imagine if it were someone you loved. What would you do?"

"Maybe the others will come."

Charity shook her head. "They won't. They took the money, and now, they won't. Said, at the last minute, it was too dangerous."

"Wonderful, it's too dangerous for a gang of rough men, but you think it's all right for us with six men we don't know?"

"I have every reason to believe these men are good chaps. A bit rough perhaps but Mr. Haze tells me they are to be trusted." She sighed and reminded, "Six men are still going. It's just these men are not as experienced. They have no idea where to meet Edward. It's not dangerous. The others are afraid of their own shadows."

"I don't think so. England and France are at war, Charity."

Charity gave a dismissive shrug. "When are they not? Those men don't know the coast as I do. They think Napoleon is hiding behind every bush."

"And that's impossible? Where else would he be but in France?"

"I'm going, Kiya. It's perfectly safe. I wish you would come with me. I'd feel ever so much better if I wasn't alone."

Kiya hated to do it. The truth of the matter being, it wasn't safe at all. Under the best of circumstances, it was exceedingly dangerous. Two women alone with six men — six men they didn't know — rowing across the dark expanse of the English Channel. God, anything could happen. "Suppose we're hit by a wave and the boat sinks. How far can you swim?"

"The weather is perfect tonight, dark but calm. And both of us can swim," she reminded her friend, for they had learn to swim together as children. "I can't wait any longer. He's not well. I have to bring him home."

Kiya knew she had no choice. She couldn't permit her friend to go alone. She didn't want to do it, but she would. For a moment, she thought to include Matt in her plans, but instantly thought better of the notion. He might very well take it upon himself to call a halt to all their plans thereby leaving Charity even more desperate.

It was best to leave a note. If the worst should happen, if disaster should strike, at least her family would know she hadn't been kidnapped from her bed. And of course, once she returned, she'd destroy it with no one being the wiser.

She left the note on her bed where it was sure to be found. Digging into her closet, she found an old pair of breeches, used years ago before she'd had riding outfits made to order, old boots and a long, dark, heavy cloak.

From the library, she took her father's two guns. The two women didn't make a sound as they moved through the house. In the kitchen, a door led to the pantry. Inside the small room, Kiya depressed one particular brick, and a wall moved, creating an opening wide enough for a man to pass through. It was no secret. All who worked in the kitchen knew of the door that led to the caves beneath the house.

Kiya took a lantern off the pantry shelf, lit the wick and, armed with two guns, led Charity though the caves to the water's edge.

The boat and six men waited for them. Within seconds, the two women were aboard and seated as the craft set out across the channel.

Charity was right about the weather, at least. It was dark — dark, foggy, wet and almost dead still. Well 'still' at any rate. Kiya didn't want to dwell on the word 'dead', at the moment. The sounds of rowing were clear above the soft lapping of water against the boat's hull. No one spoke for all were well aware that any noise carried clear and far across water, especially on a night as silent as this. It was a good-sized boat, large enough to easily fit the eight already aboard and the man they were about to rescue.

Kiya had no notion of the time. She thought an hour had passed, perhaps two. She tried to check her watch. Nothing. It was too dark to see — almost too dark to see her hand before her eyes. Three dim lights shone in the far distance. Running lights, she thought. It looked as if it were a large vessel. No doubt a warship. Kiya sucked air through her teeth. She'd seen this exact thing often enough for the English patrolled the channel nightly, guarding against the very thing they were about.

She had a feeling, a bad feeling. Somehow, she knew this wasn't going to be an easy outing. It was dangerous. Of course, she'd made this trip countless times before, but something nagged at her. Kiya couldn't have said what made tonight different.

The narrowest part of the channel measured twenty-one miles between Dover and Calais. But the night was so dark. With no stars to guide them, how could they know where they were going? She longed to ask but was actually afraid to hear their answer.

Kiya expected under good conditions this excursion might take nine hours round trip. Having retired at ten, she wouldn't be expected to arise until mid-morning. Adhering to that schedule, they should be back in plenty of time. Only she doubted it. Even though six brawny men moved the boat quickly through these calm waters, with nothing to guide them, she imagined them rowing in circles.

It was hours later that her heart picked up a beat. Perhaps she had worried for naught. It just might be they had been on course after all. A barely perceptible light flickered just ahead. Could it be they were approaching the coast already?

They were. Kiya breathed a sigh of relief and gave all manner of thanks to the Lord. It seemed, despite all her doubts and ominous feelings, they were going to make it after all.

In the dark, a shadowy form appeared huddled on a white beach. Kiya couldn't tell if it was a rock, a bush or a man, though a small lantern glowed nearby. Her hand closed over the gun in her cloak pocket.

They moved closer. It looked as if a lone man quietly awaited their arrival, but a dozen more could be hiding along the beach behind the dunes. She wasn't taking any chances. Not a word was spoken, not a sound made but for the soft scrape of the boat upon sand. The man stood and moved towards the water, even as Charity, with a soft cry, flung herself from the craft and scrambled up the beach. In seconds, she was in Richard's arms, low, desperate murmurs of relief escaping her throat upon seeing her love at last.

Kiya was happy for her friend but most anxious to be about the business of returning to the safety of England's shores forthwith. It was far too soon to relax their efforts for they might find themselves accosted by the enemy at any moment. She couldn't hurry the men enough, but in truth, there was no need. They all felt at least as anxious as she did.

* * * *

A knock sounded on Mr. Harrison's bedroom door. It was a few minutes after eleven, and as far as he knew, all were asleep. He frowned, wondering who it could be. A moment later, he opened the door to find a distraught Matthew Chase, still dressed in the clothes he'd worn at dinner. Obviously, the man had been at work in his office and had just finished for the night.

A note was thrust into the older man's hands. "She's gone."

"What?" he asked as he reached into his robe pocket for his spectacles. "Who?"

"Kiya has gone off with her friend, with no protection. She left this note on her bed."

Mr. Harrison glared at the man's daring. "And you were in her room?"

"I had just finished working and meant to wish her good night. I knocked on her door. There was no answer. I knocked again. Still nothing. She had to be awake. She and Charity were in the kitchen gathering tea and snacks only an hour ago. I was afraid something was wrong. I called out. Again, nothing. The door was unlocked. The room was empty. The bed never slept in. The note was on it."

Mr. Harrison read the note, his throat closing with fear.

Father, don't worry. I've gone on an errand with Charity. We'll be back before morning.

Mr. Harrison glanced up and thought the younger man looked at least as horrified as he felt. "What are we going to do?"

Matt couldn't respond. He'd just realised she'd left the note in case she never returned, for if she was sure of returning, there would have been no need. He made a low sound deep in his throat. "She's not sure she's coming back."

Mr. Harrison tried to deny the truth of it. "It says..." He couldn't stop his hands from trembling. "I need a drink. Have you awakened Jake?"

Matt shook his head.

"Get him, and meet me in my office."

Ten minutes later, the three men gathered there. Matt stared at the note, refusing a drink. He paced as he tried to put his terror aside, desperate to get his thoughts in order. He had to think, lest he never see her again, never know what became of her.

"This has to be something involving Charity. There's no reason I know of that Kiya would have run an errand at this time of night. Anything she needed done would have been done during the day. So, that means it wasn't something she needed. It was something Charity needed. What do you know of the girl, sir?"

"Of her personal life?" Mr. Harrison shook his head. "Next to nothing."

"She lives down the road a piece?"

Mr. Harrison nodded. "Next door actually. Mother, father, brother and younger sister, I believe. I think her brother and sister are away at school."

"Is she in a serious relationship?"

Mr. Harrison shook his head. "I've no idea."

Matt nodded. "We'll need to ask."

"What are you thinking?"

"Nothing at the moment. We need information. Without it, we haven't a chance of finding out where they might have gone."

Moments later, Matt and Jake left for the Wells' home. Mr. Harrison was almost beside himself by the time he heard their horses re-enter his drive. He was at the front door before they dismounted. "What? What did you find out?"

The men spoke as they walked into the house and returned to the library. First Matt said, "Charity's fiancé works for the government. It seems he was working undercover in France and was taken captive."

"So?"

Jake went on with, "So, the government managed, with the help of some toughs and untold bribes, to get him out of prison. It's been a little more than a week, and they haven't been able to bring him back."

"And?" Mr. Harrison almost laughed at the thoughts that were now racing through his mind. "You cannot be suggesting that Kiya has gone to save him."

Matt shivered at the thought and managed, "I don't know."

"It's impossible. It's ridiculous. A young girl? Two young girls? How could they cross the channel?"

Jake said, "A group of smugglers was set to pick him up. It appears they backed out of the deal."

"So you're telling me they rowed across the channel alone?"

Matt snapped equally as upset as his future father-in-law. "I'm not telling you anything."

"But you're hinting at it. You think she and Charity have gone to get him."

No one responded.

"Oh my God," Mr. Harrison moaned. "I'm not going to make it through this night."

"You'll make it," Matt insisted then promised, "And if she does, she's going to find it difficult to sit for a time."

"If she does," Mr. Harrison repeated as he moved to his desk and sat. The poor man looked to have aged ten years, and the night had only just begun.

"If she did cross the channel," Matt asked, "how could she manage it?"

"She couldn't. She's not strong enough to row that far."

"Suppose she had a crew. If she did, where would she meet them?"

"The tunnels," Mr. Harrison exclaimed. "Oh my God, I forgot about the tunnels." In an instant, he was on his feet and running with Matt and Jake hot on his heels.

"Wait a minute," Matt said as they entered the kitchen pantry, and he watched a wall move aside. "We have no guns; we can't go in there without protection. I'll be right back."

"This can't be right," Mr. Harrison exclaimed, having had a chance to think on their actions. "We're jumping to conclusions. The two of them probably went somewhere on horseback. She couldn't have come this way. She couldn't be crossing the channel."

Matt shook his head. "My men were guarding all exits. No one saw them leave the house. I've already asked." There was no sense arguing with the man. He simply ordered, "Stay here." And then raced towards his room for his gun.

A moment later, he and Jake returned to find the pantry empty. Mr. Harrison was gone.

"Jesus, is it impossible for anyone in this family to listen?"

The two men were poking their heads into the dark tunnel when Mr. Harrison came running into the pantry again. "Lanterns are on the shelf over your head. My guns are gone. She must have taken them."

Matt wasn't sure if he were glad or even more upset. "Can she handle a gun? Does she know how to shoot?"

Mr. Harrison nodded. "She can shoot."

Matt was relieved as that piece of information seeped into his brain. Perhaps she'd make it. Wasn't there a proverb or epigram that said, 'The Lord looks after fools and drunks'?

The trouble was, he knew from personal experience, God didn't always protect those who loved them from pain. He was going to wring her neck.

"Ow," Mr. Harrison groaned as he stumbled over a crate. "What the hell?" he muttered as the light in his hand showed dozens of crates lining the narrow passage. "What is this?"

"It looks to be Napoleon brandy, sir," Jake said, reading the markings on the crate.

"How did it get here?"

Matt didn't have to wonder. There wasn't a doubt in his mind that Kiya was involved with this. If she wasn't actually smuggling, and he thought she probably was, she was, at the very least, selling or storing smuggled merchandise for comrades. God, what had he gotten himself involved with? What kind of woman had he come to love? Who the hell was she?

"If I'm not mistaken, you'll need to pose that question to Kiya."

Chapter Nine

Amongst the rocks that bordered the channel, the three men sat and waited — the beginnings of an endless night, for Matt and Mr. Harrison. It would be the longest night of their lives. It was warm, but here at the water's edge, the air felt chilled and damp. A glance towards the channel confirmed a rolling heavy fog. Matt hoped Kiya had worn a heavy cloak or she'd find herself chilled to the bone after hours skimming over these waters.

Matt shook his head. The woman hadn't lied about her longing for adventure. Indeed he hadn't realised just how adventurous she already was.

The three estimated the round trip would take approximately ten hours. If she'd left around eleven, only moments before Matt realised she was missing, expecting a smooth trip and barring any unexpected problems, they should return no later than nine o'clock.

Matt's mind raced. The Sea Witch was docked in London, less than two hours of hard riding away. If he took it down the Thames then along the coast, would he find her? Was the tide running high enough? In the dark, would his ship ram her by accident? He gave a soft gasp. Jesus, he hadn't thought of it before. Suppose her boat *was* rammed by accident. English ships patrolled the channel. It was dark and foggy and the water cold. Would she live?

"Can she swim?" he asked suddenly. "If the boat were in trouble, and she had to swim, could she?"

"She can," her father said, relieving Matt's anxiety, but not by much. The truth was, should her boat be hit, the impact itself would probably kill her and should the boat sink for any reason, she wouldn't be able to swim for long. The Channel waters were far from warm. She wouldn't make it for more than a half hour.

Matt was torn. He didn't know what to do. Should he go? Should he not? He had to make a decision. Inaction was about to do him in. His imagination was out of control. He couldn't count the hundreds of ways and means she might die. If he had to sit here another hour, or even another minute, he go stark raving mad. He'd never known this kind of fear.

"All right," he said suddenly, "here's what I'm going to do. London is less than two hours ride from here. My ship is docked there. If the tide allows, I'm going to take it and find her."

"How long will it take to bring it off shore?"

"Five hours maybe," he shrugged. "Six. I don't care. At least, I'll be doing something."

"I'm going with you," John Harrison said.

Matt nodded. "I thought you might. Jake, you need to stay. If I miss them, I don't want her left unguarded. Let the men know to be extra vigilant. Should she return, light a fire on the cliffs."

Jake nodded, and all three re-entered the tunnel. Moments later, Mr. Harrison and Matt were on the road heading towards London and Matt's ship.

It was late when they arrived. The waterfront, usually a beehive of activity was dark, boasting a third or less of its usual inhabitants. Two women knelt in an alley and serviced a line of waiting men, while one sailor sang off-key as he stumbled towards his gently bobbing ship. It was two in the morning. Another hour or so would find the same wharf deep in peaceful slumber as sailors would have found their beds, drunks would be bedded down wherever they managed a quiet semi-private space, and prostitutes would have given up the possibility of adding to their meagre earnings on this warm night.

The night watch stopped Matt as he attempted to board. The captain had gone ashore, and Mr. Dietz, the first mate, was sent for. There was naught but a skeleton crew. Matt figured they'd have to make due. There wasn't time to search out more.

Mr. Dietz followed orders without question. The Sea Witch left for the channel with all haste.

It wasn't high tide, neither was it low, but the Sea Witch, its hold emptied just that morning, had yet to secure it's cargo– and rode high at her berth.

It was close to five in the morning, when the Sea Witch slid silently along the coast of England. The fog had lifted, and Matt could see the dark shadows of England's shoreline barely a mile off starboard. He thought they were approximately on par with the tunnel's entrance, when he ordered the ship a sharp turn to port and headed straight towards France. The wind was gentle, barely above five knots, but Matt warned against even that speed lest they inadvertently damage the small craft for which they searched. Light was extremely limited, for dawn hadn't as yet made itself known. A half dozen men stood perched upon the highest masts, straining into the murky stillness. None could discern a solid shape bobbing upon the smooth surface.

Suddenly, the clouds lifted, and the quarter moon shone its meagre light upon the water. Matt sighed with relief for the scant light cut the possibility of an accidental collision down to zero.

Matt paced, even as he whispered a bizarre mix of curses and prayers. It was impossible for him to remain still. He couldn't believe the torture this woman was putting him through. His fingers actually itched for the feel of her throat. Thank God her father had insisted he join the search. Matt didn't trust himself to face her alone.

They were almost halfway across when the sound of gunfire broke the intense silence. There was one and then more then five, Jesus God! He thought his heart would stop and almost staggered beneath the crushing weight of the worst fear he'd ever known. He stiffened with dread and silently begged The Almighty for her life, for he had no doubt Kiya was in the midst of a gun battle.

* * * *

Kiya was counting the minutes, forcing aside the need to sleep brought on by the monotonous slap of oars against the water and the stifling silence caused by the thick fog. It wouldn't be long before the shores of England would come into view. No doubt, another hour would see the sun rise to burn off this infernal fog. Perhaps an hour after that would find them home. She was on the verge of allowing herself to relax, ready to believe nothing would come of this excursion but the rescue of her friend's love, when the silence of the night was suddenly broken. A boat, almost twice their size, came at them from portside. The shock of it hitting into them was worse than the damage done. Still, no one dared say a word as the two vessels made to pull away from each other. In the near dark, it was impossible to see three feet ahead, but it was easy enough to hear—Charity's soft cry of alarm was undoubtedly that of a woman.

The men in the larger boat might have thought it unusual to find a woman upon these channel waters, but it hardly mattered to those who occupied the boat, save one. The man in charge of the larger craft was a villainous sort. He knew at first glance that his men outnumbered the others. His boat was bigger, no doubt stronger, and he would have let the incident pass, except for the distinct sound of a woman.

"Ahoy mates," he called out, while keeping the smaller craft within sight. "Be all well aboard?"

"All's well, friend. Sorry for the mishap," Richard returned, even though all knew it was no one's fault. "This damnable fog obscures much tonight."

"That it does, my boy. That it does. I take it you've a woman aboard, mate?"

Richard's lips tightened into a sneer. He was terribly ill and weak, weaker than he'd ever been in his life, and he wondered at the show of strength in his voice as he snapped, "Shove off mister."

"No need to hurry," the other man chuckled. "Is there? I'll have myself a go at the woman first, if you don't mind."

Kiya pulled both guns from her cloak pockets. Richard had his own pointed at the nearby boat, only by the looks of him, she wondered if he'd be able to hold it for long.

"That would be lovely, I've no doubt, except I do mind," Kiya managed, never knowing how her voice sounded so calm when every inch of her body trembled as if plagued with the ague.

It was dark enough, foggy enough that not a soul could see beyond three feet, so Kiya could only imagine her gun was pointed the right direction. "Hurry mates," she said, her voice barely audible, "get us out of here."

"Mayhap there was more than one." He chuckled his delight. "How many be women?"

"What matter is that to you?"

"Ah girly, there ain't nothing I like better than a feisty one. This old Harry won't hurt you none."

The men in Kiya's boat rowed madly trying to create as much space as possible between the two crafts. Because the sound carried, it was easy enough to follow them. She could hear them merely a few yards away. "Stop," she whispered.

The men immediately obeyed, and oars were held aloft. Hidden in the fog, Kiya's boat silently drifted over the small white caps, those within still. All waited for *anyone* to make a sound, anyone to inadvertently give away their location.

Suddenly, a lone voice called out, "I see her mates, off starboard."

Kiya's heart pounded with terror. *God help us.* Had they come this far just to be taken, perhaps murdered by a group of cutthroats? Kiya forced herself to wait, unable to hold back her dread or stop the pounding of her heart as she prayed he was playing them false and didn't really know where they were. groaned her dismay as the other boat slid out of the fog and next to hers.

She raised her gun. There was no way she could miss at this distance.

One man stood. No doubt this was 'old Harry', ready to jump over the side into the smaller craft.

"Pull away," she cried. "Row!" The very moment she said it, she and Richard fired their guns, one or perhaps both hitting good old Harry, and each grunting with no little satisfaction as they watched him fall upon the many boxes stacked throughout the boat, taking one with him as he tumbled into the water.

The firing of her gun did two things. It caused those in both crafts to let loose a volley of damaging shots. Plus it brought them to the attention of any who wandered these cold waters, in particular one of his majesty's frigates. Within seconds, the huge ship had hooked the larger of the two boats to its side, while the boat in which Kiya sat slid silently into the fog.

Only it didn't remain dark or foggy for long. Minutes later, the clouds above cleared. The fog slowly dissipated, and soon enough, the moon glowed gently upon the water, clearly showing their position. She breathed a sigh of relief, noticing the frigate and the men it had taken aboard were already some distance away. She was about to inquire on the damage those bullets had done, when she chanced to see yet another huge ship coming directly at them.

There was no use trying to outrun the ship. They hadn't a chance against anything this size in waters that were suddenly almost as clear as daylight.

The small boat bumped against the ship's hull, and moments later, its occupants were easily taken aboard. Kiya quickly scanned the condition of her companions. Two men had been shot, neither seriously. Richard, with an obviously distressed Charity at his side, was carried below, and the ship's doctor was summoned to tend to all three.

Kiya was dumfounded to find her father to be one of the men inquiring as to her welfare. Her arm ached miserably. She must have banged it while leaving the small boat or while climbing up the ship's side. Still, she hadn't as yet discovered exactly what the problem might be.

She was about to tell him as much, when Matt stood suddenly before her, and in her happiness and relief at seeing him, she forgot any discomfort that might assail her. The depth of intense emotion in his eyes almost took her breath away.

She couldn't quite grasp the fact that these two men were here. She was about to ask how that astonishing occurrence had come about when Matt cut off her words with, "Mr. Sanders, show Mistress Harrison to my quarters, if you would." Without another word he turned and walked away, never once addressing her, never once asking after her welfare.

Matt was so angry, so upset, he couldn't address her. In truth, he could barely make it to his own quarters under his own steam. In his relief to have found her safe, he found his legs trembled, scarcely supporting his weight. After checking her welfare for himself, he had no choice but to dismiss her and turn away lest he strangle her with his bare hands or, even worse, crush her against him. He dared not remain in her company. His want for her was so desperately powerful he hadn't a doubt should he touch her he'd likely disgrace himself with tears.

Her father fussed. Let him, Matt reasoned coldly. He hadn't a doubt that this woman would always come out on top. Almost beside himself with rage, he watched her calm smile and wondered why he'd worried. Why had he bothered?

He cut off his thoughts and entered his cabin thinking a bottle of Napoleon cognac—no doubt one of the very same Kiya had smuggled—was in dire need of his full attention. He took the bottle on deck and stood at the stern, downing one glass after another.

* * * *

Kiya was first stunned then angry. What was the matter with him? Why was he so cold? Why had he...

She pushed away any thoughts of the man. She'd have to think about that later. She wasn't feeling very good. Her father was asking her something. She couldn't hear him. What was the matter with her? Why did it sound as if his voice was coming from a great distance, while a soft, hollow roar almost obliterated his words? And why was her hand covered with blood?

Kiya turned to him.

"Father... I'm sorry, but it appears I'm not feeling at all myself," she said then before her father's astonished gaze, she suddenly crumbled into a heap at his feet. Were it not for Mr. Harrison's quick hands, her head would have slammed upon the deck.

* * * *

Kiya awoke in bed. Her father fussed as he paced the room, while a strange man wrapped her arm in bandaging. She assumed the man to be the ship's doctor.

Her arm ached like bloody hell. She moaned at the discomfort. What had happened? How did she find herself in bed? Had she fainted? Kiya couldn't imagine the possibility. She'd never fainted, not once in her life.

"What happened?"

"You've taken a bullet to your arm."

At her look of alarm, he added, "No need to worry. It's just a flesh wound, but deep enough to cause you to lose a bit of blood. With a little rest, you'll be fine." The doctor bid her to drink some awful-tasting brew and soon left her in her father's care.

Her father's face was nearly as white as his daughter's, for he hadn't as yet gotten over the shock of seeing her collapse at his feet. "You might as well know I won't soon forgive you for the fright you caused me. I couldn't imagine at first why you fainted. With you wearing a black shirt, I never saw any blood."

"I'm sorry, father. Truly. I never meant for any of this to happen."

With his help, she once again donned her shirt. The sleeve was a bit damp but growing stiff as it dried. She told him then of the night's happenings. He was far from happy but, after some explaining on her part, understood her involvement and, after gaining her promise to never do anything like this again, left her to rest. Whatever the doctor had given her soon eased her into sleep.

* * * *

An hour passed and then another, and Matt found he'd downed half the bottle, to no avail. All he'd managed to do was waste most of it and, with every swallow taken, curse the woman who had driven him to this. The liquor took the edge off his anger but, in truth, had done little else. No amount of alcohol could cloud his mind or take the damn woman from his thoughts.

What the hell was the use? Why pace this damn deck when the woman he loved more than life was but a few steps away?

Matt stepped into his cabin and locked the door behind him. Kiya was sleeping in his bed. From the men still on deck, he'd gotten most of the story. No doubt he would have been better off never knowing. All it had managed was to increase his wrath. Goddamn her! How dare she put herself in that kind of danger?

Matt watched her for a long moment before he shoved her shoulder and ordered. "Get up, Kiya. We have to talk."

"What?" she managed with just a touch of sleep in her voice as she came to a sitting position, while he moved to his desk and sat a hip on its edge.

Her trousers lay across the bottom of the bed, her boots on the floor. Matt didn't miss the fact that her legs were bare. He didn't trust himself to remain at her side. Even with half a bottle of cognac, he found himself still enraged.

"Where's your father?"

"Tired. He went to bed."

Matt nodded, knowing the man hadn't a wink of sleep in more than twenty-four hours. Last he'd seen, he'd looked the worse for wear.

"What did you want to talk about?"

Matt thought the wretch had some gall. He longed to curse her thoroughly but took a deep breath, striving to keep his temper. "Let's see," he mused. "What do I want to talk about? Perhaps the weather? No, no," he shook his head, "that wasn't it." He glanced up to his cabin ceiling as if reading the words printed there. "Oh, I know, I wanted to tell you what happened last night. It was the oddest thing."

He glared at her and began with, "After I finished working, I knocked on your door to say goodnight. To kiss you goodnight, actually. So, I knocked, and strangely enough, no one answered. Now, I knew you were awake because I'd heard you and your friend talking and laughing less than an hour earlier. Still, inside your room, it was deathly quiet. I couldn't understand it. And then I thought. God, could it be possible that someone had come into the house and taken you? Taken you and your friend? Or perhaps killed you both?" He smiled stiffly and shook his head again. "No, that's a ridiculous notion, wouldn't you say, what with the house constantly being watched," he said, answering his own questions, obviously not looking for a response from her.

"So I knocked again, harder this time, and still, there was not a sound." He looked at the tip of his boot. "I have to tell you my heart skipped a beat or two, and a chill raced down my spine. I found I was thinking the worst. Ridiculous perhaps, but stupid me, I couldn't seem to help it."

"You weren't stupid, Matt."

His gaze moved to hers, hard and dark as he remembered his terror. "I'm telling this story, right?"

Kiya said nothing but lowered a gaze filled with guilt, allowing him to finish.

"Where was I? All right, so I knocked and finally opened the door. I found the room empty. Jesus, I don't think I'll ever know fear that great again. At least, I hope to God I won't."

"Matt," she said soothingly, her remorse obvious as she came to her feet. "I'm sorry. I'm so sorry."

He ignored her response. "So, the room was empty. You know what I thought at first. I thought despite all our efforts the bastard had managed to get you. He nodded as he watched her bite her lip and move towards him. "But then I found the note. I didn't know what to think. I guess I was relieved. At least, I knew you hadn't been kidnapped, but could it be possible you were in danger equally as great?" He sighed and for the moment appeared unable to go on. Finally, he cleared his throat. "I took the note to your father. Then I got Jake out of bed. We figured something was happening involving Charity, because I couldn't imagine it was anything that involved you. We went to see her father."

Matt looked at her. Soft curls, lusciously messed, framed the most beautiful face and lay like a gorgeous gold and silver shawl over her shoulders and down her back. Her blue eyes glistened with tears.

"Matt," she said, her voice low, gravely.

"I checked with my men, of course, but they saw nothing, so you hadn't left on horseback. You couldn't have gotten past them. So how had you gotten out of the house? Where did you go? I was almost mad with worry. Your father suggested the tunnels. Nice collection of cognac, by the way. Anyway, I couldn't sit on those rocks for the next nine or ten hours hoping you might return. I had to find you or at least try or go insane with fear."

Kiya shook her head, wondering how she could have so carelessly caused this man such suffering. "I love you, Matthew."

"I rode to London. Luckily, the holds of this ship were empty so it rode high though the tide wasn't nearly what it should have been. Still, we made it down the Thames, your father and I."

"Is this your ship?"

Matt nodded.

"I love you, Matthew."

He nodded and watched as she came to stand before him, sliding between his legs.

"When we found you..." He struggled to maintain his control. "When I first saw you, I wanted to kill you." He shuddered. "At the same time, I wanted to crush you against me, to pull you inside my body and always keep you safe."

Her fingers moved to his shirt, pulled it from his trousers and unbuttoned it. Her hands slid inside, under the material, her arms around his waist, her mouth against his throat. "I love you."

"And?"

She pulled back and smiled. "I love you. No ands; no buts. I love you."

His hand reached for her head. Sliding his fingers through her hair, he grabbed a handful and, none too gently, pulled her head back, forcing her gaze to his. "And?" he insisted. "Goddamn it, Kiya. No more games. Say it!"

"And I'll marry you," she managed on a soft, trembling, almost despairing sigh. "You beast."

She meant to pull back, and tried to shove him with her hands. It was like pushing against a wall. He allowed her no quarter but pulled her closer.

She managed a sarcastic, "I'd wager no woman on earth ever suffered through a more gentle coaxing."

"You don't deserve gentle," he groaned just before his mouth captured hers in a kiss that sought to sear her soul, absorb her very essence, drink of her taste and breathe of her scent. He meant to claim her as his forever. It took only the satiny texture of her mouth for him to lose his senses.

He thought only a kiss, but a kiss wasn't enough. His mouth was feverishly hot and desperately needy. Somewhere in the back of his mind, he wondered if he'd ever touch her enough, kiss her enough, love her enough—God, he was going to love her. He had no choice. He'd waited forever. Nothing on this earth would keep him from her.

Matt pulled her hard against him, desperate for more, desperate to have all he could of her. He ground his hips into her belly.

She groaned, loving the scent, taste and deliciously hard feel of him.

His hands were under her shirt, opening the tabs of her drawers. They slid to her feet and were kicked aside. Then he touched her, his hands moving over her nakedness, his mind absorbing the pleasure and the delight of her softness. He cupped her firm derriere, squeezing the softness of her, luxuriating in the silkiness of her belly and the creamy smoothness of her thighs. Moving once again behind her, he lifted her and brought her nakedness against him, his fingers between her legs, enchanted with her sweet moist heat.

She leaned into him, helpless against his luscious investigation, as her lips, teeth and tongue ate at his chest, his throat and his jaw.

"Please," she murmured, for it wasn't enough.

He lowered his mouth to her urgent call and sighed his delight as she rubbed her lips back and forth over his, again and again, licking his taste into her. She breathed his scent, until trembling. A desperate need caused her blood to pound in her ears, throat and brain. In a frenzy of taste and touch, she sucked his tongue into her mouth with a devastating mutual groan.

One arm circled his neck; the other held to his shoulder. She held on, instinctively knowing this would be the ride of her life.

He held her against him with one hand. The other came around her hip and down her thigh then, thank you God, back up on the inside her thigh higher and higher. Gasping, he pulled his mouth from hers, his eyes blacker than pitch. He needed to watch her as his fingers moved closer to her heat. And then he found her.

She made a soft sound that resembled pain. Her eyes fluttered, and her head fell back, her neck too weak to support it. She was helpless but to give him her heart and body. He took and touched even as she wordlessly begged him for more. God, she'd never get enough of this. He parted her legs, allowing him easier access from both the front and back. Her heart pounded, her breathing growing uneven. When she managed to breathe at all, it came in short jerking pants.

His desperation knew no bounds. He was so needy for this woman that he never thought to carry her the few feet that separated them from his bed. Papers, pens, inkwell and books were swept from the desk in one swoop, and

Kiya, shaking off the dizziness from his quick move, lay upon it, gorgeously exposed to his view. In a heartbeat, his mouth was on her, her hips held high for both their pleasures. Thick, hot—burning hot—and wet, his tongue and lips sucked at her luscious sweetness, absorbing her scent, her feel, her mind, her heart, perhaps her very soul.

She was dying and didn't care. She couldn't breathe and never thought she must. She couldn't think of anything else. She had to have more. Nothing on earth had ever felt this good, this perfectly wondrously good. It was coming again. God, she hated that it should come upon her so soon. She wanted this to last. She wanted more, but her body wouldn't listen to the dictates of her mind. A tight cramp was already forming over her belly. Suddenly, his mouth was gone. Her eyes blinked open, growing wide, as she wondered what he was about.

Her gaze took in the tightness of his features. He looked harder, rougher and more darkly dangerous than she'd ever seen him. Her heart thrilled to his grimace as he held back, forcing his needs aside. She felt him tremble as he moved against her. His trousers were gone and his body was poised with unbearable power held strictly under control.

Slowly, gently, his body penetrated hers, inch by incredible inch, filling her body, her mind, her heart. She hadn't known, never had imagined. How could this feel so good?

His finger continued where his tongue had been, and she cried out in a soft sounds her delight. Within seconds, her body grew tight once again—even tighter. Her muscles squeezed at him and drew him into her. He was nearly crazed with the agony of her heat, her white-hot, scorching heat and the ecstasy of holding himself still while her body squeezed and released until madness threatened. He couldn't bear another minute and live. He groaned out his pain with every pulsing surge of mind shattering ecstasy, never knowing how he managed to keep his senses about him.

Then it was upon her at last. She couldn't bear it and never wanted it to stop. Wrenching waves of rapture tore at her insides, bringing with it pleasure so incredible it bordered on pain. She shuddered, greedily welcoming the diabolical insanity with a guttural cry torn from deep within. Her body trembled, out of control, a mindless being bent solely on gratification

Thank God, the swelling aching muscles softened, the rapture eased then gentled into sweet soothing aftershocks of delight.

Feeling the throbbing tautness ease, he pushed through the last barrier, breaking the thin shield that proclaimed her an innocent, and claimed her as his for all time. He stopped all movement at her wince. Desperate that she should know no pain, he held himself still and asked, "Did I hurt you?"

"What?" she asked, the tiny discomfort already forgotten as she came slowly from the depths of almost insane passion.

"I love you," he said. "Did you have any pain?"

"I don't know. You're not going to stop, are you?"

He grinned, while waiting for her body to fully accept his. "Greedy wretch. We need to wait a minute. How do you like it so far?"

She laughed, causing him a deep groan as her muscles tightened again, devastatingly tight around his cock. "You might say I like it well enough."

"You don't love it?"

Patricia Pellicane

"I don't know. Right now, you're not doing anything."

"Did you love what I've done so far?"

She grinned at his apparent need for compliments. "Why don't we try this? You do whatever it is you're supposed to do, and I'll take notes. Once you're done, I'll tell you if I liked it or not."

His eyes widened with humour. "Take notes? Do you think you'll be able to remember these notes? Perhaps you'd like a pen and paper."

She laughed at his wicked grin. "God, you are so bad. I suppose you're inferring I won't be able to concentrate so remembering what you're about is out of the question."

He only grinned for a response.

She shrugged and went on with, "Of course, there's always the possibility that this act is truly forgettable. If that's the case, why bother with it at all?"

Matt chuckled. "I never meant to imply what we are about to embark upon is forgettable only that you might be a bit involved, perhaps too involved to remember all the particulars," he said with pure male confidence while his mouth decided he'd waited long enough to taste her beautiful throat.

"Lord, how did a young, innocent lady ever got involved with a man so wicked?"

He pushed deeper into her warmth. "I broke down your resistance."

She moaned at the delicious movement. "You did that," she agreed. "And quite without my notice. Very sneaky of you, I must say."

Again, he moved deeper, delighting in her soft groan and forcing aside his own as the heat of her body threatened to rob him of his senses and suck him into pure enchantment. His voice was rough with the need to take her with no further delay, and still, he held back. "I wouldn't say sneaky as much as unwavering."

She laughed. "Is that what it was?"

"I'm desperate to see you. Open your shirt."

Kiya did as he asked, and Matt groaned as her breasts came into view. God, this woman was luscious. His mouth attached to one pink nipple, sucking, biting at her as if his life depended on knowing her feel and taste. He pushed deeper into her. "Put your legs around my waist and hold on. This is going to be a little wild," he managed against her soft warm flesh.

Her body had accepted all of him. Fully sheathed within her, he began to move at last. Matt thought he could go slowly, but the sweet sounds of her soft gasps, her whimpered moans and husky cries, her disjointed broken words, and the mind shattering movement of her breasts with each intense thrust, drove him over the edge of reason and into a delirious pit of aching madness.

She breathed in his hot, panting breaths, delighting in his sighs, trembled to his low trembling growls as he moved into her. All she could think was more. She had to have more. She had to have everything he could give her.

He lost all sense of time and place. His mind knew nothing but his body's wants and he wanted only the woman he loved. He tried to hold back, but there was no way. He'd heard her cry out her devastating release, and without conscious thought, he found himself racing madly to join her.

Gasping breaths, pounding hearts and soft, delirious moans of pleasure filled the room, and Kiya frowned as a thought occurred.

"Oh my God, this was too good," she moaned then repeated, "too good." She struggled to breathe and talk at the same time. "I can't imagine why I waited."

"You were waiting for me," he said in all male arrogance.

She ignored his words. "If I'd have known..." she sighed as she snuggled her face into his throat.

"Perhaps it's best that you didn't."

Kiya laughed. "You think so? You didn't wait. Look at the years of pleasure I've missed."

He forced his knees to hold his weight. Damn, if he fell to the floor he'd likely drag her with him for there was no way he would leave her. Not while burrowed deep inside her.

"First of all, not to say you wouldn't have enjoyed it, but if you were very young, it wouldn't have been this good. Second, you have to know the man has something to do with your pleasure. If you were with someone who wasn't gentle or patient, I can guarantee it wouldn't have been this good. And lastly, you weren't in love until now."

"You mean it's better if the lady loves her man?"

Matt groaned at her question. Her man. Did she realise what she was admitting? "Infinitely," he said as he cuddled her against him.

His breathing was still harsh and desperate as he suddenly swung her around so he might sit upon the desk while keeping her on his lap.

"You're going to have to stop flinging me about, Matthew. You're making me dizzy." With her head against his chest, she could feel his laughter before she heard it and smiled. "Why didn't we use the bed?"

Matt laughed aloud. "Good thinking, but once you were standing here against me, with your drawers kicked across the room, and I started touching you, I forgot there was a bed."

Kiya smiled and leaned back just a bit. "Could we use it now?"

He smiled, so enticed by her delicious charms, he never noticed the dark circles under her eyes or the paling of her skin. "My pants are at my ankles. If I try to walk, I'm bound to fall."

"Let me go, and I'll take them off you."

"In a minute," he said, as he allowed a bit of room between their bodies and began to play with one breast then the other. "Do you know how lusciously these move while I'm loving you? Do you realise how lovely they are?"

"Do you think so? I've had them for some time so I suppose I'm a bit used to them."

"I don't think I could ever get used to them."

She grinned then nodded in agreement. "I think if you had them, you'd never sleep, work or eat for playing with them."

Matt laughed. "You could be right. As a lad, I was equally fascinated with a certain part of my body. So if I had these as well, I'd likely still be in my room."

She giggled and asked, "Were you?"

"What? Fascinated?"

She nodded. "What part exactly?"

"Well, you could safely say it wasn't my head, chest, stomach, legs or feet."

"Mmm, that kind of shortens the choices a bit, wouldn't you say?"

He nodded in agreement, "Except it's not short."

Kiya laughed aloud at that. "I think I know what you're talking about. Oh my, do you think all young boys find themselves totally absorbed in their fingers?"

"Fingers?" He pulled back and looked down into wide, smiling, blue eyes, his dark gaze obviously confused.

"Well, you said you were fascinated with it, but it wasn't your feet, legs, stomach, head or chest. Right? And your fingers are long."

"You little wretch." He chuckled low, the sound deliciously sexy, while he gave a light tap to her naked rear, squeezing her breathless and nuzzling his face against the warmth of her neck, "And yes, I'm afraid all young boys are equally fascinated."

"Lord help us," she breathed, more than a bit surprised with this new knowledge.

Engrossed in his play, he pushed her shirt farther apart then stopped, stunned and momentarily puzzled.

"What the hell?" His dark finger brushed against the white bandage around her arm, and he heard her soft indrawn hiss of pain. Only then did he notice the stiffness of dried blood down one side of her dark shirt. "What is this? What the hell happened?" The last of it was bellowed into her face before she had a chance to answer the first.

Kiya slid from his lap and closed her shirt.

"Stop shouting and calm down," she said while pushing her feet into her drawers.

Matt brought his trousers up his legs and secured them at his waist. As he slid his arms into his shirt, he noticed her trembling, the dark smudges under her eyes and the white skin around her lips. Damn but the woman looked ready to faint, and he'd just lain with her. He raged on at the thought and shouted, "God damn it Kiya, don't tell me to calm down. I want to know what happened."

Jesus Christ, she'd been bleeding, and he'd made love to her. God in heaven, why hadn't she said something? "What is the matter with you? Why didn't you say something? Why didn't you tell me you were hurt?"

"Because it doesn't hurt unless I touch it, and I forgot. Because you touched me, and I forgot."

Matt struggled to clear his mind and calm down. At the moment, it was an impossible chore. God, what was he going to do with this woman?

He got her back in bed, covered her with a sheet and sat at her side, all the while wondering how much blood had she lost? How great was her injury? Exactly how had she been injured?

"Tell me," he muttered, although how he managed it, Kiya couldn't have said for his lips had grown as stiff as the rest of him and they never moved.

"If you are thinking to frighten me, don't bother. I don't scare easily."

"If I were thinking to frighten you, you'd be trembling like a goddamn leaf." He spoke softly, but his glare almost did the trick. His dark eyes gleamed like he was possessed. "Now, get on with it."

Kiya told him how she'd managed to cross the channel in the dead of night. Matt felt himself growing angry, and the longer she spoke the angrier he grew. Finally, unable to take anymore, he grunted, "Stop!" as he jumped from the bed and began to pace. "Give me a minute."

After a few minutes, he stopped his pacing but stayed in the middle of the room, for he didn't trust himself to move any closer, lest he strangle this woman with his bare hands. "Did you know these men?"

"Charity said Mr. Haze said they were good sorts."

Matt nodded and repeated softly almost to himself, "Charity said, Mr. Haze said." He turned to Kiya and asked, "And you know Mr. Haze, right? You knew him to be a man of his word."

She had the grace to lower her gaze to the sheet. Contrite, she bit her lip.

"I didn't think so. And you never thought to ask for my help?"

"I did think of it, but suppose you'd said no? Suppose you'd thought the whole of it too dangerous? Who then would bring Richard back?"

Matt took a deep breath. "Who indeed?" he said to no one in particular, wishing there was someone or something he could punch.

"Matt, please, don't be upset. Suppose it was you? Suppose you were ill and waiting for someone to come for you, but no one would? I'd be mad with worry. I couldn't let Charity go alone. I thought to be back before anyone realised I was gone, with no harm done."

"Except it didn't exactly work out that way, did it? How often have you done it?"

"What? Crossed the channel?" She shrugged as if the whole of it were of little importance. "A few times."

"Kiya," he warned.

"Once a month."

"How long has it been going on?"

Kiya breathed a sigh, knowing she might as well tell him the whole of it. The man was sure to nag her until he knew it all. "Four or five years."

Matt, who had nearly calmed was suddenly upset all over again. "Four or five years," he repeated as he ran his fingers through his hair in frustration. "For God's sake, why?"

"It started when I was in school. On a dare." She closed her eyes against his building rage. "I know. You need not tell me I was a fool."

"And yet you never stopped."

"Matt, it made so much money. How could I stop?"

Matt wondered, not for the first time, what kind of woman he had fallen in love with. This was a part of her he'd never seen before. "Are you so interested in money, then? Does it mean so much to you?"

"Doesn't it to everyone?" she asked, her tone telling him he should know better than to ask. She shook her head at his look of dawning horror and went on to explain, "Think what it accomplished, Matt. The parish nursery. An infirmary stocked like an apothecary. A full time nurse in attendance. An addition to the poor house. More than three dozen families left the poor house and are in their own homes, the fathers working at the mill. Seven men released from debtor's prison, also working at the mill. Almost two dozen children sent to school, their future schooling and living expenses paid. Children who could never hope to know a decent living. Children who will one day become doctors, bookkeepers, clerks and teachers." She sighed. "How could I stop? They needed me."

Matt took a deep breath, growing a bit calmer and despite the way she'd gone about it, thinking her the most wonderful, unselfish woman alive. "Do those in the parish know it was you?"

She shook her head. "No one knows. Money is left at the rectory with a note saying what should be done with it."

"You won't be doing it again. If you need more money, I will give it to you."

Normally, Kiya would have railed against such an order, but oddly enough she found herself nodding in agreement, in truth, more than happy to see her smuggling days brought to an end. Somehow along the way, she'd lost her need for excitement and no longer had the heart for these monthly jaunts. She'd be happy enough to give the boat to one of her crew and tell them if they wanted to continue they could, but she was done with it.

"We got off the track a bit. What happened next?"

She shrugged her good shoulder. "After the boat hit into us, we both made to pull back, except Charity had made a sound, and one of the men in the boat that hit us heard her.

"Who the hell were they?"

"Smugglers, I think. There were boxes piled high all over their boat."

"So they heard Charity and..." he asked waiting for her to go on.

"And a man identifying himself as Harry said he'd have a go at the woman if we didn't mind. Richard said 'shove off', but the man insisted. So I told him, I did mind then we tried to hide in the fog, but he found us, and when he did he tried to get in our boat, I shot him. Actually Richard and I both shot him."

"Jesus," Matt groaned. Feeling his knees about to give way, he sat again on the bed.

"Did you kill him?"

She shrugged again. "I don't know. I saw him fall on one of the boxes then slide into the water. A frigate picked them up after that."

"You mean after they shot back and hit three of you."

She nodded. "We hid in the fog again, and minutes later, it cleared and you found us."

"What did the doctor say?"

"He said it was just a scratch, to keep it clean and it should be fine. In a few days, I'm to take off the bandage."

"And your father knows?"

She nodded.

"Did he know what you've been about all along?"

"I told you no one knew."

Matt nodded. "What did he say?"

"He was a bit upset."

"Mmm. Just a bit huh? And this is just a scratch? Are you sure? You're shirt is stiff with blood."

"The doctor said..."

He shook his head. "Let's see it."

Chapter Ten

Katie Goodman had been at the bridge for almost an hour. It was getting on towards dusk. Katie hoped her ride would be along soon. She didn't much like the dark and in a few minutes it would be just that. She heard a sound behind her and ignored it. It was probably some animal. In a minute or so she'd be on her way to London. Soon the entire city would marvel at the sound of her voice. She's be adored as London's newest and most valuable asset. People would travel hundreds of miles just to hear her sing. Katie couldn't wait for the wonderful new life that awaited her there. She smiled as she saw the small dark vehicle approach in the distance.

Suddenly strong arms reached around her and pulled her backward, into the woods. Katie struggled. She kicked and bit the hand that held her mouth. She couldn't miss her ride. Her whole life depended on it. "Come on girlie; don't give me a hard time."

Katie never even supposed the man's intent was to do her harm. The thought never entered her mind. All she could think was she was going to lose her chance. The carriage wouldn't wait for her. "Stop, she murmured. "I can't go. I'm going to London. Stop!"

The thudding of a horse's hooves, the jingle of harness and over all clatter of an approaching carriage covered her already muffled cries and then a blow to her jaw cut off any further sound. The carriage came to a stop. Waited mere seconds and then started down the road again. No one noticed the small bag left near the road, nor the rustling of shrubbery just a bit farther into the woods.

* * * *

Katie moaned a low sound of pain as she slowly gained consciousness. Her arms hurt. She couldn't remember them ever hurting so bad, and wondered what she had done to cause them this ache. And then she realised she wasn't in bed, but was hanging suspended by her arms. No wonder the pain. Katie almost smiled at the ridiculous notion. Of course she was in bed; of course she wasn't hanging in some dungeon type room. And then she gradually gained her full senses and realised she was. Her pain was forgotten. Someone had taken her. Someone who had caused her to miss her chance to go to London. Why?

Had her father found out? Had he put a stop to her plans? He'd beat her to be sure, but she didn't care. After he was done, once she could walk again, she was going to London. It didn't matter if she had to crawl the whole way.

Katie frowned at the thought. Her father might very well hang her in preparation for a beating, but stripped naked?

She thought not. The truth was she wasn't actually hanging. Actually she was sort of suspended. Her arms were outstretched, her legs as well, her heels able to touch the ground and relieve some of the pressure forced upon her arms. Oddly enough she was amazingly calm, considering her present position and circumstances. She was sure now that some deprave sort had brought her here. Wherever here was. Still she didn't know any great sense of fear. All she knew was whatever she was forced to bear couldn't last forever. And once the man was done with her, she was going to London.

* * * *

Shelby watched her come slowly awake through the tiny hole in the wall that separated the dungeon from the smaller dressing room. He stood, naked, his clothes hung upon a hook at his side. It took only one glance at her helpless state, her dawning fear, to bring his cock to throbbing eagerness. Damn, but this one was a special piece. Without a doubt, he was going to enjoy this afternoon. It was a rare time when one of the pretties picked from the neighbourhood possessed this lush of a form.

In truth, he usually didn't care about form. He'd had his share, and more, of every size, age and colour, some as young as ten or eleven or as old as fifty. In the end, all that truly mattered was their fear.

Once she was fully awake and aware of her surroundings, he entered the room. He wore only a mask. Not that he was concerned that she'd ever escape or tell another the identity of her captor. No she, like the others before her, was going nowhere but, eventually, the grave.

No, the reason for the mask was simple. It fed her fear, and it was fear that most enticed him. If it were simply an afternoon's romp he wanted, he could have easily brought one or more of his lovelies from town to his mansion. And of course, that would have brought its own form of pleasure. But no, not here, not now. Now, he wanted to see the fear come alive. He wanted to watch it grow. He wanted her to beg as had the others, for it was fear that fed the pleasure, fear that made these encounters border on the ecstatic.

He grinned as she took in the sight of him, her gaze measuring the size of his cock, his tight balls beneath, and he almost laughed aloud as she spied the whip in his hand.

Her body tensed. "Wait, there's no need for a whip. I won't give you any trouble."

She cried out in pain as the whip whistled through the air and the end snapped at the inside of her thigh. A small dribble of blood began to slide down her leg.

He laughed, a low husky sound in response. She wouldn't give him any trouble. She couldn't imagine just how true those words were. Jesus, but he liked it when they shivered like that and they all did. No doubt it was due part from the cool room and part from the laying on of the whip. Or perhaps it was simply fear of the coming pain. He didn't know what caused it; all he knew for sure was that it was lovely to watch. Of course, the mask helped. Most of the time, a man wearing only a leather mask scared them spit-less. But not this one. This one was braver than most. He shrugged aside the thought. A few had been brave at the beginning. Their bravery hadn't lasted long. Soon enough they begged to be allowed to service him. The girl didn't know it, but half the fun was the whip. Both would soon gain untold pleasure because of it.

His gaze moved over her. Closer now, he truly appreciated the size of her. He liked them with big tits. The bigger the better. And the nipples, damn but he could come just looking at them. He'd always loved nipples. He reached up and took one between his thumb and forefinger.

Katie's eyes widened as she spied another enter the room. Also naked, also masked, his cock stood every bigger than the first man's. In silence, he walked behind her, while the other stood before her.

They both played with her breasts, pinching and pulling at the soft flesh. Saying nothing. Their silence was perhaps more terrifying than their actions. "Please, tell me what you want. There's no need to hurt me. I'll do anything you say."

Neither man responded to her plea. Shelby could hear the sounds of his own breath as his excitement grew. And as it grew so also did her whimpering pleas for mercy.

It was a long time before the room grew quiet again.

* * * *

Kiya blinked her surprise. She'd been measured a number of times but hadn't until now realised the dress was cut quite so low. Still, she was happy to find the short puffed sleeves covered the scar high on her arm. Her arm was healed, but the wound had left a lasting reminder of how foolishly she'd chanced death. The garment was gathered just beneath her breasts and fell in soft folds to the floor. It was dark blue, the exact colour of Kiya's eyes.

Amy couldn't claim the same delight in her wedding ensemble. Cut in much the same fashion as her two sisters, the neckline was hardly low enough. The colour was light blue and pretty enough, but the whole of it was far more sedate than she might have liked.

Blue ribbons were entwined throughout the thick blonde curls of both ladies and added to the ribbons were diamond pins that glistened beneath the candlelight. They wore no jewellery. None was needed.

Kiya left her room, intent on helping her sister finish her preparations, only to find herself waylaid by a pacing Matthew in the hallway just outside her room. "Finally. What in the world took you so long?"

She smiled. "I didn't know you were waiting out here. Why didn't you knock?"

"Your sister was in there with you."

Meaning, if she wasn't, he would have simply entered the room as he did every night. "I wanted to give you this."

Kiya's eyes widened with surprise at the small, black box. "What is it?"

"I haven't given you anything yet for our engagement."

She smiled and opened the box to find a huge emerald ring, the oval stone surrounded by diamonds. "Matt," she admonished. "What are you doing?"

"What do you mean?"

She sighed and gave him a pointed look. "I mean, this is too expensive." She was well aware the man owned a ship. Still, he didn't own it alone. He was partnered with his brothers, which meant any profits had to be split four ways. That hardly allowed him the means to afford something like this. "I know you own your business, but you'll never keep creditors from your door by spending money like this."

Matt grinned. "I'd say this was a special occasion, wouldn't you? A man doesn't get engaged but once. His future wife deserves the best he can manage. Don't you agree?"

"Not if it puts him into debt."

"It didn't. Truth is it belonged to my grandmother."

Kiya merely looked at him, unable to imagine what the man was about. His grandmother had owned this? That meant it was a family heirloom. Did that mean that he was rich? She shook her head in dismay. She was about to marry a man and hadn't a notion as to whether he could keep the wolf from their door or financially manage the family they were sure to have.

"Your grandmother?" She eyes him suspiciously. "How rich are you?"

Matt laughed. "Let's say I'm comfortable."

"Why are you working then?"

"How else could I meet beautiful ladies?" he teased.

"Ladies?" she asked.

"Lady," he confirmed. "Only one particularly beautiful lady." He nodded towards the box. "Wear it today."

She grinned. "Aren't you supposed to put it on me?"

He nodded and did as much, happy to see it fit. "I have the necklace to match. I'll put that on you, tonight."

"I could wear…"

He shook his head. "You'll wear it tonight, when we're alone. I want to see you wearing only the necklace."

Kiya's eyes widened, and she laughed at his hungry look. "Just a necklace? No matter its size, I'm afraid it won't cover much."

His gaze glowed with pleasure at the thought. Still, he remarked as if she'd just brought the matter to his attention, "Indeed?" And then in an immediately softer, more sultry tone, "I expect it won't."

She shook her head, barely able to hold back her grin. "You are so bad."

"I need to kiss you."

"Don't," she said. "You'll mess me, and I have to help my sister get dressed."

Matt grinned. Damn but she was adorable. "Kiss me then. I promise I won't touch you."

* * * *

Merry was, just as Kiya had promised, a beautiful bride. With her two sisters at her side, John Harrison knew many a reason to be proud. Within a month, Kiya would also be standing before the preacher. John wondered how he would let both these daughters go. Thank God they'd be living within a day's ride of his home — *after* the madman who prowled this countryside was caught. No one was leaving John's house until then.

After the ceremony, the wedding party and their guests returned to the manor house. An open invitation had been extended to the entire village, and all but a very few came to offer the bride and groom their best wishes. To the villagers' delight, a dozen or more white-covered tables had been set up outside and piled high with food. Two whole pigs, gutted and splayed, roasted over an open fire, while endless platters of roasts and chickens, boats of gravies, bowls of vegetables and breads stacked higher than the average man were brought from the kitchen.

The wedding party and guests did not segregate themselves from the villagers. All congregated outside gathering around the tables, helping themselves to a seemingly endless variety of breads, pies and cakes. It amazed all that so much was made available. Kegs of ale were opened and wines liberally enjoyed while giant bowls of lemonade punch were set out for the many children.

Charity and Richard, along with her family joined the celebration. Richard was feeling much more himself. Maureen, Charity's younger sister who was home from school, was suddenly at Kiya's side.

"Oh my God," she said. "The Duke of Stratford is here."

"Is he?" Kiya asked without much enthusiasm — in truth with no enthusiasm whatsoever — and never ventured to look in the direction Maureen pointed.

"Kiya, he's so handsome. You know it's rumoured that Mrs. Clark has been trying for years to get him into her bed."

Kiya laughed. "Mrs. Clark has tried to get anyone wearing trousers to her bed."

Both women laughed. "You're right on that score. Still, it's told his technique for making love is not to be compared."

"Mmm," Kiya murmured in response. "You know how these ridiculous stories begin. All one need do is be seen sipping at a glass of ale, and all of London would soon have it that you are a drunkard."

Maureen nodded in obvious accord. "Still, the ladies in question, and I understand there are more than a few, appear in agreement."

"Bully for them." Kiya thought it impossible that anyone could be better than Matt and she had no interest in another, no matter his reputation. Indeed, the greater the man's reputation with the ladies, the less favourable he appeared in her eyes, for a man who felt the need to master every woman in sight was far from a true man in her estimation.

Music began. The lively crowd danced to the enjoyment of all. The night was filled with laughter and much shouting, especially from those growing ever deeper in their cups.

Kiya's Aunt Mary and Uncle David had come to join in the festivities, along with their daughter. Because the distance between their homes was a good day's ride, their intent was to stay on a bit. Kiya was delighted. David was a few years older than Merry, and Kiya enjoyed his company very much. His stories of his years spent in His Majesty's service were told with such a flair for the dramatic and were so heavily laced with the comic they often left her teary-eyed and weak with laughter.

Some hours into the party, she left Matt's side. The sometimes wild festivities had grown to a low hum of laughter and conversation, and she finally found a moment to speak with her aunt and uncle. At her approach, her uncle grabbed her and gave her a tight hug. "So I understand you've given up your disgust of all things royal."

Kiya smiled at his teasing. "Have I?"

"Indeed. And I'm sure it's a wise decision since you'll be marrying into it."

Kiya laughed at his droll means of relating a totally absurd happening. "Shame on you Uncle. How could you tease me so cruelly?"

David grinned. "It's I who suffer teasing, I'm afraid. And it's most dreadful of you to keep at it."

Kiya's laughter drained along with much of the colour in her face as she realised he was perfectly serious. "What do you mean?"

"Sweetheart, I mean the man you love, of course. The Duke of Stratford."

"Oh, of course," Kiya replied with a weak smile, careful to keep her voice level and free of the scream that was, at this very moment, building in her chest. "I just didn't know you knew it." And just in case there was some kind of mistake, she thought to clarify with, "You do mean Matthew. Matthew Chase, am I right?"

David laughed. "Lord, you're not only going to be richer than God, you're going to love his family. They are truly good people."

"So I've been told. I can't wait to meet them. Do you know him? Personally, I mean?"

"I should. I went to school with his younger brother and spent many a lively holiday at his family home. Oh Kiya, I couldn't be happier for you."

"Thank you, dear. If you'll excuse me, I need to see to the children. I'll be right back."

How she managed to keep her wits about her, Kiya would never know. She rushed into the house. There was no time. She couldn't stop. She couldn't think. She was desperate to get away. Immediately away.

She forced herself to calm down and forced aside her horror as well as any thoughts of his betrayal. She had to think, lest she make a foolish mistake, and Matt easily find her. She couldn't let that happen. She wouldn't have him. She'd never have him. She'd never live with a liar. That she loved him was of no consequence. She'd stop loving him soon enough. Already, she felt the emotion begin to fade.

Kiya discounted the fact that she hadn't always been honest and that she hadn't lived her life in strict accordance with her ideals. If called to account, Kiya would have countered by explaining the things she'd done were for the good of others, that she'd gained nothing for herself. Because her prejudices were so extreme, she never realised that Matt had gained nothing as well in his less-than-honest dealings. Nothing but the woman he loved.

Within the hour, and through some diligence on her part, she managed a sigh of relief, of sorts. Her thoughts settled, her plan already set into motion, Kiya rejoined the celebration.

It took some effort, but Kiya managed not to raise Matt's suspicions. She pretended nothing to be amiss and played the part of a loving fiancée to perfection. She danced, she laughed, she shyly allowed his gentle handling, knowing it was expected that any future bridegroom would bestow his constant attention upon his love. The night seemed endless. She wanted to scream her rage and shudder at his every touch. She hated him beyond measure and would never forgive his treachery. As the clock ticked past midnight, then one then two in the morning, Kiya wondered if the celebration might not go on until dawn.

She sighed in relief as the festivities came to an end at last. A half hour later, she stood before her bedroom door with Matt.

"Matt," she sighed dramatically as she turned into his arms. "I'm suffering terribly from a headache. I need to take one of my powders and sleep. Would you mind terribly?"

He smiled, his heart near to bursting with tenderness for this lady. God, he loved her to madness. Gently, he held her to him and ran his hand up and down her back as he soothed, "I could hold you while you slept. We wouldn't have to do anything."

"I know, but I'd rest better if I were alone."

He looked down and, with his hand under her chin, brought her gaze up to meet his. He frowned but instantly put aside the odd feeling that suddenly assailed him. "There's nothing wrong, is there?"

"No," she smiled, careful to keep her voice sweet, light and free of the scorn that assailed her. "Of course, nothing is wrong. I just need a few hours rest is all. I'll make it up to you tomorrow night, darling. I promise."

He kissed her gently then whispered, "Good night, sweetheart."

She smiled and closed the door behind her with a sigh of relief. Barely two minutes later, she'd changed into her travel costume, pinned her hat in place and pulled her bag from beneath her bed — a bag she'd packed some hours earlier directly after finding out the truth about the man she was to marry. She divided her jewels into two halves and placed them into the inside pockets of her cloak. The money she had on hand was rolled into small packets and placed in her cloak pockets and her reticule. Until she was settled and her affairs in order, she'd need the cash.

She was ready. All she needed was for the house to quiet down. She'd probably have a good eight hours head start before anyone noticed she was gone — more if the note she left behind was believed.

Kiya took off his ring, placed it with the note upon her bed and left her room. Silently, she descended the stairs. She had to pass her father's library in order to reach the kitchen and the tunnels beyond. She silently gasped as she heard the voices. Her heart pounded like thunder. Kiya took deep silent breaths, trying to ease the hammering in her chest. Her father was in there, speaking with David, the door slightly ajar.

Idly, she wondered if her father knew the tunnels led not only to the rocky shore below the house but also to Charity's barn. Actually, once she stepped free from the tunnels, she would be barely a hundred feet from Charity's back door.

She moved quickly, soundlessly, beyond the library door. A moment later, she was in the tunnels. She needed no light. She'd used these tunnels since she was a child and knew them better than she did her bedchamber. Fifteen steps to the first turn. Thirteen to the second, another ten to her right, another twenty and then at last, thirty-three steps would bring her to Charity's barn.

* * * *

John Harrison's face turned deathly white. "What do you mean you told her?"

David laughed at his brother-in-law's question. "I didn't tell her exactly. I mean she already knew it, of course. She got a good laugh out of it though, once she realised that I went to school with his younger brother."

"Jesus," John Harrison groaned.

"What's the matter?" David asked. His eyes widened as he watched his brother-in-law come abruptly to his feet and stagger as if drunk.

"I can't do this again," John moaned.

By now, David was also on his feet. "Tell me. What's the matter?"

John shook his head. "She didn't know. Matt hadn't told her yet." But perhaps he had. John prayed to God he had.

* * * *

She'd called him 'Darling'. Matt smiled at the thought. He couldn't remember but once that she'd ever called him that before, and when she had, she hadn't truly meant it. Nor had she truly believed herself in love. But she'd said it again tonight. God, he loved her, loved her almost to the point of pain. He lay upon the bed, happier than he could ever remember, unable to stop smiling and unable to sleep. He thought he might take up his future father-in-law on his offer to join him in the library for a drink.

He shrugged aside a sudden nagging thought. Odd...hadn't Kiya told him just last week that she'd never used headache powders? That she detested...

And yet tonight she'd said... She'd said...

He tried to smile, but something was wrong. Somewhere deep down, a tightness began to form over his chest. Something was terribly wrong. He sought to shake off his fear and took a deep breath, attempting to stave off burgeoning panic. He forced his wild thoughts aside.

He needed a drink. He should have already joined her father in the library for a drink with David. Matt hadn't realised David would be there. He'd known David was part of the family, of course, but somehow had never considered...

"Jesus," he gasped. "Jesus, no, please, not again."

He lunged from the bed and tore his shirt as he tried to get his arms into its sleeves. Seconds later, he secured his trousers to his waist. Barefoot he ran to her room.

An instant later, he stood inside. He didn't need to look. He knew the bed was empty. Somehow, her essence filled this room when she was in it. Now, he felt only a cold emptiness and shivered as that same emptiness invaded his heart.

Again, a note lay on her bed. On it sat his ring. Nothing else could tell him more clearly her thoughts or her intent.

She knew. God, what was he going to do? She knew who he was.

He met John on the stairs and John knew just by his look that Kiya was gone again. In the library, he read the note addressed to her father.

Father,

I've gone to the continent. Italy to be more exact. I'm sure Mr. Chase, the Duke of Stratford, can tell you why. I'll be perfectly safe. I promise. I'll write again as soon as I'm settled. Please don't worry. I love you.

Kiya

Italy, Matt mused, his mouth forming a grim, straight line. He knew she spoke the language and it was certainly possible that she'd gone there, but for some reason, he doubted she was telling the truth.

He downed a hefty shot of cognac. "I don't think so."

"What do you mean?"

"I mean, could it be she's trying to throw us off her trail? What better way than to tell us exactly where she allegedly is? She knows I'll follow her. How often do you suppose ships leave for the Mediterranean? Do you think one just happens to be leaving tonight?" Matt shook his head at the thought. "I'll send a few men, just in case, to make sure she's not on any ship currently in port."

He tried to force aside his panic and put himself in her place. What would he do if he were running and sure someone would follow him? Wouldn't he send out false signals?

"What if, because she knows I'll follow, she actually went west instead of east? Does she know anyone west of here? Perhaps someone in Ireland?"

Harrison sighed as he shook his head. "I don't know. We'll have to ask Merry." He hesitated then said, "We vacationed just outside of Dublin a few years back. She might have kept in touch with some of the folks we met there."

"Dublin," Matt mused then shook his head. "I doubt it. Just in case we figure out her plan, she'd know we'd look up anyone she knows. I think she'll go west, but not anywhere that we might expect. She hasn't had time to work out any concrete plans. I think she doesn't know where she's going."

"If she doesn't know, how the hell will you find her?"

Matt nodded. "I'll find her. Make no mistake about that." And no one in the room doubted his word. "She can't have more than an hour head start. Jake can take care of things while I'm gone." He was on his way out of the room when he said, "I'll send you word as soon as I find her."

Chapter Eleven

Kiya, desperate for her friend's help and having whispered as much during the wedding celebration, smiled to find Charity's coach at the ready. Andrews, the family's driver, stood at its side, waiting for his passenger.

It was perhaps an hour before dawn but already light enough to see.

"Good morning, Andrews," Kiya said. "Looks as if this day will be as beautiful as yesterday, wouldn't you agree?"

"Indeed mistress," he returned as he helped the lady into the carriage. "Where might we going?"

"I thought London, Andrews, Madam Bedford's Shop then on to the stage line, if you please."

"Of course, mistress."

Kiya offered no explanation as to why she hadn't used her own carriage or why she should be travelling alone and at this time in the morning. Andrews, who had long worked for the gentry, had years ago given up trying to understand why some of them did the things they did. That they were a strange lot was a given. That it was none of his concern was equally true.

Kiya might have commented on the weather but paid no mind to it as the coach made its way towards London. At the moment, she was more intent on calming her need for violence and working out her plan. Still, she couldn't help but allow herself the delicious luxury of imagining the monster helpless in her hands. She would have given much to beat him to a bloody pulp. In truth, only so drastic an action would satisfy her, for there was no punishment that could ease her fury, the pain that wrapped tightly around her chest or the incessant pounding in her brain. Nothing but violence and the fervent, desperate hope to never see the liar again.

She knew it would take some hours to reach the city. Had she taken her horse she could have made the trip in half the time, still she couldn't have chanced it. She was enraged, but she wouldn't allow her anger to cause her a foolish mistake. Had she managed to get past the guards, she knew a woman alone could find herself in serious trouble. She might be easily abused unless she used the mind God had given her.

As the coach moved towards London, her thoughts grew a bit calmer and clearer. She'd left the note saying she was going to Italy. She wasn't, of course. Once in London, she'd buy a ticket for Glasgow, Scotland and make sure she was noticed while at it. If Matt followed her, and there wasn't a doubt in her mind that he would, if he ignored her note, which she thought he might, he'd go to Charity. She would tell him about Kiya borrowing her coach and driver.

It didn't matter. By the time he thought to look, Kiya would be long gone. Should he question all those at the stage line, one man might remember a coquettish young lady gone off to Scotland. With any luck at all, that would see Matt off to Scotland while she, veiled as a widowed lady, took a stagecoach to Liverpool. From there she'd ferry across the Irish Sea to Ireland. And on that pretty isle, she'd find a small village and settle herself there until the beast gave up and went home to his castle.

Kiya worried her bottom lip with her teeth as she imagined Matt eventually tracking her down. If he managed the feat, it was bound to take him some time, hopefully a few years.

She wished she could sleep, but her anger refused to ease, even marginally, and she couldn't relax enough to sleep. No doubt she would later, but not now. Hour after hour, as the coach bounced its way towards the city, she cursed his maggoty soul to hell. Thank God, she'd found him out before it was too late. But had she? Was it already too late? God, she prayed she wasn't with child. Kiya shook her head at the dreadful thought then realised it didn't matter. She wasn't about to marry the liar were she with six of his children. If there was a child and he should one day come to know of it, she'd merely deny it was his.

Kiya decided, once she'd got herself settled, she'd send for the children. She wasn't more than three hours away and already she missed them.

* * * *

Matt rained all types of curses upon the woman's head, even as he begged God to keep her safe. At least until he got his hands on her. It was perhaps an hour before dawn.

He was careful to keep his senses about him lest he lose what there was of his mind and she escape him forever.

He pounded on the door to Charity's family's home. No other could have helped Kiya. She hadn't left by horse or carriage. She was either still at home, hiding in some hole or another, or her friend had helped her escape.

A servant answered the door, and Charity was summoned. Matt had been pacing the foyer and stopped as he spied her coming down the stairs.

"Where is she?" he asked, knowing there was no need to further explain.

"I don't know," Charity returned, knowing it would only insult the man for her to claim ignorance. "She didn't tell me."

"How?"

"My coach."

Matt nodded. "I'm sorry to have disturbed you." A moment later, he was out the door and on his horse, racing up the drive towards London.

The sky was beginning to lighten as he pushed his horse to hurry. Perhaps an hour later, a coach loomed just ahead. The odds were nil that another coach just happened to be making its way towards London, at this time of the morning, from this particular area. He smiled knowing she was in it.

Upon reaching London, the carriage came to a stop at last and Charity's driver jumped to the ground and spoke to someone inside. A moment later, he approached a street vendor and secured two cups of tea as well as a handful of hot biscuits. He handed off half his fare to the party inside the coach, gained his seat again and ate his breakfast.

They were parked in front of a building that catered to ladies and their garments. A half hour after they finish eating, the business opened for the day and Kiya left the coach to enter the store. Ten minutes later, she was again inside the coach as it headed for London's stagecoach line. The driver was handed a folded note and obviously instructed to secure a ticket. A moment later, Kiya left the coach and stood in line to buy her own.

Matt stood some six feet behind her. Quickly, he dashed off a message to her father and handed it to a boy for delivery, promising further payment upon Mr. Harrison's receipt of the note. The boy was gone in a flash. Kiya bought her ticket after what Matt considered some unnecessary flirty conversation, no doubt meant to ensure the man's memory of the lady and the ticket she bought for Glasgow.

At the counter, Matt asked of the destination for the man, dressed as a driver, who had bought a ticket only moment's ago. Liverpool. Kiya was good, but thank God, so was he. From Liverpool a ferry could easily bring her over the Irish Sea. She didn't know it yet, but he'd be on that ferry as well.

Another message was sent, keeping her father informed that Matt would follow his lady on the long, hard trip that would cross the width of England.

He smiled as she used the lady's facilities only to exit the same some few minutes later covered in a black veil that reached her waist. The veil was dark enough to easily disguise her every feature. Yes, he thought he recognised her clothes or what little he could see of them, but he couldn't be sure. Damn but the woman gave him a terrible start. If he hadn't been watching carefully, if she hadn't stopped to say a word to the driver, he could have lost her.

Matt could have stopped her at any time, and thought more than once that he should, but to what avail? To find the minute his back was turned that she'd run off again? No. Dragging her back to her father's house would not suffice. They needed time together. She needed time to calm her temper. He needed time to make her understand why he hadn't told her the truth from the first. *Time* before she forgave him and admitted again to loving him. No, he'd wait for her to reach her destination and gain some privacy. Once she did, he prayed it wouldn't be long before he was once again in her good graces.

* * * *

Days later, Kiya breathed her relief and wondered if she'd ever sit again after the coach and ferry rides. Most certainly, she did not look forward to eventually returning home the same way she'd left. Perhaps, when it was time to go back, she'd find a ship. She'd look into it later, maybe something in Dublin.

Kiya shook her head. She wouldn't think on it now. Now, she had to find a place to stay.

"Would you like some help. You seem a bit undecided."

Kiya gasped to find Matt standing calmly at her side. It couldn't be. Had she travelled days only to find him here? For just a second, she thought she must be hallucinating, but no. No one else grinned like that. Still veiled, she dared to glance his way and muttered something in Italian.

Matt laughed. "It won't do, Kiya. I know it's you. You haven't been out of my sight in days."

"Do you think I left my home just to find you here? You're the reason I left. Go away."

"I was thinking we might as well get married since we're in Ireland. I hear tell they frown a bit on fornication in these parts."

"I hate you."

"You don't. You're upset with me. We need to talk."

"Why would I talk to you? So you can tell me more lies?"

Having just disembarked, they were standing with their backs to the water when a constable patrolling the decks walked by. Kiya suddenly and brilliantly grabbed Matt's hand and, holding tight, began to pull even as she called out. "No, please, unhand me, sir. Please don't take me away from my children."

She almost laughed as the constable quickly made himself indispensable to the poor widow lady and took Matt into custody, for with her hand in his, it had looked as if he were holding on to her and forcing her to his side.

"See here, what are you about?"

"He's…" She forced her voice to break. "He's trying to take me from my children. Please, please don't let him take me away."

"See here now. What is the meaning behind this?"

Matt took a deep breath. All this fool needed to do was look at their joined hands. Matt wasn't holding her. She was holding him. "I am the Duke of Stratford, sir. My identification is in my billfold. My lady and I are having a bit of a squabble. I'm afraid you've gotten the wrong impression."

"Please," she whimpered beautifully, her body trembling as if she'd just endured a particularly ghastly episode. "Don't let him abuse me again."

The constable's eyes hardened, his hands tightening on Matt's arm, and Kiya knew she's won. She owed him this much and more. Were it up to her the beast would rot in jail. Too bad lying wasn't against the law.

"Come away with you, sir," the constable insisted as he began dragging Matt from her hold.

Kiya knew Matt would be angry once he found her again. She didn't care. In an instant, she raised her veil and grinned while shocking Matt to silence with an unorthodox wink. A moment later, with a low wicked laugh, she picked up her case and turned away to hail a cab.

He'd find her eventually. All she'd managed was a stumbling block. The man was nearly as stubbornly determined as was she. Despite her anger, Kiya acknowledged that much about herself. But, she reasoned, if she was stubborn, the beast was that and so much more. The worst of it was he was a liar. There'd never come a time when she could believe him. God, but she couldn't abide the thought that she'd almost married a lying lord of the realm, one of the very same beasts that had so misused her sweet mother.

Now that she'd seen him again, Kiya shivered with a rage that seemed only to grow with every breath she took. Knowing only disgust, she pushed aside the obnoxious thought of marriage and forced herself to think about her immediate circumstances.

It was clear the beast would never stop trying to find her. Her only alternative was to stop running. She thought at first she might simply return home but put aside the notion for a time. She'd been travelling for endless days and needed a rest before beginning the chore again. In the meantime, why should she suffer unnecessary hardship only to be found again? The lying snake wasn't about to give up. No, he'd only search her out, insisting on a confrontation. Well, she'd give him that, she give him that and more.

She asked the driver if he knew of a cottage for rent. "Aye, lassie. Old Mrs. Reilly has a few. She, bein' a widow lady like yourself, could use the rent, I'm sure."

Kiya smiled. At least, she'd fooled somebody. Pretending to be a widow hadn't done much to keep Matt off her trail.

Mrs. Reilly was an agreeable sort. An elderly lady she was perhaps nearing her seventieth year. With pure white hair, creamy almost unlined skin, cherry cheeks and the bluest eyes Kiya had ever seen, the lady must have been a striking beauty in her youth. She had a delightful ready smile and deep, hearty laughter and found obvious delight in her grandchildren, which she didn't hesitate to show off to the newest visitor to her village. And to top off this sweet package of neighbourly fare, she made the most delicious soda bread and creamy rice pudding that Kiya had ever tasted.

As it turned out, Mrs. Reilly did have a cottage for rent. Her son — her last unmarried son, the lady was kind enough to mention — had just yesterday prepared it for its next tenant.

Mrs. Reilly lived to one side of the cottage, while her son lived to the other. She was quick to point out that fact so that Kiya would feel safe during her stay.

On her second day in residence, Kiya visited with her landlady and stayed for tea.

"I don't mind telling you, all about are filled with questions as to why a pretty young lady like yourself should be travelling alone and come for a stay in my cottage."

Kiya smiled, knowing all might be curious but none more so than her own landlady. She couldn't blame them, of course. This was the country after all, and everyone passing through was bound to be noticed, especially a woman like herself. The fact of the matter being, a lady, widow or not, never travelled alone. Therefore, how could she be a lady? Kiya hadn't missed the looks she'd gotten from all at the village market. She knew the townsfolk realised the fine quality of her shoes and clothes.

"Yes, I'm sure most are wondering what I'm about." She hesitated a moment then went on. "You see I've run from a most unhappy union."

"You're married?"

"No, I'm not married." Kiya shuddered, knowing but for a casual word spoken, she might have married the beast. "Thank God, I found him out in time."

"I don't understand. You're not married, but you ran? You left your father's house?"

Kiya nodded. "He's powerful. Very powerful. I had to leave. He pretended to be one thing but was actually another."

"Your father?"

"No, the man I almost married."

Kiya could see this was going to take some explaining. All she'd managed to do was confuse the woman. "He's a duke, a lord of the realm. I won't have him. He knew I wouldn't so he never told me. He lied."

"A duke? You left because the man you were to marry is a duke?" Mrs. Reilly like most of Irish knew no tenderness for the royals, but she'd never heard of an English woman who'd refused one.

Kiya nodded. "It's a long story. Suffice it to say, I've no love for the royals, and he knew it. Mrs. Reilly, I'd appreciate it if someone comes looking for me, if you could..." She took a deep breath. "No, I won't ask you to lie. If someone comes looking for me, could you let me know right away. Will you do that?"

"Of course, dear. Don't you worry now."

Kiya wished she *could* stop worrying. The man was sure to find her — even if Mrs. Reilly had promised to warn her. There was no way to stop him from eventually finding her.

Kiya had paid for a month but thought after her first week it was time to go. Once she'd made up her mind, she reasoned tomorrow wouldn't be too soon. That night, Kiya packed her bag. In the morning, she'd tell Mrs. Reilly she was leaving then look for the means to travel north to Dublin.

Matt found her that very morning, or as it turned out, she found him. Dressed for travelling, she opened the door to her little rented cottage, and there he was. The hated beast was asleep on her step.

A moment later, she slammed the door and locked it after having slapped his sleeping face. She'd never hit anyone in her life but had to admit slapping Matt felt wonderful. It brought a lightness to her soul and an amazing sense of calm to her entire being. She could only hope to get the chance to do it again.

Matt called her name and knocked, but it brought about no results. Had there been a back door she would surely have used it. As it was she was trapped. A moment later, he crashed into the cottage, leaving the door in a sorry state of disrepair.

"Don't ever hit me again," he warned, "unless you'd like me to return the favour."

Kiya ignored the threat and held her ground as he unconsciously sought to cower her by leaning forward, towering over her small frame.

"Don't ever hit you again," she repeated with some amazement. "The truth is I'll never hit you enough. It's all I want to do, all I'll ever want to do." At that, she pulled back her arm, her fingers locked into a fist and, as hard as she could, punched him in the stomach. She grunted her approval as he expelled a gust of breath, bent slightly at his waist and backed up a step.

"Kiya," he warned.

"I'm not afraid of you. Get out!"

"You should be afraid. I'm at my wits end and have had just about enough of your nonsense."

She sneered her hatred. "I don't care if you beat me to a pulp," she nearly growled while facing him fearlessly. "I'm going to hit you every chance I get." And with that she took a step forward, pulled back and made to hit him again.

That one punch hadn't been near enough, hadn't done anything to ease her rage.

Matt moved quickly out of her reach, knowing better than to give her another opportunity for violence and allowing her a minute to calm herself. He looked over her tiny kitchen. And just as if she hadn't slapped him awake, just as if she hadn't only a moment before punched him in the stomach and he hadn't broken down the door, he asked, "Have you something to eat? I'm starving."

And he was. Since he'd begun this journey, he had rarely slept and hadn't dared to do more than down an occasional meat pie and quick tankard of ale, lest his attention be diverted and she suddenly disappear again. Then after spending hours in jail, he'd thought of nothing but finding her again. It had taken him the better part of another week. God, the people around here were a tight-lipped sort. Most everyone was friendly enough until they heard he was looking for a particular woman. He wondered if they hadn't been warned against him, for the moment he asked about her, each and every one of them suddenly knew nothing. Thank God, he'd come across a lady at the local pub who had a soft heart and, after hearing his sorry tale of searching for the woman he loved, had pointed him in the right direction or he'd still be wandering these fields looking into every nook and cranny as he searched for Kiya. Late last night, he'd finally come upon the cottage, but she'd already gone to bed. He'd thought this morning would be soon enough to confront her, only to awaken to a slap and the door slamming behind her.

"How am I going to explain a broken door to Mrs. Reilly?"

Matt shrugged, not at all concerned. Kiya thought his arrogance an abomination and every inch that of the elite. Did any of the hated breed care for anyone but themselves? He took off his jacket and made himself comfortable in the only chair by the fire.

"You're paying for it," she informed him. "How did you find me?"

"Not an easy chore, I don't mind telling you. I've been looking into every cottage and room, big or small, on this island." He shook his head and sighed. "I'm beginning to wonder if you're worth all this trouble."

"I can tell you right now I'm not. You might as well give up and go home." Lord, if she'd left yesterday, she would have been long gone before this monster turned up on her doorstep.

Matt grinned. It would take a bit more than that one flippant comment before his interest might wane. "What did you do? Warn them that I'd be looking for you? Who did you say that I was?"

Even though she'd done just that and imagined the townsfolk had done their best to protect her, she decided to deny it. This beast deserved at least one lie in return for the misery he'd caused her. "I haven't a clue as to what you're talking about."

"I know you're lying."

Kiya shrugged. "Unlike some I've not the experience. No doubt, I'll one day grow better at it."

Matt ignored that comment and returned instead to her first question. "The first time, I never lost you." He glared his annoyance then sighed his exhaustion. "You weren't out of my sight once you arrived in London. I saw you get out of your friend's coach, and I followed the coach and sat a few rows behind you on the ferry. By the way, I didn't appreciate the way you flirted with that man."

Kiya frowned. "What man?"

"When you bought the ticket for Glasgow."

She laughed, realising the man in question. "I needed to make sure he'd remember me."

Matt nodded. He'd imagined as much. "I'm sure he did."

She frown. She'd thought she had hours. How had he known she was gone and known it so soon? "How did you know? What gave me away?"

"The little headache act. You said you were going to take a powder. On my ship, you said you never took powders. And then you called me darling. You've only once called me that."

"I'll be more careful the next time. I won't be saying that word again."

Matt shook his head. "Little witch," he said. "I'm afraid there won't be a next time."

"Oh but there will."

Matt merely shook his head again. "We should get married here, I think. Once you are my wife, I expect I can watch you closer. We can have another service and celebration once we return to your father's house."

"You cannot force me to marry you, Lord Insane, and if, by some miracle, you could I'd make your life a living hell. You'd not only rue the day we met, but you'd curse me and yourself for your ridiculous insistence in this matter. I'll disgrace you. I'll cheat on you every chance I get. You won't be able to show your face in public. I'll make you a laughing stock."

"Kiya," he said, his tone remarkably calm considering the magnitude of her threat. "That's enough of your nonsense."

She laughed without a shred of humour. "You think this is nonsense, Lord Insignificant? You're about to suffer a great shock if that's the case."

"In the first place, were I you, I wouldn't take for granted the ease in acquiring a lover. Even the hint of one would necessitate the man's early and, I'm afraid, instant demise. No doubt, the sight of one or two bodies would go far towards ensuring your absolute faithfulness and send any future prospects running."

A chill ran down her spine at his softly spoken words. She longed to tell him she didn't believe him for a minute, but he'd spoken so coldly, so lacking in emotion, while his eyes held almost maniacal fire, that it left her wondering if he wouldn't do exactly as he promised. She shuddered at the thought.

"It's you I should kill," she grated as he grabbed her hand and pulled her until she fell upon his lap. She struggled to no avail.

With his arms like a band of steel around her middle, he said, "I'm going to tell you this one time. I'm sorry I didn't tell you who I was. You were so set against the royals, that I was afraid you'd hate me, if you knew. So I figured I could always tell you later, after I was sure you loved me. I'm sorry you found out the way you did."

She tried to get up again. He gave her a little shake and turned her to face him. She refused to meet his gaze.

"Think on this, I am who I am. You loved me before you knew. A title should make no difference. The fools you knew at court were just that. You've known me for months and know better than to group me with them. I understand you're angry, but once you calm down, you'll realise I am nothing like them, nor will I ever be."

"I am perfectly calm, thank you. I need not be upset to know that I hate you. That I'll always hate you. There's nothing you can say to change my mind."

"You are little more than a spoiled brat. Were I you, I'd watch what I say. I'm tired and my patience is running thin."

"Meaning what? That you'll beat me?"

"Kiya," he sighed wearily.

"Indeed, that would settle everything, wouldn't you agree? If someone hates you, beat them. That should make all things better."

He prayed if he kept his senses about himself he just might get through to her. "Kiya, I think it's safe to say neither of us had a voice as to where or to whom we were born."

What he said made sense, of course, but she was far too angry to acknowledge the logic.

Matthew took her silence to heart and dared to ask, "So if there were no choices, why hate me?"

"I don't hate you because you were born a royal." The moment the words were spoken, Kiya reconsidered. Well perhaps she did, a little. "I hate you because you lied."

"I didn't."

"You lied by omission. Therefore, you lied."

"I explained why. Damn it, do you know how afraid I am?"

"Afraid?" She shot him a look that clearly spoke of her confusion. "What does that mean?"

"It means, brat, that you cause me to quake in my boots."

She glared at him. "It does not further your cause to spout the ridiculous, Lord Simple."

Matt grinned at her purposeful and consistent misuse of his title. "You ought to get the title right, Mistress, since, as my duchess, it will be your title as well."

She snorted a scornful laugh, "Not likely, Lord Ratford."

Kiya escaped his lap at last and went about the business of preparing tea. She set the table with one cup, one small dish, one napkin, one spoon and a towel wrapped around a huge soda bread Mrs. Reilly had given her. Matt grinned, pretending she laid the table for him. "Won't you join me, Kiya?"

"Oh, are you still here?"

Matt laughed at her less-than-genuine surprise. She would never know what it cost him not to drag her against him and crush her body to his in a hold that promised he might never let her go. She was a spitfire, a little terror who intrigued him like no other. He loved her madly. They'd barely begun their life together, and she'd already put him through hell more than once.

As she waited for the water to boil, he watched her move around the small cottage. She was a bundle of righteous fury, and he longed to take her to bed.

The woman needed someone with a strong hand, and Matt couldn't help but wonder how he might go about exerting that control while ensuring her spirit remained intact. Somehow, he'd manage, for he could only imagine the horrors that might lie in store in the years to come, should this little tormenter be allowed to run free. "So what do you suggest we should do, Kiya? I don't look forward to years of constantly chasing after you."

"Then stop," she said a bit too flippantly for his liking. "In any case, I'm sure after a time you will."

"And that's your answer? I should simply stop? What about the fact that we love each other?"

"What about it?" she asked, turning to glare at him. "Love doesn't last through all abuses. It doesn't thrive with lies. I've no doubt that in time I'll stop loving you."

Matt breathed a sigh. She hadn't denied her love for him. At least, they had that. Only he wanted a hell of a lot more from this woman. And he was going to get it. "All right, here's the thing. I love you, and you love me. We should be able to overcome anything as long as we have that."

"You'd think as much, wouldn't you?"

"I suppose that's your charming way of saying that we cannot."

She raised her hand to her cheek in a dramatic fashion. "Oh dear was I being charming?" Her obvious hope, of course, was that she was anything but.

"You're pushing. I'd advise you to ease up a bit."

"You'd advise that, would you?" she snarled, her rage barely under control. Hands on her hips, she scorned, "Here's what *I* advise, Lord Simpleton. Right now, I'm angry, in truth far too angry to carry on a civilised conversation. I'm sure to say things neither of us wants said. You need to leave. Perhaps, after I've calmed down a bit, say in a year or so, we might talk again."

"You've already had close to two weeks, and I'm not leaving."

"You will leave," she further insisted, "or I shall call for the constable."

Matt grinned. "A constable you, little witch? I owe you for that one, but sorry, that manoeuvre won't work again." He tapped his chest. "I have a letter from the chief in my pocket that confirms my identity. And what do you suppose the constable might do to you for filing a false report?"

"I wouldn't be filing a false report. It's not false to say I don't want you here."

"Nevertheless, I am here. I'm *always* going to be wherever you are. It's time you realised that fact and you grew up."

"Oh my God, I hate you," she grated through tightly clenched teeth, her knuckles white as she gripped the back of a chair in fury and wondered how the wood managed to stay in one piece for the anger she felt should have seen it crumble to splinters and dust.

She trembled with the emotion. After a few deep breaths, she finally managed in a somewhat softer tone,

"And by growing up you mean, of course, it's time for me to do what you say."

"It couldn't hurt," he said, unable to stop his grin. "The truth of the matter is you're stuck with me, so you might as well make the best of it."

"A lovely proposition, I'm sure. I'm stuck with you," she repeated half to herself. "Lord," she breathed, her gaze rising towards the heavens as if asking for guidance or strength.

In the meantime, Matt gathered his own dish, cup, napkin and spoon and sat at the table as she placed the steaming pot of tea between them, and when she prayed 'Lord', he answered with, "Yes?"

It took her a minute to realise what he was about, and once she did, she couldn't prevent her lips from curving into a very small smile. "Unbelievable."

Matt took her smile to heart and breathed a bit easier. "So when do you want to get married?"

Kiya merely glanced his way then back at the teapot. She began to pour. "How did you know I didn't go to Italy?"

"Because if I were running, I'd do exactly what you did."

Her gaze met his; her frown told him she wasn't sure of his meaning. "Set out false clues," he offered then shrugged at her obvious understanding. "But just to make sure, I sent some men to search all the ships in port."

"If I were on a ship, I'd be in disguise."

"I thought as much. They were to personally check everyone."

They sipped at their tea and ate the buttered soda bread.

"This is good."

Kiya nodded her agreement even as she did her best to ignore the emerald ring that had suddenly appeared near his cup.

Matt watched her glance towards the ring, knowing she pretended it wasn't there. He pushed it towards her. "Put it on."

He couldn't take his eyes off her, so strong was his relief that she — although not overly thrilled by any means — seemed to have gotten over the worst of her anger.

"I never wanted to get married in the first place, and now, you expect me to marry a duke? God, one of us is out of his mind."

Matt grinned at her use of the masculine pronoun. He nodded. "You could be right. Living with you might very well see me in Bedlam."

"Still, you're willing to chance it? What does that say about your common sense?"

"It says that I love a lady by the name of Kiya enough to risk my sanity and that common sense isn't all that common."

Kiya shook her head. "I can't bear the thought, Matt. You're a duke, not only a duke but the Duke of Stratford. My God, do you realise your reputation with the ladies?" She frowned, her lips curling with distaste. "The thought alone is enough to —"

"Stop! It's not true."

"What's not true? That you've jumped from bed to bed? That your reputation rivals that of Casanova? In truth, I don't want a man like you, Matt. I could never want a man like you."

"You're talking of rumours. They're not true. I swear there haven't been that many."

"Indeed? How many is 'not that many'?"

"Kiya, I'm thirty-three years old. You don't expect your husband to never have been with another."

Actually she had never given the matter a moment's thought especially since she'd never thought to have a husband. It wasn't his reputation that mattered, truthfully it was a non-issue. Still she couldn't resist, "You expect it of me."

He groaned, knowing to her way of thinking the double standard was hardly fair and yet despite anyone's wishes it remained very much in existence and probably would for some time to come. God, but he didn't need another complication in this tenuous love affair.

Matt had never felt more helpless as he said, "I swear to you, there's been a handful, no more."

Kiya thought perhaps there had been a few more than a handful. Still, it mattered not. She knew this man loved her and only her, and he wasn't about to look at another. Only she wasn't going to make things easy. She owed him for his lies. She owed him for every uncomfortable moment spent travelling from her home. Indeed, she owed him miles of aggravation.

"They say you're the best. That you have one woman after another. That none can compare with your technique. How could rumours like that abound if there's been only a handful?" She turned away lest he see the laughter in her eyes, for the more she spoke the more desperate he seemed to grow.

Again and again, he ran his hand through his hair. Suddenly, he came to his feet and paced. "That's ridiculous."

"Is it? I wonder."

"There's no need to wonder. I'm telling you." Matt was agitated beyond belief, horrified to think she might take the absolute nonsense as gospel and allow rumours to ruin their lives. He hadn't a notion how to make things right between them. "Kiya, you have to know the stories are utter rubbish."

Laughter threatened her. She fought to keep it at bay and looked into her cup. "Actually Matthew, I've shared your bed so I happen to know firsthand that they're right on the mark."

Matt frowned at the tremor in her voice. He reached for her chin and turned her face towards him. "Are you laughing?"

"Do you think this is something to laugh about?" she asked, no longer trying to control the need.

"You little wretch." He groaned as relief shuddered through his body. He pulled her from her chair into his arms. "You're killing me." He buried his face in the warmth of her neck. "My God, Kiya, have pity and marry me."

She giggled as she pressed her face to his neck. God, he felt so warm, so hard, and smelled so good. Could any man smell this good? "Why?"

He pulled back just enough to spy the wicked laughter in her eyes. "Because you're a bundle of trouble, and I can't see myself living a boringly peaceful life. Put the ring on."

Her hand squeezed between their bodies, and she smiled as she felt his body jerk with surprise as she ran her palm over his sex.

He crushed her tighter against him. "You're going to be in trouble if you don't stop this teasing."

She laughed, the sound softly alluring, her look daring as she raised her gaze to his. "Really? You know, Matthew," she said conversationally. Suddenly the picture of innocence, she pretended to smooth his shirt over his chest, even as she managed to work the ties open. "I've always thought that there was trouble and then there was trouble." She lowered her voice, the last word filled with meaning. "Which one are you offering?"

"God help us. Have I created a monster?" he moaned. "Are you going to put on the damn ring?"

Kiya reached for it and slipped it on her finger. "Nag, nag, nag. There...are you satisfied?"

"Not yet, but I'm sure as hell going to be."

Her laughter turned into a low moan of pleasure against the pressure of his mouth. Her arms circled his neck as he carried her to the narrow bed.

"It's been awhile, this might be faster than either of us would like."

"Then we can do it again."

He grinned. "I'm loving the way you think."

"Take off your clothes. I want to feel you against me."

He tore away his shirt as Kiya pulled her dress and chemise from her shoulders and, grabbing her drawers on the way, slipped everything down her body then kicked it off the bed. She was left wearing only her black stockings. She moved to dispose of them as well when his hands stalled her movement. "Don't. Leave them on."

"Kiss me, Matt."

"Tell me you love me."

"I do. God, you know I didn't want to, but I do. I love you, Matt."

He held her tightly against him, his mouth crushing her lips beneath him. "I love you," he muttered as his broke the kiss and gasped for air. "I love you," he said again as his mouth moved down the length of her. "Love you, love you," he muttered as his mouth sampled the lushness of her breasts, his teeth teasing her nipples. Her midriff, her stomach and God, at last, the sweet, moist heat of her pussy. "I love the taste of you. I can't get enough."

"Oh God," she moaned as the pleasure spread through her. It didn't take but a few minutes and she was ready. "Matt, God, Matt, I'm going to come."

"Yes," he said as he felt the first of her tremors against his tongue. Quickly, magically Kiya thought, he was inside her, his finger moving against her clit, driving her out of her mind with nearly diabolical pleasure.

And it was there. The pain twisted at her stomach, twisted until she cried out at the splendour. Her body rose up to meet his. There was no way she could stop as her body sucked his deeper, deeper into the flame of her until blackness crept to the very edges of her consciousness, until she finally collapsed beneath him in spent, delicious exhaustion.

Later, Kiya watched the ring sparkle as it caught a ray of sun coming from the window. She couldn't believe the power this man held over her. Within hours, her emotions had run the gambit. She'd gone from rages to rapture. She'd never known anger to equal it, nor the extremes of pleasure he was able to instil.

"Do you promise never to lie again?"

He was exhausted. He hadn't realised just how exhausted until the question dragged him from the edge of sleep. "Damn it, Kiya, I couldn't tell you the truth. Jesus, I swear I wanted to, but you hate the royals. What was I supposed to say? 'Oh yes, by the way, it just so happens that I'm a duke'. God," he groaned, "that would have gone over well, don't you think?"

"Poor thing, I forgive you. You couldn't help being born a duke," she said between tiny kisses spread over his neck, chest and, to Matt's delight, his stomach.

He figured he'd forgive her the less-than-subtle touch of mockery, as long as she continued on with what she was doing. In truth, if she continued what she was doing, he'd forgive her just about anything. Her mouth lowered then lowered again and just when his breath began to grow choppy, his body straining towards her mouth, she suddenly stopped and asked, "Why are you partnered with Jake? David said you've more money than God."

He smiled, at the moment, more than interested in what she was about, he tried to put her off with, "Would you have me lie about all day? Would you, dressed as you are, feed me grapes?"

Kiya turned to face him and leaned over his stomach. "That sounds interesting, but that's not an answer."

God, but she was gorgeous. Naked, her skin smooth creamy white, her breasts full and round, the soft pink tips were unbearably alluring. It took some effort to keep his mind on their conversation. He shrugged. "My mother is a believer in the Bible scripture, "to those who are given much, much is required". All her children have interests. My brothers and I, among other interests, each own more than one merchant ship."

Kiya frowned. "That's the reason you work, but why this particular type of work?"

He shrugged again.

"Are you trying to evade the question?"

"There's something I have to see to."

She shook her head and with a humourless laugh said, "Oh no, you don't. You might as well know right now you won't be treating me as if I've no mind. You tell me what it is right now, or the answer is no, I will not marry you."

"Too late, you've already said you would."

"Matthew," she warned.

"It's Shelby."

Kiya narrowed her gaze and looked into his troubled eyes. "Shelby? Do you mean the Shelby who Merry almost married?"

He nodded. "He killed my sister. I think he's probably behind the murders in your area. I've people working on proving it."

Kiya gasped. "What do you mean he killed your sister?"

"I mean he married her then he killed her."

"Matt, if that's true then why isn't he…"

"Because there's no proof. After they married, he allowed less and less contact, until there was little more than an occasional note from her. Of course, there were reasons. She was visiting friends on the continent. She was working with the poor. She'd been summoned to court, staying with his cousin, visiting friends in the Indies. The excuses went on and on. I think she discovered what her husband was about and paid for it with her life. Of course, I've no proof of that either."

"Matthew, what could she have discovered?"

"I think he's a degenerate. I think he's probably into children or masochism— perhaps both—or something equally as dreadful. She didn't live long enough to tell us. A villager found her and brought her home. She'd been terribly abused. Her clothes were in tatters, she was sick with fever and she never came to her senses. Shelby had reported her missing, of course. Oh, he played the devastated widower to perfection. I wanted to smash his face."

"Why do you think he was responsible?"

"She'd been whipped. There were old scars, as well as new, down the length of her. Where did the old scars come from? Who had beaten her? How could anyone dare to beat her and do it without her husband's knowledge?"

"Oh my God and Merry almost married him."

"No, she didn't. I would have gone to your father with what I knew and what I suspected."

Kiya took a moment to think that through then nodded. "All right, so what are we going to do about it?"

He shook his head. "I had a feeling you'd be thinking along those lines. Not a chance, lady. There is no 'we' when it comes to Shelby."

Kiya laughed as she watched him roll from beneath her arm, come from the bed, shove his feet into his trousers and reach for his shirt.

"Why are you getting dressed?"

Matt watched her kneel on the bed. Completely at ease in her nakedness, she moved to the edge and reached for his waist. He had no will against her, not when it came to this. She pulled his very willing body to hers and smiled at his low groan as she nuzzled her mouth against his stomach. "I'm not finished, Matt."

He groaned again as her fingers opened his trousers. Helpless against their mutual wants, he watched the material fall to the floor. She might not have been finished, but as her mouth slid over his cock, Matt thought there was a very good chance he was.

Chapter Twelve

Kiya sat opposite Matt as the private coach travelled east from Liverpool towards London. They had been married by special license, their vows presided over by a sleepy magistrate early that morning. "I hope father won't be overly upset that we married. I know he wanted to see me walk down the aisle in church."

"We'll still do that. I sent him a note letting him know what we are about and that we should probably go ahead with the church services as planned. Guests have already been invited. My family will want to be there, my mother especially." He shrugged. "I think your father would be more upset if we travelled together without the blessings afforded those in that holy state."

She nodded in agreement then said, "You know Matt, I've been thinking."

"I don't want to hear it."

"You don't?" she asked. Her eyes widened with surprise and a touch of hurt before growing into shards of blue ice that promised untold pain. "Is this what I can expect now that we're married?"

"I said I don't want to hear it because I know, just by the look of you, you're dreaming up some wild scenario and imagining how you, with or without my help, will take Shelby into custody."

Kiya eyes grew wider still. She looked at him for a long moment before she burst into laughter.

"Exactly," he said as if her laugh proved his point.

"I'll have to learn not to be so easy to read."

Matt grunted for a response.

"Perhaps I was thinking along those lines, but not without your help, surely. I'm not half as brave as all that."

"Not *with* my help either. You will not concern yourself with this, Kiya. I expressly forbid it."

"I only wanted to make a suggestion."

"If your suggestion involves you, I don't want to hear it."

"Matt, I was only going to say, if I came up with a plan and you watched me every step of the way, we could probably get Shelby to show his true colours. Don't you think?"

"I take it you mean to use yourself as some sort of bait?"

"I think something like that would surely draw him out."

"No."

"Matt, you don't even know what I was—"

"I said no. Kiya, if you don't listen to me, I'm afraid I won't be able to bring you home. The children will be terribly unhappy, of course, but at least, I'll be assured of your safety when I tuck you away in one of my estates."

"All right, all right, I won't do whatever it is you think I might. Exactly why are we arguing? I haven't said anything yet. I haven't even thought of anything yet."

"I'll have your solemn word, Kiya. You will not put yourself in any danger. You will not twist or turn the pledge or any wording thereof. You simply will keep yourself safe so I might retain my sanity."

"Are you a man of law? You're talking as if you're reading some document."

Matt gave her a hard look that brooked no nonsense.

Kiya gave a weary sigh. "I hope you know you'll not always win."

"I only want to win if it means keeping you safe. Have I your word on it?"

"You have."

"Good, now come over here. I want you to show me your new drawers."

"Why, do you want to borrow them?" Kiya giggled at the thought.

They had spent hours shopping this morning, and Matt had barely had a chance to glance at the new things she'd bought. "Only if you're in them."

"You won't see much if I'm over there."

Matt thought she was probably right on that score, but there were times when touching was even better than seeing.

"I could show you from here."

"That's good thinking," he said as he watched her raise her skirt.

"It's a good thing you're a duke."

Matt narrowed his gaze and raised one brow as he accused, "Who are you and what have you done with my wife?"

Kiya laughed happily, and the sound squeezed his chest, filling him with untold delight. "I only meant that if you were poor we wouldn't have a coach to ourselves and showing you my new unmentionables would be out of the question."

He nodded. "Indeed, money comes in handy now and then."

Kiya agreed, "Especially when you buy your wife unmentionables that are so thin you can almost see through them."

"Is that right?" he asked with some real interest. "Can you see through them? Shall I try?"

"You are so bad." She raised her skirt, inching the hem above a black stocking and perhaps six inches of naked thigh to the lacy edge of her drawers then quickly dropped the it back into place.

Matt raised a disappointed gaze from her skirt to her laughing blue eyes and calmly inquired, "And *I'm* bad? What was that?"

She grinned. "Did you or did you not ask to see the unmentionables you bought?"

"How can I know what I saw? I hardly got a glance."

"You might take my word for it."

"I might, and I'd be the last to doubt my lady's word on the matter. Still, I think in this instance, it's wise to take the chore upon myself."

"And you think the matter to be a chore?"

"Of course. I'd never willingly search beneath a lady's skirts."

"And of course, I'm supposed to believe you."

Matt thought it best to drop that particular subject. "Take off your dress."

She smiled. "The thought is exciting to be sure, but what would happen if this coach lost a wheel? I'd not be able to get it back on before someone saw me."

"You're right. Bad idea." He came to kneel before her. "Why don't we leave everything as it is except for your drawers? We could take them off."

Kiya felt her blood grow warm, her body heavy, as moisture began to puddle between her thighs. "We could?" she asked, pretending shock. "Why would we do something like that?"

He nodded. "That way I could see them clearly. And if this coach lost a wheel, no one would ever know you haven't got them on."

"That's a very good idea, but you'll know."

He nodded as his hands reached under her skirt. "Yes, of course, I'll know, but I probably wouldn't even look."

"Are you sure?"

His fingers worked the tabs loose. "Well, I'm not absolutely sure. I did say probably, if you remember. I *probably* won't look."

She helped him by lifting her hips as he pulled the drawers down her legs. "Well if you're probably sure, I can't see any reason why they shouldn't come off. You did buy them, after all. I think it's only fair that you should see them."

"I hope you know that talking about your drawers has gotten me all stirred up and mad for you."

"How odd. Do you always get stirred up when talking about unmentionables?"

"Only if I'm talking about yours. And only if I'm taking them off you while we talk about them."

"If talking about them so affects, one wonders what will happen once you see them." Kiya forced back a low moan as he ran his hands down her thighs, bringing her drawers to her feet.

Matt pulled them free at last and held them up for his inspection. "Very pretty," he mused, and as the sunlight shone through the material, he added, "I see what you mean when you say they're almost see-through."

"Do you like them?"

"I love them," he said. A moment later, he brought them to his face and breathed deeply of her lusciously sweet scent. "But I love the way they smell most of all."

Kiya gasped softly.

"Do you?" she asked then wondered how she'd managed even that what with the sudden breath-stealing pounding in her throat. Her pussy grew heavier, wetter. Her voice broke, but she forced herself to go on. "Everyday I learn another shocking thing about you."

Matt grinned. "Have you? What have I done to shock you today?"

"Well, I suppose it couldn't be that you like to smell a lady's unmentionables."

"I like to smell yours." He grinned. "Now that I have, I'm afraid you'll need to raise you skirt."

Kiya laughed, hardly able to hold back the need to tear the garment away. "I will? Whatever for?"

"There's a penalty to pay when a man smells a lady's drawers."

"Oh my, I had no idea."

"Now that you know, I expect you'll take care in the future."

Matt helped her lift her skirt and petticoat to her waist.

"Now that I know, I expect I'll take every precaution. I think it's simply best to leave my unmentionables in my chest of drawers lest this should happen again."

"I like the way you think."

"You are so bad. I don't think I've ever met anyone quite so bad."

"And you never will." His gaze moved over the silky naked skin above her black stockings. "God, do you know how lovely you are?"

Kiya shook her head. "I know I love it when you look at me."

Matt licked his lips in anticipation and asked, "What else do you love?"

He wanted her to say it. Kiya took a deep breath and forced the words. "I love it when you kiss me."

"Where?"

"Oh God," she moaned as he pulled her hips towards the edge of the seat.

"Where, Kiya? Where do you love me to kiss you?"

"My mouth, of course."

"Aye, but where else?"

"Here," she groaned, "between my thighs."

"Here?" he asked as he dragged his mouth over the inside of her thigh.

"Yes, there, but higher, especially higher."

"Tell me where," he groaned against her skin.

He was driving her out of her mind. Her heart was pounding so hard she could barely hear him. Still, she couldn't say it. She didn't know why he needed to hear it, but she could never say it. "Matthew, you're killing me."

"All right, show me then. Show me exactly where you love me to kiss you."

"Here," she said as her fingers came to gently part her flesh, exposing her tiny, stiff pearl of passion. "Here, please."

"Oh yes," he grated, gasping for every breath, trying to control the pounding of his heart. He leaned forward and licked her. His tongue was burning hot against her sweet moistness.

She moaned.

"No, don't take your hands away," he told her. "I want you to touch yourself. Make believe I'm touching you. I want to watch you. I need to watch you."

"Matt," she gasped. "I cannot."

"But you can. I need to see you do this."

He breathed his delight as her hands came again to her own body and began to move. Her fingertips were inside the folds of her body, gently, exploring, her eyes closed as she relished every sweet sensation. "I like it better when you do this."

"Have you ever done this before?"

"No."

"Don't stop. Let me play while you do it." He opened her legs wider and slid his tongue inside her. He wiggled it back and forth, teasing her to madness, all the while watching her fingers move. "Beautiful. God, Kiya, you're so beautiful."

His mouth was everywhere, his tongue licking her until she thought she might lose her mind. She was gasping for breath. The pressure inside her was building to mammoth proportions. She couldn't bear it a minute longer, but she didn't want it to happen so soon. "Matt, I didn't want to come this fast."

"Stop then. Stop for a minute. Let it ease up then we'll start again. We have hours before the coach is due to stop."

She took a deep but shaken breath and began to lower her skirt.

"No, don't move. Stay like this. I need to see you, to play a little."

"But…"

"I just want to play, sweetheart. I promise I won't do anything but kiss and lick just a bit."

She tried to laugh, but the sound was little more than a croak. "Just kiss and lick? Are you sure?"

He kissed her thigh and groaned as he fought against the need for more, for much more. True to his word, he played with her, daring to lick her but pulling back before anything could come of it. His teasing kept her body strung tight almost humming with need.

After some long, delicious moments, he asked, "Have you calmed down yet?"

"I don't see how I can ever calm down when you keep doing the things you're doing."

He chuckled a low, sexy sound. "All right, perhaps it's best if we finish up."

Kiya could only groan her relief as her fingers came again between her thighs. Seconds later, her breathing grew into sharp jerking pants. She couldn't stop it. His teasing had kept her body tight with need, just a heartbeat short of desperate. It took only a brief moment to bring her seconds from release again. A heavy cramp slid across her abdomen, heavier, hotter, harder than anything she'd ever known before. She wanted, wanted the madness, craved it, strained towards it.

"Matt," she gasped, "Matt, help me." Her body pulsed, trembled then with her weight on the balls of her feet, she lifted her hips from the seat, mindlessly yearning towards him.

Her bodice was undone. His fingers were at her nipples, pulling and twisting the tips just enough to drive her out of her mind. She moaned at the pleasure. Almost there, almost, almost and then she groaned and shuddered as racking, wrenching waves of incredible pleasure came to assault her senses. It tore at her insides. Too much. It was too much. It was killing her. She didn't think she'd make it. More, more, God, could she live through this?

He saw her creamy, sweet cum and licked it into his mouth, feeling her tremors beneath his hot kisses.

"Let me finish it for you," he groaned as his mouth came to replace her fingers. "Easy love," he said against her hot, wet flesh. "Easy…"

He moved his tongue madly over her, drinking in all he could, prolonging the agonising madness beyond insanity. And on and on it went. She thought perhaps she might never stop coming.

"You taste so good. God, I love the way you taste."

"Oh my God," she moaned as the tremors began to ease at last, leaving her to wonder if serious damage hadn't been done. She'd never felt the aching waves so intense, so powerfully strong, so totally engulfing. Her heart pounded wildly, and she couldn't seem to get to the bottom of her breath. "Oh my God," she gasped again, "I think you killed me that time."

He smiled as he moved again to his seat opposite her and brought her with him. "Come here," he said as if she had the will to resist, as if she had any will at all. He sat her upon his exposed erection, and they both groaned at the mind shattering pleasure.

Her senses heightened, she moaned against his neck, "Oh Matt, this feels so good. Doesn't this feel good?"

The lingering aftershocks of her climax pulsated around his sex. God, she was luscious. "Mmm," he murmured, as he pushed deeper into her. "I love you."

She smiled. "Isn't that the most amazing thing?"

"What? That I love you?"

She laughed. "Yes."

"Do you think so? I think the amazing thing is that you were still available when I came on the scene. I can't understand why some horny young buck hadn't caused you to fall in love with him."

"There was no chance of that ever happening. I have no interest in horny young bucks." And then her eyes twinkled with mischief as she said, "Apparently, my tastes run to horny, older men."

He narrowed a threatening gaze. "Are you telling me I'm old?"

"Not at all," she laughed as she fell against him, her breasts sensitive as they brushed against his clothes. "I said older, not old. What I meant was," she moaned again as he began to move into her. "I think it's amazing that of all the people in the world, two people could find one another and love each other this much. Do you think others know this kind of pleasure?"

"I don't think so. You have to love deep to know pleasure this strong."

"Oh, that's lovely," she murmured as he pushed his hips up.

"You like that, do you?"

She smiled into his dark, hungry eyes. "I think you could safely say it's better than cherry pie."

He laughed and tightened his hold on her. "Would you like to ride me, Kiya?"

She looked a bit shocked until the idea took hold and a definite gleam of interest entered her eyes. "Could I?"

"God," he groaned, "I'd take it as a personal favour if you would."

Eager to learn, she did as he asked, while he again found her tiny nub of passion and teased it to madness. His effort was doubly rewarded when she again found her release, and her tight muscles squeezed at his sex, sucked at his aching hardness bringing on bone-melting ecstasy until he helplessly emptied his seed deep into the flaming wet heat of her.

Kiya moaned weakly into his neck while gasping for her every breath. "I need a nap."

Matt chuckled in all arrogance. "This old man wore you out, did he?"

"I just need a minute."

"I'd be exhausted as well if I came three times to your one."

Kiya laughed. "Is that my fault?"

"I'm jealous, is all."

He ran both hands under her skirt, over her smooth, rounded curves, delighting in the soft firmness he found. Moments later, his mouth holding a pink nipple, he reached between them and began to play with her again. "Matt, if you want to see me live beyond this trip home, I think we should take this a bit slower."

"I can't help it. I've waited so long and wanted you for so long, I don't think I'll ever get enough."

"Let me rest a bit first."

"Mmm," he murmured into her neck, breathing in her luscious scent. "Go ahead and take a nap sweetheart. I won't bother you. You won't even know I'm here."

The soft rumbling sound of laughter filled the coach as his hands continued to wander where they pleased and his mouth sucked the tip of her breast again into blazing heat.

"Shush," he soothed. "You'll never go to sleep if you laugh."

"And you expect me to sleep while a lusty beast has his way?"

"What?" he murmured, the word somewhat muffled for his mouth was a bit occupied with a goodly portion of a soft, luscious breast. He pulled back a fraction and amazingly enough managed an innocent look, even as his mouth held its prize. "What am I doing?"

Kiya shook her head, a smile threatening. "You know, I think I've mentioned before that sleep might just be a bit overvalued."

His dark eyes smiled into hers, his teeth flashed white, even as his tongue and the roof of his mouth held fast to her and his fingers began to tease her again into helpless ecstasy.

* * * *

It was a large inn. Matt and Kiya sat at a small table in a corner of the dining room. All around them travellers ate and conversed, creating a low pleasant hum. Babies, tired from the confines of their journey, whined unhappily to be held still in their parents' arms. Children, temporarily freed from their coaches, darted amongst serving girls causing trays of hot fare to teeter dangerously over their heads.

Kiya smiled as she sipped at her ale. "The food smells delicious, does it not?"

Matt smiled in return. "Almost as delicious as you."

"Matt," she said with a small frown and a slight shake of her head as her gaze moved to the nearby tables.

He relented at her obvious censure. "I'm sorry to tease you, sweetheart. The food does smell delicious. If you're tired, I could have it brought upstairs. I was lucky to manage a room. The inn is full to overflowing."

Kiya doubted he'd had any trouble at all. Everyone, upon knowing his station, nearly grovelled before the man and he, having known the same treatment his entire life, took absolutely no notice. She hadn't a doubt they had the best room in the place. Of course, some things were easier than others to take in stride. The fact that they were sure to find themselves alone in a clean bed was indeed one of them, for upon making this trip on her own some few weeks back, Kiya spent more than one night asleep on the floor, rather than join the little creatures making their home upon the pillow and mattress that came with each room.

The food came at last, and Kiya's stomach made a most rude sound as she breathed in the scent of tempting fare. Her gaze narrowed with annoyance while still another bevy of serving girls who, upon realising their guest's station, oh'd and ah'd their way through every meal served. She and Matt been on the road some four days, and Kiya had had enough of it. Most especially, she'd had enough of women bending low before her husband so that he might glimpse their unbound breasts beyond their gaping necklines, while he conversed with a wife who sat opposite him. Apparently, she was supposed to abide such goings on and allow him these illicit glimpses as if it were his due.

The problem here was twofold. One, Kiya was just tired enough to show her objection to the despicable conduct, and two, she'd never cared for the elite in the first place and dared any of them to think watching women bare their breasts was their due.

Matt cut into his roast beef and sighed as a thick piece coated in luscious gravy nearly melted in his mouth. A moment later, to his surprise his wife came suddenly to her feet and moved to his side. She bent low, allowing him yet another glimpse of her sweetness as she moved closer then said with feeling, "Oh Matt, I'm so sorry."

He almost asked her what she was sorry about. In truth, the words were forming when her hand moved, and instantly his hot dinner burned through his trousers as it fell into his lap. He was on his feet in a flash. A few swipes with his napkin saw the food on the floor, and in helpless dismay, he watched the back of his tiny bundle of fury leave the room.

Matt hadn't a clue as to what he'd done, and for just a moment, he wished he had his hands around the little witch's throat. He left orders for dinner to be brought to their room then followed her up the stairs. When he entered the room, She sat in a chair, calmly reading a book she'd bought earlier that day. She didn't glance in his direction nor submit a word of explanation for her actions.

"I've ordered dinner to be served up here, if that's all right with you."

"It is, thank you."

Still nothing. He tried another tactic. "I've come to a conclusion tonight that it's a very good idea for men to wear black trousers."

"Have you?" she asked, offering nothing more in the way of conversation or explanation.

"Do you know why?"

"I know some things but probably not that."

Patricia Pellicane

"Indeed? Do you know why a woman would throw a man's dinner into his lap?"

"I'm sure I couldn't say."

"Couldn't or wouldn't?" he dared to insist.

For the first time since entering the room, Kiya raised her gaze to his and hissed, "I hate you."

She was angry. He knew that much, but he also knew this woman did not hate him. "Do you suppose it would be too much for me to ask why?"

"Why?" she repeated and took a deep breath ready to bombard him with her reasons, but suddenly she asked instead, "What I want to know is how many women have shown you their breasts?"

Matt was absolutely dumbfounded. Her response was so out of place that if he lived another hundred years he wouldn't, nay couldn't, imagine she'd ask such a question. What in the world was she talking about? He didn't know what to say or how to act. She had him tied in knots and he couldn't imagine how she'd done it. "Kiya, I don't—"

"You don't what? You don't know? Don't think? Don't care? Don't wonder? Don't—"

She would have gone on, but Matt suddenly pulled her from the chair and crushed her against him, pressing her face to his chest, so her lips were momentarily stilled.

To his way of thinking, the woman was obviously hysterical. "I don't know why you're upset. I don't know what I did. I swear to God, I don't."

"Let me go," she said, although how she managed she couldn't have said, what with her face squashed against him.

"Will you tell me if I let you go?"

She nodded, having no real choice in the matter. It was that or stay pressed to this man, and she had no interest in standing anywhere near him at the moment.

He let her go, and with a grimace, she rubbed at her nose, wondering if he hadn't broken it.

"Tell me," he said.

She shot him an aggravated glance as she returned to her chair and with a huge sigh said, "Every night we stop for dinner then take a room."

He nodded, wondering where she was going with this.

"And every night, bar none, I've watched women, serving girls, in particular, bend and scrape and bow before you, and every one of them did it while their blouses gaped open for you to see all the way to their waists."

Matt frowned. "Do they?"

"God," she moaned. "Could you possibly be more royal? I've no doubt the highest ranked cannot compare to you. You're a duke in every sense of the word. Have you never noticed you ask for and get the best of everything? Have you ever imagined doing without? Not having the best? Not seeing women and men bow and grovel before you once your station is known to them?"

"Not one of the women in that dinning room knows I'm a duke. They treat all people the same way."

"Hardly," she disagreed with some disgust. "Not one of them bowed before me."

"Is that what you want? Do you want them to bow?"

"Good God, are you deliberately trying to aggravate me? I can't stand watching them do it to you. I don't know what I might do if they treated me the same."

"Then what?" Matt hadn't a clue as to what her problem was.

"Here, let me explain," she said, trying for a control she wasn't fully ready to manage. "Every night, we sit down to eat, and while we are about it, you are, without fail, introduced to a new pair of breasts. Sometimes, if there is more than one server, I'm delighted to watch you enjoy two pairs of breasts, while I sit there trying to swallow my anger along with a mouthful of roast beef." She sighed her disgust. "I don't mind telling you it's becoming something of a trial to keep that anger under control.

I'm just getting a bit sick of it, is all."

Matt grinned and then looked at her, his gaze softening with tenderness. "You're adorable."

"What I am is sick of watching women flaunt themselves at my husband, and if you want to keep this wife, I'd suggest—"

"Done," Matt said, knowing there was no way to manage peace in his life unless he saw her side. "You needn't think of it again."

"In truth? How will you stop it?"

"I will simply ask any lass foolish enough to approach our table that she be so kind as to not bend over, for I have only a set amount of trousers with me and..." He shrugged leaving the sentence unfinished then grinned at her barely restrained laughter.

"How will you really?"

"I could tell them that my wife is not to be trusted near cutlery while a lady dares to display her merchandise."

"Lucky for all, I think, that the idea never occurred to me."

"Indeed," Matt said in agreement. "I could wear a minister's collar when we dine?"

She laughed at that. "And no doubt shock all about with the less than pious things you're apt to say during dinner."

More seriously, he said, "I will merely tell the innkeeper to send us his most virtuous servants. Will that suffice?"

"It should."

"For the sake of my trousers, not to mention the tender parts beneath them, I can only pray it to be so."

* * * *

They were home. The coach pulled at last to a stop, and Kiya was helped from its confines into the arms of her father.

"Thank God. I was so worried," he said.

"I'm sorry to worry you father. I swear nothing like it will happen again."

"So, you're married, are you?"

Matt nodded. "We thought it best since we had a ways to travel."

John Harrison couldn't help but agree as he kissed his daughter and shook hands with his new son-in-law. "All is ready for a blessing of the vows." And then to Matt, he said, "I've word from your mother that she and your brothers will be here tomorrow. Kiya, would you like to freshen up? I could delay dinner a bit."

Kiya nodded. "How have the children faired?"

"They've missed you, I'm sure."

She nodded again. "Let me look in on them then freshen up a bit. I'll be down to dine directly."

She found them in the nursery with Mrs Rochester insisting it was time for Seth's bath. Kiya smiled as Lizzie, dressed in a long sleeping gown, pulled at her skirts. She lifted the girl into her arms and sat in the room's one armchair.

"Have you been a good girl?" she asked a she kissed Lizzie's cheek then inhaled the sweet scent of the child newly come from her bath.

Lizzie, her brown eyes wide, answered with a solemn nod.

"I've brought you a present. I'm happy to hear you were good because only good little girls and boys can have presents. Isn't that right, Mrs. Rochester?"

The nurse smiled. And as she took Seth by the hand guiding him towards his bath, Kiya asked, "Mrs. Rochester, you do allow one of the grooms to sit with Seth while he bathes, do you not?"

"Oh indeed, Duchess, he is never left alone."

Kiya groaned, definitely ill at ease with her new title. "Oh please, you must call me Mrs. Chase. I'd much prefer it."

"Certainly, Duch...Mrs. Chase. If you prefer it, of course."

"And Mrs. Stevens? Is she about?"

"In the kitchen I believe."

"Fine, I'll speak to her later."

Seth soon returned to the nursery, dressed in long johns and a short nightshirt. A half hour passed as Kiya spoke with the children, catching up on what they'd been about while she'd been gone. "And have you practised riding?"

"I have," Seth said, his dark eyes bright with his growing accomplishments. "And Adam says I'm the best he's ever seen. Daisy likes me to rub her down."

Kiya smiled. "I've no doubt. And you do it after every ride, am I right?"

He nodded.

"Good boy," she said. "And what about you, Lizzie? Have you been driving your buggy?"

"Adam says I don't need him to walk by my side anymore. He says I can do it by myself."

"And what about your studies? Have you begun them?" she asked both children, only to grin at Seth's obvious dislike.

Lizzie said, "I can write my numbers to ten."

"Isn't that wonderful?" Kiya cried then hugged and kissed her again. She turned towards Seth and asked, "Is there something you don't like about your studies, Seth?"

"I don't see why I need to know where China is. Why should I care if so many pecks make a bushel?"

"Well," Kiya reasoned, "suppose a man wants to buy a bushel of blueberries from you. But he says a bushel is five pecks. If you believe him, if you didn't know that four pecks is a bushel, then he will cheat you."

"But I don't have any blueberries."

Matt laughed from the doorway. "I think he has a point."

"Don't take his side, Matt."

Seth beamed as Matt came into the room carrying two brown-paper wrapped packages. "I found these in your bags, Kiya. I'm afraid I've quite forgotten who they were meant for. Do you remember?"

Seth had a serious case of hero worship and grinned all the more as Matt sat on the edge of one of the beds and placed the boy on his knee. On Kiya's instructions, he handed Seth his gift while Kiya helped Lizzie open hers.

Kiya smiled as Seth watched her, apparently waiting for permission to open his own gift. "Go ahead. Open it."

Both children were delighted, and Kiya was pleased that she'd thought of them while in the midst of her own wedding purchases. Lizzie cuddled her new doll to her chest, while Seth looked with awe upon a carousel that could, when wound up, turn by itself and play music. He'd never imagined such a thing.

Kiya allowed both children to enjoy their gifts for a moment before she went on with, "And as far as knowing where China is, suppose you want to go there some day. How will you do it, if you don't know where it is?"

"If I want to go to China, I'll tell the captain of a ship to take me there."

Matt laughed again.

Kiya shot him a glare. "You're not helping."

He forced aside his amusement and asked, "Suppose you are the captain of a ship. Won't you need to know then?"

Seth's eyes widened. Obviously, he hadn't thought of that circumstance. "Could I be a captain of a ship someday?"

"Of course, you could," Kiya returned. "You can be anything you want to be. Only, you'll have to learn your numbers. All grown ups know their numbers, and most everyone knows where China is, especially captains of ships."

A few minutes later, with kisses good night, Kiya left the children to play and went to her room to freshen up. She took a soapy cloth and a pitcher of water behind a screen then stripped away her travelling dress and stepped into a tub. Having no time to take a leisurely bath, she soaped her body then rinsed off the suds. When she came from behind the screen, wrapped in a linen towelling, she smiled to find Matt gathering pillows behind his back and making himself comfortable as he stretched out on her bed.

"Are you tired?" he asked.

"No. Why?"

"I thought we might have dinner in your room then you wouldn't have to dress."

Kiya laughed. "And you thought that all by yourself, did you?"

Matt grinned. "Brilliant of me, don't you think?"

She laughed again as she dropped her towel and pulled a thin chemise over her head. Her skin was still damp so she had a time of it smoothing the material over her hips.

Matt couldn't deny his disappointment as he watched her dismiss his words and dress. "I take it you don't agree."

"Actually, I think you're terribly brilliant and your thoughts quite amazing. It's just that I haven't seen my family in more than two weeks, nearly three actually. Of course, I could claim exhaustion soon after dinner. After all, I have been travelling. Suppose we have dessert in bed. Have you an objection to me feeding you grapes with a bit of wine?" She pulled her dress in place and buttoned the bodice. She glanced in her mirror to make a few quick adjustments to her hair then turned to face him, unable to hold back her grin at his obviously interested look as he came towards her.

"You mean you'll feed me grapes because I'm a duke?"

"I'll feed you grapes because I love you and you're my husband. I try to ignore the duke part as much as possible."

Matt laughed. "But you will dress the way I like you dressed?"

She smiled. "You did promise me the necklace to match my ring, and if I remember correctly..."

"God," he groaned as he pulled her against him, for he remembered quite clearly how he'd asked her to wear the necklace. "Don't move," he said as he quit the room.

A moment later, he returned with a large, black velvet box in hand. "You need to wear this tonight."

"Matt, it's lovely," she said as she turned her back so he could secure it at her throat.

Through the mirror, she watched his tanned hands brush against her throat as the emerald and diamond necklace settled into place. "It's beautiful," she said, delighting in the gold set with diamonds and small emeralds and a very large single emerald that dropped from an intricate gold extension at its centre, almost to her cleavage. She loved it and said as much. "How did you get it? I mean when did you…"

"I sent one of my men for it. My mother knew which one I wanted."

She frowned. "Which one? Does that mean you've more?"

"A trinket or two." He dismissed the subject with a shrug.

"A trinket or two," she repeated in disbelief. "No doubt."

"Will you fault me on this, Kiya? I wasted no money and saw no women bow before me. These were very simply my grandmother's."

Kiya kissed him then promised, "I have something for you as well, but I'm giving it to you after dinner."

"What is it?"

She shook her head and smiled.

"Will I like it?"

"I have every hope that you'll love it."

"I can tell you right now that I will," he said suggestively.

"Oh I'll give you that, too."

"What?" he asked, as she dropped a quick kiss to his jaw and opened her bedroom door, leaving him momentarily behind, with a puzzled frown wondering what his lady had in mind.

Chapter Thirteen

The walls and floor were of stone and mortar, allowing nothing in the way of comfort or warmth. Katie Goodman huddled naked into a corner of the dungeon-like room, dazed with pain. Her body trembled and jerked uncontrollably with the chamber's chill, added to the memory of a degree of torture she'd never known to exist.

She'd never before imagined that a body could live through the horrors she'd come to know. Every night, she prayed for death and every morning, to her acute disappointment, found herself awakening to face yet another day of horror. The two who came to her were brutal in their ministrations. Their obvious delight in her pain knew no bounds. Indeed, the more she cried out the longer they played their games. They found her moans, her cries, her pleading uproariously entertaining, and they laughed aloud as they took turns abusing her body.

Once they appeared, the two would set upon her like rabid dogs for hours. Katie had never been with a man before this impossible horror and hadn't imagined any could maintain this lust, this hideous need that lasted hours at a time. Somehow they seemed never to tire, to never know satisfaction. Indeed they appeared, even to a girl of no experience, to be in some sort of competition as to which one could last the longest. Never did they say a word. All she ever knew above the silence was the horrid sounds of their laughter, their excited breathing, the putrid stench of stale breath and sexual sweat.

She sat huddled on the cold floor with her chin upon her knees, her arms around her legs, hugging them tightly against her. Shivering, she tried as best she could to hold the meagre warmth she knew tightly within. Idly, she wondered how much a body could live through in the way of abuse and wasn't happy to realise, lest she took ill from the constant chill, she could probably go on like this for years. With silent tears streaming over rounded cheeks, she found herself begging the Almighty to end her suffering soon and in any way he chose.

She dozed in fitful slumber and never realised the two familiar figures once again slipped silently into the room. One moment she was alone, the next her two leather-masked tormenters stood naked before her. The shorter one reached for her hair and pulled her to stand before them. Without a word spoken he shoved her beneath the two hooks that protruded from the low ceiling beam. Her arms were raised. He was just ready to attach the chain on one wrist to the hook above when a knock sounded on the thick wooden door. "Sorry sir, but you have a visitor," came the timid voice of one of the servants.

"Who is it?"

"It's the constable, sir. He insists he must speak with you."

"Fuck," the man before her growled as he moved away. "Tell him I'll be along directly." As he spoke, he gave Katie a shove, leaving her forgotten as she fell upon the stone floor. She lay there perfectly still, fearing to move an inch, as the man above her muttered, "What the hell does he want?"

He left the room ready to see to the visitor. In his anxiousness to hurry and dress, for the first time, he did not remember to lock the door.

Katie moaned. There wasn't a place on her body that didn't hurt, most especially her legs for she'd fallen forward, but her feet were still spread apart, held in place by...by Katie couldn't remember what it was that held her. She wasn't sure she'd ever thought to look.

She did then. She looked to her right and then her left. A rope around her ankles connected each to a metal circle embedded into the stone floor. Could she untie the rope? Dare she? Katie laughed aloud at her thoughts. What might they do to her that they hadn't already done? The only thing left was to kill her, and she couldn't find it within her to care if that happened. Indeed were she forced to choose between future tortures or certain death she'd gladly welcome the latter.

It took her some time, but she finally managed to untie her feet then groaned at the exquisite pleasure of bringing her legs together. A moment later, she staggered towards the door. It opened silently on well-oiled hinges. She knew only shock. Had it always been left unlocked? Had she simply been too battered too horrified to think about escape? Had they known the shock to her mental abilities? Had they realised her mind was easily as battered as was her body and therefore never bothered to lock her in? She prayed it hadn't always been so, for she'd suffered some many weeks and might have made good an escape if she'd known the door was not locked. Outside, a door stood to her left. Straight ahead was a long hallway. At the end of the dark hall a small light shone. Beyond that light was another door.

Katie tried the closest first. It was a small changing room that held nothing but two chairs and hooks from which were suspended whips and leather masks. She moved down the hall and tried that door, again marvelling at the fact that it was open as well.

She moved on silent feet into a tiny brick room that held a dozen mops, brooms and pails. The sight brought her a measure of hope. A utility room had to mean she was close to the kitchen. She prayed for it to be so. If it were, she'd be sure to find a door that led outside.

She was barefoot and naked. She couldn't have cared less. She had to get out of here. It didn't matter who saw what. It only mattered that she find her way home again.

She opened the door ahead and gasped to find a man standing there. A tall man with blonde, almost white hair. She tried to slam the door again, but he quickly jammed his body forward hitting her and pushing her hard into the brick wall. Katie screamed reflexively, for she wasn't afraid. There wasn't anything this man could do to her that would cause her to know fear, nothing except perhaps to drag her back to the horrifying room she'd just left.

"Help," she screamed then suddenly abruptly stopped as a knife plunged into her throat. He'd killed her. Her eyes bulged with the horror of knowing she was about to die, but even knowing her end was near Katie suddenly found the strength to fight back. She hadn't been able to do it before. Two grown men against one young girl always bound, drugged, or asleep, she'd been an easy target. Now it didn't matter. She was dying. What more could he do? She hated this scum and wasn't about to leave this life without returning at least a tiny piece of her own justice.

She swung a fist hoping to hit his throat as the knife sank again into her body. This time it slipped from his hand to clatter to the floor while her blood pumped over the two of them. They stood in a puddle of it. Just as she swung at him, his foot slipped and he stumbled just enough for her blow to miss its target and land instead on his arm. To her surprise he cried out in pain.

He slipped and fell back, his good arm reaching for the pain in the other. She ran by him into the kitchen. Katie dashed to her right towards a door. In a flash she was outside, gone into the night.

* * * *

In the main part of the house, just inside the front door, Shelby explained that yes, he not only knew the man, but Mr Connery was his guest.

The constable nodded, "Well, if you're sure, my lord, I'll leave him in your care." He then added, "I'd suggest in the future that he'd be more careful. Trying to climb your wall is bound to cause any a second glance."

Shelby nodded and shrugged, "The gatekeeper sleeps like the dead."

The sheriff knew that for a fact. It had taken almost fifteen minutes of nearly hysterical barking dogs before the man had managed to stumbled from his bed.

The earl smiled. "Thank you, Sheriff. I know I'll sleep better tonight just knowing you patrol the roads of this county."

The sheriff smiled at the compliment and smiled yet again as the earl slipped several pound notes into his hand and said, "For all your trouble."

The sheriff gave the earl a short bow. "Thank you sir and good night to you," he said as he turned towards the door.

Moments later, Shelby stood alone in the hall wondering what had kept Connery so late. He found him a minute later at the kitchen table, covered with blood. "What the hell happened?"

"She got away."

"What? How could—"

"I don't know how. I cut her pretty bad. Still I saw her dash over the back wall."

Shelby muttered a stream of curses. "The sheriff's at the front door while she runs out the back? Jesus!"

"I stabbed her a number of times, but the bitch wouldn't go down."

Shelby nodded. A moment later he shrugged. "It doesn't matter. It's dark. There's little chance of her finding help. And if she does no one will ever trace her back to us. We'll find another. What kept you so long?"

Connery grinned as he remembered the little package he'd left outside. "I've brought you another one. This one's a little young, but I didn't think you'd mind."

"How young?" Shelby asked, not really caring, for age made little difference.

Connery shrugged. "Maybe twelve."

Shelby figured maybe ten considering Connery's evil grin. "Use the back gate to bring her in and tell Menkens to let the dogs loose again after you do."

* * * *

It took her some time to find her way. Katie never knew of the dogs' existence. Even had she known, even had they currently prowled the property, Katie would still have made the attempt. Anything even death was preferable to the suffering she'd endured. There was a wall to climb. Quite a high wall actually. Still Katie figured it would have had to be a mountain before it gave her pause.

With the help of a few thick vines, she soon left the mansion and its protective stone structure behind. She held tightly to her wounded throat and ran as fast as she was able. She never noticed the cool night air against her body. She never felt the dozen or more sharp stones cut into her feet, the hundred stickers and sharp twigs that scratched at her legs.

It took less than half an hour, and she was pounding on the door to her family's mercantile. She was gathered in her father's cloak and hauled instantly across the road to the physician. She was covered in her own blood, but thankfully, most of the bleeding had eased, for miraculously no arteries or major veins had been cut. A few quick stitches saw the wound closed.

Outside the earl's mansion, just beyond the back stone walls and small gate, Susie Tenor lay unconscious in the woods. She was nine years old and had left her house an hour or so after her family had gone to bed. Susie needed to use the outhouse. The small wooden structure stood barely ten feet from her back door.

Tonight, she left the outhouse, quietly closed the door behind her and to her amazement found hulking hard arms close silently around her. She'd screamed in terror, for he instantly had her arms bound at her sides. She meant to call out to her father for help, but her cry was cut short as a fist slammed into the side of her face. Susie knew nothing as a man carried her away from her sleeping family.

She lay in the woods on a thick bed of leaves. It was dark. Above her, she could see the stars. She shivered with the cold for she wore only her everyday chemise and wondered how she had fallen asleep outside. She'd never done it before. She tried to sit up and found her arms bound to her sides, by a thick rope that wrapped around her from shoulders to knees. For a moment, she couldn't understand what had happened. She couldn't remember. Then she did.

Wide-eyed, Susie looked around her. She was alone. Her heart thundered in her chest. She didn't know where she was. She only knew someone had taken her from her home.

A horse trotted nearby, perhaps only twenty feet away. Desperate for help, she tried to call out. It was only when she heard her own voice muffled and low that she realised something was tied around her face, preventing her cries.

Susie struggled to her feet. She was tied to her knees, but the bottoms of her legs were free. She ran, even knowing she had nothing to protect her should she take a fall. She didn't care. She had to get back. With every step she took, the possibility of returning home grew stronger.

The moon shone bright, but deep in the woods, it wasn't bright enough to prevent her from running into an occasional tree. She fell a number of times but managed to scramble to her feet again and again. She didn't care. Her head was bleeding, her legs and feet as well, but Susie would have gladly suffered a hundred wounds, a thousand, if it meant she'd get back home again.

She reached the dark, quiet village. It was scary. Her family lived on a small farm north of here, well beyond the cobbler who owned the last building in town. She longed to reach her own home but dared go no further. She needed help. She needed it desperately. The man who'd taken her might come upon her at any moment, for she stood far from the protection of the woods and totally exposed to any who might pass by.

The first building in town was the church. No one would be there at this time of night. She ran next door to the parsonage. She couldn't knock. She couldn't call out. With her back to the door, she kicked it with her heel until she heard Reverend Simmons on the other side.

"Who's there?"

Susie's muffled response was hardly worth the effort. She thought her head might explode from the pressure in that scream.

He never heard her. Again, he called out, "Who's there?"

All Susie could do was kick the door again. She continued kicking until the preacher gave up asking and, with a heavy stick in hand, finally opened the door.

* * * *

Kiya laughed as she came from her bath and wrapped herself in linen towelling. A mischievous twinkle in her eye, she only hoped she had the courage to go through with her plans. Never before had she even thought to do something so wicked. Quickly, she pulled his gift from its box and slipped it beneath her pillow.

A knock sounded at her door.

"Who's there," she asked, her voice low and far more suggestive than she realised.

"Kiya, it's me. Why is the door locked?"

"Are you alone?"

"So far. I won't be if I have to stand here much longer," he returned.

She opened the door and posed herself dramatically with one hand on her hip and the other palm open as if displaying an object at her side. Only Matt never even glanced towards her side. He gasped then in a low voice croaked a shocked, "Jesus!"

Quickly, he stepped inside and closed the door behind him.

She heard the lock turn, as he leaned against the door. She grinned at his frozen expression and shook her head. "Sorry, it's just me."

"What?" he asked, obviously a bit dazed at this unexpected, glorious vision.

"It's not Jesus. It's just me."

He tried to smile, but for some reason, he couldn't get his mouth to work. All he managed was a jerking muscle in his cheek.

"What are you..." he began and never noticed that his words dwindled down to silence.

"A man told me once that he liked the obvious, so I thought I'd give him some."

This brought a huge grin. "And I take it you're under the impression that a naked woman is obvious."

She shrugged. The movement caused her breasts to sway. God, he loved it.

"A man told me once that a naked lady is exactly that."

"Brilliant of him, I'd say."

She ignored his comment and went on with, "And that he'd like it should a naked lady happen to answer his knock."

Matt groaned. "I think I remember him saying something like that."

Kiya smiled. "You look a bit dazed. Could it be you're somewhat partial to naked ladies?"

"Most men are."

"So, I wouldn't be exaggerating if I said you look as if you love it."

"You're right. I do love it."

"Of course, I have only your word for that."

"And you'd be wanting something more than words, I take it?"

"Oh words are very good, but they are better if accompanied by actions."

"Is this my present?"

"Part of it."

"I can tell you right now, I don't need anything more. You are every man's dream."

"But I have wine and grapes."

"Do you? I don't see them."

"You could if you blinked then looked towards the bed."

"If I were looking at the bed, I'd have to stop looking at you, and I was hoping you might have hidden them on you."

"Did you?" she laughed softly. "As you can see there's no place I could have hidden them."

"Are you sure?"

"Very sure."

"Why don't you come over here so I can see for myself?"

"I could do that, I suppose, but we might never reach the bed if I do."

"We'll get there," he promised. "Eventually."

She moved closer. "I don't mind telling you that I'm not all that comfortable standing here naked while you're fully dressed. My mind is far too clear, not having been kissed and all."

"What? You mean to say you're naked?"

"Possibly it's too dark in here."

"It's perfect. You're perfect. Come over here."

She did as he asked, even as she asked, "Why? What do you want?"

"I want you and anything you can do to me. But right now I was thinking of those grapes and the wine you promised. I'm sure you have them on you somewhere."

Kiya grinned. "I love this necklace."

"I like the way the emerald lays between these," he said as he nudged the giving flesh a bit. "But I should have bought you something new. Something that would cover a bit less of you."

"It only covers my neck."

"But I love your neck. With all this glitter, I'll never be able to kiss it the way I want."

"Hmm, you know that does sound interesting. Did I ever tell you how much I enjoy neck kissing?"

"Do you?

She nodded. "Very much. It was one of the first things you did to me. Do you remember?"

"I remember you telling me you enjoyed my kisses more than cherry pie."

"Did I say more? What I meant was at least as much."

Matt laughed. "I suppose I should be happy with 'at least as much'."

"If you knew how much I love cherry pie, you'd be more than satisfied."

"Oh I expect to be satisfied, sweetheart. I expect we'll both be *more than* satisfied." He laughed at the way her brows rose and fell in quick succession and asked, "Are you tired?"

"No. Why?"

"I thought you might like to take my clothes off if you weren't tired."

"You thought that did you?" she asked as she started to untie his cravat. "And is there a reason why you can't do it yourself?"

"Oh usually I can do it myself, but what has happened is I've sort of sprained my wrists and…"

"How?" she asked

"Ah, yeah, how. I was just going to tell you how."

"You mean, after you think of something?"

He shot her a stern look. "I should know how I strained my wrist, Kiya."

"I love you. Do you know that?"

"You'll never make me believe anything else. Not after the way you opened the door."

Matt's hands held to her breasts, his thumbs teasing the nipples to hard nubs, as she tried to pull his arms from his sleeves.

She looked at him then his hands. "Something is going to have to give here."

"I know. I'll let go in a second."

"Why don't you do this…let go with this hand," she nodded towards his left, "and I'll pull your sleeve down." He did as she asked then immediately sought out her breast again. "And now, you can let go of the other." His jacket joined his cravat on the floor. He still wore his shirt and trousers and Kiya thought she was probably going about this all wrong. Instead of trying to undress him, she merely slid her hands under his shirt. "You're so warm God, I love the way you feel."

She grinned as he nearly tore his shirt in an effort to get it off, then laughed as she fell against his chest. She seductively rubbed her chest to his. "You're so easy."

"I know," he returned helplessly.

"Does this feel good?" she asked as she rubbed herself over him, delighting in the feel of his chest hair against her.

He held his arms wide, not daring to touch her, lest she stop. "Damn, I couldn't stand it if it felt better."

"I know."

"I wish I could tell you how much I love this. I wish you could rub these all over my whole body. I want to use them for a pillow. I want to lick them, bite them, suck them." His eyes closed, and his head fell back against the door. "I don't think I'll ever get enough."

"I think we should move to the bed."

Matt hadn't the strength to argue. She took his hand, and he followed her to the bed. Once there, he pushed down his trousers and was delighted beyond measure to see Kiya turn and with his foot between her legs began to pull his boot off.

With one booted foot, he pushed at her naked rear to help her along. Once that was done, she pulled the leg of his trousers off and then took the next boot between her legs. Matt had a better idea considering her present position. He brought his foot all the way back towards the bed until he was able to capture her hips in his hands. Naked, she stood with his leg between hers, her back to him and allowed him the most delicious investigation of her pussy. "God, I love this," she said as she felt herself grow moist and then wet, heavy with need for more of his luscious ministrations.

"I think we should have taken your boot off first." Her delight was obvious as she struggled with her words. "Now, I don't see how we'll ever get it off you." She knew from past experience that she'd be too tired to do more than yawn once they were done.

What boot? He didn't care and for just a moment he couldn't think what she meant. His pulse thudded thick in his throat, causing his words to slur. "Bend over a little more."

Kiya did as he asked even as she muttered weakly, "You are so…wicked… Oh my God, Matt. What are you…?"

With one arm around her waist to steady her, he pushed three fingers into her soft wet pussy and finger-fucked her with maddening speed. Her knees almost instantly gave way. Suspended by his one arm, she was helpless but to cry out her pleasure. She couldn't stand; there was no way she could keep her balance. She trembled after finding almost instant release, then his hands were at her hips, lifting her over his body, so his tongue might reach her pussy.

On her knees, she knelt over him, his mouth where they both wanted it most, Kiya's laugh grew somewhat strangled as she asked, "Do you think we might have accomplished this position by simpler means?"

He only moaned for an answer, his mouth otherwise occupied. Enthralled with his magic, her body humming with the pleasure, she leaned down, reaching for his cock, and they both moaned as she took the satiny length of him deep into the heat of her mouth.

Sometime later, she moaned as he shoved her shoulder.

"You'll have to stay that way," she murmured sleepily. "I haven't the strength to take my hair out of my eyes never mind take off your boot."

"I'll look pretty ridiculous if there's a fire and I have to limp down the stairs with one boot on and the other leg bare while my trousers trail behind."

Kiya laughed at the picture his words brought to mind. "You could always slide your leg back into your trousers. You'll only have one boot on, but your trousers will be in place."

"That sounds fine to someone who doesn't wear trousers. But for your information, it's not easy getting my leg back into them now that it's out."

Kiya chuckled into her pillow. "I'm not moving from here, so you might as well stop begging."

"Begging? Me? I think we both know who does all the begging around here."

"Do we?"

"Of course.

"And what might his name be?"

"Her name might be Kiya."

"Go away."

"Oh, so now that you've finished using my body, you find no further need of me?"

"I'll need you again later. Don't go far."

Matt chuckled, knowing the truth of that statement. He'd never imagined a woman so hungry for his loving, and the more they came together, the hungrier she grew. "The problem is I can't go anywhere. I've only got one boot on."

"Oh my God, no doubt I'll not get a minute's rest unless I accede to your wishes. I mean, after all, you are a duke and no doubt have someone specially hired just to take off your boots."

Matt grinned as he watched her roll from the bed and pull off his boot. Suddenly, she stopped all movement as asked, "You don't, do you?"

"Don't what?"

"Have someone just to take off your boots."

He grinned at her question, knowing the meaning behind it. Knowing she wasn't the least bit happy that he might have someone to see to his every whim. "Other dukes might, but I think that kind of thing is more the duty of a wife." Grunting a few unintelligible words, she flung the boot across the room. A second later, she was again on the bed, her face pressed deep into her pillow.

Matt shook off his trouser leg and turned to her, his gaze moving over her naked form. She lay on her stomach, her arms under her pillow. He couldn't resist the soft flesh that plumped deliciously from the sides of her chest. "I love you."

"Matt, give me ten, will you?"

"Ten minutes?"

"Hours," she returned, her voice muffled as she spoke into her pillow.

Matt laughed as he moved closer, his hand siding down the length of her to settle deliciously between her legs and enjoy the warm, moist flesh he found there. He wondered if there'd ever come a day when he'd have enough. "I think from now on I'll be a little less generous. Just about every time, you manage to come three times to my one."

"I don't mange it. That's just the way it works out."

"That's just the way it works out because I make it work out that way. And to what end? To find you too tired? I think from now on I'll be a bit more selfish. It wouldn't hurt to leave you wanting some."

Kiya turned to her side and grinned. "No, you won't."

"Won't I?"

"I think you like to watch me almost as much as I like what you do to me."

"You might be right," he laughed. Faced with the lady, Matt found no reason to resist her lovely attributes and sought out one sweet, warm nipple, twisting it gently until it hardened to a stiff bud of pleasure. She made a soft sound and moved just enough to allow him to bestow this pleasure with equal fascination upon the other breast.

"I also think you have a valid point. I think you deserve a reward for your efforts."

"Do you? What kind of a reward?"

"I was thinking we should try something."

"What?"

"Well, I really love what you're doing, but you'd need to stand at the side of the bed."

"Would I? Why?"

"Because then I'd be able to reach everything I need to reach."

"Should I do it now?"

"I think you wouldn't be sorry if you did."

Matt eagerly acceded to her request, and Kiya came to her knees. "You need to come closer. I can't reach you from here."

He moved obediently forward, his knees butting against the mattress.

Kiya began at his mouth, teasing it with light airy kisses as she asked, "Would you like me to give you your wedding gift now?"

Patricia Pellicane

His eyes were closed as he awaited the coming pleasure. "Mmm," he moaned, unconsciously jutting his hips forward just a bit. "Yes. I'd love it now."

Kiya reached beneath her pillow and pulled out what she'd bought him—a gold watch and chain that he would wear in his vest pocket. She'd earlier secured the chain to itself, creating a small circle. As she kissed his neck and chest, she slid the chain over his erection then burst out laughing as she spied the watch hanging between his legs. In a fit of giggles, she fell back upon the bed. "I would have hung it around your neck, but the chain wasn't long enough."

"What did you..." It took Matt a moment to clear the lust from his mind and realise what his wife was about. He felt the cold hard metal against him and looked down. "What is it?"

"Your gift. Weren't we just talking about the wedding gift I was giving you?"

His brow furrowed in confusion, "But I thought..."

"Yes, you thought I'd make love to you, and I'm certainly going to do that, but I wanted to give this to you first."

He grinned as he reached for her gift. "Should I always wear it there?"

"You could, but you'll have a problem checking the time if you do, especially if you're out in public."

"But every time I checked it, I'd think of you."

"You'll think of me anyway," she said in all confidence. "Open it."

Matt held the watch in his hands as he sat at her side and examined it closely. "It's beautiful, Kiya. How did you? We haven't been apart for more than a minute in days. Where did you get it?"

"I bought it when I went to buy my books and you went to send another message to father."

The workmanship was extraordinary, the scrolling over the lid the most beautiful he'd ever seen. He could tell by the weight of it, it had cost her a fortune. "This had to cost a pretty penny."

Kiya hadn't taken much with her. It had taken all the ready cash she'd had plus she'd found it necessary to add her much-loved pearl necklace to defray the cost. Still, the look of pure amazement in his eyes was worth any amount. She shrugged for an answer.

"I never expected anything."

"Isn't it usual for a bride to give her husband a wedding gift?"

"I suppose, but..."

She laughed at his dumbfounded expression. "You're staring at it as if it's your one and only. Has no one ever given you a gift before?"

He shook his head.

"Matt, be serious. Of course, someone must have given you a gift."

He looked at her for a long moment before he said, "My mother, I suppose."

Kiya shot him a look that clearly told of her disbelief.

"I'm a duke. Dukes give gifts. No one has ever given me anything."

"Well, we won't have any more of that, will we? Everyone needs a gift, now and then."

He grinned then flipped open the watch. His gaze took in the inscription. Kiya watched as his look of amazement grew into a smile which soon became a grin and then a laugh as he read:

More than cherry pie.

"I told you you'd think of me, every time you opened it."

"You're right about that, but you said before, not more but at least as much as."

"I know. I lied." She moved towards him. "Lay back, I need to do something."

He looked at her for a long moment, the love he knew never more evident. "Are you going to make love to me now?"

"I've been thinking on it. You said before that you wished I could rub myself over your whole body. I thought we might try that first."

Matt swallowed, finding it harder than usual to breathe. "Where should we put my new watch while you're at it?"

She only laughed for an answer as she held out her hand. They both knew where she would put it.

Chapter Fourteen

A coach made its way up the long drive to the Harrison's mansion, accompanied by three large men on horseback. The men looked in varying degrees much like the Duke of Stratford. The driver pulled his vehicle to a stop, and two young liveried and wigged footmen jumped from the back to open the door and lower the steps.

A woman who appeared to be nearing forty, but in truth was closer to fifty, was handed down into her son's welcoming arms. Kiya was surprised to see the tiny lady, a woman smaller than herself and as dark as Kiya was blonde. She flashed a smile — the very same smile that had more than once convinced Kiya to see to her husband's way of things — as she hugged her son then hit his arm as she said something Kiya couldn't hear.

Matt laughed and grabbed the woman in a crushing bear hug and gave her a quick dizzying spin before depositing her suddenly before his bride. Steadying her a bit, he said,

"Mother, I'd like you to meet your new daughter, The Duchess of Stratford."

"You big bully," the lady managed amid helpless laughter before she turned towards the newest addition to her family. "I hope you don't let this hoodlum intimidate you."

Kiya laughed, liking the lady on sight. With a short curtsey acknowledging his mother and her station, she replied with a sharp look shot in her husband's direction, "Not likely."

Matt groaned, looking slightly uncertain and more than a bit concerned as he suddenly realised the two had instantly formed a bond of sorts. He knew right then he was sure to find himself no stronger champions or tougher critics. "Have I made a mistake? Should I have kept the two of you apart?"

The two women laughed at his dismal expression then hugged as if they were long lost friends.

The moment his mother had been introduced to Kiya's father and sisters, Matt turned and boxed a few quick mock rounds with his brothers while all four boasted they could take each other with one hand behind his back until the last and smallest insisted, two hands and one leg behind his back.

The four laughed at the last remark as their mother groaned in despair. "You mustn't pay my boys any mind, Mr. Harrison. I swear there's not a lick of sense amongst all four. Except for Matt choosing your lovely daughter, I declare I'm at my wit's end with these ruffians."

Amy's eyes rounded with awe as the rich sound of male laughter filled the courtyard, and once again, the youngster found herself madly in love, but this time, she couldn't decide which of the handsome three had stolen her heart.

"You certainly have beautiful children, Mr. Harrison," Madelyn Chase remarked as her host ushered her inside the huge house.

"Thank you, Duchess. I've my wife to thank for that, I'm afraid. Please, call me John."

"Nonsense, I'd submit all three ladies look much like their father," the duchess acknowledged. And as she took in the house, the richly appointed scrolled ceilings, the polished wood panelling, the marble floors, the Chippendale chairs with tables to match that adorned the wide foyer, she went on with, "And you've a lovely home as well."

"Thank you, Duchess. I hope you'll be comfortable during your stay."

Their voices lowered as they drifted deeper into the house. "Madelyn, please, and I'm sure I shall."

Matt, with his arm around Kiya's waist, pulled her closer to his side and spoke softly near her ear. "Did you see that?"

Kiya grinned. "She's a sweet lady, Matt. You're so lucky to have her."

He nodded. "I'm thinking your father most especially agrees with you."

She laughed as she realised his meaning, for the older couple stood quite a bit closer than might be expected, their expressions clearly revealing their interest, their attention solely on one another. "Wouldn't that be something?"

The three men followed them into the drawing room. and Matt said, "Let me introduce my brothers, Luke, Mark and Jack."

It took only a second for Kiya's eyes to widen. "Jack as in John?"

The young man smiled and nodded.

"As in the gospels?"

All four men laughed aloud, and Matt returned with, "Our mother had high hopes, I'd say."

"And was doomed for disappointment, I'm afraid," the duchess remarked as a smile danced around her mouth and her dark eyes softened with affection. "Not a clergyman amongst the brood."

Kiya might have thought that was odd indeed, for with every family, the oldest always inherited whether titled or not, while the younger male siblings often went into the militia or the clergy, but in this case, Kiya remembered Matt mentioning his brothers were in shipping as each of them owned multiple merchant ships.

Minutes after their entrance, all four women sat on the settee and two arm chairs while the men brought more chairs from separate groupings throughout the room. Two trays were wheeled into the room, each loaded with teapots, cups and dishes, scones, jellies and a variety of small cakes, while a third tray held glasses, an array of liquors in crystal decanters and a pitcher of water.

Merry, as the oldest daughter presided over tea, with her proud husband hovering nearby, while Matt and two of his brothers indulged in a small glass of brandy along with their tea as all quickly caught up on family news.

Over the next half hour as Kiya was welcomed into her new family, she came to know what it was to be teased by brothers.

"Of course if I would have seen her first," Luke said with a teasing grin and Mark quickly interjected, "Or I."

Matt shot both brothers dark, threatening looks. "I promise you it wouldn't have mattered."

All three brothers grinned, knowing the truth of those words by the soft looks exchanged between Kiya and Matt.

* * * *

"You know the Turner place?"

"I do," Kiya returned as she continued folding delicate silk undergarments and placing each in the trunk at her feet. "Matt, I wish you'd tell me where we're going. How can I know what to pack?" It was three days before the celebration and blessing of their vows, and she'd barely begun to pack. Granted, they wouldn't be leaving for a honeymoon immediately, but they would within a week or so, and Kiya was the type of woman who, when able, planned things down to the last detail.

"You're not going to need much in the way of clothes." He picked up an almost transparent nightdress and matching robe and flung it to the other side of the bed. "And you won't be needing this at all."

"Leave that alone." Kiya frowned and slapped his hand. She reached across the pile of clothes and pulled the nightdress back.

"I expect we'll be leaving the bedroom on occasion." She laughed at his ogling look and insisted, "We will if there's a fire."

"You won't be wearing that if there's a fire."

"Matt," she groaned in warning.

"All right, pack for warm weather," he said as his hand reached under her skirt and began to slide up her leg.

Kiya laughed and shook him away. "Stop, God, you are so bad."

"And I've every intention of showing you just how bad I can be, but for now, what do you know about the Turner place?"

"The Turner place," Kiya repeated. "Let's see. It's been empty for years."

Matt nodded. "I understand the house is in dire need of repair, the property overgrown, but it's just come on the market at a very reasonable price. The heirs are suddenly in a hurry to get rid of it."

"All this time and now they're in a hurry?"

Matt nodded. "I heard there was a problem finding them. They live in America, I think. I thought we might take a look at it. It sits almost exactly between Jake's place and your father's, probably a half hour from either one. I thought you might like living close to them — at least for most of the year."

"Most of the year? Where else would we live?"

"At my estate."

She was slightly taken aback. What in the world had she been thinking that she hadn't thought of it until now? He was a lord of the realm, a duke. Of course, he'd have an estate. "Where is it?"

"About two days ride northwest of here. It's quite large."

Kiya frowned, knowing Matt to be a master of understatement. If he said large, she could only imagine huge. "How large is quite large?"

He shook his head. "We don't have to live there but for a few months total of every year. Perhaps the summer months and a week here and there. You'll like the summers there I think. There's a lake to swim or fish, if you've a mind, and miles of trails to ride."

"How large, Matt?"

He shrugged and looked distinctly ill at ease when he mumbled, "You said you were once at court."

It took her a moment before she realised his meaning. She gasped, "Oh my God, we'll never find each other."

He shook his head in the negative. "It's probably not that big."

"You grew up there?"

He nodded.

"How big was your room, say in comparison to mine?" Kiya figured she'd get a more accurate idea of the size of the place if she knew at least that much.

Matt frowned. "I didn't have a room exactly. It was a little more than that. More like a small group of rooms."

"Good Lord," she groaned and then shook her head as she sat hard upon the bed. "What does that mean, a group of rooms?"

Matt figured she might as well know the whole of it. "It means a bedroom, a dressing room, a smaller room where my servant slept—"

"You had your own servant?" she interrupted, her eyes wide. She'd never known anyone who had their own personal servant. "He worked only for you?"

Matt didn't comment on that, but instead went on. "It also has a room to hold my clothes, another for bathing and a small kitchen and eating area."

"You have your own kitchen and dining room? In your bedroom?" This was worse than she'd thought. "Why? Did you have something special made if you didn't like what your mother…" She was going to say if he didn't like what your mother served, but realised his mother, being a duchess, wouldn't have served anything and, as a duke, he probably was offered everything and anything a young man might desire. All she managed was another far more sickly, "Why?"

Matt shrugged. "All the apartments have one."

"And we have to live there?"

Matt shook his head in the negative. "We don't have to live there, but we do need to be in residence now and then."

"Oh my God. Be in residence. Do you realise you sound just like a member of the royal family?"

"Kiya, I have tenants who are forever looking for me to settle one dispute or another. There are acres of land where sheep graze, others we farm, a racing stable to maintain. Someone has to look after it all."

"And you've no manager?"

"I do. Mr. Pennyworth is very efficient and does an excellent job of running things, but it's still my responsibility to oversee it all."

"Do you have liveried servants at every door?" she asked, almost afraid of his answer.

Matt shrugged. He'd forgotten about that. Having grown up with them, he never really noticed or given them a thought.

"You do," Kiya groaned. "This is a catastrophe!"

"They're not at every door, only some of the main rooms. You'll get used to it."

She shook her head. "I won't. I'm sure I won't."

Matt figured she didn't have much of a choice. Actually, she had no choice. Still, he thought he would let the subject rest for the time being. "All right, back to the Turner place. Would you like to look at it tomorrow?"

Kiya nodded, obviously far from happy. She didn't look his way.

"We'll ask Jake and Merry to go with us and we'll have a picnic. Would you like that?"

She shook her head, her thoughts on his style of living. "Matt, you're so much more…" She shook her head again. "I mean, I never thought…" She looked up, taking in yet never realising his troubled gaze that easily matched her own. "You should have married someone closer to your own station."

"I should have and did marry the lady I love. Station doesn't matter. If I owned the security firm and only that, would you love me more? Would you love me less?"

She shook her head. "Of course not."

"Then why is my money so important?"

"It's not the money. It's the way you live, the way you've always lived and how you take that lifestyle for granted. I'll never get used to having young men open doors for me every time I want to enter a room."

"If we spend summers there, if you invited your family to join us, we could make every stay a holiday."

"Suppose your brothers want to visit."

He nodded. "There's more than enough room."

Kiya merely closed her eyes and groaned unhappily as she imagined the size of the place.

Matt laughed as he pulled her to sit on his lap. "It's not as bad as all that. I promise you it's not."

"Does your mother live there alone?"

"She'll move into the dowager house, now that I've married."

Kiya shot him a sharp glance. "From a palace to a mere house, and how big is that?"

"It's about the same size as your father's."

Kiya sighed. "I see now why no one ever gave you a gift. How many gold watches do you have?"

"None like yours."

"Matt, you already have everything there is. I'll never be able to buy you—"

"Until I found you, I had nothing at all."

"And you never would have had me had I an idea of who you really are."

He shook his head, disagreeing. "Yes, I would have. Never believe anything would have stopped me. Once I saw you, having you was a forgone conclusion."

* * * *

Kiya craned her neck trying to see the top floor of the Turner place. The mansion was larger than she'd remembered. The building itself was of Tudor design and three stories tall, almost entirely covered with ivy. The property boasted of acres of woodland, plus huge lawns both front and back and a cobblestone circular drive. A formal garden complete with Romanesque benches and statuary surrounding a murky pond stood just outside the library doors. The stables were in shambles, as was a good part of the house. The conservatory was roofless, most of its windows broken, and the detached summer kitchen was in appalling disrepair. The house and all its outer buildings would need some concentrated effort to restore it to the showplace it had once been.

While the men first inspected the outer building, Kiya and Merry took in the spacious home—the three drawing rooms that opened one upon the other to create a space of mammoth proportions, the billiard room, library, a huge dining room she imagined would seat nearly a hundred guests, the pantries, kitchen, the butler and maid's sitting rooms, the ballroom and gallery. The bedroom suites were on the second floor. The nurseries, governess and maid's quarters were on the third.

The house was at least twice the size of her father's and his was large enough.

The two men caught up to their wives on the second floor. "I'd say the size of this place should satisfy you," Kiya remarked. "I counted five bedroom suites, besides the master bedroom."

Matt grinned. "How many children do you want?"

"Why? Are you looking to fill them up?"

"You might say that. Actually, I thought it couldn't hurt if two or more shared each one."

Jake laughed at Kiya's shocked expression.

"Two or more?" she asked, clearly shaken at the very thought of having ten to fifteen children. She took a deep breath. "Why don't we leave that up to God. Whatever he gives us should be just fine."

After two hours of looking into every nook and cranny the mansion had to offer, the four sat in a circle of sorts on a large blanket, enjoying their picnic lunch. "What do you think, Merry? Is it big enough?" Kiya asked, the sarcasm in her voice clearly evident.

"It could be wonderful. I particularly love the fireplaces especially those in the smaller rooms and the wood. Everywhere you look you see beautiful wooden walls and doors and they can only grow more so with a little care. Don't you agree?"

"Kiya has a problem with houses — with most things in fact — that are ostentatious."

"Do you think it's too big?" her sister asked.

Kiya only shrugged for an answer.

"It's a lovely place, Kiya. You'll make it into a beautiful home."

"She doesn't like it," Matt concluded, not at all happy with the thought.

Merry frowned. "Why?"

"It's hard to explain," Kiya said.

"Here, let me try and do it for you," Matt offered. "As it turns out my wife is a bit prejudiced against the rich. And she's only recently realised that as a duchess she'd be part of the elite. And the elite being very well off hardly fills her with delight."

"Well off," Kiya mocked. "I'd say it's a bit more than that. And I'm not in the least prejudiced. It's going to take some time to get used to things is all."

"I think it doesn't matter how much or little a person owns. It's far more important that everyone treats each other with respect and consideration," Merry offered.

Matt turned to Kiya and said, "Your sister has it right."

Kiya smiled. Her sister was so sweet. Kiya thought, except for their mother she'd never known a more gentle soul. "I know, but the simple truth is most of the wealthy don't treat others with respect and consideration."

"The good ones do," Merry returned. "The others we don't need to associate with."

Matt and Kiya looked at each other. Kiya smiled at his hopeful expression. Soon enough, her smile became a grin then a laugh. "You win. I think I shall be very happy here."

"A wise decision, Duchess," Matt said then sipped at his drink.

Kiya frowned at his address, and to the amusement of all, she explained on a dismal sigh, "He only calls me that to aggravate me."

* * * *

About five miles from London a man entered the Boar Inn. It was dark inside and smelled of body odour, rancid grease and stale whiskey. Years of smoky fires had left the unwashed ceiling black with soot. The floors fared hardly any better, and rather than wash them as needed, sawdust was simply thrown over the filthy surface.

The sign outside read Inn, which spoke of food and rooms to rent, when in truth the place was little more than a dilapidated hovel that boasted cheap liquor and cheaper women, mostly unkempt and a step beyond ugly. Here was a place where the disreputable gathered to indulge, whether it be in drink, cards or the flesh — if man were brave enough or desperate enough to visit the rooms upstairs.

The man who entered on this day was desperate indeed but for matters that had less to do with the flesh than with his empty pockets. He was average looking. His clothes, having seen better days, were in dire need of washing. Still he fit into his surroundings well enough. He was a stranger to these parts, but not to Jim Willis.

Tony Edwards and Jim Willis had been cellmates for a short spell in their youth. They had once been detained on minor charges by a country constable some miles north of London and spent two uncomfortable nights awaiting a magistrate's hearing. The small cell had been hardly big enough for one. Their stay had been brought to an abrupt end when a far more dangerous criminal had needed accommodations. The two had been set free with a warning to leave the area — an order which they were happy indeed to obey.

The two men hadn't stayed in touch, and though the years of overindulgence in drink had somewhat altered their features, each immediately recognised the other.

They sat together and nursed tankards of ale as Edwards blubbered his sorry tale. His children had been taken, and the bitch that had done the dastardly deed was an uppity sort who thought her money and power were enough to take from him his own kin. He'd tracked the shrew to this area. Her name was Harrison. He wasn't sure how, but he was going to get the little bastards back. He could hardly keep a roof over his head or a bottle on his table without them. If he could kill the cow at the same time, so much the better.

As the two spoke of old times and their brief acquaintance back then, the waitress was ordered to bring yet another tankard. The two never bothered to lower their voices, especially Edwards for his hatred of Kiya and her man was almost more then he could bear. The other man, however, noticed that the waitress took in every word.

* * * *

Kiya sat in her father's library, a frown marring her lovely features as Matt's solicitor, Gerald Parker Esquire, spoke in the most monotone, expressionless manner about the death of the man at her side. Every so often, she shot that very man a look of desperation only to see a grin for a response. Finally, unable to bear another moment, she interrupted.

"I'm so sorry to interrupt, Mr. Parker, but please, might I have a moment with my husband?"

"Of course, Duchess. I'll be right outside. Call me when you're ready to continue."

Kiya waited for the door to close behind the solicitor before she said, "What in the world is this about? What are you doing?"

"I though that was clear, Kiya. I've had papers drawn up declaring your personal properties to be yours unequivocally, as well as the house and surrounding properties, my wedding present to you. Should I die, you'll also receive a portion of the jewels and an annual amount to see to your care. Should we have an heir, all other properties and funds would be held in trust until he is old enough to inherit. If not, my brother — "

"Oh my God, do we have to talk about this?" Kiya moaned.

Matt smiled at her obvious distress. "Do you believe talking about it might cause my imminent demise?"

"Matt," she shivered.

He smiled as he gathered her to him and sat, placing her upon his lap.

"Matt, please, I don't want to..." She spoke against the warmth of his throat, her arms around his neck.

"Nothing will happen. I promise you won't be rid of me so easily."

She only moaned her response.

"Come on. Let's see one of your ravishing smiles."

Her smiled was a bit peaked. Still it was a smile, of sorts. "I know I'm acting like a fool, but I truly cannot listen to this." She took a deep ragged breath and managed, "I've only just discovered that I love you, and now, we're discussing the most godawful circumstances."

"I need to know you'll be cared for, Kiya. It will take only a few more minutes." With his finger beneath her chin, he forced her gaze to his. "I did promise to sign papers that you might keep your property, did I not?"

She nodded.

"That's part of it."

"What about the house and property?"

"I told you. It's my wedding present to you."

"Oh that's fair, isn't it? I bought you a gold watch and you bought me a house."

"Are we in competition? Are you trying for repayment in kind here?"

Kiya just shook her head. "Hardly that, Matthew. I could never compete with a man of your means."

"Good, allow me that at least."

"What do you mean?"

"I mean, you're the prize. I was lucky enough to find you. I want to give you everything."

She shook her head. "But I don't want everything. This marriage was supposed to be equal, remember?"

"Do you mean to say I can't give you a gift unless you're able to buy it yourself?"

"No," she shook her head. "I suppose…I'm just a little confused. I never thought things would get so out of control. I never thought my husband would actually give me a house."

"If it makes you feel any better, you can give it to our first daughter." He shrugged. "Or our second son or our third or our—" His laughter effectively cut off his ability to go on, especially when accompanied with one of Kiya's killing looks. "What?"

"How many children are we having?"

"Well, I think we've already mentioned the possibility of ten or fifteen. Why don't we compromise with twelve?"

"If I remember correctly, *we* did not mention it at all. You did."

"And you said whatever God would allow. In this instance, I believe in the adage, 'God helps those who help themselves'. What else would we do with all those rooms?"

"There are only five."

"Yes but each suite is big enough for two or three beds."

"Lord, help us," she groaned.

"I fully intend to. How else could we have twelve babies if I don't?"

"Beast, I was referring to the heavenly kind."

A knock sounded at the library door, and Matt called out, "Enter."

Beauchamp, the family butler entered and, upon seeing the young couple so familiarly displayed, dropped his gaze and said, "There's a woman to see you, my Lord."

Kiya came from Matt's lap and touched a hand to her hair smoothing already smooth curls. "Show her in Beauchamp, and thank you."

"If you don't mind, I've asked her to wait in the kitchen. She looks to be a servant of some kind."

Matt shrugged and followed the butler from the room with Kiya behind him.

The woman who waited for them was unknown to either Matt or Kiya, and upon entering the room, Matt nodded at her curtsey. "How can I help you, madam?"

Sally Brady shook her head. "No sir, I've come to tell you and your lady something." She looked around the room at the half-dozen kitchen helpers taking orders from cook as the huge woman prepared dinner. "Could we find a place where we could talk, sir?"

"Of course," Matt returned then he and Kiya led the way to the nearest sitting room. Once inside, he showed the woman to a chair. Kiya sat across from her, Matt to Kiya's side.

"Would you care for something?" he asked, "A drink, perhaps?"

"Oh, no, thank you, sir. I'm sorry to bother you, but something 'appened at work, and I thought you should know. I work at the Boar Inn."

Matt frowned, and Sally realised he thought she worked upstairs. "In the barroom, I serve in the barroom."

He nodded and waited for her to go on.

"Last night, a man came in. I never saw 'im before, but 'e soon took up with one of our regulars. Jimmy 'is name is."

Matt nodded again and said, "Go on."

"Well, this man, the stranger was very angry. 'e was a talking about a lady from these parts. Said 'e tracked 'er to this area. Said the lady took 'is children — "

Kiya gasped. "No!"

"Said 'er name was Harrison."

Matt's entire countenance stiffened before he managed again, "Go on."

"Said 'e'd like to kill the... Well, 'e called 'er some bad names."

"I'm sure he did."

"Did he say how, or what his plans were?"

"No, sir. 'e was drinkin' and kept repeatin' over and over that 'e needed 'is kids."

"What's your name?"

"Sally, sir. Sally Brady."

"Well, Sally, I've an offer for you. Of course, I'll be rewarding you for your efforts, but if I could ask a favour,

I'd be eternally grateful and would certainly make it worth your while."

"Anything, sir."

"If the man should return, I'd ask you to get word to me immediately."

"I will, sir."

"And after you do, I'd ask you to come to work for my wife and myself. We'll be taking the old Turner place once it's put to rights. We'll be needing help to keep it in good order. What I was thinking, in particular, was we'll need someone to take charge of the kitchen girls and their serving. Would you be interested in the position?"

"Oh, I would, sir. Thank you."

"Of course, it would mean more responsibilities, but you would be earning quite a bit more than you do now. I take it you wouldn't mind."

Sally laughed. "No sir, I wouldn't mind. Thank you, sir and thank you, missus."

"Have you a boy on hand, Sally? Someone who could come for me if the man shows again?"

Sally shook her head. There was no one. By the time, she got a chance to go for help, the man might be long gone.

Matt nodded. "That's all right, Sally. I'll put one of my men in the barroom. He'll go for help when you tell him."

He loaned Sally a horse and asked one of his men to accompany her back to the inn. Once there, the man was to settle himself discreetly in a corner of the barroom, blend as best he could into his surroundings and wait for Edwards to show himself.

As the two left the Harrison estate and turned north towards the Boar Inn, Kiya remarked, "He must be desperate to come here."

"You took his livelihood from him. I thought to throw a scare into the bastard, but like you said, he's desperate. And desperate men are dangerous."

"No more than myself."

Matt grinned and responded to her comment with a nod. "I've no doubt about that. I, for one, wouldn't want to go up against you."

Kiya shook her head, dismissing his remark. "That's because you love me."

"No, it's because you scare me, especially when in one of your tempers."

"Matt," she sighed, "this is hardly the time to talk nonsense. I'm afraid. What if—"

"He won't. I promise you, he won't. I'll have the men take extra care. He won't be taking them. I promise."

With his arm around her waist, they re-entered the house. "Matt, do you think it's him? Do you think he's behind the murders?"

"It would be convenient if he was, but I don't think so."

Kiya shot him a questioning look.

"First of all, he's only just arrived in the neighbourhood." At her puzzled look he explained, "Remember he said he'd tracked a lady to these parts. Said her name was Harrison. Everyone around here knows this place and you. The man we're looking for knows the area well and has been here for some time. Secondly, Edwards might be able to murder a woman, but he hasn't the place or time to do the things that were done to them. He'd need privacy. The women weren't murdered where they were found. Their screams would have carried."

Kiya shivered.

"Don't be afraid. Nothing is going to happen to you. Just promise me you'll be careful."

Kiya nodded.

"And as far as Edwards goes, we'll get him. I can promise you that."

Chapter Fifteen

"I told ya. Didn't I tell ya? She 'eard us and told the bastards."

Two men stood some few feet into the woods, blending unnoticed into their shadowy surroundings. From their concealed position, they could see the drive to the Harrison estate between thickly leaved branches. They watched with pinched, angry lips and muttered promises of retribution as the woman in question rode from the mansion towards the Boar Inn with a man at her side.

"Fuck! They sent a bloke to watch 'er."

"Take it easy. It don't matter none what she said or who's wit 'er. Nobody stays on guard all day every day. We got all the time in the world. You'll get the little bastards back all right. In the meantime, I've got plans for that bitch."

Edwards shot his colleague a glance then laughed aloud. "What are we going to do?"

"First, we'll have ourselves a bit of fun then I'll hand 'er off to someone who will take care a 'er for good."

* * * *

"They found another body."

Kiya turned from her mirror and frowned as she saw the grim set of Matt's mouth. "Oh my God, who was it this time?"

Matt shook his head and gave a helpless shrug. "No one can say. She was dressed as a servant, but no one has been reported missing. She was badly beaten. Unrecognisable in fact. It's possible someone was trying to hide her identity."

Kiya frowned. "Beaten?" She couldn't remember hearing the same about the others. "But the others —"

"No. This one is different. It doesn't look as if she's been abused, except of course for her face. All her clothes were left in place. The doctor said she was strangled and appears to have been beaten after she died."

Kiya shivered at the horror of it. "Lord, maybe it wasn't the same man."

"Jesus, I don't want to think there are two murderers in these parts. Let's hope it was." His eyes widened with pleasure as he noticed her dress. "God, you look gorgeous."

Kiya smiled and teased, "Thank you. It's just a little something I found in the back of my closet."

Matt chuckled. "Did you? Are you sure you never wanted to marry?"

"Why?"

"It seems odd that a woman, who never wanted to marry, would keep a wedding gown in the back of her closet." He eyed the lace veiling draped over the bed and reiterated with, "A gown and veil."

Kiya hit his arm. "Matt, it was my mother's. Merry wore this exact dress barely a month ago. Don't you remember?"

Matt knew some surprise. He remembered Merry looking very pretty in something white on her wedding day, but she hadn't look anything like this. There wasn't a doubt in his mind that the woman he loved obviously occupied his thoughts to the exclusion of all others. "I remember she was wearing something white."

"Oh my God. How could you not remember?"

Matt gave her a blank look and a helpless shrug.

"Why in the world would a woman dress for a man? They don't see a thing," she muttered in some disgust.

"It's best when women don't—or at least my woman doesn't—dress at all."

Kiya ignored his remark as she ran her fingers over the creamy silk, pearl-trimmed garment. "It is beautiful, isn't it?"

"It is, but not as beautiful as you."

Kiya gave a sudden gasp. "What are you doing here? It's bad luck for you to see me before the wedding?"

"It might be I suppose, except we're not getting married. We're having our vows blessed. And I saw you this morning. If I remember correctly, I saw quite a bit of you this morning."

Kiya giggled at his ogling as she unconsciously smoothed her hand over his already flat lapels. "You are such a beast."

"Don't call me names. It makes me hot."

"Everything makes you hot. Go away. I need to finish dressing." Despite her words of warning, he reached for her, but before he could pulled her securely into his arms, she fussed, "Matt, I'm about to grow angry. If you wrinkle me, I'll be upset. You don't want to upset your bride, do you?"

"A quick kiss and I'll leave you be."

Kiya smiled and leaned forward, raising herself to her toes to meet his descending mouth. She moaned a soft sound of pleasure, and just as her heart stumbled and thickened into a heavy throb, he tore away his mouth and forced himself to move towards the door. "I'd better get out of here, or we'll have to delay the ceremony a few hours."

Kiya giggled.

"Oh, I meant to tell you, your sister is waiting outside."

Kiya rolled her eyes towards the heavens. "Tell her to come in."

* * * *

As with Merry's wedding, the festivities were held outdoors. The tables, if possible, were piled higher than ever with every kind of food and confection imaginable. No one would leave the festivities without rubbing their painful stomachs and cursing their gluttony. More tables were added as a seemingly endless stream of guests arrived. Kiya thought she'd never seen so many in one place before. The townsfolk were again invited, and the rich and mighty mingled easily with the poorest souls over barrels of ale, bowls of wine punch and pitchers of lemonade. Kiya watched her husband's relatives, friends and acquaintances mingle easily with barkeeps and parsons, coopers and smithies without a shred of disrespect shown on either side.

"Are you enjoying yourself?" Matt asked. It was a rare moment when he found her alone, for she'd been constantly surrounded by relatives or friends and well wishers since they'd returned from the church.

Kiya nodded and smiled. "Did you see the Prime Minister and his entourage arrive?"

"I did. Robert Jenkinson and my father were great friends. Come along, I'll introduce you."

Kiya knew no little amazement as The Earl of Liverpool and his friends—many of them also lords of the realm—bowed before her, even as they warmly and sincerely wished the loving couple lifelong happiness.

The festivities promised to continue long into the night, at least as long as the ale continued to flow, and it was hours before Kiya and Matt managed a rare moment to be alone. "I like your friends."

"Do you? Are you aware half of them are titled?"

"I know. That's what makes it all so amazing." Kiya shook her head. "Where were they when I was at court? I swear there wasn't one who—"

Matt interrupted her coming tirade. "Apparently you met a different breed. If I'd have known you were there, I would have sent in a few of these folks. It might have saved me a pack of trouble."

She smiled. "Would you have done that?"

"I would have done anything to shine in your eyes."

Her eyes widened. "What? From the first?"

He nodded. "From the first. How didn't you see it? I was besotted with one glance."

She shook her head. "I was too young, too inexperienced. I think you were too dark, too big, too much of a man for my taste. I could barely look you in the eye."

He chuckled.

She poked his chest. "I didn't know it then, but I think you were too full of yourself."

Matt laughed. "It's as I thought. You were afraid."

Her back stiffened at what she considered an affront to her character. "I never said I was afraid. I was leery is all. I'd never met a man like you before."

Matt smiled as his arm loosely circled her waist and allowed her to lean back thereby causing their hips to briefly brush together. He groaned at the momentary contact but managed to keep a respectable distance from her. "Thank God for rain storms or I might have never brought you under my spell. God, you were so skittish. I could barely get you to answer a question."

"Thank God for cabins," Kiya added.

"Mmm," Matt agreed with a teasing leer. "Most especially for cabins."

Kiya burst out laughing at the fire suddenly glowing in his eyes.

"What?"

"Stop thinking about it. I'm not going upstairs with you."

"I'm afraid I'm always thinking about it. I just manage to do the things I must while I'm thinking of it."

"You do not," she said in disbelief.

Matt's laugh clearly spoke of her innocence in the ways of men.

"You do? Do all men?"

"I'm afraid they do, darling."

"Oh Lord," she groaned, "I'm sure I could have gone quite happily through my entire life and never known that. Thank you very much. Now I'll be thinking that they are thinking... Dear me, I'm sure my cheeks will be stained red forever."

"You look delicious with red cheeks. Shall we step inside where I can show you other parts of you that look equally delicious while red?"

"Be good, Matthew," she said exactly as she might to one of the children.

Matt laughed. "If I were good, we wouldn't be married."

"Just be good for the next few hours. I want to enjoy my wedding party." She looked to her left and spied Sally Brady filling her plate. "Did you see Sally and her beau?"

"They make a lovely couple."

Kiya laughed and snapped her finger before his face. "Wake up. You're eyes are still glazed. And you didn't hear a word I said."

"I did. You said Sally and her beau are here. Sally who?"

"Matt," she admonished. "Sally, the woman who was here yesterday." She looked at him, waiting for recognition, then offered, "The one who works at the Boar Inn."

"Oh, yes. Is she here?"

Kiya breathed a despairing sigh and dropped the subject. "Have you seen Seth and Lizzie?"

"I saw Nurse Rochester with them a few minutes ago."

Kiya nodded. "I didn't have the heart to make them stay upstairs. Poor little things were so anxious to join the party."

Matt knew she worried for their safety, especially since their father was looking for them. "I wouldn't worry. Mrs. Stevens and Nurse Rochester are taking turns watching over them."

As it turned out, Kiya had every reason to worry. Somehow, the two caretakers had gotten their signals mixed, and each for the length of about twenty minutes, thought the other had the children with her. During that time, Seth made for his favourite place, the barn, with his sister trailing behind. Inside the dim enclosure, the smells of horse, hay and earth mingled pleasantly.

Seth went to Daisy's stall and, petting his nose as the horse looked over the low door, he offered a small treat taken from the pastry table. The horse quickly disposed of the broken piece of cherry pie and licked the boy's hand free of crumbs. Seth laughed at the feel of Daisy's huge tongue on his palm. Too late, Lizzie thought her little pony deserved a snack. She was just about to turn and run back to the party when heavy hands grabbed both children at their shoulders.

"Not a word out of you, little bastards." In an instant, he grabbed a chunk of their hair. He pulled hard, causing both a painful gasp. "If you know what's good for you, you'll keep your traps shut and listen to your da," he said as he dragged both by their hair into the back of the barn where none could see if passing the huge open doors.

"What?" Seth asked his voice trembling. "What do you want?"

Tony Edwards smiled at the boy's tremors. He was terrified. And terrified was exactly how he wanted the boy. "Happy I found you, I take it."

Lizzie whimpered.

Edwards looked down at the five year old. "Shut up girl, or feel the back of me hand."

Lizzie knew better than to disobey. She forced aside any need to cry aloud. Her body trembled as she waited for him to go on.

"You like it here, girl?"

Lizzie nodded, or tried to since his hand held her hair, preventing any real movement.

"And you, boy? Do you like it here?"

Seth nodded. In doing so, his entire body nodded along with his head.

"And you want to stay here? You don't miss your dear old da?"

Edwards laughed at the two, knowing at a glance they were afraid to speak the truth.

"All right, so you want to stay, fine, but I want something for letting you stay." He waited ten seconds for each to understand his words, and when they were smiling again, he released their hair and said, "Bring me something from the house. I want something every day. I don't care what. A piece of silver, a spoon, a vase, a trinket. Something. Only don't let anyone see you take it. You can leave it in the back of the barn, outside by the woods. Do it, and I'll let you stay. You understand me?"

Eyes wide with terror, both children nodded.

"One more thing, if you tell your new mum, I'll have to kill her. I might not want to, but I'll have to do it. And if I kill her, it will be your fault. And if she's dead, you'll be back with me. No one else wants you."

Moments later, he disappeared amongst the bales of stored hay at the back of the barn then moved through the small door that led to the woods. The two children ran for the doorway. Lizzie fell and allowed her tears to escape at last.

It was then that Mrs. Stevens found them. "Oh my, I've been looking everywhere. Where did you go?"

She wiped Lizzie's tears with her hankie as Seth said, "I brought Daisy a treat. We were only gone for a minute."

Mrs. Stevens felt almost faint with relief and fought to control the desperate need to gasp for each breath. She couldn't imagine going to the duchess with the news that her charges were missing. Thank God, she'd found them unharmed. She looked Lizzie over. The child had fallen but there were no open wounds.

"Are you all right?" she asked as she smoothed the hair of both children into place.

Lizzie nodded as she brushed her hands together, shaking off the hay that clung to her.

"Your mother said you might stay up late tonight. But you must promise me you'll never leave the party again. Terrible things could happen to young children if they're not being watched."

Both children nodded, each all too aware of what could happen if they weren't being watched. The children did as she asked, even knowing their lives were about to change yet again.

* * * *

"Mummy wants us here. She wants us to stay. I don't want to leave."

The room was dark; the children were in their beds. "I don't either," Seth whispered in return. "But what else can we do? If we tell on him, he'll hurt mummy, and if we steal, we'll go to prison."

"Tell Matt. He'll know what to do."

Seth was the first one to think Matt was everything good, powerful and strong, but he didn't think even Matt could help them now. Now that their da knew where they were, no one could help them.

"If I tell him, he might fight with Da. Suppose he gets hurt. It would be our fault." Seth shook his head, unwilling to chance it. "I'll bring Da something tomorrow, something every day next week. After that, maybe we can think of something."

* * * *

The party finally dwindled down. Perhaps an hour before dawn, near the house, the gardens were brightly lit with torches. Deeper into the gardens, the footpaths grew less distinct while shadowy alcoves protected an occasional lover from sight as he dared to steal a kiss. Upon these footpaths, John Harrison walked with Matt's mother at his side. "I was wondering, if you've nothing pressing at the moment, if you'd like to lengthen your stay a bit."

"That would be very nice, John, thank you. I think I shall. I rarely see my son these days and will probably see him even less now that he's married. And your beautiful daughter... I'd very much enjoy getting to know her."

"And your host, Madelyn? Could he hope that you might wish to know him better?"

She shot him a quick tantalising smile. "Word has it he's a bit of a rascal."

John laughed with some surprise that she might have heard such talk. "Is that right?"

"What have you to say on the matter?" she asked.

"I suppose some might believe it so, but you must concur, an eligible man is often the brunt of ridiculous tales."

"And you profess them to be ridiculous?"

"Exaggerated at best. And you have neatly avoided answering my question."

She bit her bottom lip and looked up to his shadowy gaze. To John amazement, she smiled shyly just as if she were a young girl. "I confess I'm not adverse to the thought."

John laughed aloud in relief. "Have you anyone, in particular, waiting for you at home?"

Madelyn smiled and shook her head. "There is no one."

"Indeed, madam, that's hard to believe. I would have thought a woman as lovely as you would have many admirers."

Madelyn laughed. "Thank you, but I never said I have no admirers, simply no one in particular."

"Are you teasing me?"

She laughed as she tapped his arm with her closed fan. "Perhaps, just a little, John."

The lady quite stole his breath with an entrancing combination of shyness and sophistication. John wondered if he'd ever known another half so lovely. She looked a good ten years younger than her actual age. In the moonlight, she appeared even younger than that. Despite his short acquaintance with the lady, he already knew her to be witty and charming, a woman with a delightful sense of humour. He could hardly wait to know her better, most particularly, if possible, to know her in the biblical sense. "I must tell you I look forward to many days spent in your company."

"And perhaps at the end of each day another delightful walk in your lovely gardens, John?"

He took her hand from his arm and brought it to his mouth. His lips lingered against her skin longer than they should have. John knew immeasurable relief as she smiled, and he found it impossible to hold back an answering grin. "Indeed, madam, I can hardly wait."

* * * *

"Something is wrong," Kiya said as she and Matt walked towards the barn.

"What do you mean?"

"I mean Seth. He's not his usual self."

"Kiya, he's six. Do you know how a six year old acts?"

"For one thing, they don't look terrified at every encounter. At least, he didn't until the party. And they don't start crying every time I talk to them." She nodded as if confirming a fact to herself. "No, something is definitely wrong."

"Perhaps he thinks now that you're married he won't be welcome to stay with us."

"I told him he's always going to stay with us."

"Maybe it will take some time before he can believe. Would you like me to talk to him?"

"Oh, would you? I truly don't know what more I can say. He's acting so nervous and jittery. He never laughs. He hasn't been finishing his meals."

"I'll see what I can do, sweetheart."

At the barn's doorway, he put down a picnic basket as Kiya asked the two children inside, "Is there anyone in here who would like to ride today?"

Seth and Lizzie were both brushing down their pets. Seth looked up, and even in the dim light of the barn, Kiya could see something was wrong. He tried to smile, tried to act like he always did, but he couldn't quite meet her gaze. He merely nodded for an answer.

"We could have a picnic. Would you like that?"

Lizzie laughed with joy and did a quick spin. "Bloody hell would, Mummy."

Matt grinned as he moved past his bride and stepped into the barn. "You might consider some extra time spent on Lizzie's conversational skills, Mrs. Stevens."

"Indeed, your lordship, we've been working on it. I've no doubt that we'll soon have it under control."

"Cook packed us a giant basket full of goodies," Kiya remarked as she eyed the basket Matt had left at her feet. "She won't be happy unless we bring it back empty. Do you think we could eat it all?"

"We could, Mummy, we could," Lizzie exclaimed, her enthusiasm knowing no bounds. "Seth could eat everything we don't finish."

"Could you, Seth?" Kiya asked.

Seth shrugged. He'd never known such guilt. All around him people laughed, but he only wanted to cry. His new mum gave him everything he'd ever wanted, and he was stealing from her. Early this morning just as he had for the last three, he'd taken a silver spoon from his tray and hidden it under his shirt. Once in the barn, he'd slipped easily outside for just a second and left it near the barn's back door.

Every day, he left something, and every day, whatever he'd left the day before was gone. He couldn't keep taking spoons and forks. Before long, someone would notice and ask where they were. What would he tell them? Would he lie and say 'I don't know'. He would. Of course, he would, for to tell the truth could only lead to something even worse.

They stopped the buggy at a small meadow after following a narrow path about a half mile into the thick woods. Beside the meadow, a stream bubbled noisily as it rushed on by. After eating their fill, Matt and Seth sat on rocks at the water's edge and fished. Seth looked up at Matt in awe. Matt had given him his own fishing pole. Never in his life had he imagined he'd one day have a fishing pole.

Their lines slipped down the stream perhaps ten feet from where they sat, pushed by the rushing water. They sat side by side, while Kiya and Lizzie wandered off a bit under the watchful eye of their guards to collect an assortment of wildflowers. Lizzie said she thought they should give the bouquet to Cook because Cook gave them a treat with a hug every time they went into the kitchen.

Kiya smiled as the little girl went on about the best treats ever and watched Matt as he began a conversation with Seth.

"Do you know that I'm your father now?"

Seth nodded. "You married mummy."

"Do you know that now that I'm your father you can tell me if you have a problem?"

Seth shrugged for an answer.

"Have you got a problem, Seth? If you tell me what it is, I'm sure I can help you."

Seth sighed, his gaze upon the moving water before him. Silently, he shook his head. His new father couldn't help him. No one could. And if he told, mummy would be killed and Matt might get hurt. He shook his head again.

"It doesn't matter, Seth. I don't care what it is. We'll take care of it. We'll take care of you."

"I ain't got any problem." Seth dared a quick guilty glance towards the man at his side. "I ain't."

Matt sighed. Kiya was right. Something was wrong, but if Seth wouldn't tell him, there was little he could do. "All right. I won't press you now, but I want you to remember one thing. You're part of my family now. You're always going to be part of it."

Seth shuddered as emotion swept over him. He was only a little kid. He didn't know what to do. Tears gathered and slid silently over his cheeks. He wanted to tell. He wanted to tell so badly, but he couldn't. It took a moment, and with a deep shuddering breath, he pushed the matter aside and asked, "Should I call you Da?"

Matt smiled and ruffled his son's hair. "Whatever you like. You can call me Da or Matt or father. It's your choice."

Seth shook his head. "I don't like Da. I'll call you Dad."

Matt smiled. It would take a little time, but he hadn't a doubt that he'd soon find the root of Seth's problem. That the boy had a problem could not be denied.

Kiya and Lizzie braided long pieces of grass and flowers together forming a crown for Lizzie's pretty hair. "Do you like it here, Lizzie?"

The girl nodded. "Oh I do, I really do," she said enthusiastically and gave her mother a smile that twisted Kiya's heart. One front tooth was missing. Kiya thought she'd never look sweeter.

"What do you like about it?"

"Lots of things. I like the food, the soft bed, my toys. I don't like a bath so much or naps, but I like learning my numbers. And most of all, I like you and Mrs. Stevens."

Kiya smiled. "You wouldn't think of leaving me, would you?"

"I wouldn't want to," she said, her childish exuberance waning.

"But you might have to?"

Lizzie shrugged. "I don't know. I really don't want to go, but Seth says…" Her voice trailed off to silence.

"What? What did Seth say?"

"I can't tell you. It's a secret."

"But you can. Now that I'm your mother, you can tell me anything. That's what people do when they're part of a family. And you're part of my family."

Lizzie shook her head. "I can't tell anyone. He said he'd kill you if I told."

"Me? Who said that?"

No response. At the suddenly thick silence, Kiya felt a chill of foreboding race down her back. She cleared her throat and forced any trembling from her voice. "You know, Lizzie, now that Matt is your father, I think—"

Lizzie shook her head and interrupted her mother. "Seth said Matt might get hurt. We can't tell him either."

* * * *

Matt entered the room and sighed. "I can't get him to open up."

Kiya nodded. "Lizzie is the same. Except that she said she loves it here and doesn't want to leave. Apparently, she's afraid she might have to. There is a secret. Someone threatened to kill me if she told."

"What? Kill you? And she didn't say who?"

Kiya shook her head. "She's very afraid."

"Jesus, I wish I knew what the hell is going on."

"Seth won't tell you because he's afraid you might get hurt." Kiya breathed a sigh. "I think only one man could have frightened them this badly."

Matt nodded in agreement. "He's here."

"I think so."

"We'll have to be extra cautious. I'll let the men know."

"He spoke to them, Matt. I don't know how, but I can't imagine what else could frighten them like this."

"How did he do it? Someone is always with them." He cursed. "I'm going to talk to Mrs. Stevens."

"Wait! Let me do it. We won't get any information out of the woman if you scare her to death."

"I'm going with you."

She shot him a look of warning.

"I won't say anything." And when she continued to look at him, he said, "I promise. All right?"

* * * *

"Is there a problem, duch…I mean, Mrs. Chase?"

Matt might have smiled. If the situation weren't so terrifying, he would have even as he wondered when his wife would grow used to her title.

"I hope not, Mrs. Stevens, but I'm not entirely sure. The children have been acting oddly of late. Wouldn't you agree?"

"Yes, a bit, but they're children. It's usual for children to act strangely most any time."

"I understand, but I think it's more than acting a bit strange. I think they are afraid."

"Good Lord, afraid? Why?"

"That's what I wanted to talk to you about."

"Do you mean to say I'm making them afraid? Are they afraid of me?"

"No, no, not you." Kiya shook her head. "Not you at all. But something is frightening them. Do you remember if they were left alone at any time recently? Most particularly while outside. Have you run off to the kitchen for just a second or perhaps left them to speak with one of the servants for just a moment. Can you remember anything like that since the party or perhaps during the party?"

"I never left... Oh, but at the party, I couldn't find... But it was only for moment..."

"When," Kiya and Matt asked in unison, causing Kiya to shoot him a sharp look.

Mrs. Stevens looked horrified. "Do you think something happened to them? I swear they were only alone for ten minutes, perhaps less."

"When?" Kiya asked again.

"During the party. I thought Nurse Rochester had them, and she thought I did." Mrs. Stevens twisted her hands together nervously. "I don't know how that happened. Oh God, I never thought anything... She was crying." She bit her lip worriedly. "When I found her, Lizzie was crying. She said she fell. Do you suppose someone was there, in the barn? Someone who frightened them?"

Kiya moaned softly and shook her head, while Matt muttered curses almost beneath his breath.

"It appears someone spoke to them," Kiya said. "Someone gave them a scare. They won't talk about it."

"I'm so sorry. Seth said he brought his horse a treat. I thought nothing of it. I was upset when I couldn't find them, but everything appeared to be fine when I did."

"There's some talk about the possibility that they might have to leave."

"Leave? What do you mean leave? Where would they go? Who would they go with?"

Kiya shook her head. "I only know that they're very frightened. And because of that fear, it's possible they might take it into their heads to run, thinking that would solve their problem. I'd be grateful if you could keep an extra vigilant watch."

"Oh indeed, Mrs. Chase, I won't leave them for a minute. You may be sure of it."

* * * *

Sally Brady took a much needed moment in order to soothe an aching back as well as feet that burned like fire. She leaned against the bar that ran almost the length of the room, her rounded hip upon a rickety stool and surveyed the dinner crowd — crowd being a relative term since the dinning area held only five tables, all of which were filled with men suffering varying degrees of inebriation. Only one or two dared to sample the evening's fare which boasted of black bread and a particularly greasy stew that smelled, to her mind, just a bit too ripe.

Except for an occasional fight, on most nights, the place would quiet some as the hour grew late. Most of those currently imbibing would join card games or visit the women upstairs while the rest would find themselves sleepy enough to give her little trouble. It was Thursday, usually her day off. Nora, the girl who came in on Thursdays, had earlier sent word that her baby was feeling poorly and she wouldn't be able to make it tonight. Sally sighed. She'd had plans for tonight — plans that had included Tim and her and the little room she was allotted upstairs.

Tim had come calling again last night. She'd seen him every night since the wedding last Sunday. She hoped it wouldn't be long before he'd ask her to marry him, and she could leave this job forever.

It wasn't that she didn't want to work. She simply didn't want to work here. She'd be leaving in any case thanks to the duke and his promise that she would oversee his kitchen serving girls. The trouble was she didn't want to wait. She hated this place and the low-life crowd that frequented it.

Tim was a shy one. It was going to take some work on her part or she might never get the man to the altar.

Sally held no false expectations. She wasn't about to attract a string of beaus. She knew she was passably pretty but far from a beauty. What she did have was good skin and dark brown eyes. Men often commented on her eyes, but what men really liked was plenty of curves. And she had curves in abundance. She was counting on those curves to catch a man like Tim.

Vince Hennings sat at the bar, nursing a tankard of ale. Like last night and the night before and the night before that, he'd sat there the entire night. He didn't so much watch over her but he watched every man who approached her — watched and waited for her to point out the man who had threatened the duchess. Sally knew his job wasn't to protect her, still she felt immeasurably safer just because he was there.

There was something about the man, Sally thought, something that greatly attracted her. In truth, he wasn't handsome. His skin was marked with deep craters, scared from his teenage years, but his features were good, his hair dark, straight and thick but left long and a bit straggly. His clothes could have been cleaner. But it was his eyes, Lord, they were beautiful. Deep brown, they seemed to draw her closer. If it weren't for Tim, she wouldn't think twice about having a go at this one. Sally looked at his hands. For a moment, she studied the long tapered fingers and couldn't help but wonder what it would be like if those fingers...

Lord, she gasped at the wayward thought and took a deep breath. Those were dangerous thoughts, very dangerous thoughts. A smile touched the corner of her mouth as she noticed his gaze move slowly over her from her hips and waist to linger at her breasts. His gaze reached her eyes and again moved to settle upon her lush curves.

Sally moved towards him and asked, "You ready for a refill?"

"Damn," he muttered almost on a groan, "I'm ready for something."

"My Tim is coming soon."

"Is he?"

She nodded, finding it harder to think, harder to speak the longer this man looked at her.

"Your Tim, I mean. Is he yours?"

She knew better. This man promised her nothing but a few minutes of pleasure, and there was no way she was giving up Tim for that. "He will be."

Vince smiled. "And you want that?"

"What?"

"To belong to Tim. Is he the one for you?"

Sally shrugged. The truth of the matter was she didn't know for sure, but he seemed to want her. She'd be a fool to give up that possibility for a few stolen moments no matter how luscious those moments promised to be. "He could be."

A smile curved Vince's usually brooding mouth. "Could be? Does that mean you're open to other suggestions?"

A pulse hammered in her throat, and she found herself saying exactly what she'd promised she wouldn't. "Depends. What have you got in mind?"

"We could take a walk outside and see if we could come up with something."

Sally smiled and allowed her gaze to drop to just below his belt. Her mouth went dry, and the pulse in her throat hammered harder than ever at the bulge she found there. Her voice trembled with excitement and she knew, God she just knew, she was going to do something real stupid. "Oh, I haven't a doubt that you could come up with something," she said, almost on a sigh of despair. "The problems is, Tim and I have this thing."

"But no promises made yet?"

Sally shrugged. The movement caused her breasts a luscious sway, and Vince to groan. "Not yet."

"So?" he asked, while waiting for her to take him up on his offer.

Sally couldn't remember a time when she'd felt half this excited or half this needy. She was out of her mind and suddenly didn't care. "So, I haven't too much time, but I suppose I wouldn't mind a small sample of what you've got in mind."

"It's better if it takes some time, and I can tell you right now, it ain't small."

Sally's laugh was slightly strangled as she moved towards the back door. Her plans for Tim were suddenly forgotten. God, but she couldn't wait to feel this man's mouth and hands on her.

Just outside the back door, Vince pulled her hard against him and groaned, "Jesus, you're so soft." He tugged the neckline of her blouse down. His hands were on her breasts, weighing the heavy, soft flesh. "I've wanted to do this since the first moment I saw you."

It wasn't yet dark. Anyone entering the yard could have seen them, but for the moment, neither seemed to notice or care. Suddenly Vince seemed to realise what he was about. His boss would skin him alive for playing around while on duty. But his boss didn't have a piece like this one, begging for it. He dragged her towards the privy and pushed her up against the back of the building. There wasn't all that much privacy here either but for a shrub or two on each side. Still the woods at his back offered some and anything was better than standing in the middle of the yard.

"Are you married?" she asked and realised she'd waited too long before asking. Right now, she knew it didn't matter.

"No," he said as his mouth slashed hungry and hard across hers. And it just so happened that he wasn't, but the truth of the matter was, even if he was married, he would have denied it tonight. All he knew was the softness of her body, all he heard was the pounding of his blood and the harsh sounds of their breathing. Damn, he had to have her. And it had to be now.

"Sorry baby, but you've got me so hot." He bit her nipple and smiled at her low groan of pleasure. "I can't take it slow." He pulled her skirt up and reached for her hot, moist flesh. "I'll make it up to you. Next time, I'll—"

He didn't hear the footsteps coming from the woods behind him—never heard them until it was far too late.

* * * *

"I assume you enjoy that."

Kiya smiled as she held the shank of her pipe, bringing the bit to her mouth as she lit the packed tobacco within its bowl. A thin, aromatic blue stream of smoke was aimed at the ceiling when she nodded. "It tends to sooth the nerves."

"But what of the taste?"

"It's an acquired taste, I'm sure."

Madelyn grinned, her gaze bright with amusement as she looked upon her spirited, new daughter. "I've no doubt," she said in agreement and then, "I think I'm going to like you, Kiya."

"Madam, please," John Harrison interrupted on a groan. "Do not encourage the girl. I've had trouble enough with her outrageous actions and opinions. Thank the Lord, she's no longer my responsibility."

All three adults glanced towards Matt and the wicked grin he shot his bride. "If you're waiting for me to complain, you apparently have me confused with a man far more courageous."

Kiya allowed a low mysterious chuckle, which caused all in attendance to laugh aloud.

"I should never presume to object to my husband's preferences," Kiya remarked almost offhandedly. For any less perceptive, the thin thread of steel in that seemingly simple comment might have gone unnoticed. Not one in the room could claim ignorance.

"And of course, you expect the same consideration in return," Madelyn finished for her then added with obvious delight, "I believe you've made an excellent choice Matthew."

"I think so," he said as he exchanged a warm look with his bride.

Merry entered the room with Jake and sat on the sofa while he hovered nearby. Tea was rolled into the room moments later, and because only the family — Madelyn, of course, was considered family — was present the children soon followed attended by their nurse to take their tea with the adults. Merry presided while the children, fresh from their naps, were seated at a small table set quickly in place for them. All enjoyed the light offering of sandwiches, sweet cakes and cookies.

Madelyn smiled at the children who quietly enjoyed their treats. "You are a big boy, Seth. Do you take care of your sister?"

"Yes, ma'am," Seth returned.

"Does he?" she asked Lizzie, looking for confirmation from the little girl sitting across from her brother.

Lizzie shrugged for a response.

"When I was young, my brother always pulled my hair." She eyed Lizzie's long, silky, blonde pigtails. "Does Seth pull yours?"

"Not bloody likely. I'd kick him in his ba — "

"Lizzie!" came a sharp response from her mother. "A simple, 'No duchess', would have sufficed."

Matt grinned. "Lizzie hasn't as yet quite grasped the niceties of polite conversation. It's bound to take a bit of time, but we won't stop trying, will we, Lizzie?"

Madelyn grinned well aware of what the youngster was about. "Refreshing, I'd say."

Matt and Kiya were laughing when Beauchamp interrupted. "I'm sorry to interrupt, your lordship, but there's a man to see you. He appears most disturbed."

Matt, with Jake at his heels, followed the butler to the large hall just inside the front door. Tim McGrath paced nervously. Something was obviously wrong. Matt moved quickly towards him and asked, "What is it?"

"They've got her."

"Who?"

"I wish the hell I knew."

Matt shook his head, confused. "What are you talking about?"

"It's Sally. Someone took her."

Matt finally realised where he'd seen this man before. He was Sally's friend. The same who had accompanied her to the wedding celebration. Matt shook his head again in denial. "Vince... I've a man watching her."

"Someone cracked his head. I sent for the doc."

"Jesus," Matt gasped. "What the hell? How?"

He shrugged. "I found him outside by the privy and Sally was gone."

Chapter Sixteen

Matt sat beside the bed in a second floor room of the inn and shook his head in disgust. Vince looked as if he'd been hit with a boulder, perhaps an avalanche of boulders. A cap of white bandaging covered most of his dark hair. Both eyes were swollen, his nose looked to be broken while a gash near his mouth was crusted over and leaked blood every time he moved his jaw. How had they gotten the jump on him like this? "What the hell happened?"

"Jesus, Matt, I'm sorry. I don't know what happened?"

"What do you mean you don't know?"

"I mean I followed her outside, and someone came up behind me. I never heard him until it was too late."

A glance at the man's hands told the truth of it. Vince hadn't fought back. He hadn't had the chance. Matt frowned. He knew there was more to it than following her. There had to be. Vince had worked with the firm for years, had had dozens of confrontations and nothing like this had ever happened before.

"So you followed her outside and then what?"

Vince looked his boss in the eye and, to Matt amazement, flushed. Suddenly sheepish, he looked away, cursed then groaned. "Damn it, Matt, do you know how soft she is? Christ, I don't think I've ever had a woman so…"

Matt grunted and, with a mingling of annoyance and understanding, nodded. "I get it." He came to his feet and said, "Get some rest. Doc said you'll be fine. You just need some healing. I'll see you in a few days."

"Wait a minute. No one told me. Is she all right?"

Matt shook his head. "She's gone."

"Christ!" Vince said as he struggled to come to a sitting position.

Matt pressed a hand to the man's shoulder. "Stay there. You've got a cracked rib or two. Once you can sit a horse, come back to the manor house. You're no good to anyone right now. Don't worry, we'll find her." Both men knew Matt or one of his men would do just that. The real question was would they find her in time.

* * * *

Ten miles west of the Boar Inn, a ramshackle hut of rotted mostly see-through slats of wood somehow managed to remain erect in the midst of a lush field of high grass and higher wildflowers.

Inside the hut, a woman moaned in pain.

Sally Brady awoke dazed, disoriented and shackled by a short chain to a bolt imbedded in the hut's wall. Her muscles were sore, her joints achy, for her position hardly boasted of comfort. She'd slept on her knees, her side against the wall, her chin on her chest. The bolt was high.

Even on her knees, it kept her arm suspended well above her head.

Her hand and arm were asleep. She had to move. With the help of the wall she leaned against, she slowly came to her feet and groaned at the pain in her knees and hips, as well as the painful pins and needles sensation that filled her arm from shoulder to fingertips. She cried out. The degree of pain was enormous. Its intensity damn near stole her breath. For a moment, it alone occupied her every thought. It was some moments before Sally noticed her surroundings. A man lay dead near her, a puddle of blood congealed at his side. She groaned with the knowledge of where she was and the memory of what she'd suffered through last night.

She was naked and covered with his blood. Her skirt and blouse were torn and strewn upon the floor. Other than herself, a dead man and those few ragged pieces of cloth, the building stood empty. Empty and eerily silent.

Sally shivered as the memory of last night washed over her. One moment, she'd been tightly pressed between Vince and the wall behind her, and the next, a fist slammed into her jaw. Hit hard enough to render her cries to little more than a low guttural moan, she was flung over a shoulder. Helplessly, she watched in horror as Vince slumped to the ground, a huge rock slammed upon his head once, twice, perhaps more. In seconds, two men, the same two Vince had been sent to watch for, carried her away. Her hands and feet were tied, a dirty rag shoved into her mouth, and she was flung over the back of a horse.

They'd travelled in silence. She couldn't say for how long, but it felt like hours. Finally, they pulled her from the horse.

Inside a shack, a candle was lit. The small room was empty but for the two men and herself. She knew they would kill her. Nothing could save her. No one knew she was missing. No one would know where they'd taken her.

She was shoved to the floor, a chain twisted around her wrist. The chain was secured to a bolt in the wall. A moment later, her clothes were torn away. It was obvious what these two were about. She didn't cry out and gave little resistance. To do so would only ensure greater abuse.

The two stood above her. Both leered at her nakedness. She shivered at their evil grins. They argued who would take her first. Jim insisted. Without further ado, he pulled his member from his trousers and manipulated it for the time it took to sink to his knees and shove her legs apart. A moment later, he hovered above her.

Sally knew she only had seconds before he forced his body into hers. With her free hand, she raked the side of his face, screamed then kicked out madly in her struggles to get him off. Sally was amazed when he suddenly fell on his back moaning in pain, for she had inadvertently kicked him in his groin. His friend offered no help, but laughed and quickly took his place.

A moment later, he was flung to the floor as Jim again on his knees positioned himself above her. "Hold her legs, you stupid fuck," he ordered.

Sally's scream was instantly cut off as a punch slammed against her eye and another to her mouth. He was on her, his rage and aching pain making it far harder than it should have. Her hand fell by accident upon his knife sheathed at his belt. Without thought, she pulled it free and shoved it as deep as she could into his side. Below his ribs, it encountered no resistance and sank a full five inches to the base of the handle.

Jim Willis looked puzzled. He gained his footing, while his blood flowed over her. He kicked her and Sally moaned as she heard in the distance, "She stuck me. The bitch stuck..." his words drifted to a stop as his eyes rolled into his head and he fell at her side.

Thankfully, he was already weak, weak enough that the foot that smashed into her face only knocked her out.

It was the last thing she remembered before awakening a few minutes ago.

She twisted her hand in a half-hearted attempt to find comfort in a still aching wrist and was amazed to hear the wood groan as it gave just a bit. She pulled again, more to investigate the oddity than in the belief that she might free herself, and gasped as the rotted wood suddenly splintered. A moment later, with a far more aggressive yank, it completely gave way. Her hand was free. Attached still to the chain and bolt, the small slab of wood hung uselessly at her side.

In seconds, Sally had on her skirt. Her blouse took a bit more effort as the wood and chain refused to move through the sleeves as was needed. The blouse tore. She didn't care. Within seconds, she was outside and running towards the thick forest, frantic in her need to hide should her abductor return.

She had no idea where he went, what he'd done. All she knew was she had to get away.

Anxious not to bring attention to herself, Sally kept to the woods and ignored the occasional road for fear that her kidnapper might more easily find her should she use it. She came across no one and had no idea where she was. She'd been unconscious when she'd been brought to the hut. All she could do was watch the sun. She lived within a few miles of the coast, and she knew she couldn't go too far off if she kept the sun behind her.

She slept in the woods that night, but near noon the next day, she managed to find a small cottage. The lady who lived there took pity and gave her a cup of tea and a thick slice of bread covered with strawberry jam before directing her towards the Harrison mansion.

Sally forced herself to take her time. She followed the road the old lady had pointed out but walked three feet and more into the woods. She was terrified and took no chances lest she be abducted again.

It was almost dark by the time Sally stumbled out of the woods to find herself about three feet from a barn. She stepped inside, breathing deeply of its warm earthy scents. A few men congregated at the other end beyond a stack of hay. They were laughing as they teased one another about the attentions of one of the house maids. A huge black stove stood at the barn's centre, while a metal chimney ran to the ceiling and out the roof. A sturdy set of stairs led to the loft. Unlike most barns the loft held no hay, but instead had bunks used by the many men who guarded the house and its occupants.

Sally shivered as her cold, damp skin was enclosed in warmth. A young woman gave a lusty laugh, and Sally silently peeked from behind a bale of hay and watched as a man closed off that laughter with a kiss while his hand played under her skirt and another man obviously enjoyed her exposed breasts and nuzzled his face into her neck while she in turn used both hands to work their male members. While she was about her business, three more men impatiently waited their turns.

Sally knew neither the master nor the mistress would be happy with this kind of goings on. She thought even the women at the Inn weren't this bad. At least, they had the decency to take care of their men behind closed doors.

"Lay her down, mates. I'll have a go at her while she works you two over."

Happy to leave this scene behind her, Sally made for the small back door only to find herself stopped in her tracks at a sudden and loud, "Jesus Christ!"

She stood perfectly still. She knew the duke had entered the barn.

"Are you out of your minds?" he roared. "Do you realise my wife or one of her sisters or, worse yet, one of the children might have walked in here?"

Sally watched the three men come instantly to attention as they adjust their clothes while the woman fixed her blouse and smoothed her skirt. Matt glared at the woman. "You'd best go back to the house."

The maid curtsied and murmured a soft, "Yes, your lordship. I'm sorry, sir."

Matt shook his head as she moved quickly to obey. Silently, he promised himself he'd make sure that one wouldn't work here for long. He didn't care if all she ever did was dust the library. There was no way he'd allow her near his wife or the children. Once she was gone, Matt turned his annoyance on his men. "I hope the hell you know what you're about. If she's willing to take on all of you almost at one time, I wouldn't be surprised to find her diseased. If you don't mind finding yourself with the pox, that's your business surely, but the next time you want a woman, leave the housemaids alone and have the decency to bring whomever you chose up to the loft. And for God's sake, be quiet about it."

Sally shivered at the thought of the pox, for she'd manage, just barely and with God's help, to escape that possibility last night.

Quickly and quietly, she left the barn by the back door and turned a corner. She was standing there waiting for the duke to exit the barn when a lone rider rode slowly into the yard. Sally pushed her back against the barn wall. It was too late to move. There was no where to hide. She closed her eyes for a long second and wished herself invisible then smiled upon opening them again as she realised who the rider was. He dismounted and came towards her. Battered and bruised, it didn't matter. To her way of thinking, his grin was adorable. His head was bandaged, both eyes were still swollen and circled with a multitude of colours, his nose was a little more crooked than when she'd last seen him and still he managed to look unbelievably cocky. His teeth flashed with a grin. "I believe we have some unfinished business."

Sally's laugh was short and choppy and filled with surprising emotion. "We might have to wait a bit on that."

Vince nodded as he took in the results of obvious abuse. One of her eyes was black and blue and swelled almost shut while her lip was cut and swollen to three times its normal size. Her hair hadn't seen a comb in days. She wore the same clothes as when she'd been taken. Dirty and ripped, she looked as if she'd suffered major trauma. His gaze softened as he asked, "Are you all right."

Sally tried to hold back the tears, but once his concern made itself known, she couldn't quite manage the feat. Her hand the one with the chain and wood still attached to her wrist came to wipe away her tears and succeeded in streaking the dirt over her cheeks. "I am."

Vince took her hand in his and looking at her wrist, asked, "What the hell?"

"They kept me in a hut. The wall was rotted. When I woke up, one was dead, the other gone. I pulled at this and it broke away from the wall."

Vince pulled her against him. "Jesus," he groaned as he gently snuggled her battered face against his neck. "It was my fault."

"It wasn't," she countered. "No one knew they would come for me. I didn't know they saw me come here."

"Who did it?" Vince had no need to ask what they'd done. Her torn clothes made what happened all too clear.

"Jim Willis. He's dead. I don't know the other one's name," she said then surprised them both with a sob as she pushed herself even closer. Into his shirt, she murmured, "He was the one who threatened the duchess and the children. They tried to rape me."

"Tried?" Vince asked.

She nodded. "I stabbed Jim, and he died. The other must have run off."

Vince pulled back and looked at her for a long moment, oddly relieved, then wondered at the depth of that emotion. Certainly, it was important that no woman should suffer abuse, but why should he feel relief to this degree that this woman had escaped the worst of it?

"Both of you come into the house," Matt said, suddenly at their side

The kitchen was warm. The last meal for the day had been served, and the room put to rights. "Sit down. You look near dead on your feet."

"Aye, I've been walking a bit."

"How long?"

"Since yesterday morning. I slept in the woods last night."

Matt nodded. "Let me see your hand." He nodded as he examined the chain and bolt. "Stay here. Both of you. I'll get the blacksmith." He started for the door and stopped. "First, let me get my lady."

Within minutes, Kiya stood in the kitchen and Matt was running towards a small cabin beyond the formal gardens, next door to the gardener's. She smiled at her guests. "Sit. I'll make tea."

"I need to clean up, Duchess."

Kiya nodded and opened the door to the sitting room behind the kitchen. Inside, four young women sat laughing at something one of them said. Kiya interrupted with, "Peggy, have one of the girls draw a bath please. The empty bedroom next to yours will do nicely, I'm sure. Also, see to it that the bed is made up with fresh linens." She smiled as the girl came to her feet, curtsied and nodded at her mistress. "Yes, ma'am."

"Thank you," Kiya said then turned towards the kitchen again, only to find Sally on her feet about to follow the girl. "Wait, have something to eat first."

"Oh no, Duchess, I can't—"

Kiya took her by her arm and directed her back to the table. "You can listen to me. A bit of pampering won't hurt right now."

And because she was being pampered, because someone obviously cared, because Sally needed it more than she'd realised, she began to cry again.

Vince came from his chair and pulled the woman into his arms. As he rubbed a comforting hand up and down her back, he said, "You can't be too nice to her. This happens every time."

Sally gave a watery chuckle into his shirt.

Kiya grinned as she placed a steaming pot of tea to steep then set the table with the appropriate utensils, cups and plates. A moment later, with the larder near emptied, the table held two loaves of fresh bread, butter, jams, slices of roast beef, hard-boiled eggs and small bowls of hot chicken soup that had been had for dinner.

Kiya sliced more bread as the two ate and asked as appetites were appeased, "Are you feeling a little better?"

"Much better, thank you, Duchess."

"I'd appreciate it if you called me Mrs. Chase."

"Of course, Duch…Mrs. Chase."

"You'll stay here from now on."

"But…"

Kiya shook her head. "You'll stay here. My husband tells me one of the kitchen girls will be leaving us. You can take her place, if you'd like." She smiled and added, "Until the work is finished on our new home."

Matt returned with the blacksmith and a few tools. Within minutes, the chain was broken and Sally's wrist was free.

"I sent for the doctor," Matt said.

"Oh no, please. You and your lady are making too much—"

He shook his head at her objection. "We owe you. And we're happy to do it."

An hour later, after a luxurious bath using lavender soap, Sally dressed again in a clean chemise, skirt and blouse walked into the kitchen. Vince sat still at the table waiting. She smiled to find him there. "Were you sleeping?"

"No. I was waiting for you. What did the doctor say?"

"Nothing more than I already knew. Lots of bruises, nothing broken. He said I'll be fine." She looked at him, noticing his grimace of pain. "You should be in bed. You're in pain."

He shook his head. "I'm better now."

Sally smiled. "I bathed with lavender soap. I never did that before. It was lovely."

Vince smiled at her delight. "You should always use it. It smells good. You smell good."

Sally laughed aloud. "They gave me a beautiful room. It has a fireplace. They gave me clothes and shoes, and I'll work here until they fix up the Turner place."

"If you married me, would you want to keep working?"

Sally gasped. "Vince!"

He pulled her to sit on his lap. "I know, I think I'm as shocked as you are."

She shook her head. "You don't mean it. You hardly know me."

"I expect I will know you." He shrugged. "You'll be working around here. I work around here." He laughed. "And once you get to know me, I imagine you'll want to marry me, all right."

Sally laughed. "Will I?" She turned a bit to see him more easily. "Can you tell me why I'll want that?"

"You won't be able to help yourself. You'll love me, of course," he teased with a thread of real confidence.

"Oh, of course," she agreed, joining him in this light banter. With a smile, she ran a finger over his cheek and studied the nearly healed cut near his mouth. His face was that of a man who'd lived a hard, rough life, but his eyes... God, they were something. Dark and warm, they promised tenderness and more, much more. Sally wondered if his easily spoken words weren't right on the mark. "I've no doubt that all women love you once they get to know you," she said, thinking they probably did.

He shook his head. "Women never get to know me. I don't stay around that long."

She blinked her surprise. "But you expect you'll be stayin' this time?"

"I'm thinkin' I will."

Her smile was tender as her fingers moved gently over his battered face. "Your nose is crooked."

Vince nodded. "Ain't likely to win any contests."

"We look a lovely pair, wouldn't you say?"

"I'd say you're a pretty lady, and a few bruises don't matter none."

"No one ever told me I was pretty before."

"No man you mean?"

She nodded.

"That's 'cause men are dogs and are lookin' for only one thing. They never got around to lookin' at your face."

Sally laughed. "But you did?"

He breathed a long sigh. "It took me awhile."

She licked her lip. "Every time you make me laugh my lip bleeds."

Vince took a breath, pretending despair. Despite the pain in his ribs, he cuddled her closer against him. "If I'm gentle, you cry. If I make you laugh, you bleed. There's no pleasin' some."

Sally closed her eyes and breathed deeply of his scent while gratefully allowing his gentle soothing. "I think I'm going to like getting to know you."

He kissed the top of her head. "Didn't I tell you?"

She laughed even as she snuggled closer yet.

"You want me to carry you to bed?" Vince thought that would hurt him some since his ribs were even now aching miserably, but he'd do it if she asked.

"You'd better not. I'll just sit here for a bit, if that's all right."

Vince thought sitting here was better than all right. What was even more all right was the fact that she hadn't once mentioned Tim.

* * * *

Kiya stood at the kitchen window and watched as Seth ran to the barn, his hand holding something against his chest, under his shirt. She waited no more than twenty seconds, and he was on his way towards the house again. He dashed into the kitchen and raced for the back stairs that would bring him to the nursery on the third floor.

"Seth," she called as his foot touched the first step, his hand on the newel post. "Come here for a minute, will you?"

"Mandy," she said, addressing one of the kitchen girls. "Please tell Mrs. Stevens that Seth is with me."

"Certainly, ma'am," the girl replied with a curtsy and left to do Kiya's bidding.

Seth moved slowly and reluctantly towards his mother. She poured a glass of milk and put two cookies Cook had just taken from the oven on a plate. "Come with me, Seth."

With plate and glass in hand, she moved down the hall that led to the small sitting room. She closed the door behind them and motioned for Seth to sit. She placed the milk and cookies on a low table nearby and sat across from him. "I saw you go to the barn."

That was all it took for a flood of guilty tears to erupt. Kiya ached to go to the boy. Obviously, he was suffering, but she couldn't help unless he told her what the problem was. She was afraid to move, to say anything, lest she inadvertently say the wrong thing and watch him close up again. When he began to quiet some, she asked, "What have you to say?"

"He made me do it. I swear I didn't want to. I don't want to go to prison."

Kiya was almost beside herself with the need to ask who and exactly what Seth had done. She decided instead to bluff her way through for a bit longer. "Do you think you belong in prison?"

He shrugged.

"Why?"

Seth cried all the harder, his little shoulders were shaking with his sobs. "Mummy, please, I don't want to go."

Kiya's heart broke. She forced aside her own tears, her heart wrenching at his suffering. "Suppose I promise that you won't. Suppose I tell you I'll never send you to prison. Would you believe me?"

He nodded, his eyes shining, his lashes spiky with tears as he looked up from twisting his fingers. "If you promise."

Kiya handed him her handkerchief and waited for him to wipe his face and blow his nose. She was dying to ask him straight out but knew it was better that he should think she already knew. "All right, so now that I've promised, what have you to say?"

"I won't do it again. I swear I won't."

Kiya nodded, having no idea what he was talking about but continuing her bluff. "That's good, but what do you think will happen now?"

Seth shrugged. "I don't know. I didn't want to do it, 'cause I didn't want to go to prison, but he said I had to do it. He said he'd kill you if I told and that Lizzie and I couldn't stay if I didn't give him something every day." He shrugged again. "I guess we'll have to go back now." He looked up truly puzzled. "How did you find out?"

Kiya's quick mind assimilated the facts. No doubt Seth was talking about his father when he said 'he'. Give him something? Apparently, considering the short trip, he'd just left something in the barn. Something small. Silverware? "How many forks and spoons did you give him?"

Seth moaned. "I knew someone would notice they were gone, but I couldn't fit anything big under my shirt."

Kiya breathed a sigh of relief. At last. The truth was no one had noticed anything, with the exception of his all too short visit to the barn. The stealing might have gone on for some time. If Seth had been less sensitive, for he'd been close to tears for more than a week, no one would have imagined anything was wrong. "I understand why you didn't say anything to me. I know he threatened to hurt me—"

"Not hurt." Seth shook his head. "Kill."

Kiya nodded. "I know, but why didn't you tell Matt? Don't you trust him?"

"I didn't want him to get hurt."

Kiya nodded, a smile touching the corners of her mouth. He thought he was protecting them. God, what kind of a monster put that kind of pressure on a child? She glanced towards the low table and asked, "Would you like those cookies and milk now?"

Seth smiled and reached for the snack. A moment later, both the cookies and milk were but a memory. "I think Matt is in his office. I want you to tell him what you told me."

Seth shot her a look of obvious fear and trembled as more tears gathered.

Kiya hugged him close and rocked him for a long moment. "Don't be afraid," she soothed as she brushed back his hair. "Matt is here to protect us. All of us."

"It will be my fault if he gets hurt."

She smiled even as she wondered how the boy could have grown to love him so deeply and so fast. "He's not going to get hurt. And even if he did, it could never be your fault."

Down the hall, Kiya knocked and entered Matt's small office.

"Good morning, Kiya," he said then noticing an obviously distraught Seth with her, he added, "I see you've brought a young gentleman with you. Are you looking for employment, sir?"

Seth giggled as only a young boy can, and the sound squeezed at Kiya's heart. "It's me, Dad. Seth."

"Oh, so it is." Matt returned, pretending surprise. "You've been growing so fast, for a moment, I didn't recognise you." He pushed back from his desk and patted his knee. Seth didn't hesitate. In seconds, he was on his father's lap. Moment's later, the boy began his story.

When he finished, Kiya said, "He didn't want to tell you in case you got hurt."

Matt nodded. "I'll be fine, Seth. So will you, Lizzie and your mummy." He pushed a lock of hair from the boy's forehead. "You never have to worry about that again."

Seth looked with nothing less than awe at his mother and, in a loud whisper, said to his father, "I don't know how mummy found out."

"Mummies often know things, and most of us never figure out how they did it."

Seth glanced at Kiya.

"Tell me where you leave the spoons," Matt said.

"Outside the barn's back door, against the wall."

"And they're gone every morning?" he further inquired. Seth nodded.

"You won't have to do it again."

"Are you..."

"Don't worry, Seth. I'll take care of it," Matt promised.

The boy smiled and breathed a deep sigh of obvious relief.

"Your mummy has been worried that you might leave. You won't run away, will you?"

Seth's eyes grew huge and solemn as he shook his head then looked at Kiya with some amazement. "How did you..."

"I told you mummies always know," Matt reminded.

* * * *

Later, after Annie brought Seth back to the nursery, Kiya asked, "What are you going to do?"

Matt nodded in agreement. "Good thinking. For a moment there I thought you were going to say, 'what are *we* going to do'?"

"I've already done most of the work," she reminded with a healthy dose of arrogance.

Matt chuckled as he tugged her close and pressed his face against her belly. "I love you."

"I know, but you haven't answered my question."

"I'll have half a dozen men secreted in the woods near the barn. He won't get away."

Kiya breathed a sigh of relief.

"How did you get him to talk?"

"I didn't have to do much. His guilt did just about all of it. All I said was 'I saw you run to the barn' and he burst into tears."

"And you bluffed your way through the rest?"

Kiya smiled. "You said yourself that mummies are smart."

"I don't think I said smart, exactly."

She pulled back some and asked, "No, what did you say exactly?"

"I think I said we never figure out how they know things. But what I meant was mummies are brilliant."

Kiya laughed as he reached under her skirt, quickly releasing the tabs on her drawers. He helped her keep her balance as she stepped out of them. Then he leaned back and tugged on her skirt, drawing her closer, guiding her to sit upon him, facing him while placing her legs on each side of his lap.

"A lady would never sit like this."

"She would if she were a mummy."

"In truth? I didn't know that."

"That's why you have me."

"Is that why? Only this morning I was wondering."

Matt grinned in all confidence. "You were a bit busy this morning. It's a wonder you had time to wonder."

She laughed. "Actually it was later that I wondered."

He nodded. "Well, you needn't wonder any longer. It's my job to tell mummies…" His words came to an abrupt stop at the sudden sharp warning in her eyes. "What I meant was, because you're new at being a mum, my job is to tell you how to sit."

She chuckled at their nonsensical conversation. "And you know how mummies are supposed to sit?"

Matt nodded. "I've once read a book about it."

"Did you?"

He nodded again.

"What was the title?"

"The title was…let me think."

Her legs had pinned her skirt between her and Matt's chair. He pulled at the fabric. Kiya knew only too well why. "Would you like to come?"

She blinked her surprise. "That's the title?"

He grinned. "No, that's a question."

"Where are we going?"

Matt chuckled. "I have a special place. After a few minutes, I'm going to show you where it is."

"God, you are so bad."

"I'm bad? Was it me who answered my knock stark naked?"

"I don't see how you could answer your own knock or why you should knock in the first place, if you were only going to—Matt the door isn't locked."

"No one can see anything, except for a wife sitting on her husband's lap. And don't change the subject," he said as he finally managed to pull the skirt from beneath her knees allowing room to slide his hands underneath.

"What was the subject?" she groaned as his hands moved up her legs and found the moist heat of her at last.

"I was trying to remember something."

"What?"

"What?

"What were you trying to remember?"

"Oh, yes, well that's the thing, isn't it? If I remembered it, I won't be trying would I?"

She smiled. "Are we speaking in English?"

"I don't know," he said as she released the tabs of his trousers and wrapped her hand around a huge erection. "It sounds a little like English."

"What does?"

"I don't know," he said again, giving up any hope that he had the power to continue this conversation as she slowly moved her hand up and down his cock. He couldn't hold back a shudder of ecstasy as her hands moved deeper into his trousers and cupped his balls. "Oh God, that feels so... Wait, don't touch me. I want to play a little first."

"Doesn't this feel good?"

"I'm sure I haven't a clue as to what you mean." She leaned back against his desk, her eyes half closed as she luxuriated in the feel of his hands playing with her, his fingertips teasing her clit and the entrance to her dark tunnel and back to her clit again. Her pussy grew hotter, wetter and heavier. God, this was so good.

"You're sure about that, you say?"

"What?"

"You said you haven't a clue."

"Did I?" she groaned softly. "What didn't I have a clue about?"

Kiya never remembered moving. Suddenly, she was half lying on his desk, her legs on his shoulders, his mouth where his fingers hand been.

A steady throbbing began in her brain, the sound pulsed and obscured much of anything else, connecting somehow to her belly, to the rhythmic motion of his tongue. She grew tense, desperate in her building need. Muscles tightened as her anxiousness mounted. Her breathing became short, shallow pants. She leaned farther back, allowing him easier access.

His mouth, nose and jaw were wet with her juices as he ate at her pussy, while one finger played against her pretty little puckered hole. Gently, he entered her, with first one knuckle then two. He finger-fucked her ass, and Kiya was helpless but to allow him anything he desired.

"Open your dress. Hurry. I need to suck you."

The bodice came undone, Kiya never remembered how. She was simply, suddenly, wantonly, totally exposed to his hungry gaze.

He pulled his mouth from her, leaving one hand to replace his tongue, while the other continued to finger-fuck her ass. His mouth took her nipple deep into a furnace of heat.

She arched her back. "I'm coming. God," she gasped, "I'm... Bite me." She trembled, her body stiff, hard, aching in her need. "Bite me...hard," she groaned as she pulled his face closer nearly suffocating him as she shoved her nipple into his eager mouth. She strained into the need, hungry for it, desperate for it. "Matt, oh God, Matt." It was almost there. Just a second...more...and... Her body shuddered as continuous waves of ecstasy rolled over her.

Kiya could only groaned as he brought her to his lap and slid her pussy over his engorged erection. He cuddled her exhausted form against him and smiled as he watched her slowly regain her senses. "So what do you think?"

"I think you are possibly the most wonderful man I've ever known."

He grinned at the compliment then frowned. "What do you mean possibly?"

Sometime later, after her breathing settled some, Kiya moaned, delighting in the feel of his mouth and the gentle playful suction he put to her nipple. "That feels so good."

"I love it myself." His words were only slightly slurred.

"It's amazing how you can talk with my nipple in your mouth."

"It's not that hard." Again the words could have been clearer.

She moved her hips against him and grinned. "It feels like it is."

"I don't know how you can accuse me of being bad when you are sitting like this wiggling against me. I'm only a man after all."

"Yes, poor dear. And you're managing so wonderfully under the strain of it."

"I thought so."

Chapter Seventeen

Edwards froze in his tracks. What the hell? He crouched low to the ground in silence. Someone was in these woods. Was it a trap? Had the little bastard told? He waited. It felt like hours, and still, he made not a move. Steadying his breathing, he strained to listen. Finally another sound. This one came from his left. Someone cleared his throat, but the sound was almost lost in the nocturnal chirpings of crickets and cicadas. Had he not been listening for it, he might never have heard it. But he did. A man was out there all right. More than one man. Good God, he'd almost walked into a trap. A thin film of cold sweat instantly coated him from forehead to toes. The woods were probably full of men just waiting to pounce on him. There could be no other reason for these two — and there were at least two — men to sit silently in the woods. A warm barn and bed awaited them yet they sat here. There could only be one reason why.

When he got his hands on that little bastard, he was going to kill him. He was nothing but a useless shit and deserved to die for turning on his da.

Edwards crept back from whence he'd come. Some good distance from the Harrison property, a small fire blazed in a clearing. Hannah Walker sat by the fire dressed only in a chemise, awaiting his return. "The little bastard's sold me out," he complained. "My own flesh and blood. I don't know how many, but there were men in the woods. If one of them hadn't coughed, I'd be on my way to Newgate right now."

Hannah had taken up with Edwards only minutes after she left the Harrison place. Of course, she'd known she'd be asked to leave once she was found out. What she didn't know was why? Who was she hurting? No one suffered under her ministrations. In truth, the men only grew happier and because of their satisfaction paid closer attention to their work. She shook her head at his odd comment, not having a clue as to what he was talking about and caring even less. "It's a sad day when a man can't trust 'is own kin."

Hannah laid back on a blanket spread over a thick layer of pine needles. She made herself comfortable as she reached into his trousers for Edward's limp member.

He looked down at her as she played with his cock. "What are you going to do?"

She shrugged. "I don't know. Get a job, I suppose."

"I think we should have made camp farther away from the Harrison place. What if one of the guards comes across us?"

"What if they do? Maybe they'll want to join in the fun. The more the merrier, I always say," Hannah returned in her heavy accent.

Edwards grinned as her mouth closed over his sex. He certainly didn't fight off her advances but it wasn't a woman he truly wanted. It was money, money to keep him in his cups and those two little bastards had been the perfect ticket to fill his pockets and then some. But no, now that they lived with the upper crust, and they thought they were too good for their da. Well they were going to pay for telling. Somehow, someway, he was going to get even with them and the bitch who took them.

Edwards pushed Hannah's chemise to her waist and played with her huge soft breasts. A moment later, the woman quickly shook off the garment. Edwards just stood there watching. When she parted her legs clearly exposing the moist, warm, inviting flesh between her thighs, Edwards decided he watched long enough. Later, would be plenty of time to plan his revenge.

* * * *

Hours later, they sat in the inn, enjoying meat pies and ale.

"Tastes all the better when you don't have to cook it yourself," Hannah remarked.

Tony Edwards suddenly realised a possibility. He asked, "You worked in the Harrison kitchens?"

"Aye, and glad I am that I'm out of there."

He almost smiled as a thought took hold. "You know the children there, of course."

She frowned. "Of course. What about them?"

"They belong to me."

"Bloody hell," she said with a half laugh, her tone all doubt.

"They're mine all right. They took them."

"What do you mean? Who took them?"

"I mean the bitch that just married, took 'em and told me right to me face, they were 'ers 'cause she 'as the money to say so."

"Bloody hell," Hannah gasped in shock. "Did you go to the sheriff?"

Edwards shot her a long look. "Who do you think the sheriff will believe?"

Hannah shook her head. She knew they were a prudish bunch, especially the duke, or she'd still be working there. Even so, she never would have imagined they'd actually steal children from their own father. "What are you going to do?"

Up until half an hour ago, Edwards hadn't a clue as to what he was going to do. But now that he realised Hannah knew the children and she could probably still get into the house, maybe even unseen, just maybe things might turn out the way they should have in the first place. "Can you get into the house?"

Hannah shrugged. "I suppose. I wouldn't want to get caught at it though."

"What about the barn? You could get into that, couldn't you?"

Hannah laughed. "That's why I don't work there any more. The duke walked in on our little party, and that was the end of things."

"Would the men like to see you again?"

She laughed again. "You might be safe in thinkin' that."

"What if you paid regular visits to the barn? Suppose you're still there one morning when the children come to see their pets?"

"And?"

"And suppose you take one with you and meet me on the other side of the woods behind the barn?"

"I could take the girl I suppose. The boy would fight me and make a ruckus to be sure."

Edwards was interested in money, not his daughter's welfare, still he knew he'd never get a penny from the bitch if the girl ended up dead. "You have to make sure she doesn't get hurt."

Hannah nodded. "They never go outside without their nurse. She's bound to make a fuss if she sees me take her. Someone will have to keep her quiet."

"And you couldn't?"

Hannah laughed. "I can do many things, but the woman is almost three of me."

"I could wait in the woods for a signal. Once they were in the barn you could take Lizzie and I'd stop the nurse from calling out."

"What about the men in the woods? The ones that were waiting for you?" she reminded.

"Shit!" he'd forgotten about them. "Damn. It can't be the barn. Where do they ride?"

"I worked in the kitchen. I never asked where they went."

This was going to take longer than he'd expected. If the little bastards hadn't told, the woods would be safe enough for him to hide. Now, he'd have to think. "The only thing I can do is wait for them to ride away from the house. And that might take months." And he didn't have a month to spare. The little money he had wouldn't last that long.

"They only take one guard when they ride, 'cause they never leave the Harrison estate. If they go into town, they take three."

Edwards considered the possibilities. Three was obviously impossible to combat. It had to happen on the Harrison estate. "All right, so it has to be on Harrison property. How do we get away?"

Hannah shrugged.

Edwards mused in thought, "Suppose I shoot the guard and take the girl. I'd leave the nurse with a warning, telling her what I want." He returned his attention to his companion. "How much to do think I can get?"

"What are you saying? You're kidnapping your own kid and holding her for ransom?" Hannah knew this man was nothing to boast about, but she hadn't imagined him to be this bad.

Edwards explained, "I'll never be able to keep her. I haven't anything. No court would give her back to me. I might as well get something for all the years I took care of the little bitch."

"I don't think…" Hannah began doubtfully.

"They won't even let me see them. Is it right for them to do that to their da? Should they always get what they want just because they have money?"

Hannah nodded. She had no love for the rich. Most were inconsiderate, beyond arrogant and eager to show her she was far beneath them. Still, she wasn't sure. The folks she'd worked for weren't so bad. And the men that were hired to protect the womenfolk were good sorts. "You could watch from the woods at the back of the property. You can see everything from there. But I won't be no party to shootin'. If you mean to shoot the guard, count me out."

"All right," Edwards nodded. "I'll work out something. No one gets hurt."

Hannah didn't believe him for a minute. There was no way he could take the girl from her mother or her nurse while a guard watched over them without someone getting hurt. Still, she made sure the man didn't doubt her. Her smile was all teasing and natural as she ran her hand up his thigh. "You want to go down by the river, baby? I could use a bath."

Two days later, Hannah awakened to a deserted camp site, empty but for her small carpet bag and the blanket on which she slept. Edwards was gone. Hannah hadn't a doubt the man was about the plan spoken of a few days back. She also knew someone was going to get hurt.

Hannah had no liking for the rich, especially the aristocracy, still she didn't think they deserved what Edwards had in store for them.

She knew she could walk away and, if she did, would soon take up with another. But Hannah possessed more character than even she was aware. Instead of heading towards London, Hannah turned southeast. She was heading back. Unsure for now of what might happen, she knew one thing. She couldn't let a little kid be kidnapped, even if the kidnapper was her father. There had to be a better, safer way.

The sun was low in the sky by the time Hannah stepped on Harrison property. Two of the men she knew grinned at the sight of her, and she couldn't help but to grin back. Damn, she would have loved to have a go at the two of them for a few hours. But that would have to wait. She had something to say first. Something this family had to know.

It took some time and insistence on her part before Beauchamp finally listened to her and notified the duke she was here. Both the duke and duchess came to the foyer. She was invited in and brought into one of the small sitting rooms near the front door. "I'm on my way to London, but I had to stop and let you know."

"Let me know what?" the duke asked.

"I was with…" Hannah hesitated when she saw the warning look in the duke's eyes. "What I mean is I met a man who told me that 'is children were taken from 'im."

"Not again," Kiya groaned.

"'e said you were rich, and 'e didn't have a chance of getting 'em back. 'e's plannin' on takin' 'em." Again, she hesitated. "Well, take Lizzie anyways. I think 'e's going to ask for ransom once 'e 'as 'er."

"Oh my God, this is never going to end."

"Why do you think he's going to ask for ransom?" Matt asked.

"'e asked me how much do I think 'e could get?"

Kiya moaned.

Matt nodded. "Did he say how or when?"

Hannah was smart enough to keep her part of that conversation to herself. But she did say, "'e knows men are waiting for 'im in the woods. I don't know 'ow. So 'e's waiting for Lizzie to ride. Said 'e'd shoot 'er guard and take 'er."

"Jesus," Matt muttered.

"She won't be riding. Not until we know he's gone forever," her mother insisted.

Matt looked at his wife, nodded and smiled. "We'll keep her safe. Don't worry." And then, looking at the woman before him, he said, "The last woman to tell us about Edwards ended up badly hurt."

"Oh 'e won't 'urt me none."

Matt nodded. "You might be right, but there's no need to take a chance. Stay here. I'll be right back."

Matt left the room. Kiya smiled at the girl. "Why did you leave us, Hannah?"

"I got an offer for a better position, ma'am."

"Did you? And it had nothing to do with the men in the barn?"

Hannah's eyes widened with shock. "But you weren't supposed to—"

"I know. My husband likes to believe I'm a bit simple."

Hannah shook her head. "Not simple, Duchess," she said with amazing insight. "I think 'e's thinkin' innocent."

Kiya laughed. If anyone in this house had a clue as to what went on behind their bedroom door, innocent would be the last thing they'd imagine of their mistress. "You might be right. When you secure your next post, I'd make sure the men…"

"I'll be a bit more discreet next time."

Kiya smiled and nodded her approval.

"'ow did you find out?"

"You should know nothing gets by the servants."

Hannah laughed.

"I'm sure I knew long before my husband walked in on you."

Matt re-entered the room. "I've a coach waiting to bring you to London and the stagecoach line. Plus you'll take this to see you over," he said as he handed her a generous stack of pound notes.

"Oh sir, it's too much."

"Take it," Kiya insisted. "It's not too much." Turning to Matt, she added, "Matt, please give her a letter of reference."

He nodded, wrote a sentence or two on a sheet of paper, signed it and sealed it with a few drops of wax and the impression of his ring.

* * * *

They stood on the mansion's steps as the coach pulled away with two men riding, one on each side. If they were eager to be about this chore neither man let it be known.

"How long do you think before they stop?"

Matt frowned. "Stop? You mean before they reach London? Why should they stop?"

Kiya let the question go for a minute. "You know, I rode in a coach once. Only I wasn't alone. A man sat across from me. You know what happened?"

Matt grinned at the wicked glance sent his way. "What?"

"It was the most shocking thing. The man asked," she shrugged, "well sort of insisted actually, to see my unmentionables simply because I happened to mention that they were almost see-through. Can you imagine?"

"Truly it's hard to conceive of such a happening. He was a bold fellow."

Kiya laughed, the sound clear and lovely. "Oh, he was that indeed."

Matt's heart filled to overflowing. He couldn't believe how much he loved this woman. "But how does that—"

"It's not at all the same, except for the fact that a lady rides in a coach. That particular lady," she nodded towards the coach as it turned from the drive towards London, "likes men well enough, and there are two riding alongside." Kiya glanced at her husband, offering a dazzling grin, implying the woman would have no choice now that the men were there.

"She's a nice woman, I've no doubt, but she's no lady, Kiya."

"No, a lady would never take men two at a time in the barn, while others awaited their turn."

Matt took her by the waist and turned her to face him while laughing in surprise. "Why you little... How did you find out?"

"I think the real question here is why were you keeping it a secret?"

"I wasn't." And at the narrowing of her gaze, he reconsidered. "All right, perhaps I was. I thought you'd be horrified."

"I might have been if a certain husband of mine was a bit less frisky."

"A certain husband? Have you more than one, then?"

"I've only one," she returned then added wickedly, "at the moment."

"Witch," he said with a little shake then guided her inside and down the hall towards his office. "I need to look at a few papers this afternoon. Do you think you could lend me a hand?"

This was the first time Matt had ever included her in his business dealings. Her eyes widened in surprise, for she hadn't an iota of how she might help. "In truth?"

"Would you like to learn about my business interests?"

"I would like that."

Matt nodded. "Then I shall show you all you need to know. But for today, I'll need a little more than your hand."

"What do you mean?" Kiya should have known what he meant. If she'd looked in his eyes, she wouldn't have been left with a doubt.

"I'd take it as a personal favour if you could spare me a moment or two."

She narrowed her gaze again. "A personal favour? That sounds familiar, don't you think?" The door closed behind her, and she found herself suddenly pressed between it and her husband. "Could it be you're about to grow frisky again?"

"I love you."

Kiya laughed. "I know. I thought we were going to look at a few papers."

Matt reached behind her and locked the door. He then took a step or two to his right, grabbed a few sheets of paper and threw them on the floor. Returning to her, he nodded at the fallen papers. "We could look at these."

Kiya laughed. "I'm sure we could, but I'll need my spectacles especially since they're so far away."

Matt grinned as he reached for the buttons of her dress. "I've a thought. We could move closer to them. You're adorable."

"That is a thought," she returned in agreement then added, "and thank you."

"When were you going to tell me you knew what was going on."

"You mean with Hannah?"

He nodded as he took off his jacket and loosened his cravat.

"I didn't want to disappoint you. You were doing such a lovely job of protecting me. If she hadn't come back, I might never have told you."

Matt grinned, looking deep into her blue eyes as he shook his head. "Do you think we might spend the rest of our lives protecting each other?"

"I hope so. I thought you were very sweet."

"Sweet? Not exactly the characteristic I'd boast on."

"Well, if you're looking for my thoughts of you, I can tell you you're not only sweet."

"No? What am I then?"

"Indeed, I wouldn't be far off the mark if I said, domineering, obnoxious, controlling, delicious, gorgeous, gentle, and the man who stole my heart."

Matt laughed as his merits good and bad rolled off her tongue. "Stole it? I thought you gave it to me."

"You took it first then I gave it to you." The sweet sound of her laughter was cut off by the pressure of his mouth. His heart pounded in his chest, and Matt wondered if there would ever come a time when he'd feel sated, when he'd finally touch her enough, kiss her enough and love her enough. So far, their coming together had only caused him to want her more, to want her beyond anything else in his life.

Her eyes were half closed with passion as her mouth rose to meet his, and she made a tiny sound of satisfaction as she easily pushed his lips apart and found nothing to bar her way into the depth and heat of him. Her tongue savoured his taste and texture. She moaned her appreciation as she rediscovered every mysterious nuance of his clean mouth.

On their knees, she sucked his bottom lip into hers and ran her tongue over it, adoring the flavour and feel of him. Then her mouth moved to his jaw to his throat. He arched his neck, allowing her complete access.

"I love you," she murmured. "I really love you."

"Open my shirt."

She did his bidding without thought, kissing her way down his chest as the fabric parted.

"Now yours," he said. "Open your bodice."

Kiya quickly opened her bodice and rubbed her breasts against the crinkly hair on his chest.

"Oh God," they uttered in unison, neither hearing the other, as hearts pounded, obscuring all else but the touch, the feel of each other.

Her mouth dragged over his chest, leaving a trail of hot, wet kisses as she worked her way down to his waist and the edge of his trousers.

He was gasping for his every breath, desperate for her to take the next step. He wanted her. God, how he wanted this woman.

The tabs at his waist were quickly undone and his trousers and drawers were pushed to his knees, while he helped her pull away her own clothing. "My cock, Kiya, please, my cock."

"Yes," she murmured. And again, she said, "Yes," just as she took the satiny length of his cock deep into the heat of her mouth. And as she licked and gently nibbled his shaft, her hands moved over his body as if memorizing all she touched. Open wet lips ran from the base to the tip of his cock then sucked as deep as she could manage while she weighed and played with his balls.

She was driving him out of his mind. He couldn't take any more. He had to have her, and it had to be now. "You got me so hot, Kiya. I'll die if I can't take you now."

"Then do it. Do it now," she said as she leaned back, her legs wide for his delight. Her hands spread open the lips of her wet, pink pussy, displaying all to his delight, her actions inviting him more than any words could. He shuddered at the sight of her. And wondered how he managed not to lose his seed right there on the office carpet.

"Hold it, damn it. Wait," he said more to himself than his love, as he watched her hands move over herself. "I need to see you. I need to watch you touch yourself."

Kiya laughed. "Do you? What would you like to see?"

"Hold your pussy wide just like that. Jesus, God," he groaned as she did as he asked. "Now rub your fingers inside."

She was wet, wetter than he'd ever seen her. His mouth watered, wishing there was time for him to taste her. Her juices glistened in her tiny curls, running over her fingers and thighs. His gaze widened with newborn delight. He'd taken this woman innumerable times, and he'd never seen her so damn hot.

It was beyond his power to further resist her siren's call. He entered her with a powerful thrust and heard her low, guttural moan.

"Was I too rough? Jesus, Kiya, I didn't hurt you, did I?"

"No, it felt good. You didn't hurt me," she somehow returned over the pounding of her heart and the roaring of her blood. "Don't stop, Matt. God, just don't stop."

And he didn't. Her legs were around his waist, and he didn't stop as the pleasure mounted and grew to torment. And then the torment raged on and on until nothing was left but mind-shattering bliss.

Some time later, Kiya shifted then sighed as she felt the papers rustle beneath her. "I don't think we got much work done."

"Jesus, I haven't got the strength to lift a pen."

"I don't think that's necessary. I've not a doubt that your signature is clearly written upon my backside." She laughed. "Should you need it written anywhere, I'll simply sit on the paper for you."

Matt moaned, his mouth holding to the lush softness of a generous breast, as he reached for the object in question. "Shall I turn you over and look?"

"Perhaps later," she gasped as his fingers found the moist heat of her ass impossible to resist. She squirmed. The movement only caused him to press more deeply into her warmth and his finger two knuckles deep inside her ass. And still he continued to play.

"Right now, I've better things to do with your rear than write upon it."

Kiya laughed in delight as he rolled her over the small office floor, playing with her delicious ass and pussy until the dinner bell brought them back to their senses.

Chapter Eighteen

"He's threatened to shoot the guards in order to take Lizzie. As you can imagine, neither child will be riding for some time."

Jake nodded his approval then shook his head in disgust. "Damn, we don't need this added aggravation. I want to bring Merry home. How the hell much longer?"

One of the guards raced into the yard and dismounted in a cloud of dust almost before his horse came to a full stop. "Just heard, another girl is missing. Half the town is out searching for her."

Both Matt and Jake grated horrified curses as they shook their heads in disgust. "Who was watching Shelby last night?"

"Gus Evans."

Matt nodded. "Tell Evans I want to see him, will you?"

Moments later, Gus Evans walked up to the two men, and Matt asked, "Anything happen last night? Did you see or hear anything?"

Gus shrugged and replied, "Yesterday, just before sundown a man came to the back gate on horseback and hauled a canvas bag over his shoulder as he went inside. Couldn't see what was in it."

"Might it have been a girl?"

Gus shrugged again. "Could have been, I suppose. Didn't know anyone was missing until now, and I didn't think about the possibility at the time."

"Who was he?"

"I don't know him, but I've seen him bring other packages inside."

"Larger packages?"

Gus shrugged. "It was always at night. I could never tell," he nodded. "But larger yeah."

Matt nodded. "You've got someone watching the place around the clock," he said. It was less a question than a statement of fact.

Gus nodded. "Have been for a while."

"Good. Keep it up."

Gus walked away, as Matt muttered, "If I could think of a reason to get into that place..."

Jake shrugged. "He was once your brother-in-law. You could always stop in for a friendly visit."

Matt grinned. "You think the earl might be pining away, waiting for me to drop by?"

Jake had a difficult time controlling his need to laugh. "I'm not sure, but I think he might."

* * * *

"I understand congratulations are in order."

Matt forced a smile—the same smile he'd pasted across his face from the moment the bastard's butler had ushered him inside. "You were invited. A pity you had previous plans."

Shelby shook his head in supposed dismay and said a bit woefully, "Yes, that was unfortunate. Couldn't be avoided, I'm afraid. Pressing business matters." He allowed a smile, the same slimy smile he always exhibited. Matt imagined the man believed his smile to appear sincere. "I would have loved seeing your lovely mother again. I heard it was the social event of the season."

"I suppose it was."

"You have friends in high places. I read even the Prime Minister was there."

"He was." Matt shrugged. "My father's friend, you know. He was at your wedding, as well."

Shelby nodded. "I remember."

Matt sipped at the cognac, even as he wondered if the bottle had come from one of the many cases his wife had smuggled in from France. "Smooth," he said as he held the clear amber liquid up to the fire.

"I don't mind telling you it cost a pretty penny. Until this war ends, everything costs more than it should."

"I'm surprised to see you've never married again."

The earl gave a shrug of sorts. "You have to know the loss of your sister was my greatest heartache. I don't mind telling you it's been years, and still... Well, let's just say, I'll never forget her."

Matt barely contained his rage. He wanted nothing more than to slam his fists into this man's lying face, to hit him until his arms ached from exhaustion. He forced his expression under control. He wouldn't give this maggoty sack of shit the satisfaction of knowing his rage.

The earl took a moment before he went on. "It took a long time before I could think of marrying again. Actually, I was engaged for a short time, but that didn't work out."

Both men were aware of the reason why, and both men were conscious of the fact that the other knew. Still, they continued to pretend civility.

"I'm leaving the country for a bit. When I return, I think I'll look over the next crop of beauties London has to offer."

Matt knew the season wouldn't begin for some time. "You'll be leaving for some months then."

"I will. I've a friend who owns a place on the islands. I'm to visit with him for a spell."

"You've heard, of course, of the killings, the young girls who've been murdered?"

"I have." Shelby shook his head in dismay. "It's a terrible thing."

"Another was taken last night."

"Good God, another?" Shelby almost laughed aloud as he heard the shock in his own voice then bemoaned, "What is this world coming to?"

"A good question, I sometimes wonder." Matt took another taste of his drink. "You know the ones we found were whipped. They had the same markings on them as my sister did."

"Jesus! Are you saying it's the same man?"

"It appears it very well might be."

Matt decided it was time to leave. Finally, he mentioned the trumped up reason for this visit. "Oh, I almost forgot the reason for my visit. My mother was wondering if you had anything of my sister's. Something you might be willing to part with, of course. Something personal. Perhaps the ring my mother gave her the day before she married. Anything, even a hanky, or perhaps some needlepoint she was working on when she disappeared?"

"I'll have to look through my things. I'll find her something, I'm sure. I always thought your mother was a lovely woman. You will tell her I sent my regards, won't you?"

"Of course. It was nice to see you again. If you like, I can come back in say a week to pick up the item."

"That won't be necessary. I'll send it on, probably by the end of the week."

Matt smiled. If one didn't look too closely, the hatred in his dark eyes might be missed. Shelby had looked and couldn't help but wonder why either one of them bothered to pretend. They hated each other's guts. Shelby knew Matt believed him behind his sister's murder. The only problem was he couldn't prove a damn thing and he never would. Shelby almost laughed at the younger man's obvious frustration.

He grinned as Matt departed then laughed his relief, knowing he had pulled it off. There wasn't much he could do about the fact that the man obviously didn't believe him. Truth was he couldn't have cared less. He listened with glee as Matt's horse trotted away from his property. In a day or two, Shelby would be leaving for the island, and his mother-in-law could drop dead before he'd give the bitch a thing.

Right now, he had himself a little treat waiting. It was growing late. He thought he wouldn't keep her waiting any longer.

* * * *

Later that same day, after dinner, John Harrison and the dowager Duchess of Stratford strolled again through the formal gardens behind his mansion. She'd been here three weeks. During that time, their initial attraction had grown as the two had become more comfortable in each other's company. Still, Madelyn thought it well past time to return home. "I find I must leave by the end of the week, John. I'm afraid I have innumerable appointments I'm no longer able to postpone."

"Have you been postponing them?"

She allowed him a charming smile. "I have, and I can only hold you to blame for keeping me away so long."

"I won't be happy to see you go. Not since my wife have I so completely enjoyed a woman's company."

"Indeed?" she returned in obvious doubt.

"Not a woman like you."

Madelyn laughed.

"I hope you've enjoyed your time here."

"Oh, I have. Truly. Your girls are delightful. I've lost my daughter and I'm so happy to find another in Kiya. I'm so pleased, John. I don't think Matthew could have chosen better. I only hope my other boys will be half so fortunate."

John nodded his agreement. "I think they've found a true match in each other. But what about your host?"

She smiled. "What about him?"

"Are you pleased to have gotten to know him?"

"I am."

"How pleased?"

"Pleased enough to invite you and your girls to my home for the holidays. If you've made no other plans, we should have a lovely time of it. Most of my children will be there as well as many friends. There are large expanses of woodland, and the men hunt most every day. The festivities stretch late into the night."

John frowned for the holidays were yet months away. "And there will be no chance for me to see you before then?"

She offered a tantalising smile. "Would you prefer we met sooner?"

"I'd prefer you never left at all."

"I've long promised a trip to the continent with my cousin and her husband. We'll be leaving next week. If you've no plans, perhaps you'd care to join us. We're touring northern Italy. Have you ever been there?"

"Not with someone like you." John thought quickly. As far as he could remember there was no pressing business. And he didn't give a damn if there was. He was not going to refuse her invitation. "When are you leaving?"

"On the fifth."

"And I can't convince you to stay on until then?"

She laughed and offered him her most tantalising smile. "I've had a wonderful stay, I'm sure. But I've already stayed well beyond what I should have. Indeed, I've no doubt you'll only know relief to see the last of me."

John groaned, and without thinking of the consequences, his arms came suddenly around her small waist and brought her unresisting body to press tightly to his. They'd had many teasing conversations and spent hours alone in the darkened gardens, but until this minute, he had never touched her. Madelyn could only sigh her relief that he had finally done so.

"Don't go. God, I don't know what I'll do if I awaken every morning knowing you won't be here. I know it's too soon, but I have to tell you I admire you above all women."

His mouth nuzzled her cheek and jaw and she moaned softly as she not only accepted the caress but turned just enough to allow their lips to finally meet.

He groaned as his mouth took possession of hers at last. Hungrily, he twisted his head then twisted again so he might find greater access. "God, Maddie, God," was all he was able to manage as his tongue smoothed over her lips and eagerly sought entry to her sweet mouth.

Madelyn shivered at the barely checked passion, unsure if it were hers or his that slammed with terrible urgency into her stomach. She opened her mouth at the slightest pressure of his tongue, eager to know his taste and his scent. Her head reeled by the time he brought the wildly ecstatic moment under control.

"Lord help us," she sighed into his warm neck, "but it has taken you an exceedingly long time to do that."

John smiled, pulled back and blinked his surprise. "Was I moving too slow?"

"Any slower and I'm sure you wouldn't be moving at all."

He laughed. "If a certain lady had offered a man a clue as to the direction of her thoughts, he might have moved a bit faster."

She joined him in his laughter, the sound low, sultry and far sexier than she might have imagined. "A lady is at a definite disadvantage in circumstances such as these."

"I wanted you from the first moment I saw you. You had to have noticed my interest."

"I noticed."

"And yet you did nothing."

Madelyn leaned back, allowing a most intimate embrace that brought his hips and obvious arousal into bold contact with her stomach. As she spoke, she idly smoothed his shirt front, forcing her hands away from what she wanted most to touch. "I stayed on at your request, did I not? I've walked with you in these lovely gardens every night after dinner. What more can a lady do?"

John was aware of his arousal and the fact that it was pressed against the tiny lady though she made no mention of it. He held her loosely, but she did not step away. Rather, the opposite was true for she stirred ever so softly against him, enticing him to take further liberties. He took hope in her gentle movement and dared to ask, "Is it too soon, Maddie? Might I visit your room tonight?"

She grinned at his plea. "You might, I suppose. It is your house, after all."

"Don't tease me, sweetheart. Jesus, I feel like a lad again. I'm desperate to have you."

"Are you? I'd say you hide your needs well. You've kissed me only once and
have yet to touch me?"

"What are you saying?"

"What I'm saying is you needn't treat me as if I'm made of porcelain."

"Oh my God," he groaned, knowing she was giving him permission to make the next move. "Step over here for a moment, will you?" he asked as he brought her into the deep shadows beneath a tree.

She laughed as he nearly dragged her into the alcove of dark shrubbery. "Is there something in particular you want to show me, Mr. Harrison?"

"You'd best stop teasing me, Duchess."

"Or?"

"What?" he asked, his mind having a time of keeping up with his body's wild needs.

"What will you do if I refuse to stop teasing you, John?"

"I'm afraid I'll have no choice but to do this," he said as his mouth swooped down and effectively cut off her laughter. His hands found the deliciousness of her breasts and delighted them both as he pushed her dress lower, freeing the lush softness and groaning his pleasure as the generous mounds tumbled into his all-so-willing hands.

He tore his mouth from her tempting lips, gasping for breath and eager to discover charms so wondrously displayed. His thumbs had already brought the sweetly giving flesh to hard aching nubs.

Suddenly, his gaze took in the soft glow of red against the dark woodland far beyond his house. He frowned at the sight, his mind somewhat muddled and unable for a moment to comprehend. He blinked, clearing aside a bit of his passion, and wondered at the peculiarity that the sun should glow in just one spot upon his property, especially since the sky had already turned to night.

And then he realised the truth of the matter.

"What the hell?" Fire. There was a small fire burning in the distance. Had a vagrant stumbled upon his property and made himself at home with a campfire?

"Maddie," he said

"Mmm," she murmured, unwilling to be drawn from this ecstatic state of near-diabolic pleasure.

Quickly, he readjusted her dress and, with one last quick kiss and breathless hug, said, "We have to go. Someone has started a small fire."

Within minutes, they were in the sitting room, eyes wide with growing dread. Both greatly feared the fire might be part of a plan to see harm come to this family.

Matt came instantly to his feet when told of the fire and ran to his office for his gun.

"Oh dear, you will be careful, won't you, Matthew?" his mother said as he reappeared armed.

"I'll be fine, mother. Don't worry. He kissed Kiya and without another word was gone in a flash out the French doors that led to the barn and the back property, with Jake hot on his heels. With six men, Matt and Jake race towards the flames. Within seconds, they beat the fire out, but just as the last flame disappeared into a puff of smoke, a shot suddenly rang out. Matt cursed as he grabbed his left arm with his right hand. He felt little but a dull throbbing ache at first, but knew he'd later suffer some true discomfort. "I've been hit. Watch yourselves."

* * * *

Tony Edwards had grinned as he'd watched the men run towards the woods out back. Within seconds, he'd lit the dry debris stacked along the side wall of the house and laughed as it took hold in a flash and began to climb the walls just outside the sitting room.

He heard the women scream and watched flames jump into the room and catch one of the chairs on fire. Quickly, he ran around the house to hide in the shrubbery just outside the front door a few steps from his tethered horse.

He knew most would exit the house by way of the front door, except for the servants who would no doubt use the kitchen door. Well, he couldn't be in two places at one time. His best chance to grab the kid would be at the front door.

He didn't have long to wait. The women screamed as they ran from the place. He counted four ladies and a number of servants, plus what appeared to be the kid's nurse and governess. And then the kids themselves. It looked as if the master of the house and any male servants had stayed behind, no doubt trying to extinguish the flames.

Edwards grinned. Damn, he hadn't imagined it was going to be this easy. In seconds, he grabbed his little girl and started for his horse. The governess or nurse or the kid — he wasn't sure which — screamed.

Lizzie's cry caused Kiya's chest to squeeze. All about were in hysterics. Men were dashing in and out of the door, pulling out people and items that were flammable. The entire scenario was chaos plain and simple. No one but Kiya, Mrs. Stevens and Sally heard Lizzie's screams.

A woman ran towards Edwards and jumped on his back. He tried to shake her off, but she held on and, in a heartbeat, gave him two punches to his face, hitting him solidly in the nose and causing blood to gush over his mouth and shirt and the little girl held tightly in his arms. He shook the woman off and delivered a punch that would see her unable to fight anyone for time, only to find another in her place. He dropped the girl who ran screaming back to the group near the house as he fought the bitch who had taken her in the fist place. With no little satisfaction he left her unconscious with a quick, hard punch to her jaw.

An instant later, he was pulled into a circle of men, the last thing he remembered were lights flashing as one of them, slammed a fist into the side of his face, while the unconscious woman was temporarily ignored.

* * * *

Connery returning from another hunt, this time without the prize he'd hoped to gain, watched from behind a wide hedge as men ran to and fro and women screamed at the drifts of smoke that escaped the mansion. The scene was pure wild confusion.

No one noticed the small woman laying unconscious near the hedge. No one was there to stop him. All it took was some quick movement on his part, and he had her in his arms. A moment later, he mounted his horse and sped into the night.

* * * *

Seth stood there in shock. The women were screaming. Everyone was screaming even as the men called out orders. Seth tried to tell them that the bad man had hit his mummy and another had taken her on his horse. Only no one could hear him. No matter how much he yelled, no matter how much he tugged on skirts, no one even saw him. He gave up and dashed for the barn. He had to get Daisy and follow his mum.

It was quiet inside the barn. Too late, Seth realised Daisy was unsaddled. He was too little to saddle her by himself. He had no choice. He opened the door to the stall and climbed the short wall. With some grunting effort, he finally managed to settle himself on Daisy's back. In seconds, he was heading his horse down the road trying to keep up with the man who'd taken his mum.

It wasn't hard to keep up. Daisy was a good horse and Seth's gentle urgings moved her along nicely. The problem was Seth had never ridden bareback before and was having a problem staying on. Desperately, he held to the horse's mane, leaning low he hugged Daisy's neck even as he tried to keep his seat and stifle the soft, terrified sobs he couldn't completely control.

Finally, he saw the horse turn into the woods by the big house with the high stone fence. Seth had to get help. He had to find his dad.

He turned Daisy around and headed back.

In the meantime, Matt had returned to the house. Even in the near dark, Matt had no trouble recognising Edwards. "Take him to the barn. Tie him to one of the posts and keep watch over him. This one is headed for the colonies." His laugh was closer to a jeer, his voice low and purely taunted. "Just like I promised."

The fire was out. He was amazed to find the inhabitants outside on the front drive. Sally, in her man's arms, had recovered enough to explain. "He was taking Lizzie. I had to try and stop him. Your missus must have seen what I did. He hit me, and as I was falling, I saw her jump on him. When I woke up, Lizzie was still here, but Mrs. Chase was gone. Someone took her!"

Matt realised the fire out back had been a ruse. A needed diversion to ensure the chance to take Lizzie, only their plans had been deterred by two women who were far too brave. God damn it! When he got his hands on Kiya he was going to... *Oh Jesus, please let me get my hands on her. Let her be all right.*

He was beside himself. He couldn't think. He didn't know what to do, where to go, how or where to begin his search. He was as close to hysterical as he was ever likely to get when he watched in nothing less than amazement as his son rode up the drive and almost fell as he slid from Daisy's back. With tears running down his face, he ran to his father. "Dad, he got her. A man came and took mummy."

"She was lying on the grass. The other man hit her and then the big man took her." It took only a few seconds to explain, only a few for Matt to understand the boy through his sobs of terror. He hugged the boy tight against him, and Seth cried into his father's chest.

Matt looked at Jake. "Get the men ready to ride. All of them but for a few we'll leave to watch the house. Tell them to surround it."

He knelt before Seth and hugged the boy against his chest. "You did good, Seth. If it weren't for you..." He took a deep shaken breath. "You did better than any of the guards. Don't tell them I said so." The last of it he said close to the boy's ear, bringing about a huge, proud smile amid hiccupping sobs.

As far as the lad knew, the man took her to a house where the road separated into two. A big house surrounded by a high stone wall.

Matt knew there was only one big house with a high stone wall where the road forked. A man had taken his wife to the earl and, in doing so, had signed both their death warrants.

"Matthew, you've been hurt," his mother reminded as she noticed his torn jacket and the blood coating one sleeve and hand. "What happened?"

"Edwards. He's tied up in the barn. I'll send for the constable later."

"But..."

He nodded at her concern. "It's already stopped bleeding, mother. Just a nick I think. I'll have it seen to when I get back."

"But..."

"The most important thing right now is to bring Kiya back."

Madelyn nodded, keeping her fears to herself. A man brought Matt's horse to the front. In seconds, three dozen men joined him. He mounted the horse and, with a long look sent his father-in-law's way, told the man without words he'd do exactly what he said he would. Without another word spoken, he led the way as they raced out of the yard.

* * * *

Kiya was dazed. Her first thought upon awakening was pain. Her jaw ached terribly then she remembered. And when she remembered, she stiffened, almost causing the man who carried her to drop her.

"Take it easy. No one is going to hurt you," the man whispered above her.

Kiya screamed. Did he think her a fool? Of course, she didn't for a minute believe a word the man said. He was right about one thing though. No one was going to hurt her if she escaped. She screamed again. She was inside a building. Surely someone in here would help her. Surely a servant would come to her rescue.

Another powerful blow came to her cheek. Kiya groaned at the jolting pain until another came. This one, heavier and harder still, promised escape. A thick, heavy, blackness surrounded the edges of her consciousness. It beckoned that she succumb, that she give over and Kiya hadn't the strength to refuse.

* * * *

God, her arms were killing her. What in the world had she done? Was Matt laying on them? Was she? Why should they…

Kiya came fully awake to the sound of male laughter. A man stood before her. A naked man wearing a leather mask. Two naked men, she quickly corrected as she glanced to her right and watched the nightmare of a masked man laughing as he left the side of a bloodied girl.

Kiya shuddered at the sight. The girl wasn't conscious. For that, Kiya could only thank God, as she watched blood gush from the tiny, pitiful frame.

Kiya wished she could faint. She didn't want to see this. She didn't want to even know about this.

A hand slid over her breast and pinched hard at her nipple. She moaned with the pain and tried to push away her assailant. It was then that she realised her hands were above her, tied to something, holding her in place, preventing her from managing even the most feeble protection.

"Big, brave, strong men," she muttered. "Can't find a woman who will want you? Can you only manage the act if a woman is tied and helpless."

Both men knew what she was about. They knew she was terrified and sneered her remark to bolster her own courage. Despite the harsh words, she couldn't hide the tremor in her voice.

Both men laughed at her bravado. Both knew it wouldn't last long. Soon, she'd be whimpering like all the others. Soon, she'd beg to be allowed to die.

"You know, of course, that my husband will kill you for this."

"She talks like a duchess, all right."

"Like her bitch sister-in-law."

Both men chuckled, knowing it was best when watching the high born grovel. There was something about the power. The higher born, the more the power they felt.

Eventually, even a duchess would do exactly as she was told. It was amazing how low a person could grovel when the whip was laid to them and pain filled their every waking moment.

"She needs a little touch. Let's see how brave she is after that."

They laughed as they each picked up a whip.

Kiya whispered a quick prayer, knowing nothing and no one but God could help her get through this. The whip whistled through the air and struck her high on her naked thigh. She screamed as the tail snapped, causing the skin to break.

* * * *

Matt had almost reached the earl's mansion when he spied a man on a horse racing towards him. "Your lordship," the man said as he brought the horse to an instant stop. "A man brought a woman to the back gate. He carried her inside."

"My wife?"

Pete wasn't sure who the lady was. He hadn't been close enough to see. With a quick, helpless shrug, he offered weakly, "I couldn't see her face."

Matt forced himself to ask, "Was she awake?" He couldn't bring himself to ask if she lived. He had to believe that she did.

Pete shook his head. "She looked to be unconscious. The man was careful with her," he added.

Matt took heart at this bit of information. She was alive. There'd be no need to deliver a corpse. And certainly no need to be careful. Careful had to mean she was alive.

His lips tightened with rage. Murder flashed in his dark eyes. He could hardly wait to get his hands on the man who took her. It was better, far better that he keep his mind on Willis. If he concentrated on the murderous rage he felt for Shelby and Willis, there was little time left to worry.

They reached the front gate at last. The dogs were loose, ferocious and beside themselves with the need to attack as they jumped and slammed their bodies against the gate. The barking and growling was enough to awaken the dead, yet the gatekeeper never showed his face.

There was no way that Matt would wait. He ordered five men to take care of the dogs while a sixth man jumped the gate and opened it.

The men rushed in. Pounding upon the huge front doors brought about no results. The place appeared empty, but Matt knew better. The servants were quartered above the carriage house, no doubt to enable Shelby to do his dirty deeds unnoticed. It didn't matter. He needed no one to let him in. He nodded towards Pete who stood at his right. "Take out that window. I'm not waiting another minute."

Pete broke through the window. Within seconds, the men filed into the house. "No unnecessary noise. You," he pointed to Travis, "take five men. Search the second floor. You," he nodded towards Mike, "take another five to the third floor and attics. And when I say search I mean every closet, crawl space, nook and cranny. You got that?"

Matt nodded as the dozen men took off to do his bidding.

"What are you thinking?" Jake asked.

"I'm thinking between the dogs and the noise it took to break in, he should have shown himself long before this. That means he didn't hear us." Matt looked around the huge centre hall and watched his men raced from room to room. "Maybe he's not here."

"He's here," Jake insisted.

"I mean maybe he has a special place, but it's not in the house." He thought for a few seconds trying to figure where... Where... "Suppose it's underground. That would prevent anyone from hearing screams if he was torturing..." Matt shivered, unable to finish the sentence.

"All right, say you're right. Say he has a chamber underground. The best place would be here."

"Tell me why," he implored, desperate to hear they were at least on the right track.

"The servants sleep over the carriage house, right?"

Matt nodded.

"It wouldn't be there. Too dangerous. They might hear or see something."

Matt nodded his agreement.

"The   gardens   are   out   as   well."
Matt waited for his reasoning.

"Too easy to be seen coming and going. No, it's definitely here, in the house."

"Tear this fucking place apart."

Jake called out, "Listen to me." Every man within his hearing stopped. "After you check everywhere, do it again. The duchess is in here. Behind a wall, in an attic, somewhere that would stop any cries from being heard. Hurry up!"

Steve Parker searched the kitchen. There wasn't much to see. A small utility closet and a larger pantry. Two others had opened the trapdoor leading below to the cellars. Five more joined the two. There were three cellars, in all, one stored root vegetables such as potatoes, squash and such, another held shelves of jars containing preserved vegetables and fruits, while another was filled with free standing racks of wine. All seven men pushed at shelves, tapped on walls, hit floors but found nothing. There was no cell, no small room. Nothing but solid brick walls in a cellar that led nowhere.

They were disappointed but undeterred. They would find her. Nothing was going to stop them from finding her.

Matt was tearing at a wall, hitting against it with an iron curtain rod searching for something, anything that would give them a hint as to where she might be held, when he suddenly stopped.

"Jake," he said to the man across the room. "Jake," he said again as he turned to face him. "Listen to me. Who would know this house at least as well or perhaps better than the owner?"

Jake shook his head. "If you're thinking the man who built it, forget it. This place is about three hundred years old."

"Right, but who else?"

"The housekeeper, the butler?"

Matt nodded. "The butler. He sleeps over the carriage house, right?"

Jake nodded, and to another of his men said, "Harry, bring him here."

Harry was outside and running towards the far end of the drive and the carriage house before Matt finished his order. No light shone from the rooms above, but Harry pounded on the door. He was still pounding on the door when inside the kitchen another door suddenly opened.

Steve Parker had searched the room twice already. He checked the stove, wondering if it were possible that the heavy thing rotated on some sort of device. Maybe a small room stood behind it. Maybe a large one. Maybe a priest hole. Most of these big old houses had them. But Steve could find nothing. No scratches on the floor, telling of something being dragged about. No walls that moved. Nothing. He shoved with all his might, but the cast iron object remained firmly in place. Next he went over the pantry and closet again. Nothing. God, there had to be something. There just had to be. Accidently, his foot kicked a pail and it fell over. Oddly enough, the small amount of water inside instantly disappeared and yet the floor remained dry. How the hell? The water had run behind the wall. That fast? Why? Steve pressed against the wall. Nothing. He tapped it. Was it his imagination? Did it sound hollow? He moved to his right and stumbled on a mop. He grabbed at a hook to keep his balance, and the back of the damn closet suddenly moved. In amazement, he stared at a narrow brick hallway, lit by a lone, small torch embedded into the wall. Steve moved quickly towards the main room to find his boss, his whistle was loud and piercing as he went.

Three men were instantly at his side. He whistled again and Matt and Jake were there, as well.

"What have we here?" Matt asked a with a hard smile as his gaze took in the utility closet.

Steve nodded towards the closet. "There's a tunnel behind that wall. It opens when you turn that hook."

Matt nodded and watched as the back wall opened. "Jake, just you, come with me."

Every man there knew why the boss wanted only Jake with him. If the lady was in trouble, and there wasn't a man there who believed otherwise, he didn't want anyone to see more than what was absolutely necessary.

A small torch sat in a sconce upon a brick wall some three feet into the hallway, another some twenty feet further along allowed light to what would otherwise be a pitch black tunnel. There were no windows, nothing but wall, floor and ceiling all of brick.

The two men moved silently into the tunnel. At the end stood a wooden door. Neither Matt nor Jake made a sound as they walked the tunnel's length. Then suddenly a blood-curdling scream tore through the silence and nearly froze Matt's heart, for he hadn't a doubt who had screamed.

He was at the end of the hall, his hand on the door before he realised he'd moved. Jake stood immediately behind him.

For just an instant, Matt couldn't take it in. He opened the door and stood with gun in hand in obvious shock.

The most shocking, of course, was the fact that his wife stood to his left with her arms stretched wide, her wrists tied with rope that was secured to steel rings imbedded in a heavy overhead beam attached to the ceiling. She was naked and stood before two equally naked, sexually aroused men.

The men wore leather masks, no doubt thinking to increase their pleasure by further terrorising their victims. They laughed as a red welt began to seep a thin trail of blood upon his wife's thigh, and tears ran freely over her rounded cheeks. None of the three in the room noticed that another two had joined them.

Matt knew he was on the verge of madness. He fought against the insane need to kill these men, to kill them now without another word spoken. Only he wouldn't. He had something in mind for them. First and most important, he had to cover his wife. Later, he swore, oh yes, later he'd coolly and calmly extract his revenge.

He signalled his partner with a nod, silently directing Jake's attention towards the two men then came to stand soundlessly before his wife. He pressed her against him as he quickly removed his coat. His body covered the front of her, his coat the back, as he reached for the bindings on her wrists.

"Matt, oh God, Matt," Kiya sobbed, her face pressed against his chest.

As Kiya cried, he heard the shocked, "What the fuck," behind him.

"I wouldn't, mate," Jake warned, quickly at his partner's back. "Let's put down those whips, shall we?"

When Kiya was free, completely covered in his coat, Matt held her tightly in his arms. "It's all right now, sweetheart." It was then that he noticed the bruise at her jaw and another just under her eye. "Who hit you?"

"The man who brought me here. I don't know him."

Matt nodded and soothed as he ran his hand up and down her back. "No one is ever going to hurt you again."

Matt tightened his lips as he turned his gun on the two masked men, who oddly enough no longer sported erections. He laughed coldly as his gaze dropped to each man's suddenly limp sex.

"The two of you, move apart and turn towards the wall."

"Are you all right? Can you stand?" he asked his wife.

"I'm fine." She nodded towards the two naked men. "They hadn't done much of anything yet."

Matt had seen the red welt on her thigh and the small trickle of blood that oozed from it and knew they had done something. She was naked, and no one had to tell him that they had touched her. That again was something, far too many somethings in fact. Neither one of these pieces of horse shit impersonating humans realised it yet, but both were dead.

"We weren't going to do anything, Matthew."

"That's right. We weren't," the taller of the two said. "The whip slipped, is all. It wasn't meant to touch her."

"No, I'm sure it wasn't," Matt returned in disbelief. "It must have been my imagination to find my wife naked and tied up."

"Will you kill them, Matthew?" Kiya asked, only slightly surprised at the thought for she'd warned from the first that her husband would do just that.

"They touched you. They looked at you."

"Not a killing offense, I'm sure."

"What would you have me do, Kiya?"

"I don't know." She shivered as she forced her mind away from the horror of this day. Somehow she managed to redress. She leaned against Matt when necessary. Kiya might have said she was all right, but she trembled uncontrollably and found it most difficult with to button her dress with her shaking fingers. As she finished, she looked again in their direction and shuddered, "Make them take off their masks."

"Do what my lady says."

The two were ordered to turn from the wall. They did as told.

"Oh my, what have we here?"he asked in feigned surprise. "The Earl of Binghamshire? Who would have thought to find you in your own home?"

For the first time, Kiya realised where she was and who the men behind the masks were. She was held at her husband's side, fully dressed and amazingly calm, considering the last forty five minutes. She recognised the taller of the two without his mask. "He's the one from the county fair."

"The one who shot Johnston," Matt said.

"Call for the constable," she urged.

Matt shook his head. "Kiya, he killed my sister and a dozen others. Young girls. Innocent young girls. Do we want to leave dirt like this alive to one day grab one of our own?"

"If he's arrested," she offered, "and maybe sent to a penal colony…" She let the sentence hang.

"There's no proof. No court will convict a lord of the realm. He'll lie his way out of it and might get off even if you testify." He shook his head again. "There'll be no trial. The two of them are going to die."

Kiya understood his reasoning. Still, she wouldn't be a willing participant to this. She knew they would have killed her if Matt hadn't found her in time. The two were less than animals, for animals never harmed or killed for pleasure. She wouldn't argue for their lives. Perhaps in weeks to come, she'd rethink her decision, but for now the horror was too new, too terrifying. She simply turned towards the three men who suddenly filled the doorway and said, "I'll wait outside."

"No, wait. Don't leave. Don't let him kill me," Shelby pleaded.

"Steve," Matt said to one of the three men, "attend to the duchess, if you will. His lordship boasts an excellent supply of Napoleon brandy. See to it she has at least two fingers then find two men to take her home."

* * * *

Hours later, Matt entered the kitchen at the Harrison mansion and smiled to find his wife and mother serving the family tea. His arm circled Kiya's waist, his free hand whispering gently over her bruises. "Are you all right?"

"I'm perfectly fine," she promised as she turned into his embrace, "or soon will be." She hugged him tight against her. "And you?"

Matt nodded. "Relieved that it's over."

"Are they...?"

Matt nodded. "Dead."

Kiya never asked for the particulars, and Matt never offered the information. Instead, he held her tighter yet and kissed the top of her head, delighting in the clean, warm scent of her. His relief that this terrible day was over and his wife was safe knew no bounds.

It was very late. The children and most of the staff were asleep. Kiya, her sisters, Jake, Madelyn and John sat or stood around the kitchen sipping at cups of tea or glasses that held a slightly stronger brew.

Matt poured himself a drink from the bottle on the table as he came again to his wife's side and said, "I stopped by the doctor. He took a look at my arm." He nodded towards his arm and showed Kiya the bandage.

Kiya knew some surprise for she hadn't known he was injured. She'd been upset enough while being rescued not to have noticed much of anything but the need to get dressed and away from that awful place.

"I'll tell you later," he told her at the question was in her eyes. "Just know we got Edwards."

"What will happen?"

"Let's say he'll be spending some time abroad. Perhaps not as luxuriously as he might have liked." Matt turned to the others. "The villagers know who was behind the murders. Before I left, between the servants and a few from the village, the place was already on its way to being cleaned out." He placed a small brooch into his mother's hand and leaned down to kiss her cheek. "I found this in her jewellery box. I thought you'd like to have it."

Madelyn smiled sadly and held the brooch in her fist pressed close to her heart. Her dark eyes misted a bit. "Thank you, dear."

Matt sighed. "I have the rest of her jewellery. I'll give it to you later. I think every granddaughter should have something of hers."

His mother smiled her agreement.

"Whatever's left of the place will no doubt be gone by tomorrow." He shrugged. "Perhaps the building, as well. There's talk of burning it down."

"I can't believe it's finally over," Merry said. She glanced at her husband and covered the hand that rested on her shoulder. "It's finally safe to go home, Jake."

"I don't mind telling you I'm not happy with the thought of you leaving. It's been very nice, not to say most lively, having my girls around here," their father said.

"I'll only be an hour away, father. You can come for a visit every day if you like. And once the Turner place is finished, Kiya and Matt will be living between the two of us. We'll be able to see each other quite often indeed."

John laughed at that. "The truth is I expect to be a little too busy to do much visiting."

All looked at the man waiting for him to explain. All but for Merry who smiled and Kiya who grinned. "It can't be the mills, father, I'm sure," Kiya remarked. "Your managers do an excellent job running them. One can only wonder why you'd be too busy to visit your daughters."

"I see by your smile you already know."

"I'm sure I don't," she said then offered her most wicked laugh, "even if you haven't been the least bit subtle."

John looked happier than any could ever remember seeing him. He grinned as he looked at his two oldest girls and took in their knowing expressions. He shook his head "Never could get anything by you girls."

"You got it by me," Amy said obviously confused. "What's happening?"

"Amy, I think you were looking in the wrong place again," Merry offered.

"What? What do you mean?"

"Merry means, I've asked Madelyn to marry me, and to my delight, she has agreed."

All were smiling with pleasure and offering their best wishes as Amy came to her feet. "What? Aren't you too old for that sort of thing?"

Matt grinned as he took his mother in a tender hug and shook hands with his father-in-law.

"I probably should have waited to ask you first," John said.

Matt laughed aloud. "You would have wasted your time. I know my mother, and when she makes up her mind, nothing can stop her."

"Had you already made up your mind, Madelyn?" John asked.

And to everyone's delight, she returned, "I'm afraid I did, John."

"Another wedding. I'm sure the neighbours will begin to wonder if there isn't something in the water around here."

"Wonderful, just wonderful," Amy remarked, and if she could have sounded just a bit happier, no one paid her any mind. "And I'm the only one around here who wanted to marry."

Epilogue

Matt looked in on his son, saw he was still awake and smiled as he took him from the bed and set him on his knee again. Matt spoke low so as to not awaken Lizzie. "I want you to know that you're the bravest boy I know. If it weren't for you, your mummy might have died today."

Seth's chest swelled with pride. He didn't think he could love a man more than he did his father.

Matt knew the guard he'd placed at Shelby's place would have told him that a woman was brought there, but he didn't know who she was. And Matt could only wonder if he would have found her in time?

"And she's all right?"

"She has a few bruises, but yes, she's all right. She's better than all right and the smartest lady I know. Imagine what might have happened if she hadn't found you, if she hadn't brought you to live here."

Kiya stepped into the room and smiled at the boy. "You should be sleeping."

"I stayed awake because I wanted to see if you were all right."

"I am and I have you to thank for that, Seth." She hugged him tightly against her. Your dad told me you followed me."

Once she'd let him go, and to his parent's amusement, Seth asked his father, "Are we going to take mummy on her honeymoon now?"

Moments later, the boy was back in bed, and his parents were on their way to their room. "You know your father said he and my mother might take a wedding trip to the islands."

"Not at the same time we're going, surely."

Matt shrugged. "I only know my mother mentioned the place we have there."

Kiya laughed. "Between the children, who you've already promised can go, and now my father and your mother, servants and nurse and governess, it might be wiser to let them all go and we could stay here."

Matt grinned as he watched his wife drape her nightdress and robe over a chair and face him wearing exactly what he liked best. "You might have a point."

"But you promised to show Seth how to steer a ship."

"I know." He sighed as he opened his shirt. "Looks like we haven't got a choice."

Kiya laughed. "We could take a trip to Ireland when we get back."

"You mean for a few weeks of privacy?"

"If I remember correctly, we had all the privacy needed when in the coach."

He frowned. "Um, are you sure? I can't say as I remember."

She grinned. "Can you not? Would you like me to refresh your memory, then?"

Matt raised and lowered his brows in quick succession. "That might prove helpful."

Kiya giggled like a young girl at the enthusiasm he didn't bother to hide. "It might spark a memory if you move those two chairs so they face each other."

Matt did as she suggested then asked, "What happens now?"

"You should probably sit in one, and I'll sit in the other."

She sat and he asked, "Like this?"

"Exactly like this," she said.

"Were you dressed like you are now?"

Kiya's shrug shivered her breasts. Matt loved it.

"I might have been wearing a bit more than this."

"I have to tell you I love it when you shrug like that."

"Do you? Perhaps I should shrug more often then."

"I'd take it as a personal favour if you would."

"Another personal favour?"

Matt ignored her question and remarked instead, "It might help my memory some if you scooted your hips forward a bit."

"Might it? I thought you said you didn't remember."

He knelt before her and moved her legs to his liking, and to Kiya's laughter he said, "I think it's beginning to come back to me."

About the Author

Patricia Pellicane lives on Long Island in New York with her husband and family. She enjoys reading, travelling in her motor home and especially enjoys her grandchildren. "Too bad we can't have grandchildren first. They're a kick." Most of all she loves to write.

Most of all she loves to write. "Life's tough we all need a bit of fantasy now and then. For myself, I love a happy ending."

Patricia Pellicane loves to hear from readers. You can find her contact information, website details and author profile page at http://www.total-e-bound.com

Total-E-Bound Publishing

www.total-e-bound.com

Take a look at our exciting range of literagasmic™
erotic romance titles and discover pure quality
at Total-E-Bound.

www.ingramcontent.com/pod-product-compliance
Lightning Source LLC
Chambersburg PA
CBHW022204030726
47494CB00019B/176